Praise

"A compelling, satisfying romantic adventure."
—*Publishers Weekly* on *Echo North* (starred review)

"Epic and engrossing. Magic pulsates through every page . . . a lush, captivating new twist on beloved fairy tales."
—*Kirkus Reviews* on *Echo North* (starred review)

"A fantasy novel that packs an emotional punch as it explores how doing the right, kind, and gentle thing can require far more courage than waging war."
—*BookPage* on *Into the Heartless Wood* (starred review)

"Brimming with lush prose, endearing characters, and soul-stirring stakes . . . completely irresistible."
—Rebecca Ross, #1 *New York Times* bestselling author of *Divine Rivals* on *Into the Heartless Wood*

"Breathtaking and beautiful."
—*Booklist* on *Wind Daughter* (starred review)

"Weaves a powerful, beautiful spell in a storyline threaded with fairy-tale magic and heartwarming romance. A rich, romantic tale of identity, agency, and love."
—*Kirkus Reviews* on *Wind Daughter* (starred review)

WHILE THE DARK REMAINS

OTHER TITLES BY JOANNA RUTH MEYER

Beneath the Haunting Sea

Beyond the Shadowed Earth

Echo North

Wind Daughter

Into the Heartless Wood

The Winter Dark, Book One

WHILE THE DARK REMAINS

JOANNA RUTH MEYER

47N❋RTH

This is a work of fiction. Names, characters, organizations, places, events, and incidents are either products of the author's imagination or are used fictitiously. Otherwise, any resemblance to actual persons, living or dead, is purely coincidental.

Text copyright © 2025 by Joanna Ruth Meyer
All rights reserved.

No part of this book may be reproduced, or stored in a retrieval system, or transmitted in any form or by any means, electronic, mechanical, photocopying, recording, or otherwise, without express written permission of the publisher.

Published by 47North, Seattle

www.apub.com

Amazon, the Amazon logo, and 47North are trademarks of Amazon.com, Inc., or its affiliates.

EU product safety contact:
Amazon Media EU S. à r.l.
38, avenue John F. Kennedy, L-1855 Luxembourg
amazonpublishing-gpsr@amazon.com

ISBN-13: 9781662530692 (paperback)
ISBN-13: 9781662530685 (digital)

Cover design by David Curtis
Cover illustration © Shannon Associates Inc

Printed in the United States of America

*For anyone who has ever felt alone in the dark:
Look to the east—the sun is rising.*

And for my siblings: Daniel, Corrie, and Andrew. I don't know what it says about our relationship that I'm dedicating a book about an evil king keeping child prodigies in cages to you three, but here we are. Millennial power. Or something. I love you guys. (And I will be only a tiny bit offended if you never read this.)

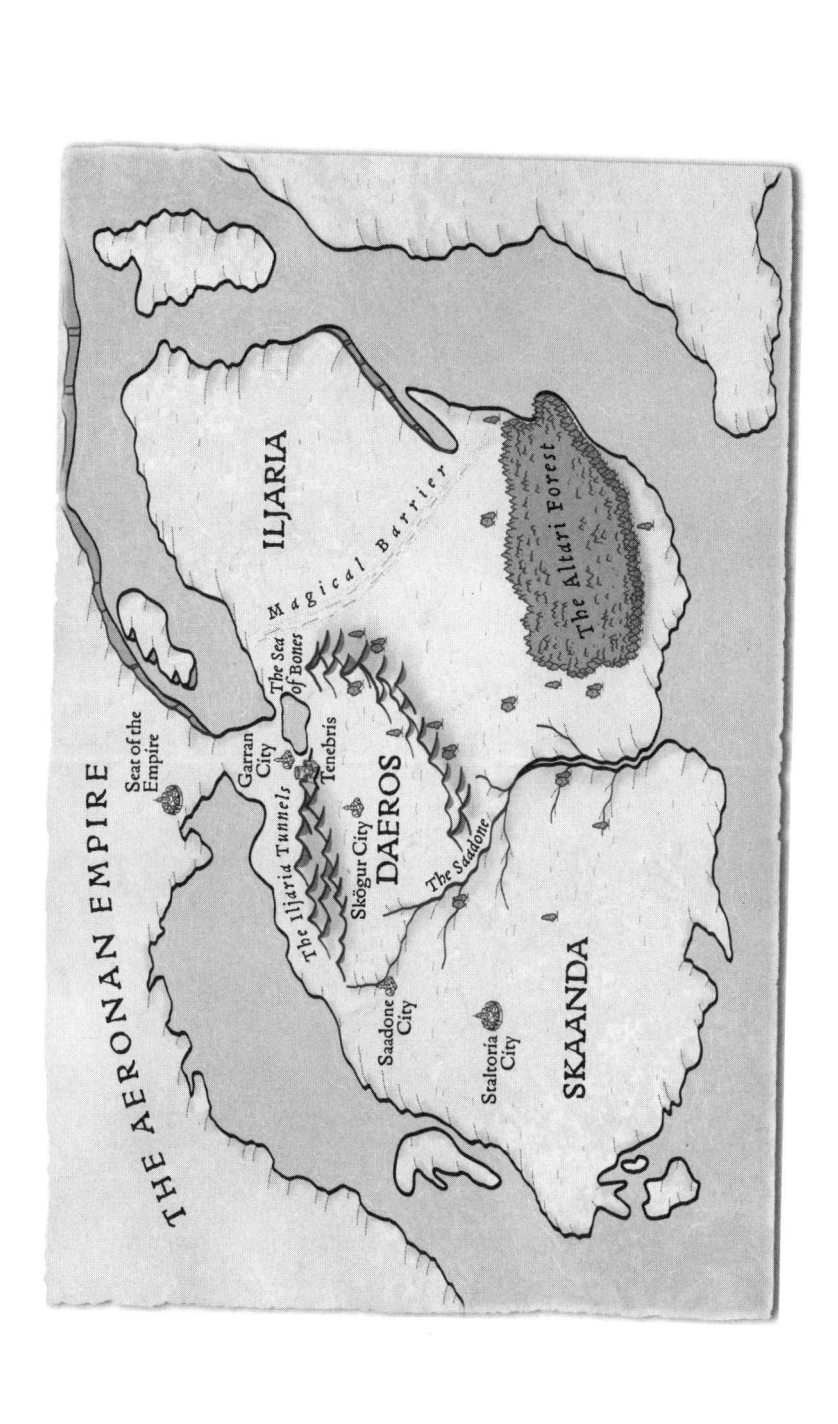

PART ONE

Gods' Fall

TEN YEARS AGO

YEAR 4190, Month of the Violet God
Skaanda—a ruined village

This might be the last day I ever see the sun.

The falling light dazzles me as I clamber up onto the roof of what was once a Skaandan public house, abandoned in the war and half tumbled down. The entire village is empty of everything but dust and memory, its small knot of buildings and ruined central fountain gilded all in liquid orange. I want to stand still and tilt my face to the sun, let the light seep into me before it vanishes entirely for the whole of winter. But that is not why I am here.

I squint at the rope that stretches taut between where I perch on the roof of the public house and the small temple across the street, its white pillars cracked, its roof tiles loose and crumbling. Despite the chill in the air, the dark curls at the nape of my neck are damp with sweat. I don't know the feel of the rope, don't know which spots on the roof are safe to put my feet. It's been a week since I last practiced my routine, and this is a far cry from the arena at home.

"Get on with it!" the king shouts from the ground, thirty feet below me. His impatience is just this side of rage.

I don't dare glance down at him. If I do, I'll lose courage. I'll fall.

I take a breath. I shake my muscles loose.

I leap into a sequence of back handsprings along the peak of the public house roof, slicing my hand on a broken tile and barely stopping myself from careening down into the caved-in portion. The pain hardly registers as I hurl myself back the other way, doing flips and cartwheels and landing with both feet on the taut rope.

I don't stop. I can't.

I run across the rope, getting the measure of it, the fibers rough on my bare feet. Adrenaline courses through me, and when I reach the roof of the temple, I flip backward onto the rope, catching it with my hands because my feet miss it.

I swing up, launching myself onto the temple, skidding on the loose tiles and turning it into a dance. I jump and flip and cartwheel as the tiles slide from the roof and smash on the street below.

And then it's one last mad dash across the rope and I shimmy back down to the ground, doing three front flips and a final somersault before landing in a perfect bow at the king's feet.

I try to quiet my raging heart as I study the hem of his robe, red velvet stitched with silver. I'm slick with sweat, my insides jelly. Dust swirls up, sticking to my skin. The last rays of the sun fade from the world, and the king's soldiers light torches. They stink of sulfur; the smoke burns my eyes. I dare a glance up at the king: His pale skin and dark hair and beard make him look like a specter in the torchlight.

"I told you she's remarkable," says the Skaandan woman who brought me here, rings on every one of her milky-brown fingers.

The king scoffs. "I thought she would fall."

"But she didn't."

I bite my lip to keep myself still. I bite deep, deep, until I taste blood. For the first time since leaving home, I am horribly, wildly afraid. I didn't know, before. I didn't *understand*. But it's far, far too late now to turn back. That choice was taken from me the moment I was presented to the king.

"I don't have an acrobat," he finally says, turning on his heel away from me. "I suppose I will take her."

"It will cost you," says the Skaandan woman.

The king snaps his fingers and his steward, a tall, pale Daerosian man, tosses her a pouch that clinks when she catches it.

I tremble before him, everything in me screaming to run. Yet I am still.

The Skaandan woman opens the pouch and counts the coins in the torchlight. I wonder what she means to do with them, what the price of my life is worth to her. The steward hauls me up by the arm while she's still counting and shoves me into the waiting cart. Then he climbs into the driver's seat.

The Skaandan woman turns away without another word. She is no one to me, but she's my last link to home. I have to clamp my jaw shut to keep myself from shouting for her to come back. I huddle between a sack of grain and a mound of wool blankets. There is another Skaandan child in the other corner of the wagon, a boy scarcely older than me. He's crying quietly. I shift my body so I don't have to look at him.

The king swings up onto his horse, flanked by his soldiers, with the lurching wagon following behind and the torches blurs of orange against the burgeoning stars. We head northeast, toward the mighty river that divides Skaanda from Daeros. From there we will travel on to Tenebris, the king's mountain palace.

I tell myself that all will be well. I tell myself there is nothing to fear, that I will find my way home again soon enough. Goddess of death, it's a lie.

The Skaandan boy can't stop crying, and I despise him for it. The king is not known for his kindness—tears will not help us now. I turn my back on the boy. I try to remember the feel of sunlight on my face.

But there is only darkness.

CHAPTER ONE

YEAR 4200, Month of the Bronze God
Skaanda—Staltoria City—the royal palace

"Brynja. *Brynja!*"

I jolt awake to find light slanting through a warm chamber. My sheets are silk. The room smells of oranges. Tears drip down my cheeks, and the mad pace of my heart makes the world wheel. I squeeze my eyes shut again to try and block it out.

"Breathe, Brynja."

A cold glass is pressed into my hands, damp with condensation from the ice that must have slowly melted overnight. I focus on the texture of the glass, on the scent of oranges and the steady voice of my friend. My pulse slows. I open my eyes.

Saga's gaze meets mine, the memory of our shared horror written all over her face. I've clearly pulled her from her own bed—she's wearing her sleeping shift, and her hair is wrapped up in a swath of purple. There are tears on her cheeks, too. Her hands wrap around the glass just above my own.

I take a shuddering breath, and for a few moments we breathe together, in and out, long and steady.

I remind myself that we are not in Daeros anymore but safe in Skaanda, far out of reach of the cruel king who haunts our sleep.

For now, at least.

Saga sets the glass back on my bedside table. "Breakfast in my room. Five minutes." Her words are certain, but her voice wobbles. "Then to the training arena."

Saga is a big believer in working your body until you're too exhausted for traumatizing memories.

"Thanks for waking me," I tell her.

She squeezes my hand. "Always. Now hurry and get dressed, will you? I'm starving."

She slips away through the door that joins our chambers, and I drag myself out of bed.

I stretch, first thing. It's a habit I haven't been able to shake, even though it's been a year and nine months since Saga and I escaped from Kallias's mountain and I'm not forced to perform anymore. I broke nearly every bone in my body in order to make it mind me, and the thought of losing my acrobatic skills entirely panics me nearly as much as the idea of facing Kallias again.

"Breakfast!" shouts Saga from the other side of the door, just as I'm pulling on loose trousers and a linen shirt.

I splash water on my face and join her in her room, kneeling with her at the low round table that's laden with more than enough food for two. We eat while her maids fuss around her, unwrapping her hair and dabbing the smooth dark skin of her face with cosmetics, no matter that she'll sweat it all off in the arena. Saga is the crown princess of Skaanda, and she's not allowed to appear in public looking like "a disheveled mongoose," as her mother so lovingly puts it. She's regained her composure since waking me, locked her shadows tightly away, and become, at least in appearance, the confident princess she was before Kallias broke her.

She watches me over the table as she sips tea and eats berries, absently swirling her oatcake in a bowl of cream until the soggy pastry breaks apart and the pieces float away. "Brynja," she says pointedly.

I stare at my own breakfast, not having much of an appetite.

"By the time we reach the mountain, it will have been two years, you know," she says.

It was a three-month journey from Tenebris to Skaanda; the return trip will take another three months. I brace myself for the argument I've heard many times. I take a bite of an oatcake.

"You look completely different," she goes on. "You have hair now, for one, and you've got *curves*, Brynja! You no longer look skinny enough that a child could snap you in half like a twig, and I *swear* you've grown a couple inches. I doubt your own mother would recognize you."

I grimace and she does, too, because she didn't mean to needle at the sore subject of my family.

"Sorry."

I shake my head. She's right, though. I've changed a lot since we fled from Tenebris—eating proper, hearty meals and not living in a cage will apparently do that to a person. I have filled out in unexpected places, gained weight and acquired hips; I frequently run into doorframes and furniture because I'm no longer quite sure of the shape of my own body.

"Is that why you don't want to come?" says Saga softly. "You want to stay and keep looking for them?"

My parents, she means. My brother. I think of the empty house in the tangled streets of Staltoria City. Saga went there with me, when we first arrived back in Skaanda. She was heartbroken that I was robbed of the joyful reunion she had had with her own family. There was nothing in that house but dust and shadows.

"I won't find my family here," I reply.

"Why then?"

I stare at her, at a loss for words, as her maids sweep her cloud of black hair back into a headdress and dab cerulean powder on her eyelids. She's so much braver than I am, voluntarily revisiting the place of her greatest torment without so much as flinching. If I told Saga that, though, she'd point out that she was only in Kallias's Collection for a year, while I was there for eight—nearly half my life—but that doesn't mean the horror was any less for her. I don't know how she can even bear the thought of it."

"We will be perfectly safe, Bryn. Vil will be there with us the whole time, and we won't be there for too long anyway before the army arrives, and then—"

"I know," I say wearily. "Daeros will be annexed into Skaanda. The war will end once and for all. We'll have trade with Aerona, free access to the Altari Forest, and all the Daerosian gems and metals and inventions we could ever want."

Saga nods. "Kallias won't hurt anyone ever again. He'll be tried for his crimes, and executed. His spirit will be doomed to labor outside the gates of paradise for all eternity."

I gnaw on my lip.

Her face is tight, grim. "If we don't face our demons, they'll haunt us forever. *Please*, Bryn. Say you'll come. We need you."

I'm the only one who can move around Kallias's mountain palace undetected, eight years of experience giving me intimate knowledge of the paths through the false ceilings. I have access to any room, including the king's private chambers. I wouldn't have to wait for the army to come. I could kill him in his sleep our first night there, if I wanted.

"Please," says Saga softly.

I rub at my eyes to make my headache go away. I have endured many things in my twenty years in this world. But I don't know if being in the same room as Kallias again can ever be one of them.

"I'll see you in the training arena," I tell her, and leave my best friend to finish her breakfast.

Knife throwing helps. It's satisfying to dig my heels into the sand, to hurl blade after blade at the painted targets across the arena and watch them thud into the wood, handles quivering. It helps keep my mind steady, to keep the blinding panic from overwhelming me like a flood.

Saga's brother, Vilhjalmur, watches from the fence bordering one end of the arena, sword at his hip, the neck of his shirt gaping open. He's already had his practice bouts this morning, judging by the sweat glistening on his dark skin. My face warms. Every inch of him is muscle, finely tuned, like the hunting lions in the royal menagerie.

Vil is two years older than Saga, but he wasn't the one the oracle chose as Skaanda's next ruler. He doesn't seem to resent her for that, though, or for her sudden reappearance a year and a half ago, when the entire country thought she was dead. He immediately relinquished the title of heir he'd been given in her absence and resumed the endeavor he's most passionate about: improving the working conditions on the hundreds of farms, spread all across Skaanda, that are so crucial to feeding the population.

Vil's the one who concocted the plot to annex Daeros, and he'll be the one to govern it if the plan is successful. It would more than suit him, I think.

"You've improved," he calls over to me, catching my eye.

I flush anew at the praise but give Vil an impassive nod and throw the last of my knives, then trudge through the sand to collect them. Saga is conspicuously absent, and I would bet a hefty sum it's intentional.

He joins me at the target, quiet as I pull the knives out. I am overly aware of his proximity, of his heat and his scent: sweat and dust and the citrus-perfumed cream he rubs into his jaw when he shaves.

Vil doesn't prevaricate, and after weeks of increasingly pointed requests, I don't expect him to. I like that he doesn't play games. I respect him for it. "We leave at dawn, Bryn. We can't do it without you."

He touches my arm, and I try to ignore the way my skin pricks beneath his fingers. "Of course you can. I drew you maps of the palace layout."

"Brynja."

I look up to meet his dark gaze, and it burns through me. He stands head and shoulders taller than me, but he has never once made me feel small. The jewels in his ears glitter in the sun. "I'm not coming," I say. My words are petulant, unyielding. I trace a circle in the dirt with one foot.

Vil lightly shoves my shoulder. "What do you intend to do all alone in Staltoria City? Rattle about the palace having tea with my parents?"

"I have no intention of presuming upon your family further, Vil. I won't stay."

"You're not presuming. You never have."

I don't reply, hunching my shoulders, fighting not to be caught once more in the grip of my nightmare: an iron cage, a cruel king, the fear of falling, so sharp I can taste it.

"Hey." He tips my chin up with one finger so I'm looking at him again. He sees the tightness of my jaw, the way I'm so fiercely trying not to cry. He's kind enough not to comment on it. "We're indebted to you, Bryn. You brought Saga back to us. Without you"—he smooths my cheek with his calloused thumb—"without you, the world would be so much smaller. Don't shrink it back down to nothing."

My heart beats too hard, too quick, his nearness overwhelming me. Vil is safety, strength, peace, and I know that's what he would give me if I let him. But it scares me too much.

I take a step back, putting distance between us. "Being here, with you and Saga—" My throat catches. "It has meant everything to me, Vil. Truly. But it's past time for me to go now."

"Go where? Back to the family that abandoned you?" His voice is hard. "Come with us, Bryn. Come with *me*. Don't waste the life the gods gave back to you. Do our country proud. End the war. Take revenge on the man who treated you so cruelly."

Anger twists down my spine. I grip the collar of his shirt and yank him to my eye level, close enough that I can see the stubble already showing on his chin, the curl of his dark lashes. Close enough that I can't deny I want him closer still. "The gods didn't give me my life—I took it back myself. And I have no intention of wasting it."

He looks at me, daring in his eyes, and my belly twists. "Then don't," he says.

I let him go and stalk back to where the throwing line is marked with red powder in the sand.

A year and a half ago, when Saga and I arrived back in Skaanda and couldn't find my family, she insisted I stay with her. She was more than happy to adopt me as her sister—doubly so, I suspect, where her brother is concerned—but Vil or no Vil, my feet have been itching to leave.

I know I can find my family. I just don't know if they'll want me back. Bile burns in my throat, and I start hurling knives again before Vil is quite clear of the target.

Skaanda and Daeros have been warring for decades. It's not all-out war, all the time, but frequent skirmishes over border towns, river trade routes, and logging efforts in the Altari Forest have taken a toll. Daeros is a smaller country than Skaanda, bordered by mountains on three sides and the mighty Saadone River on the fourth. By all accounts, Daeros is running low on the food that Skaanda has in large supply. But Daeros trades with the Aeronan Empire, our mainland neighbor to the north, and so seems content to keep squabbling with Skaanda indefinitely.

Iljaria, the third country to occupy our peninsula, lies to the east of Daeros and stays out of our eternal feud. The Iljaria claim pacifism almost religiously and are a people blessed with long life and inherent, powerful magic, every member of their race marked by their white hair. Centuries ago, the Iljaria erected a magical barrier that permanently cut them off from the rest of the peninsula. So they don't fight because they don't need to—and that's only one of the reasons Skaandans despise them. But even *without* the magical barrier, Skaanda would never dare march on Iljaria. Ordinary swords and spears are of little use against a people who can bend earth and rock, beasts and trees, the air in your lungs, and the very beats of your heart to their will. So it's Daeros Skaanda squabbles with, locked in seemingly endless conflict over land and resources, while the Iljaria dwell ever apart, essentially an island unto themselves.

The plot to take Daeros is twofold: Vil will lead a party of ambassadors overland to Tenebris—the mountain palace in Daeros—to make overtures of peace and secure a cessation of hostilities between the two nations, while keeping tabs on the key players within the mountain. The Daerosian nobility will be staying in Tenebris during Winter Dark, and Vil means to make allies with them where he can, laying the groundwork for a smooth transition of power. At the same time, the Skaandan army will come secretly through the labyrinth of mountain tunnels Saga and I discovered during our escape. When the army arrives, Vil will seize Kallias and claim Daeros for Skaanda—hopefully with minimal casualties. It's a good plan, one I've helped Vil and Saga fine-tune for the year and a half I've been here. But I still don't want any part of it.

If I ever see Kallias again, it will only be long enough to drive a knife into his heart and look him in the eye while I do it. I would want him to know exactly who it is who ends him, as he once threatened to end me. I don't want to play at being an ambassador and hope Kallias doesn't recognize me while I spy for Vil. I don't want to spend a single minute more in that damned mountain. Eight years was enough.

Tonight there's a feast in the great hall to send off the ambassadorial party. I sit on Saga's right, across from Vil, who is wearing a sleeveless blue robe embroidered in silver, whorls of gold painted all up and down his tautly muscled arms. There are rings on his fingers, and his ears are heavy with jewels. He looks every inch the chiseled statue of a god, as he did the first time I saw him the day Saga and I arrived back in Staltoria City. He has grown more human to me since then. We've become friends.

But I'm not sure he understands the enormity of the thing he's asking me to do.

While the Dark Remains

Vil catches my eyes across the table, and I can read his thoughts as easily as if he spoke them aloud, because they're the same things he says to me over and over: *We need you, Brynja. Skaanda needs you. I need you.*

I flush and look away, playing with the fringe of the tablecloth and hardly touching my food. I stare at my pale, freckled hands and wonder if Saga is right—maybe I *have* changed so much my mother wouldn't recognize me. Maybe that means Kallias won't, either.

Skaandans, like the magical Iljaria with whom we share a common ancestry, run the gamut of skin tones, from light like mine to dark like Vil's and Saga's, and every shade between. It's my freckles that worry me the most. They are neither very common nor very *un*common in Skaandans, but I am certain Kallias would recognize mine. Indridi, Saga's handmaiden, promises she can cover them with carefully applied cosmetics.

But despite the cosmetics and my curls, my added weight, and my newly acquired curves, Kallias would know me. Wouldn't he? How could he not?

Saga's father stands from his place at the head of the table, the crystal-and-sapphire crown that marks him as king of Skaanda resting on his close-cropped, silvering hair. He toasts the Skaandan army, then toasts Saga and Vil. They rise from their seats, regal and shining, ready to end the war—and Kallias—forever.

A cheer roars through the hall, and every soul present lifts their wine goblet to their lips. I take a hefty swallow, and the alcohol burns all the way down my throat.

Pipes and drums and tiny, tuned cymbals strike up music for dancing, while a host of servants shove the dining tables to one end of the hall and couples rush to the floor.

I look up to find Vil beside me, the jewels glittering in his ears, his fitted robe accentuating his muscular frame. "Dance with me, Brynja?" he says, holding out his hand.

My mind snags on the image of a blue-eyed boy with white-and-black hair, pulling me toward him in the dark. I taste the heat of his kiss, of his magic, fizzing blue and silver inside me. Longing floods my senses. This is why I keep distance between me and Vil. The blue-eyed boy is why. But all that is over. I will never see him again. Vil is the one here, in front of me.

I forcibly shove the memory away and fold my hand in Vil's.

"I'm not going to Daeros," I insist as Vil leads me to the outskirts of the dancing.

He shakes his head and smiles a little. "So you say."

He puts his other hand on my waist, tugs me close against his chest. His heat pulses through me, and he smells of his shaving lotion, of our dinner wine. It would be easy, I think, to melt into him. To forget everything else.

And yet I can't forget the boy in the dark. Fingers in the stubble of my newly grown hair. Blue eyes and sparking magic. Unshaven cheek scraping against my smooth one. Lips like fire, desperate and wanting.

"I need some air," I choke out, pulling away from Vil. I fairly run through the hall and out onto a high balcony that looks east, toward Daeros, faint stars scratching already at the night sky. I breathe deep and slow, trying to come back to myself.

As autumn deepens across the peninsula, the days will grow shorter and shorter until the onset of winter, when the sun won't rise at all for three months. The Iljaria call this long period of darkness *Soul's Rest*, we Skaandans *Gods' Fall*, and the Daerosians the rather-unimaginative-if-you-ask-me *Winter Dark*.

Saga and I escaped from Daeros during Gods' Fall a year and nine months ago. Vil's plan is to arrive at Kallias's mountain in time for this year's. He means to infiltrate the palace while the dark remains and seize Daeros as the sun rises again, marking the beginning of a new year—and the beginning of Vil's governorship over a new territory.

Up on the balcony, I blink into the night, a cool breath of air sliding past my neck.

"You know you're coming with us," says Vil, stepping up beside me, but at a thoughtful distance.

My throat tightens. I don't look aside at him, because I can't quite bear to. "I know," I say.

TEN YEARS AGO

YEAR 4190, Month of the Gray Goddess
Daeros—Tenebris

There is a cage waiting for me when we arrive at the mountain palace. I suppose the king sent word ahead.

The mountain devours us, a maw of cold, unfeeling stone, and the Skaandan boy and I are dragged into the great hall, where the king keeps his Collection. The boy is shut, weeping, into a cage made of reeds, while I am shoved into one made of iron. It seems enormous to me, until the door is locked and the king nods at his steward, who hauls on the chain looped through the top of it, and I find myself hoisted, spinning, up into the air.

I wrap my hands around the cold metal bars, peering dizzily below me and trying not to be sick. The cage stops when it reaches the ceiling, some thirty feet in the air. The steward must do something to secure it, because he lets go of the chain and the cage does not fall, though it keeps spinning slowly.

My heart leaps and dives within my chest. I barely hold back a whimper. I huddle in a corner of the cage, dimly aware of a metal sleeping ledge, a short set of climbing silks, and a rope that's stretched from one end to the other. The king means me to practice my routines, I suppose, as well as I can in here. The cage must be ten feet square, far larger than the boy's away below me. But ten feet square is my whole world now. And that is not very large for a world. The others at least are together, in their cages down on the cold floor. Mine is the only one suspended from the ceiling.

I listen to my breathing. I count the beats of my heart. My body grows stiffer and stiffer until my limbs start to hurt and I'm forced to uncurl myself, to move, carefully, toward the sleeping ledge. My legs are asleep and I fall, making the cage lurch and sway. I nearly lose my lunch. But I haul myself up to the ledge. I massage my legs until the feeling comes back into them, needles of pain so sharp they take my breath a bit.

I gaze down into the hall, vast and echoing, the entire back wall made of glass. It looks into the glacier valley, a frozen wasteland the king's guards referred to as the Sea of Bones. Stars burn cold above the Sea. The winter will be long and lonely. My stomach pinches in hunger, and I wonder how often the king feeds the children he keeps in his Collection. I remember that I am part of that Collection now. I remember that this is not a joke or a game. I'm trapped here, and I am wholly, irrevocably, alone.

I curl up on the sleeping ledge, my cheek pressed against the metal. Just this once, I allow myself to cry.

I watch them work from between the bars of my cage: a dozen men on scaffolding, strapped in with harnesses and ropes so even if they fall, they will not die on the marble floor far below. They drive iron rings into the ceiling and hang equipment from them: chains attached to wooden platforms, thick knotted ropes, red and gold and blue aerial silks, swinging bars. They stretch wires from one end of the hall to the other, at varying heights. They do it all for me.

I study the apparatuses, ice in my belly, trying to map out a routine in my mind before I force my body to do it. I am not sure I can—maybe the king *wants* me to fall. But I picture the arena at home, where I spent hour upon hour practicing. I remember that I am remarkable and that I must not fail.

I expect to be let out of my cage; I expect a chance to practice properly before I am called upon to perform. But I am not.

The first time the king's steward hauls on the chain and brings my iron cage down to the floor, it is the fifteenth hour—evening, if it were not winter. He fits his key into the lock and turns it with a click, then heaves on the chain to bring me skyward again. The door creaks open, and I stare out at the wires, the platforms, the silks. Fear slides through my bones.

The king is here, of course, with a handful of Daerosian nobles, pale men and women overburdened with furs and glittering with diamonds. They sit in a semicircle of chairs in the midst of the room, ready to marvel at the king's prodigious Collection. Lamps skew orange shadows across the floor, and the time-glass in the back wall—a marvel of Iljaria magic—pulses with its own red light. When the Iljaria abandoned Tenebris, they left quite a number of magical items behind, and the magic that they set in motion all those centuries ago still endures. That is the power of the Iljaria—eternal, until the world's ending.

The king tilts his face up, up. He frowns at me. I try not to shake, but I do. I know what happens to the children in his Collection who fail to please him: He slits their throats and throws their bodies down into the Sea of Bones, where it's said the Ghost God and the Gray Goddess walk together, keeping watch over the dead. That is the terror woven into every part of me. That is the only reason I step from my cage and leap onto the first wooden platform.

My routine is shaky, at best. I don't even use all the apparatuses. But I don't fall. And when it's over, the king nods for me to be locked back into my cage. I collapse onto the sleeping ledge, slick with sweat. I have passed this first test. But I know I must do better next time. I know I must be braver, bolder, showier.

Below me, the other children perform. I don't watch. I curl into the tightest ball I can, and I pray: to the Violet God, god of time; to the

While the Dark Remains

Bronze God, god of minds; to the Prism Goddess, goddess of all things; to the Ghost God, god of nothing. I am clumsy at praying. I am not good at it, I am not used to it. Perhaps that's why they don't answer.

I rub my aching arms. I plot out my next routine, over and over in my mind. I tell myself I will live through it. I tell myself that I will not fall, that the king will be pleased with me, that the Sea of Bones will not be my ending.

I tell myself all these things, but I don't think I believe any of them.

CHAPTER TWO

YEAR 4200, Month of the Bronze God
Skaanda—the tundra

It's raining when we leave Staltoria City, Skaanda's capital, a miserable, cold, dripping rain. I hunch under the hood of my cloak and try to ignore my roiling stomach as my horse trudges gloomily eastward on a road of churning mud.

The great swaths of farmland scattered liberally across Skaanda will be glad of the rain, as long as it doesn't go on for too long and cut short the precious days of dwindling sunlight. Vil has been working with the top Skaandan engineers on crafting huge lamps to simulate the sun for the fields, but so far they can't find a source of sustainable fuel to make them burn long enough to be of any use.

Daeros solved this problem years ago, constructing greenhouses on its much more limited land, the lights inside allowing crops to grow even during the winter months. They won't share the secrets of powering those lights with Skaanda, though by all accounts it's this very knowledge that they trade to Aerona for the food they're always in need of—because even with the greenhouses, Daeros doesn't produce enough to feed its entire population. This is yet another reason Vil is eager to annex Daeros into Skaanda—food for Daeros's people, miracles of engineering for Skaanda.

We pass fields as we go, workers harvesting crops and piling them in huge wagons, which will be taken to storehouses outside of Skaanda's largest cities. New brick structures with shining tile roofs line one end of the fields, housing for the workers so they don't have to travel long hours every day back and forth to their homes during the busiest seasons.

This is one of Vil's innovations, paid for out of his own pocket, and there are similar buildings going up all across Skaanda, ushering our country into a new era of prosperity. It makes me fiercely proud of him: his ingenuity, his generous spirit.

Saga rides beside me on the muddy road, bristling with nervous energy, oblivious to the damp. Vil is in the lead, his shoulders square and strong against the dreary day. I am not quite brave enough to nudge my horse up next to him, unwilling to confront the tangle of emotions he inspires in me quite so early in the morning. And anyway, I am more than content to stay with Saga. We have grown fiercely close in the year and a half we've spent together in Staltoria City. She's nearly a sister to me and understands me far better than my actual sister ever did.

Rounding out our company are Indridi, Saga's handmaiden, who has been attending me all the while I've been at the palace, and two soldiers: Pala, a woman of forty or so who seems distant and severe, and Commander Leifur, a man only a few years my senior who is eager to prove himself and be named Vil's general one day. Our party is small enough to travel quickly and to appear unthreatening to the Daerosian army encampments we will have to pass on our way to Tenebris. We can't risk getting caught up in any skirmishes, and it's the season for war: light to see by, blood running hot.

At least when it's not raining.

At Saga's beckoning, Indridi rides alongside us, her tight dark curls dripping water in her eyes. She's twenty-three, just older than Vil, and I don't miss how often her glance drifts in his direction. I can't blame her—Vil is hard to not look at—but I don't like the way it plants a seed of jealousy in the pit of my belly, hard and tight and small.

Indridi has lived in the palace since she was thirteen years old, and in addition to being Saga's handmaiden, she's one of her very best friends. I have gotten to know her, too, these past eighteen months, and have appreciated her quiet humor and steady good sense. Now, however, she sits tense in her saddle, her shoulders tight, her forehead creased. Her skin is a medium brown, halfway between my light and Saga's dark, and raindrops cling to her high cheekbones. There is misery in her eyes.

"All well, Ridi?" says Saga, peering at Indridi in concern.

"Of course, Your Highness," Indridi returns, not meeting Saga's gaze. She grips her reins too tight, knuckles straining against her skin.

"Long way to Daeros," Saga presses. "If there's something bothering you, I hope you'll tell me."

Indridi makes an admirable effort to smile, though she doesn't quite manage it. "I am fine, Your Highness. Thank you." She gives a little bow from her saddle, her eyes briefly sliding past mine, then holds her horse back until she's riding behind us again.

Saga leans sideways in her saddle and pokes my arm. "What's bothering *you*, Bryn?"

There's no point in lying. "I'm not sure I can really do it, Saga. Pretend to be something I'm not. Face Kallias again."

Saga waves my comments away like so many flies, though I don't miss the tension in her own frame. "Of course you can! Vil and I will coach you in the finer details of Skaandan royalty the whole way there." She chews on her lip, giving me a piercing glance and a glimpse at her own fear. "We're not kids anymore. He doesn't have any power over us, and we will never be part of his Collection again. You know that, right?"

Fear squeezes my throat, and for a moment I feel like I'm falling, shards of ice and rock waiting at the bottom to dash me to pieces. I take a jagged breath and swipe rain out of my eyes. "I'm afraid I'll ruin our ploy the first moment I see him."

"How?" says Saga.

I shrug and stare at the mud churning under my horse's hooves. "I'm afraid I'll drive a knife into the bastard's heart."

Saga gives a grim laugh. "You'll have to beat me to it."

"Saga, you promised you'd behave," says Vil, voice light with forced humor. He glances back, and for a moment I'm caught fast in the intensity of his gaze. He smiles at me. "No stabbing," he says, "either of you."

"God of fire," swears Saga, but without any real heat. "You are no fun at all."

Vil calls a halt at midday, and we do our best to eat lunch in the still-pouring rain before it can get too soggy: sweet brown bread and cheese with figs, salty rice cakes with sweet-spicy dipping sauce. There's no chance of a fire in all this wretched wet, but that doesn't keep me from feeling grumpy at the lack of tea or coffee. When we've eaten and all taken a chance to relieve ourselves, we ride on.

Vil sings an old Skaandan ballad in the rain, his voice a rich, strong tenor that burrows inside me and makes my chest ache. After a few minutes, Saga joins him, hesitant at first, then growing more certain, her voice twining around her brother's in a hauntingly beautiful counterpoint. I haven't heard her sing since Tenebris, since Kallias locked her in a glass cage like a canary and forced her to trill at his command. She was remarkable, then. She is more so, now. Tears press at my eyes. I blink and swallow until they're gone.

My thoughts drift in the rain, in the music. There was a time when I wasn't made up of anger, every cell in my body stitched together with rage. I was happy, once. When Kallias is dead and I find my family, I can be happy again, and everything that happened in the last ten years will fade to a half-remembered nightmare. Won't it?

Rain seeps under my collar and crawls down my spine. It's going to be a long journey.

Saga has been praying to the Red God and Yellow God and Prism Goddess all day, but they don't seem to have heard her by the time we make camp for the night—it's still raining. Saga grumbles but helps the rest of us erect canvas tents in hopes of staying relatively dry until morning. When they're up, we unfold more lengths of canvas over the soggy ground inside the tents, and then the six of us huddle together in the larger one to eat our cold dinner. We'll separate for sleeping, the four women in this tent, the men in the smaller one.

"Gods I want a fire," says Vil. He stretches out his long legs in front of him and scowls at his food.

"I can try and build one," Indridi offers, the color in her cheeks deepening.

"In all this wet? I think not."

My stomach twists and Indridi ducks her head.

"Let her try, oh grumpy one," Saga admonishes her brother. "What's the worst that could happen? Toasted cheese and hot tea?"

"Fine," says Vil shortly. He rubs at his temples, and I wonder what's gotten him so out of sorts.

Indridi slips back out into the rain and gathers some of the wood from our mound of supplies, which is protected beneath yet another length of canvas. For a moment I watch her uneasily through the tent opening.

Pala and Commander Leifur finish eating and leave to check on the horses, and Saga mumbles something incoherent and conveniently leaves, too.

I briefly eye Vil before plopping down beside him, careful to keep space between us. "You all right, Vil?"

He shrugs a little ruefully. "This is taking so *long*."

I laugh. "It's only been a day. And it won't rain the whole time. Probably."

He turns to grin at me, and he's close enough I can feel the heat of his breath on my face. My own breath hitches as his eyes flick down to my mouth.

Outside, Indridi lets out a little whoop, and I start away from Vil. Flames lick up from her woodpile, hot enough to burn even in the rain. I don't think it's my imagination that the rain starts to slacken, bit by bit, as the fire grows brighter, until it's hardly dripping at all.

I leave the tent with Vil at my heels, and then there is indeed tea and toasted cheese, enough to warm my belly, enough to ease the prick of ever-present fear in my heart and dispel a bit the tension of whatever it is that's building between Vil and me. He sits on the opposite side of the fire and I'm able to relax, to enjoy the hot cheese and scalding tea.

I'm full to bursting when Saga slips away from the fire, rummages among our supplies, and returns with a tray of jewelry and an alarmingly sharp-looking needle. She thrusts the tray into the firelight and orders me to scoot closer, too, so she can see better.

"Gold or sapphire?" she asks.

I laugh. "What?"

She rattles the tray and shoves it nearly into my face. "Sooner we do this, sooner it heals. Now. Gold or sapphire?"

I focus on the tray and the dozen or so earrings spread out on it. Some are simple gold twists, some are heavy with jewels.

I look at her in absolute confusion, and it's her turn to laugh. Vil's laughing, too, into his tea on the other side of the fire.

"You're posing as Skaandan royalty, Bryn," says Saga. "If you don't have an earring or two, your story will fall apart pretty quickly."

"Oh." I take another look at that needle. "Will it hurt?"

"Nothing you can't handle."

"That means yes!" says Vil helpfully.

Saga swears at him and then turns back to me. "Will you please pick out the ones you like? Two or three will do to start. I would have done this weeks ago, but you only decided you were coming this morning."

I sigh, studying the earrings carefully, then choose two simple gold rings and a single flashing ruby.

Saga nods approvingly. She uncorks a bottle of strong-smelling alcohol and pours it on a cloth, which she then dabs onto my left ear. She jabs the needle in without any sort of warning, and a bright prick of pain shoots through me. I curse perhaps more vehemently than the situation requires, up and down the pantheon of all twelve gods. Saga just laughs and pierces my ear twice more. Then she fits the earrings in and hands me a fresh mug of tea by way of apology.

Vil winks across at me, his eyes glittering. "No one else lets her touch them with needles anymore."

"I did a *fine* job!" Saga objects.

Vil ignores her. "They look nice, Brynja."

His compliment warms my belly nearly as much as the toasted cheese, but it doesn't do much to dull the smarting pain of my ear. I chase down the tea with the remaining contents of that potent bottle.

The rain stops altogether, and stars prick through the clouds. We sit around the fire, everyone but Pala—she and Commander Leifur will trade off standing watch through the night. Indridi keeps glancing at Vil. Vil keeps looking at me, a question in his eyes, wanting perhaps to continue our interrupted moment from inside the tent.

But I'm tired and my ear hurts and I don't know what I want. *A river rushing in the dark. Blue pebbles in the palm of my hand. His magic bursting bright inside of me.* I push the memories away with an inward curse.

Saga has brought out her carving things, her fingers deft in the firelight as she works on a knife hilt. I squint to see what she's carving: a sun design, the rays wrapping around the hilt. It's beautiful, and the familiar snick of her knife cutting into the wood comforts me. Saga is not a great advocate of being still. When she has to be, she carves to keep her mind steady and her hands busy and, she informed me once, to keep from shouting at whoever is making her be still in the first place.

"Stories," Saga declares, blade glinting. "Before we sleep. You start, Brynja."

Vil smiles across at me, and despite myself my chest goes tight. Indridi pokes at the ground with one finger. The fire seems to flare a little hotter.

I stare at Saga's hands, at the carving taking shape, and stop myself from tugging at my throbbing ear. "The Black God ruled in his darkness," I begin. "He covered all the world with it, ignoring the pleas of the other gods. So the Red God, the god of fire, and the Brown Goddess, the goddess of the earth, came together and made between them the twelfth god—the Yellow God, the god of light. He was powerful, nearly as strong as the Prism Goddess, but he was yet very young. All the gods and goddesses agreed to send him to defeat the Black God, but they didn't understand quite what it would cost."

"No one *ever* understands what something might cost," says Saga agreeably. *Snick snick snick* goes her knife.

Vil is watching me so steadily I have to fix my eyes on a distant point in the night sky, lest I get too distracted to finish. "Light and darkness met on the highest mountain of the earth," I go on. "Little by little, the Yellow God defeated the Black God. Thread by thread he stole the darkness away, until what little was left of the Black God was able to be bound into a pillar of smoke. The other gods and goddesses appeared, congratulating the Yellow God. The Prism Goddess encased the smoke of the Black God in glass, and the Brown Goddess buried it deep within the mountain.

"But none of them had counted on the boundless power now contained within the Yellow God. When there is no darkness, how can the world sleep? When there is only light, how can you see the stars? The world was too bright, and the Yellow God too powerful.

"So the gods and goddesses reached a compromise. The Brown Goddess dug into the mountain and retrieved the smoke bound in glass. The Prism Goddess cracked the glass, enough so that every night the Black God could seep out and blanket the world, for a little while, with his darkness. But no one ever saw him in his true form again, for the greater part of his power, the very spark of his soul, dwelled within the Yellow God."

I fall silent, watching the flames—the mark of the Red God—spin up into the night. I can still feel Vil's eyes on me, but I don't raise my own to meet them.

"I've heard that story many times," sighs Saga. "But no one tells it quite like you do, Brynja."

I shrug, but I'm pleased at her praise.

"Indridi next!" Saga crows. She puts down her carving knife and blows shavings off the hilt. The design is finished now, and I know from experience she'll lacquer it, then fit it around the blade. Then it will be done, and she'll start carving something new.

"Forgive me, Your Highness," says Indridi tightly. "I don't have any stories."

"Of course you do. You've told them lots of times. What's going on with you?"

Indridi's lips pinch together and she doesn't answer, her hands twisting together in her lap.

Knots pull tight in my stomach.

"Leave her be, Saga," says Vil after a moment. "It's late. We should all get some sleep—early start in the morning."

Indridi shoots him a grateful look, and I forcibly shove down another pulse of jealousy.

Saga gives a very overdramatic sigh but acquiesces, packing up her carving things and leading Indridi and me back to the big tent.

"Indridi, what's wrong?" Saga asks quietly when the three of us have folded ourselves into our bedrolls. Pala will not join us until later, when Commander Leifur relieves her watch.

"You know you can tell me anything," Saga goes on. Her voice is infinitely gentle.

"There is nothing to tell, Your Highness. Truly."

Saga sighs. "You didn't have to come, you know, if you didn't want to."

For a moment silence spins between us, broken only by the distant pop and crack of the fire.

"I wanted to come," says Indridi.

No one says anything more.

We sleep, and I dream, as I often do, of falling.

TEN YEARS AGO

YEAR 4190, Month of the Ghost God
Daeros—Tenebris

I grow braver, bit by bit. Sometimes, when I am performing, I dare to slide all the way down the aerial silks and ropes, to cartwheel across the floor and tumble past the king and whatever dignitaries he's invited to view his Collection. My fingers are as quick as the rest of me: I filch hairpins and jewels and, once, a small knife.

The king never speaks a word of praise—not to me, not to anyone. But mostly we're all locked back into our cages when we're finished performing. Mostly he lets us live.

I use the knife, first. I cut off my hair, and then I scrape the blade against my scalp again and again, until I have no hair left at all. I do it because I am terrified my hair will get caught on a chain or a rope or a silk when I'm performing, that I'll get trapped, choked, that I'll break my neck. I do it because I am afraid and because, here, it is the only thing that I can control. I feel lighter when I've done it. Freer. Like not everything I am has been taken from me.

I've been a full month in the king's Collection before I finally dare to use the hairpins, which I've been hiding in the weave of my blanket. I poke them into the lock on my cage, wiggling and twisting and pushing until the lock clicks open. Then I'm free, gripping the chain that holds

While the Dark Remains

the cage aloft, shimmying down it and shaking with terror until my feet are planted firmly on the floor.

I slip up to the double doors that lead to the rest of the mountain palace but freeze with my small hand on the latch. There are guards on the other side of the door; I hear them shift where they stand, sword belts creaking.

I scamper back across the hall and climb, quick as a spider, up to my cage again before I am quite aware of my intent. I crouch on my sleeping ledge, heart raging in my ears.

But no one comes. My trespass is not discovered.

So the next night, I do it again.

And the next.

And the next.

And the next.

※

I become aware, little by little, of the others below me. I don't mean to, but I cannot be wholly, forever alone, with only my own thoughts and fears to occupy my mind.

So I notice the other children in the Collection; I learn their names and their abilities. I see how broken they are, the cold numbness in their eyes. There is Corinna, a brilliant Daerosian painter. Eirene, a Daerosian singer. There are Edda and Frida, twin Skaandans who dance with swords. There is Tier, the Skaandan boy who came in the wagon with me: He's a harpsichordist. There is one Iljaria, a young boy named Dagmar, who is blessed by the Red God and can make fire out of anything. He is kept in an iron cage, the only metal that can dampen his magic and keep the king and his court safe.

The king and the guards call the children not by their names but by their ability: So there is Painter and Singer and Swords. There is Harpsichord and Fire and me, Acrobat. But the children tell each other

33

their names, refusing to forget these precious pieces of themselves. I don't tell anyone my name. I keep it hidden safe in my soul.

The king has four wives. Pelagia and Elpis are both Daerosian, and Unnur is Skaandan. Gulla is Iljaria, and I hear her story shortly after the king first locks me in my cage.

Gulla was once part of the king's Collection. She claimed the White Goddess—goddess of music—as her patron, and boasted that she could make the king and his entire court go to sleep with just a note of her magic. She did, and when the king woke up, he cut out her tongue.

And then he married her.

The story makes me sick; it is too like what happened to the Bronze God, who was left mutilated and alone. I don't like to see her, powerless and mute, trapped in the mountain.

The king has children: four sons, two daughters. They're young, no older than the children in his Collection. They like to come into the great hall, gawk at us in our cages, poke things through the bars, laugh at us. All except for Gulla's son.

The first time I notice him is on an evening the Collection is called upon to perform, trotted out like prize horses and made to show our tricks and our teeth. I perform next to last, confident enough in my routine by now to end it with a flourish at the king's feet, sweeping him an elaborate bow as I gulp for breath and try to slow the mad pace of my heart.

The king eyes me coolly, his blue eyes sharp against glacier-white skin. He waves a hand, dismissing me, and as I am stepping back into my cage, I see the boy. He looks about my own age of ten, his skin a perfect blend of his father's light and his mother's dark. His hair a mix of theirs, too, the loose curls a tangle of white and black. There are swirls of blue tattooed onto his arms, marking his power as coming from the goddess of animals, whom the Iljaria call the Blue Lady.

He paces to the ivory throne waiting for him in the center of the room, as Daerosian nobles and the king's wives and children look on. The throne is writhing with snakes.

"Get *in*," barks the king's steward to me, prodding me in the back with the handle of his whip.

I obey, climbing into my cage, barely aware of the key turning in the lock, losing my balance as the steward hauls on the chain to send me spinning back to the peak of the ceiling.

My eyes are fixed on the scene below, on the throne, the snakes, the half-Iljaria boy.

He sits without fear, the snakes sliding harmlessly around him, hanging on his shoulders like a cloak, circling his brow like a crown.

The king laughs and claps from his place among the onlookers, and the rest applaud politely. The king frowns, displeased that his audience is not as keen on this show as he is. He jerks up from his seat, stalks over to the throne.

"They are not amazed, boy," says the king. "Of course the serpents do not hurt you, with your barbarian magic. Let them clothe me instead."

The boy turns wild eyes on the king. "Father," he says in a hoarse, choked voice. "What if they hurt you?"

"Then I will kill you," says the king frankly. "So you had better see that they do not."

The nobles laugh at this. I guess they're the only ones who don't realize the king's threat is not a joke.

The boy stands from the throne. He trembles before his father. He shuts his eyes. Slowly, the snakes slide from him and creep up the edges of the king's robes. Slowly, they coil about the king's arms and legs, transform themselves into a crown.

The king turns to his audience. He bows with a flourish while the sweat pours from his son's head and the snakes hiss with anger. The nobles clap loudly.

Then the show is over. The animal handlers come to shut the snakes in wooden crates. I can't help but wonder what will become of them.

The noblemen leave and the wives file out until there is only the king, and the boy, who stands there and shakes. The king slaps him, hard, across the face. The boy bows his head, hands clenched into fists.

"Don't question me again, Ballast," says the king.

The boy nods, staring at his feet. "I'm sorry, Father."

The king stalks from the hall without another word, and the boy collapses to the floor. He weeps, for a while, though his tears are soundless even in this vast, echoing room. Then he slips away. This is how I learn that the only difference between Ballast and the rest of us is he doesn't sleep in a cage at night.

But he is every bit a part of his father's Collection, all the same.

CHAPTER THREE

YEAR 4200, Month of the Bronze God
Skaanda/Daeros—the Saadone River

We're two weeks on the road before we reach Saadone, the city built on the banks of the great river that shares its name. We've passed scattered villages and acres of sprawling farmland on our way, more of Vil's housing abandoned half built beside the fields. Already the sun sinks a little earlier each night, and if the crops aren't harvested before Gods' Fall, they'll be left to rot. The housing will have to wait, much to Vil's dismay.

I've been keeping my distance from Vil since that first night. I don't know how to untangle the snarl of my own emotions, and I can't allow myself to get close to him before I've sorted them out. It wouldn't be fair to him—or to me—and the nearer we get to Tenebris, the less certain I am about anything: Vil. Me. Our mission. It's all confusion and uncertainty and dread.

So I put space between us, as much as is possible in our little company of six.

It's midafternoon when we ride into Saadone City, the stink of the river thick in the air, the sudden press of people jarring and overloud after the long quiet of the road.

"With any luck we should be able to catch the last ferry," Vil calls from the front of our group. "Then we won't have to wait till the morning."

I glance back at Saga, who twists her fingers in her horse's mane. The Saadone marks the border between Skaanda and Daeros. Once we cross, we'll be in constant danger—and close to the site of the disastrous skirmish that left her at Kallias's mercy.

"I'm fine," says Saga brightly.

Indridi and I exchange a knowing glance.

"Why don't we stop early today?" I say to Vil. "Stay at an inn, sleep in a real bed." I give a little sigh at the thought. A year and a half in a royal Skaandan feather bed has made me soft—I haven't slept well since we left Staltoria City.

"As much as I would like that," says Vil, with a pointed look at me that makes me flush at my accidental implication, "we can't afford the time. Besides, the inns are sure to be full on account of the holiday."

It takes me a minute to remember what holiday he's talking about: the Bronze God's feast day, a celebration of the harvest. But the feast has more to do with the time of year than it does with the god of minds.

I shift uncomfortably in my saddle. I've never liked the Bronze God's story. There's certainly nothing *celebratory* about it. But like anyone, I suppose, Skaandans skew religion to fit their desires, instead of the other way around. If pressed, a priest might explain that it's a commemoration of the Bronze God's banishment and the return of people's free will. Although if *that's* the case, it would make more sense to honor the Prism Goddess—she's the one who banished him, after all. But maybe the Prism Goddess has too many feast days already. And the most religious among us are proud if they can afford clothing in every color of the pantheon—when would they wear bronze, if not now?

"If I may, Your Highness," says Pala.

Vil nods his permission.

"I would suggest having a meal in a public house while I secure us passage on the ferry."

"We won't miss it?" Vil asks.

"Not if you're at the docks in an hour."

"I'm happy to go to secure passage," Indridi says quickly.

Pala frowns at her for speaking out of turn but doesn't otherwise acknowledge her offer. "An hour, Your Highness." She salutes Vil and nudges her mount down one of the twisting, clay-tiled streets, and quickly disappears from view.

Vil leads the rest of us through the milling crowd to a three-storied building made of earthen brick. The hanging wooden sign carved with the symbol of a woman and a blooming rose, both painted bright green, marks it as belonging to the Green Goddess. There are hundreds of such public houses scattered across Skaanda—this one is hardly unique. It hits me anew how such a pious people as us Skaandans can dedicate temples and drinking places to the same deity and not be struck down for blasphemy.

A pair of half-grown boys trot around from the back to take our horses, and then we file into the public house, Vil and Leifur leading, with me and Saga in the middle and Indridi bringing up the rear.

It's noisy inside, raucous laughter and steady conversation fighting for dominance over the trio of musicians in the corner playing fiddle, drums, and piercing pitched bells. Incense from the obligatory altar to the Green Goddess coils up from its place in the center of the room, a green basin on a simple plinth, with vines growing up from the base of it and leaves trailing over the basin's rim.

Both Saga and Vil pull scarves over their heads and train their eyes low to keep from being recognized—their official portraits have been published widely enough for that to be a concern—while Indridi and Leifur go up to the counter to order food from the proprietor.

Then we all squeeze ourselves into a corner booth with a little circle window that looks out over the water. At nearly ten miles wide, the Saadone River might seem like the ocean, I think, to someone who had never seen the real thing. It's brown and green, a slow-moving mammoth that runs chillingly deep.

Somehow, in the rush to fit into the booth, I find myself scooted all the way against the wall with Vil next to me, his hip touching mine. The heat of him sears me. I carefully don't acknowledge him, but look up to find Saga grinning at me across the table. She waggles her eyebrows suggestively.

Indridi is sitting next to Saga, watching Vil with a hopelessness that simultaneously angers me and makes my heart twist. Leifur is on the other side of Vil, nervously jiggling his knee. He's not used to eating with Vil and Saga, and his hand keeps going up to his left ear to touch the gold bar that marks him as a royal guard. He watches Indridi watch Vil, and I want to shake the lot of them.

Thankfully, the food arrives and we inhale it, red rice and spicy lamb stew, candied figs and little square orange cakes glazed with honey. There's mead, too, clear and sweet, and marvelously strong coffee.

I try not to be aware of Vil beside me, but it's impossible not to be, his hand grazing mine as we both reach for more candied figs, the way his lips look stained with mead, or the way he stirs just the right amount of cream and sugar into my coffee because he knows exactly how I prefer it. He doesn't move his leg the whole time we're sitting there, like the two of us have been fused together.

By the time-glass on the wall, we still have half an hour before we're due to meet Pala, so we stay awhile longer in our booth, sipping drinks and imagining we have room for more of the orange cakes that tantalize us from the table. Vil and Saga take this opportunity to quiz me on my fake persona for when we arrive at Tenebris, and I'm grateful for anything to distract me from Vil's heady proximity.

I'm to pose as Vil's cousin, the stepdaughter of Vil and Saga's mother's sister, which explains my lighter coloring. Memorization has always come easily to me, which is good because Saga and Vil insist I know the Skaandan royal lineage all the way back to the beginning, some four hundred years ago, when the threat of genocide drove them out of Iljaria.

Along with Indridi, Saga will act as my handmaiden, too certain that Kallias would recognize her to pose as an ambassador with Vil and me. Everyone in Daeros still thinks that the crown princess of Skaanda is dead, and unlike mine, Saga's appearance hasn't changed much since her captivity.

So she will stay out of sight, while I hope my mop of dark curls that have begun to brush my shoulders and my altered figure and the cosmetics Indridi practices applying every few evenings will trick Kallias into thinking I am exactly what I claim to be.

"We never did decide on how to round out your history," says Vil thoughtfully when I finish my recitation of Skaandan royalty. "Some talent or particular interest, in case Kallias pokes holes in your story."

My mouth tastes suddenly sour.

Vil's face softens at the horror in my expression. "There must have been something," he says gently. "Before Kallias. Before—"

I blink and see my parents, my brother, my sister. A house on a hill. An untainted sky. The gleam of sunlight on the water. "My talent is acrobatics," I say roughly. "I was ten when Kallias took me. I was a child, Vil. Reckless and impatient and filled with boundless energy. I could never be still enough to learn painting or memorize poetry or whatever it is *you* did when you were ten. I don't have any particular interests."

He lets my anger roll off him, then shrugs a little and says, "By the time I was ten, I was skilled enough in my weapons training I could kill a man in fifty different ways if I wanted."

Indridi makes a choked noise while Saga glares at her brother. "You're not helping, Vil."

"I *didn't* want to," Vil clarifies, glaring back. "I only mean to say I had no special interests at that age, either. I just did what I was told. Please forgive my thoughtless question."

My throat hurts. Vil takes my hand under the table and squeezes it, his fingers warm and rough. My pulse quickens in his palm. I wonder if I ought to reconsider my resolution to keep him at a distance.

It would be so easy to allow him nearer, to sink into his steadfastness and security. I would want for nothing, on the arm of Skaanda's prince. I've had a taste of it already, these last eighteen months: belonging, purpose. Maybe even love. I'm not assured of any of those things, even if our mission in Daeros is successful. I wonder sometimes if I ever had them, even before Kallias stole my life away.

"You have a mind for stories," Vil says, breaking me from my thoughts. "We can always tell Kallias you've studied as a historian."

I glance at Indridi, who fiddles with her coffee cup, lips pressed tight together.

"We'd better go," I say abruptly, pulling my hand from Vil's. "If we're not to the ferry in time, Pala will kill us."

※

The ferry is essentially a giant barge, with a pen on one end of it for horses and other livestock that need to cross the river. I stand shoulder to shoulder with Saga by the knee-high rail, a coveted position away from the central knot of passengers, who are packed in so tight together it's hard to breathe. The stink from the river itself doesn't help any. I stare into the murky water and will us to reach the opposite bank faster than the promised quarter hour. We lost Vil and the others in the initial press to get onto the ferry, but will find them again as soon as we reach the other shore.

Saga and I both tilt our faces west, where the sun sinks over Skaanda, already half vanished behind the horizon.

"Is this all a mistake?" Saga says, low in my ear.

I think of all the decisions that have led us to this point, of all the ones still left to make. "Maybe," I tell her. "But it's necessary."

She nods, holding tight to my arm. It feels right that we're here together, that we mean to end as we began. Vil might be leading our company, but the mission is mine, and Saga's. She is the only soul in the world who understands me. Apart from—

While the Dark Remains

But I shove that thought away. "We're going to end him," I tell Saga. "We're going to make him pay for what he did to us."

"Yes," Saga whispers. *"Hell yes."*

The sun disappears wholly from the horizon, and a sudden chill permeates the air. I think of winter, of unending cold and unending darkness. There are two months, yet, of light left, but already I am longing for the sun to rise.

There's a chaos of confusion when at last the ferry reaches the far bank. Torches flare, passengers clamor to reunite with their parties or claim their livestock. We find Vil and the rest without trouble, though Pala does a good deal of shouting at the ferry master and still has to hand over an additional pouch of coins before he relinquishes our horses and packs and we're back on our way again.

We ride away from the majority of passengers, who are returning home to the villages scattered along the banks of the Saadone. Technically we're in Daeros now, but Skaanda has controlled this section of the river for a handful of years. Many Skaandans work in Saadone City and live here, where it's cheaper, protected by the small Skaandan army encampment a little ways to the south. We should be relatively safe, for the night at least.

But we've only just made camp when a Daerosian rides up to our fire, recognizable by his blue sleeves and scale-armor breastplate. A lantern that pulses red with Iljaria magic hangs from his saddle horn, illuminating him in an eerie glow. He hefts a spear in one hand, eyes glittering beneath his steel helm.

"By whose authority does an armed Skaandan company tread on Daerosian soil?" the soldier demands. His free hand twitches to the bone whistle that hangs on a cord at his neck, ready to alert his own company.

Beside me, Saga seethes, hand on her sword hilt, though she ducks her head out of the light.

"By this token," says Vil, fumbling for the peace banner that hangs on his belt for just such a challenge. He unfurls it quickly, so the

Daerosian scout can see the gold lily on the white field—an ancient symbol of peace. Vil jerks his chin at Pala and Leifur, who sheathe their swords and step back with twin reluctance. "Surely you recognize me," Vil adds, looking hard at the scout. "I'm the crown prince of Skaanda."

His brazenness makes my heart race, but I trust him to keep his cool.

Indridi is stirring a pot of soup over the fire, her cheeks traced with orange light. Her hands shake, and the fire seems to burn a little fiercer than before.

The Daerosian scowls at Vil and the banner in equal measure. "You will come and show your token to my commander, and explain to him your presence in Daeros."

Saga practically radiates anger at this, and Vil's eyes flick backward, willing her to keep her peace. "We'll come," says Vil.

"Just two of you," the scout objects, glancing uneasily at Pala and Leifur.

Vil shrugs. "Astridur, with me."

It takes me a moment to remember that *I* am Astridur, a false name chosen in case Kallias ever knew mine. The shape of it feels strange in my mind, in the pulses of my heart.

I fight down my rising panic and step to Vil's side.

We walk on foot after the Daerosian as the stars appear over the wide expanse of autumn meadow, our boots flattening the grass and clouds of gnats swirling up.

I wish Pala and Leifur were with us. We have no guarantee that the Daerosian commander won't take one look at us and clap us in irons— or worse—peace banner be damned.

Vil strides tall and confident beside me, and I find myself steadied by his strength. His eyes flick briefly to mine as he takes my hand. The touch of his fingers sends a familiar heat through me, coiling down to my toes.

Too soon, the Daerosian camp comes into view below the ridge of a hill, sprawling and vast, thousands of fires stretching into the distance. I am suddenly, wildly afraid that Kallias is here with his army, that he will see me, know me. That he will drag me back to his mountain palace, back to my iron cage.

Vil senses my panic and tightens his grip on my hand, mooring me to the present, holding me here, with him. I let his stability cover me like a cloak.

The scout leads us down a winding path and into the valley, where raucous soldiers sit around roaring fires, eating their evening meal and passing wine bottles back and forth. The air reeks of smoke and alcohol.

We halt at a huge tent the color of the autumn grass, and at the scout's call, his commander steps out, a tall man with lines pressed into his pale face. His scale armor is traced with gold, the hilt of his sword encrusted with jewels. He's clearly been pulled away from his dinner, too, crumbs in the corner of his mouth, lips stained with wine.

Vil lets go of my hand and kneels before the commander, though I know it must grate on him. He holds the peace banner outstretched in both hands. I don't kneel. I can't make my body bend. I just stand there and try not to let the panic drown me, while sparks from the nearby campfire leap out and sizzle to nothing in the dirt.

"We come as ambassadors to your king," says Vil in his tenor-rich voice. "We come proposing peace between our nations, and ask for free passage across Daeros."

The commander folds his arms across his chest, wholly unimpressed. "Have you some other token, boy, beyond your word and this worthless rag?"

Vil's body goes tight, but there is no other sign of his anger. He works his seal ring off the first finger of his left hand and shows the commander the eight-pointed red star worked into the metal. "This, sir, and the weight of my blood as crown prince of Skaanda." Vil takes the dagger from his belt, pricks his finger, and presses the spot of blood onto the truce banner.

The commander scowls, considering. Such a pledge is binding, the blood invoking the gods as witness. Daerosians don't believe in the gods, but they've seen enough Iljaria magic to be superstitious, and in any case their treaty with the Aeronan Empire requires them to abide by offers of peace. Although that still wouldn't keep the commander from slitting our throats and burning the banner right here, right now, with none the wiser.

In the end he just utters a curse and pricks his own finger, smearing his blood next to Vil's. Then he thrusts the flag into Vil's hands and orders us the hell out of his camp.

Vil and I walk back under a star-spangled sky.

It is some minutes before my racing heart quiets a bit, enough for me to hear the crickets in the grass. Vil takes my hand again.

Somehow, he knows my thoughts. "I won't let that bastard king touch you," he says, low and feral. "I won't let him. Do you believe me, Bryn?"

I tilt my face toward his, his earrings flashing in the light of the rising moon. My heart beats, beats. I want to fold myself into him. Borrow his strength because I am not sure I have any left of my own. "Yes," I whisper. "I believe you."

We stop walking, and he gazes down at me in the moonlight, one finger tracing the line of my brow. My skin sparks where he touches me.

"Brynja," he says, his voice uneven, a question in his eyes.

I give him the smallest of nods because I find I can't speak, and then he's leaning his head down, crushing his mouth against mine. I kiss him back, raw and wild, and his hands are on my shoulders, pulling me closer. He tastes of salt and wanting, of the mead we drank at the public house and the slight tang of spiced lamb stew. He holds me so tight there is no space for breath in my lungs, and suddenly I am not here anymore, in the moonlight with Vil. I am down in the dark by a rushing river. I am—

I break away, panic jolting through me.

Vil looks at me, breathing hard, his whole body trembling. His eyes spark with hurt. "Brynja, I thought—"

"My fault," I manage. I'm shaking, too. I gulp desperate mouthfuls of air.

"There is no fault," he says roughly. "There is nothing wrong with—" He waves one hand between us. "This. You and me."

Something sticks in my throat, and I want to cry. "I know."

"Then what is it? Why did you pull away?"

I don't know how to explain it to him. I don't know how to explain it to myself.

Vil's jaw tenses. He kicks at the ground, and another cloud of gnats swirls up. "I don't know what the king did to you, what his damned son did to you, but I'm not them, Brynja. I would never hurt you. I would never—"

"Ballast didn't do anything to me," I say to the grass, my raging pulse not quite back to normal.

Vil curses. "We both know that isn't true."

And there it is. I flick my eyes up to him. "Saga told you." Her betrayal hurts, but it isn't, I guess, unexpected. We have peace, Saga and I. Understanding. In all things but this.

Vil's throat works and he looks away, fighting to regain control of himself.

"I'm sorry," I say miserably, helplessly.

His eyes find mine again, and the anger has already ebbed out of him. "It's all right, Bryn. You've been through a lot, and it makes sense that you need time to . . . understand it all. To understand yourself. I'll wait for you. I don't mind."

I bite my lip, the tears pressing hot. "Thanks, Vil."

He gives me half a smile, but I don't miss the sorrow in it. "You don't need to thank me."

We walk side by side the rest of the way back to our camp. He doesn't take my hand again, and I know that I'm selfish for wishing he would.

"You were gone long enough," Saga says when we finally step up to the fire. "Thought you'd gotten yourselves killed. Or . . . lost." She grins at us, and my face washes hot.

But Vil doesn't let her bait him, which I'm grateful for. "Bit of a walk, both ways," is all he says.

I feel hollowed out as we eat our dinner. Vil catches my gaze across the fire and smiles at me, this time in earnest. I'm the one who looks away.

When we've eaten, Saga makes tea and asks for another story. Vil tells it this time.

"The Bronze God lived on an island in the sea. He was god of minds, and so could speak to the minds of all things, manipulating people and animals and even matter into doing his will. But he grew weary of friends and lovers who stayed with him only because of the power that seeped out of him whether he meant it to or not, ensnaring them to his will.

"So he lived for a time alone, eating fish that willingly swam into his nets, listening to choirs of birds who sang for him all day long, because he once had a stray thought that it would be pleasant if they did so.

"But one morning, he woke to find that his island had moved through the sea and joined itself to the mainland, answering the unspoken pain of his loneliness. There he found the Prism Goddess in her wondrous garden. Of all the pantheon, the Prism Goddess is the most powerful, for she holds within her pieces of all the other gods' magic. And so the Prism Goddess was the only one among men and gods who could resist the Bronze God's power. He fell in love with her, but she did not return his love."

Vil lapses into silence, and I feel heavy and wretched. He could have chosen any story at all, and *this* is the one he picked?

"I know it's the Bronze God's holiday and all," says Saga, "but you could have told a cheerier tale."

Vil shrugs, and I carefully don't look at him. He'll wait for me, he said. Does he mean like the Bronze God waited for the Prism Goddess?

Saga doesn't ask him to finish his story. None of us do. Instead we bid each other good night and crawl into our bedrolls, which we've laid out under the stars because the weather is clear.

The rest of the Bronze God's story has always haunted me, and sleep stays far away as it blooms unbidden in my mind, tangled up with the echoing sensation of Vil's kiss.

The Bronze God sought to win the Prism Goddess's love, though she told him many times it was not to be. He moved mountains for her. He sent her whole villages of people who plucked out their own hearts to display his true feelings. Thousands of people died for his love, and finally the Prism Goddess had had enough.

She called to her the Gray Goddess, goddess of death, and the Ghost God, god of nothing. Gray and Ghost held Bronze between them, while the Prism Goddess maimed him: She put out his eyes and cut out his tongue and cut off his ears. She cut off his feet and his hands. She healed his wounds so he would not die. And then she returned him to his island and sent it back into the sea.

If the Bronze God still lives, he has never shown his ruined body to anyone, ever again.

And yet every autumn there is feasting in his name, incense burned on his altars.

Vil's words whisper through my mind. *I'll wait for you.* I am drawn to him, to the strength and companionship he offers. With Vil I would have a true home, the belonging I never quite found with my own family. I want that, I *yearn* for it. But there is far too much ahead and behind to make that choice just yet.

I sleep at last. My dreams are not kind.

NINE YEARS AGO

YEAR 4191, Month of the Yellow God
Daeros—Tenebris

Gods' Fall is over. The sun returns, and the year begins anew. I don't welcome it. At least the days are still short, the light brief. I watch the hours climb up the Iljaria time-glass in the wall and shrink down again. I keep myself limber in my cage. I scrape the stolen knife against my scalp. I pick the lock every evening when the palace has gone to sleep. I stand a long while at the door, listening to the guards on the other side, angry that I am still trapped in a cage, even though I can get free of the iron one.

Most nights I step up to the great glass wall opposite those doors, and stare out into the Sea of Bones, watched over by the stars. Sometimes I stand with my hands splayed out on the glass, pressing against it until I can no longer bear the coldness. Sometimes I just sit and stare, feeling lost, alone, afraid.

Forgotten.

I am here at the glass wall one night, slumped on the floor, when someone touches my shoulder and I nearly jump out of my skin. I wheel to see Gulla, the king's Iljaria wife. She looks silvery in the starlight, her white hair almost seeming to shine.

I blink at her, heart slamming against my rib cage. She gives me a gentle smile and holds something out to me.

It's a slab of soap, a clean rag. She points at my head, mimes shaving it with a knife, then folds the soap and rag into my hand.

My heart pricks. I don't know how *she* knows how uncomfortable it is without soap, how I have cuts everywhere along my scalp.

"Thank you," I tell her softly.

Her smile deepens. She lifts her fingers, moves them slowly so I can see, and repeats the same motion several times. Then she points at me. I mimic the gesture with my own fingers, as best as I can.

"Does that mean 'thank you'?" I ask her.

She nods.

That warm feeling in my heart expands. "Teach me more," I say.

And she does. She teaches me how to shape the alphabet with my hands. She teaches me the words for *star* and *ice* and *dark*. And then she smiles yet again, squeezes my arm, and slips soundlessly away.

I watch her weave among the cages of the king's Collection and see that she has taught most of the children her finger speech already. They all have a kind word for her, and she's brought most of them trinkets she pulls from her pockets: bone charms or bits of ribbon, scraps of paper, stubby pencils. The children hoard her gifts and thank her sincerely.

Then she slides away across the hall, knocking at the doors to be let out.

She comes like this, every few nights, and I realize she cares for all of us in the king's Collection because she was once part of it, too. The only one, it seems, who has ever left the Collection and not ended in the Sea of Bones.

She brings me more slabs of soap, when she senses I have run out, and little treats: candies or nuts or, once, half a slice of cake, with frosting so sweet it nearly made me sick. And she continues to teach me her finger speech until her nimble hands have trained my clumsy ones, and I begin to understand her.

The ceilings, she tells me one night.

We're again sitting by the glass wall, bathed in moonlight. She's snuck me a piece of crumbly sweet bread. I meant to make it last but devoured every bit of it immediately.

"Ceilings?" I ask her.

They are false, she tells me.

My heart begins to race. "False ceilings."

She nods. *Palace carved from mountain. Ceilings false. Keep rooms heated.*

I try to tamp down my excitement. "Heated rooms."

Gulla nods again. She spells out her next word: *Vents.*

I turn to stare at the doors that have held me captive in this hall for so many weeks. My eyes slide to the time-glass beside them, to the grates above the time-glass that I've never thought much about before.

Gulla gives a silent laugh.

I make the sign for *thank you.* I hug her, sudden and tight.

She looks at me knowingly when I pull back and slips off to make her rounds with the other children.

I don't wait. I climb up the chain that leads to my cage and leap across to one of the swinging platforms. From there it's a few quick steps along the wire to the aerial silks hanging near the doors. The time-glass is designed with branching metal to look almost like a tree, the twenty-four veins that mark each hour encased in glass to trap whatever magic the Iljaria set within it long ago.

The metal branches protrude from the wall, each one nearly as wide as my foot. I leap from the silks without thinking, scrabbling for purchase and cutting my hand on one of the branches, which is sharper than I expected. But I ignore the pulse of pain as I take one of the filched hairpins from my belt and work on loosening the screws that hold the vents in place. The vents are an elaborate filigree of metalwork.

And they are large enough to climb inside, with room to spare.

My heart pounds as I slip into the upper vent, the metal freezing against my arms and legs. I pull the vent cover over the opening again, slipping my hand through the filigree to tighten the screw enough to keep the cover from clattering to the floor while I'm up here. Then I crawl forward, afraid that darkness will utterly consume me, but it doesn't.

The vent shaft opens up into a rocky domed space, rough wooden planks creating the ceiling for the room below me. Irregular knots in the wood allow chinks of light to shine through. I crouch there, shaking. A whole world has opened suddenly before me. *Finally.* I could cry, but I don't.

I take a deep breath.

I explore my new world.

CHAPTER FOUR

YEAR 4200, Month of the Red God
Daeros—the plains

There are more Daerosian camps after that first one. Vil has to show the peace banner every few days, and soon there is more red on it than white. I hate looking at it. Blood turns my stomach.

The daylight grows steadily shorter, but we can't afford to decrease our traveling time to match, so we ride an hour and then two in the early dark. We aren't as tired, though, our bodies hardened by the travel, and Saga decides to add another element to my royal education: dancing lessons.

I have danced some, of course, in the eighteen months I spent with them in the palace, but I am severely lacking in the years of formal training an actual Skaandan princess would have had. Since the Bronze God's feast day, Vil is the one who has been keeping his distance, and I suspect Saga has had enough of it. When she explains her plan, though, Vil doesn't take much persuading.

He teaches me the steps, solemn and steady, one hand on my shoulder and the other on my waist, the points of his fingers grazing my hip and sending heat through my veins. His eyes never leave mine.

We spin and sway under the stars, to the music of crickets and the rhythm of Saga's carving knife, while Indridi mends our clothes and Pala and Leifur keep a sharp watch beyond the circle of our fire. Every

While the Dark Remains

time Saga declares our practice is over, Vil releases me and strides off to his tent, glancing back as if daring me to follow. I never do.

One evening, when we've been at this for a few weeks, Vil pulls me into the dance as usual. Saga sings as she carves, and Indridi sews, never lifting her head.

Tomorrow our road turns north, toward Tenebris.

Toward Kallias and everything I want to forget.

Vil's hands are heavy and warm in their usual places: my shoulder, my waist. It is easy, dancing with him. Familiar and safe, for all it sends my heart into a desperate riot.

Vil has been impossibly kind to me, ever since the day Saga and I showed up at the palace with a regiment of the Skaandan army, in borrowed clothes and helms too big for us. They'd been eating luncheon, Vil and his parents, in the private dining room with an open balcony looking out over the menagerie.

I had halted in the doorway as Saga rushed in, and then the four of them were a big tangle of arms and legs and disbelieving shouts and grateful tears and it was Vil who looked back and saw me there, uncertain, lost, Vil who said, "Who's this, Saga?"

And then Saga broke away from them and ran to grab my arm and tug me back, explaining all in a jumble who I was and what had happened. She didn't make a whole lot of sense, but they understood that I had saved Saga, that I had brought her back to them. The queen wept on my shoulder and the king said something about a reward and Vil looked at me, tears brimming in his eyes, and thanked me sincerely.

After that Vil made a point to seek me out. He showed me the palace and the city. He gave me a horse and taught me how to throw knives in the arena. He would sit in the library when I was there, reading, not imposing or pestering me in any way, just offering his steady company. And then of course there were the strategy meetings with his parents and their generals and Saga as we concocted the scheme to seize Daeros. There were the many afternoons he and Saga and I would sit poring over the maps of the tunnels, tracing out the best route for the army to take.

Vil would take care of me, I know, if I let him. With him, I would be profoundly loved, unutterably *safe*. And yet I still cannot forget the blue-eyed boy, down with me in the dark, though with him there could only ever be danger.

Out on the star-drenched plain, Vil and I dance. His eyes pierce me through and I feel something like shame coiling in the pit of my belly.

"Where did you go just now?" he asks me quietly. "I wish—" His forehead creases. "I wish you would let me know you. The *real* you. The one you hide."

I meet his eyes in the shifting firelight, heart racing. "I don't hide from you, Vil."

"Then tell me. Tell me everything. About your childhood and your family before—before the mountain. About what you want and what you dream of. You've told me some, but I want to know it all. I want to know every piece of you, Brynja Sindri. Give me something." His voice pitches lower. "While I wait."

I take a breath, hyperaware of the pressure of his fingers at my waist, of the intensity in his eyes and the warmth of his breath, whispering past my cheek. "My father is a mirror maker, and my mother is an architect. Or they were ten years ago, at least."

"A mirror maker?" says Vil.

I shrug. "Someone has to make them."

"True."

"I'm the youngest of three siblings. My brother is a scholar, and my sister was a mechanical genius."

"Was?"

"She died when I was small."

He waits to see if I will say more but doesn't press me, which makes my chest hurt.

He wants to know the real me, so I tell him. "She was trying out one of her inventions, but it failed and . . . and she fell."

"What was her invention?"

My breath hitches. "A pair of wings made of canvas and wood and wire. They were beautiful. But they failed her. They killed her. It's why—" I fight to say more, trembling as we both heedlessly follow the pattern of the dance. "It's why I'm afraid of falling."

Vil's throat works, and his fingers press a little harder into my shoulder, sending a trail of fire down my spine. "I'm so sorry, Brynja. It must have been awful for you. When we thought we'd lost Saga—" He shakes his head. "I was not well, for a long time."

I fight down the old horror, that familiar sense of despair ready to drown me anew. "In my family, we were expected to be remarkable," I tell him quietly. "I had no talent for books or inventions. But my body would mind me. I could bend it to my will. So I did."

"Your acrobatics," says Vil.

"Yes."

Saga has stopped her singing now and is chatting with Indridi by the popping fire, knife blade flashing in the light. Vil and I keep dancing; the motion grounds me—if I stop, I fear I will fall apart.

"I wanted to make my family proud, like they were proud of my brother and my sister. I trained religiously. I made myself remarkable. But there was a woman." There's a sour taste in my mouth that I can't get rid of. "She saw me performing in my village, and she—she told my parents she had a place for me in her traveling troupe. She promised them a hefty sum, said I must only perform with the troupe in the summers, and the rest of the year I could be at home."

"You were a *child*," says Vil, voice tight with anger. "Surely your parents didn't—"

"They needed money to pay for my sister's funeral expenses, to buy my brother more books. My father's business was slow, my mother's practically nonexistent. This was a way for me to be useful, a solution sent straight from the gods."

"Gods' bleeding *hearts*," Vil swears.

My own heart pricks that he would feel such fierce emotion on my behalf, when my own family did not.

We dance, dance, while the stars look down.

"Perhaps it would have been different," I say quietly, "if they'd known the woman meant to take me straight to Kallias, to sell me for twice the sum she'd promised them. I like to believe it would have been different."

I chew on my lip. I'm not going to cry. Not in front of Vil. Not ever, if I can help it. I don't want him to think that I am weak.

"They never looked for you," he realizes. "Or if they did, they never found you."

I stop dancing, suddenly, and he stumbles but does not fall. He holds so tight to me it almost hurts. "And when you finally went home," he says, "they weren't there." He's breathing hard, harder than his small stumble merits.

I am, too. "No."

"But you know where to find them?"

"I think so."

"Then why are you here with us, instead of searching for them?"

A sudden wind seethes over the plain, blowing smoke at Saga and Indridi and causing them to choke and swear.

I blink grit out of my eyes. I don't look away from Vil. "I prayed for the gods to send my parents to rescue me, for years and years. I begged, groveled, made vows and spat curses. But they never came. I don't know if my parents stopped caring for me, or if the gods did." It isn't grit in my eyes now. I gnaw the inside of my cheek.

"My parents aren't here to slay my demons, Vil. So *I'm* going to. Maybe when Kallias is dead, I can sleep at night. Maybe when he's gone, I can finally prove to my family that I am every bit as remarkable as my siblings. Every bit as worthy of their regard."

"Brynja," says Vil, gently, face stricken.

"They don't feel like my family anymore. You and Saga are my family, Vil. And I mean to see this through."

He pulls me against his chest, and for a moment I allow myself to sink into him, his heart beating fast under my ear, his scent soaking into my skin.

"There is too much," I whisper into his shirt. "There is too much left to do. I can't—"

"I know," says Vil. He presses a kiss into my hair and releases me.

I walk past Saga and Indridi, hyperaware of their eyes on me, infinitely grateful for the cover of night so they can't see how red my face is. I crawl into my bedroll, curling tight into a ball and gritting my teeth until I can be sure I'm not going to cry. I don't want to think about my parents, my brother, my sister. I don't want to think about how all this started. I just want it to be over. Gods, *gods*. I just want it to be over.

Maybe then I can be what Vil wants. Maybe then I will know what I want, too.

In the morning we start on the road to Tenebris. We have several weeks to go yet, but this is the last leg of our journey. No more twists and turns—just straight on to the mountain.

We don't run into any soldiers, but we pass groups of Daerosian farmers or merchants who glower and swear at us as we ride by. The bloodied peace banner hangs plainly from Vil's saddle, keeping them from hurling anything more harmful than insults and a few unripe apples. One hits me hard on the arm, and I know I'll have a bruise to look forward to later.

In the afternoon, the daylight already fading, we glimpse a glittering company riding toward us on the road. Beside me, Saga's whole body hardens; ahead of us, Vil curses. My heart jerks sideways, and I suddenly find it hard to breathe. Pala and Leifur both draw their swords. I can sense Indridi tremble.

The company is Iljaria, easily identifiable by their white hair. Their banners are sewn with tiny mirrors that refract the sunlight in every color, making it painful to look at them. What the *hell* are they doing here? They're supposed to be safely on the other side of their magical barrier. The Iljaria leave their country only rarely, and it seems like more than some sick chance that their path would intersect with ours.

They draw nearer, and panic drums against my breastbone. There are too many of them for us to subdue, especially considering their magic, and in any case it would violate the terms of the peace banner to attack them. I tangle my fingers in my horse's mane and will myself to be steady.

Saga is a pillar of rage on my left, while Vil sits tense, wary, watching the Iljaria approach. They rein in a few paces from us, their horses stamping and blowing, dust rising up from their hooves. The Iljaria themselves regard us with glittering eyes, like we're of no more consequence to them than worms.

There are ten Iljaria in all, clothed in elegant robes the colors of their patron gods, whom they call Lords: green and blue and violet, bronze and black and yellow, brown and white and gray. Their leader wears red, the color of the god of fire. Their skin tones range from light to very dark, with every shade between. The youngest of them looks hardly fifteen, the eldest no more than fifty, though in reality he could be much older. They wear their white hair in all different styles, some short, some long, some bound, some loose. Five are men, and five women.

The Iljaria leader doesn't look much older than me. He sits tall in his saddle, his long white hair twisted into braids, the ends crimped in metal bands. His skin is smooth and light, with a spattering of freckles on his nose that somehow hardens instead of softens him. He teems with magic, and it is so strong I can feel it crawling under my own skin, and I want to be sick in the grass.

"Hail," says Vil finally, when the Iljaria show no sign of speaking. The word is cold and bitter.

The Iljaria leader raises one pale eyebrow, and the ends of his braids spark with sudden flame.

Behind me, Indridi gasps, but I don't dare look back at her. The leader's magic rages through me, and I fight the urge to scream, to flee.

One of the Iljaria, a young woman with dark skin and a blue robe, has a venomous snake wound about her shoulders, kept docile with her magic. It lifts its head and hisses at us. An older man dressed in green flicks his wrist, and vines burst out of the earth, twisting near us and our horses, who shift uneasily.

"Turn your mounts off the road and let us pass," Vil grinds out. "You have no right to ride here."

The Iljaria leader gives an exasperated sigh and waves his hand at the rest of his company. The flames in his hair wink out, the vines retreat back into the ground, the snake lowers its head.

"We ride to the shrine of the Gray Lady to honor our revered dead," says the Iljaria leader. "Our passage was bought through free trade with the king of Daeros, and by the order of the Prism Master, from whom we hail."

I draw in a sharp breath, earning a fleeting glance from the Iljaria leader.

Vil holds firm at the mention of the Prism Master, though I know his mind must be wheeling. The Prism Master is the most powerful of the Iljaria, commanding more magic than even their queen, if not as much authority. Like the Prism Lady, from whom he claims his magic, he holds a piece of every other god's power, save for the non-magic of the Ghost God. The stories say he could level the whole earth with a word, if he wanted.

"What do the Forsaken do here, so far from your chosen home?" asks the Iljaria leader.

Vil clenches his jaw at the Iljaria's name for Skaandans. "We ride to Tenebris, to treat with the king of Daeros." He lifts up the peace banner. "Now let us pass."

The Iljaria leader scoffs. "At last you forsake your violence. I will send an Iljaria envoy to help negotiate peace."

"That is neither wanted nor needed."

The Iljaria gives Vil a thin smile. "Our paths will cross again." For a moment the Iljaria's gaze roams past Vil and fixes wholly on mine. His eyes narrow, and fear and magic both sear through me, so painful I have to bite my lip to keep from screaming. But then he looks away, and the pain is gone.

The Iljaria ride past us without another word. We're all rattled and continue our journey in silence as the sun sinks over the rim of the world. Darkness blankets us. The stars come out.

"Bastards," says Saga hotly. "They claim not to meddle in our wars, and yet they trade freely with Daeros and think to help *us* negotiate *peace*! If they had stepped in, even briefly, they could have ended our war with Daeros *years* ago!" I hear what she doesn't say: If the Iljaria had helped us, Hilf and Njala needn't have died.

"But they're pacifists," Indridi puts in unexpectedly. She's riding beside Saga and me now, her brow creased.

Saga scowls. "That didn't keep them from slaughtering Skaandans and driving us out of our own land."

"That was over a millennium ago. Who's to say it's even true?"

Saga stares at Indridi, mouth dropping open. "Do you doubt our history? Our people?"

"Of course not." Indridi worries her lip. "But it seems that histories grow with the telling and the passage of time; it may not have been the genocide we were taught growing up. There are two sides to every story."

Saga shakes her head, incredulous. "What other side could there possibly be, Ridi?"

Indridi doesn't answer, just shrugs unhappily.

My stomach clenches. The histories say that, long ago, the Iljaria and the Skaandans were one people. But when some of their children were born without magic, the Iljaria feared that these powerless had been cursed by the First Ones. They feared that these children were damned to live a life devoid of magic, robbed of the chance to attain that which all Iljaria seek: to become as the First Ones, immortal, omnipotent. And they feared that this lack of magic was a disease that might spread to them and bind them to the same fate.

So the Iljaria considered it a mercy to kill their powerless children, thereby giving them the chance to be born anew, this time gifted with the magic of their birthright. But some of the children were hidden and, in time, banded together and fled Iljaria, settling in the far west of the peninsula.

To them, the killing of their powerless brothers and sisters was not mercy but genocide. They held that magic was not the only form of strength, and they became a kingdom of warriors. No longer did they claim the First Ones as their ancestors; instead, they worshipped them as gods. They thanked the gods for taking away the curse of magic, for saving them from the trap of arrogance and false superiority that led the Iljaria to slaughter their own kind.

And so Skaanda was formed.

Indridi *is* right—that was hundreds of years ago, and it might not be the whole truth. But I still don't like to think about it.

"The Iljaria are hypocrites," says Saga. "Heathens. They claim lineage and power from the *gods*, and yet they pen themselves up in their corner of the world, giving no help to the people who share their own blood, all the while trading goods with godsdamned *Daeros*."

"Would Skaanda trade with Iljaria, even if they offered?" Indridi asks.

"Why are you taking their side?" Saga demands.

"I just think it's rarely as simple as one side being evil and the other righteous. The Iljaria are taught pacifism from the very beginning of their long lives. It's as close to religion as they come. Isn't it a *good* thing, to shun war?"

"Pacifism is a sham," says Vil tightly from his place in the lead. "If a man raises arms against another man's daughter, will the second man stand by and let her be slain? Will the daughter shut her eyes and do nothing?"

"If they truly believe in peace," says Indridi, "then yes, yes they would."

Vil shakes his head. "What would that accomplish, Indridi?"

She fixes her eyes on him. She fixes her whole *being* on him, and it makes my gut twist nastily. "Perhaps the first man will see that they do not fight back, and be ashamed, and stop his violence."

"And if he does not stop? If he kills them?"

"Then he will feel shame at what he has done, and he will stop his violence then."

Vil laughs. "How very un-Skaandan of you, Indridi. And how little you know of the hearts of men."

He glances at me as he says this, and I shove my discomfort down into the deepest recesses of my mind so I won't have to examine what it means.

Indridi, for her part, gnaws on her lip and looks away.

I have often thought it strange that the three peoples who share this peninsula have such wildly different beliefs about the First Ones, the original twelve beings to inhabit the world. The Iljaria, indeed, claim them as their ancestors, the beginnings of their power, and refer to them as Lords instead of gods. They believe that if they are faithful to their traditions and their people, that if they nourish and grow their power, they themselves will become immortal after death and join the ranks of the First Ones. If they are not, they will be reborn powerless. Damned. Skaandan.

The Daerosians don't believe in the First Ones at all. They believe in nothing, no one, and hold that the world knit itself together, and will one day likewise tear itself apart. They scoff at the idea of life after death, resigned to their assertion that there is only emptiness. Darkness. Nonexistence.

But Skaandans revere the First Ones as gods. We build temples and shrines and write books of truths and prayers. We fight wars in the gods' names, and we believe that if we are devout enough, they will reward us with eternal paradise after death. If not, we are damned to dwell outside the gates of paradise, our backs bent with eternal labor, tormented and ashamed.

Not for the first time, I think that none of us have got it quite right.

※

Saga is the one who tells the story tonight, as we huddle close to the fire against the growing chill in the air. Vil is, as usual, sitting opposite me, and I wish I were brave enough to go and join him, to let his warmth banish the cold and the dark together. But I'm not brave enough. I stay where I am.

"For a time," says Saga, "when Skaanda was first formed, there was peace. The Iljaria couldn't be bothered to pursue us to our new home, or they did not like the idea of slaughtering adults as they had slaughtered children, their precious pacifism finally coming into play."

Indridi frowns into the fire, her fingers making short work of repairing a tear in Vil's cloak. Leifur sits closer to her than is strictly necessary, but Indridi has eyes only for her mending.

"They ruled from Tenebris, the mountain palace they carved from ice and rock. Some say they pulled the mountains themselves up from the earth and scattered the bones of the deep places in the glacier sea." Saga is carving a design into the shaft of Pala's spear, her knife quick and vicious, her eyes glittering as she talks.

"And then invaders came from over the sea, their eyes on our land, our resources. The Iljaria held to their damn pacifism. They abandoned Tenebris and retreated like cowards into the east, erecting their magical barrier and refusing to take part in the long wars between Skaanda and Daeros. And there they hide still, gifted with impossible power and using none of it to aid anyone but themselves."

"The legends say they buried something in the heart of the mountain, before they left," says Leifur unexpectedly.

For a heartbeat Indridi's hands still over her work.

"What did they bury?" asks Saga, interested despite herself.

"Doesn't matter," says Vil, a little too quickly, but Saga waves him off.

"A weapon of impossible power," Leifur answers. His eyes are on Indridi, who is making the last few stitches into Vil's cloak. "They could have ended everything in a heartbeat, but that kind of power—it couldn't be contained. It would have destroyed all life, so the story goes. So they hid it. They chose peace. That speaks to their sincerity, if nothing else, does it not?"

"It's just a story," says Vil dismissively. "If such a weapon *truly* existed, only a fool would hide it."

Indridi ties off her thread and snips the end. She hands the mended cloak to Vil, who takes it with a nod of thanks.

"Kallias believes it exists," I offer.

Everyone's eyes snap to my face.

Vil frowns. "How do you know that?"

"I've overheard him discussing it with his engineer. He's been digging into the mountain, looking for it."

A tension comes into Vil's body, his eyes glittering in the firelight. "Why didn't you say anything about it until now?" he demands.

I shrug, raising my eyebrows. "It's just a story. I didn't think it was important. And I'm telling you now. *Is* it important?"

For another moment he stares hard at me, but then he shrugs and gives a forced laugh. "Just a story, indeed. The dark must be addling Kallias's brain. In *any* case, we're going to do what the Iljaria did not. We're going to drive those Daerosian bastards from our shores once and for all."

Saga nods, a fierce light in her eyes. "Damn right we are." She yelps as she slips with her knife and slices her finger.

Indridi curses softly and digs for a bandage in her sewing kit. She binds Saga's finger while Vil paces over to me. He grabs my hand and tugs me a little away from the others. My heart races, my lips remembering our moonlit kiss weeks ago.

Clouds knot over the stars, and the wind is bitter.

"What is it?" I ask him, warring with myself over whether to pull my hand away, or pull him closer.

His eyes fix on me, sharp and clear, and my stomach clenches. "I wanted to make sure you were all right," he says. "After our talk last night. After we ran into the Iljaria today. You've been . . . quiet."

I find myself staring at his mouth.

"The Iljaria's presence doesn't change anything. We continue on as before." He lets go of my hand and puts both of his on my shoulders. There is precious little space between us now. "You have nothing to fear, from Iljaria or Daeros, either. You know that, right? I'm going to keep you safe."

My throat catches and my eyes fill. "I know."

Vil takes a breath, lifting one hand to smooth his thumb against my cheek. I shut my eyes and lean into him, tucking my head under his chin. He holds me like that for a little while. His heart beats out a mad rhythm beneath my ear.

Before I'm quite ready, Vil pulls away, pressing a brief kiss on my brow before heading toward his tent. I take my jumble of emotions to the tent I share with the other women. I tug a comb through my curls, change into my sleeping shift, and crawl into my bedroll. I stare up at the ceiling of the tent. Sleep feels far away.

Saga comes in a little while later, Indridi conspicuously absent. I wonder if she's lingering by the fire, hoping for the chance to speak with Vil. Nausea churns in my gut.

I shut my eyes and pretend to be asleep, but Saga isn't fooled. She pokes me until I sigh and sit up, looking at her in the light of her lantern. My fingers go unconsciously to my ears. They've healed well, due in part, I'm sure, to Saga making me clean them with alcohol every night for the first six weeks.

Saga presses a cup of tea into my hands. "So, are you going to tell me what's going on with you and Vil?"

I fight down a surge of annoyance that Saga feels entitled to this information. I sip the tea. "Nothing's going on, Saga."

She presses her lips together and fiddles with the hem of her shirt. "You and I both know that isn't true. My brother has feelings for you. Do you return them or not?"

I shove down the urge to curse at her. "What do you want me to do, Saga?"

She folds her arms across her chest. "I want you to figure out how you feel about him, so you can either claim him or cut him loose so he can find a way to heal his broken heart."

I sag. "I don't—I don't *know* how I feel, Saga. How am I supposed to feel about anything? How am I supposed to *feel*, at all?"

"That didn't keep you from kissing that bastard son of Kallias in the tunnels," she says viciously.

I grind my jaw, tears pricking hot. "That was different."

"Why?"

I blink and see sparks of blue and silver; I taste magic, enough to light the dark. I don't want to parcel out my feelings, lay them on a tray like Saga's earrings, pick out the ones I want to keep. I don't even know how.

"Ballast was my friend," I say quietly. I have no other excuse to offer.

Her anger is palpable, and tears shine on her cheeks. "He killed Hilf, Brynja. *Murdered* him. I don't understand why that doesn't matter to you."

I duck my head, knotting my fingers in my blanket. "It does. It haunts me. But you know that wasn't his fault."

"Now you're *defending* him?"

I take a breath. Try to steady myself. "He was trapped in Kallias's control. Just like the rest of us."

"He was *nothing* like the rest of us. Hilf is gone. Hilf is *gone*. Because of *him*." She collapses, sobbing, and I put the tea down and scoot over to her, pulling her tight against me, holding her as she shakes and cries.

"I'm sorry, Saga," I whisper into her hair. "I'm so very sorry. If I could bring him back to you, I would. You know I would."

I hold her until she grows still, my heart cracked in two.

She blows out the lantern, and we both crawl into our bedrolls, Indridi still not joining us.

Saga's breathing evens out. I think she's asleep, but then she says: "I'm so scared to go back to the mountain, Brynja. So scared Kallias will put me back in my cage. Slit my throat. Throw my corpse into the Sea of Bones."

My throat works as I fight to breathe. I find her hand in the dark, and I squeeze it tight. "I'm afraid of that, too."

"I know." She takes a shaky breath. "We're both of us just learning to be normal again. Maybe this was a mistake."

"Maybe," I say. "But we can't let him go unchecked any longer. Someone has to stand up to him. Someone has to stop him doing to anyone else what he did to us."

"You're right," says Saga. "Of course you're right."

Silence flows between us and I stare into the dark, trying to understand something, *anything*. "I kissed Vil," I confess at last.

Saga squawks. "When were you going to tell me *this*?"

"It was weeks ago. After the river crossing. But I *don't* know how I feel. And it wouldn't be fair to him to promise him my heart when I don't understand it."

She's quiet a moment. "You need to figure it out, Bryn."

I count the beats of my heart. "I know."

She falls asleep after that, but I'm still awake hours later when Pala bursts into the shelter, lantern swinging from one hand.

"Brynja!" she says, "Saga! Your Highness!"

I'm on my feet in an instant and Saga the next. We stare at Pala in the lantern light.

"What is it?" Saga asks, voice rough with sleep.

Pala's face is all hard lines. "Indridi is gone, Your Highness."

Saga blinks at her. "What?"

"She's fled. Taken a horse and gone in the night."

Saga rubs her forehead, confused. "Why would she do that? Where is she going?"

"East, Your Highness. Toward Iljaria."

My stomach twists. I'm going to be sick.

"But *why*?" says Saga, voice high and frantic.

Pala looks grim. "Because she's an Iljaria spy."

NINE YEARS AGO

YEAR 4191, Month of the Blue Goddess
Daeros—Tenebris

Slowly, I explore the mountain palace, every night when the king and all his courtiers are sleeping. I squeeze through heating vents and creep across wood ceilings, learning the layout of the rooms, making a map of them in my head. Now there is hope, beyond my despair.

    I know where the king's council chamber is, the warren of rooms where his wives live, and the connecting warren that houses his children. I have found a library, a treasury, a dining hall. There's a laundry, of course, a kitchen, a wine cellar. There is an endless maze of corridors, the arched hall that boasts the main entrance. Side doors lead to gardens that thrive even in winter. Huge lamps keep the plants growing and the gardens illuminated. They're mechanical, the product of some genius like my sister, but they still *seem* like magic.

    Beyond the gardens are the stables, the army encampment, and the road to Garran City, which is the capital of Daeros and lies just north of the mountain.

    Every night as I creep my way through the ceilings, I ponder escape. But every night I return to my iron cage and sleep away the remaining hours until dawn. Because there are guards at every door. There is no sanctuary in Garran City. I would die alone on the tundra, long before I ever found my way home. And if I were caught trying to escape, the king and the Sea of Bones would be my ending. It is better to wait. To plan. To hope that I'm not truly forgotten.

To pray that someone is coming to rescue me.

One night I slip into my vent as usual, back aching from the steward's rod, face bruised where the king grabbed my chin, nails digging deep. He'd been displeased with my performance. He was displeased with *everyone's* performance. Even Ballast's. My stomach twists. The king made him call the rats up from the cellars, and the palace cats from their various sleeping corners. Then the king made Ballast compel the cats to slaughter the rats, until the floor was sticky with blood. There weren't any courtiers tonight. Just the king and his foul temper. He had Ballast beaten, too, when all the rats were dead.

Maybe this is what makes me follow the paths toward the wives' wing of the palace, wriggling my way through the narrow space until I find myself just above Ballast's room. I peer down at him through the knotholes in the wood. He sits on his bed, which is shabby and plain, drawing patterns in the fog on his window. There are spots of rat blood on the front of his white shirt, and streaks of his own on the back. Books are scattered all about the room: on his bed, the floor, his small dressing table. I think of my studious brother, and my heart wrenches.

I swear I don't make a noise, but something makes him glance up and see me through the cracks in his ceiling. He has the king's startlingly blue eyes, Gulla's square, solemn face. There are tear stains on his warm brown cheeks.

For a moment we stare at each other, and I try not to think of the rats, screeching as they were torn to pieces.

"What's your name?" he asks me unexpectedly. His light and dark hair is mussed, curls springing out in every direction.

I blink at him, feeling the ache in my shoulders, knowing his are aching, too. "Brynja," I whisper.

He takes a breath, fiddling with his sheet. "Every time you do your routine," he says quietly, "I am always afraid you will fall."

My chest tightens. I tell him my secret: "I am, too."

He nods and looks to the window again. "You should get out of here, Brynja. Before my father kills you. Before you *do* fall."

My heart thumps too hard, and I fight off the sudden press of tears. "Why don't *you* leave? Why do you let him . . . hurt you? Command you?"

He doesn't answer and I think of Gulla, teaching me her finger speech while we gaze down into the Sea of Bones.

"Your mother," I say.

"When I am big enough," says Ballast viciously, "when I am older and stronger, I'm going to kill him. Then he won't hurt her anymore."

I hear what he doesn't say: *Then he won't hurt* me *anymore.*

"Not if I kill him first."

He blinks at me, chokes on a laugh. "All right," he says. "Not if you kill him first."

There's nothing to say, after that, so I squirm my way back through the ceilings, wriggle out of the vent, and climb up the chain to my cage. I lather my head with Gulla's soap and scrape away at the dark hairs growing from my scalp. When it's smooth again, I wrap myself in my blanket and curl up on the sleeping ledge. But every time I shut my eyes, I see the twisted, bloodied bodies of the rats.

I don't intend to go and visit Ballast again, but not three evenings later I find myself once more crouched in his ceiling, peering down at him through the knothole.

It's quite late, past the twenty-first hour, yet he's sitting on his bed reading in the yellow glow of an Iljaria light globe. I watch him for a while. Something shifts beside him, and I realize it's a cat, the same white as his sheets. My stomach wrenches.

"Are you going to come out?" he says softly, turning another page.

I hesitate for only a moment before wriggling through his vent and hopping down into the room. I eye the cat uneasily, but it just stretches again and tucks its paws over its head, purring as it sleeps.

Ballast closes his book and looks up at me. He smiles. "I was hoping you'd come back," he says. "I've blocked the door, just in case."

I glance over to see that he's shoved his dressing table up against it; there is no lock. Fear coils through me. "Does . . . does he come here?"

Ballast shrugs, but there's no missing the echo of my terror in his eyes. "Not often."

Which means *sometimes*. I turn to scramble back up into the vent.

"Wait," he says.

I turn back.

He rubs at his temples, the blue tattoos on his arms shimmering in the glow of the light globe. "Please stay. Just for a little while." His voice breaks.

"All right," I whisper.

Wordlessly, Ballast scoops up the snoozing cat and slides all the way over to the wall, leaving plenty of space for me on the bed. I sit gingerly on the opposite end, jiggling my knee. The mattress feels impossibly soft, like it's made of clouds, or dreams—I have grown somehow used to my iron sleeping ledge. And it seems I have forgotten how to talk to another human being. There is a long silence before I manage to say, "Did you call it here? With your magic?"

The cat has settled into his lap and is making little whiffly noises, whiskers twitching.

"No," he says. "She just found me. Kind of like you." He gives me half of a smile.

I try not to see the king's eyes peering at me out of Ballast's face. I try not to think about the rats. Power hangs on this boy like a coat, and I wonder what would happen if he were ever to truly wield it. "What are you reading?"

"A book of Iljaria myths. From my mother. I'm not sure where she got it."

I understand without him having to tell me that if his father were to find him with such a book, there would be hell to pay. He scoots it over to me, and I touch the pages with careful fingers.

"You must get bored," he says.

I turn a page of the book, studying an illustration of the Yellow God battling the Black God on a high mountain peak. The artist was skillful, or perhaps imbued the illustration with magic—the Yellow God's light seems to glow, the Black God's darkness seems to writhe and devour.

"Do *you* get bored?" I counter. I turn another page, this one all text, but written in shimmering colors.

"I have tutors," he says. "Weapons training. Every day."

Another difference, then, between us. "I try to sleep. I practice my routine, as best as I can."

"As best as you can in a cage, you mean."

My heart pulses faster at the bitterness in his voice. "At night, I'm free."

"You could be free always. You could leave this cursed mountain. I could help you."

I gnaw on my cheek. "He'd kill you for that."

Ballast doesn't deny this; we both know it's true. He pets the sleeping cat, and there is anguish in every line of his frame. I shove the book back toward him, and in a blink I am leaping up into the vent.

"Brynja," he says.

I pause but don't turn back.

"Come again. Please."

I pull the vent into place without answering and crawl back through the ceilings, to the great hall and to my cage. I curl up on my sleeping ledge, but I lie there a long, long while, before dark dreams at last find me.

☼

He's waiting for me the next night, when I hop down from his vent. He has tea on a scratched wooden tray, and a plate of little round cakes dusted with purple icing sugar. I sit on one end of the bed and he on the other, the tray in the wide space between us. We eat and drink without speaking, but the silence is a comfort. There is a bandage on the left side of his neck, and his white cat is nowhere to be seen. I hope it's safe somewhere, but from the slump of Ballast's shoulders and the red seeping through his bandage, I doubt that it is.

When we've finished what amounts to the most dazzling feast I have had since long before the king shut me in an iron cage, Ballast takes out a deck of playing cards. They're beautiful, Iljaria made, with the usual eleven suits—one for each god except Ghost.

"Would you like to play?" asks Ballast, the first words he's spoken to me tonight. His voice sounds rough, like he's been crying or screaming or both.

My gut clenches with hatred and horror. I don't understand how anyone can be such a monster to their own son. "What game?" There are many that can be played with these cards. I know only a few.

"War," he says.

I smile. "Isn't that against Iljaria philosophy?"

His jaw goes tight. "I am only half Iljaria."

I didn't mean to upset him, and tell him so.

He shrugs this off. "Do you know how to play?"

"It's been a while."

Ballast reminds me of the rules, explaining the hierarchy of the gods' colors, of points won by different sets, runs, or pairs when laid down, with cards from the Prism suit being highest, and of course the Prism Goddess card—whom he calls the Prism Lady—trumping anything else. This deck has one wild Ghost God card that, if played, makes the points of any cards the other player holds in their hand turn negative.

We play, quietly taking our turns in the glow of his light globe. As the deck dwindles down to nearly nothing, Ballast plays the Prism Goddess card, which I counter with the Ghost God card.

We play another round. He has the Ghost God card this time, but I have already laid out my cards, so the points can't be counted against me.

"When you come again," says Ballast, after I beat him a fourth time, "we will have to try a different game."

I laugh, feeling a strange kind of contentment coiling in my belly. I wonder if this is what it's like to have a friend.

※

I don't come every night. I can't afford the risk. But I come more than I ought to. I think he waits for me every night, I think he's disappointed when I don't come, though he never tells me as much. He always has food ready, sometimes something sweet, like the little cakes, other times something savory, like fried spiced lamb bites or roasted vegetables with fiery dipping sauce. As time spins on, his offerings are almost always savory, often some kind of meat. I think he realizes what awful fare the king's steward gives me, and means to make up for it as best as he can.

We play games, every one we know of that uses his deck of cards; we even make up a few. One night he has a Lords and Ladies set waiting, the wheel of the board painted in alternating blue and yellow, the pieces themselves intricately carved. He won't tell me where he got it, and I can only assume he stole it from his father.

Sometimes we read, him on one end of the bed, me on the other. He brings me all sorts of books from the palace library, trying, I think, to find the ones that interest me most. But I am equally greedy for poetry and history, science and myth. I cannot read them fast enough. The books are a gift, as is his steady company, and I feel human for a handful of precious hours every few nights.

And sometimes we talk, though haltingly, and never again about his father. He tells me about his mother, how she instructs him in his magic and teaches him about his Iljaria heritage. He tells me that, one day, he wants to sail with his mother to Iljaria and leave Daeros behind forever. He tells me that his half siblings hate him.

I tell him that I'm beginning to forget what my home was like, that I'm afraid I will never get to go back. I tell him that my brother hates me, that my sister is dead. I almost tell him I don't think my father loves me at all, but that is too close to the topic of *his* father, so I keep it to myself. I don't tell him that he's starting to feel more like home to me than my family did. I was alone then. I'm not now. He sees me, understands me, in a way no one else ever has.

On the nights I am made to perform, or Ballast is made to show off his Iljaria magic in the great hall, I don't come to his room. I want our time to be ours. I don't want him to be thinking of me at his father's command, slick with sweat and terror. I don't want to be thinking of him obeying his father's every whim, no matter what it costs.

YEAR 4191, Month of the Black God
Daeros—Tenebris

Gods' Fall comes, blanketing the mountain palace in bitter darkness. I have been in the king's Collection for over a year now. Were it not for my visits with Ballast, I think I would have succumbed to despair. But as it is, there is hope in his quiet company and subtle humor, in his careful, earnest friendship. It makes everything else bearable.

One night we sit, as we always do, on his bed, him on one end, me on the other. It has been a few days since I last came to see him, and a heavy silence weighs between us. There's a half-healed cut on his left cheek from two nights ago, when the king cut-slapped him with his heavy signet ring because Ballast couldn't make the royal hounds stand on their hind legs and serve soup to the king's dinner guests. I know because I was watching.

While the Dark Remains

I was made to perform that night, along with the other children in the Collection, and the king was in such a foul mood that afterward he ordered all of us beaten. I still have sore spots on both my shoulders.

Ballast has laid out the Lords and Ladies board on the bed, but he doesn't seem to have much interest in playing tonight.

"Why don't you stand up to him?" I ask quietly. "You could, you know. You are far more powerful than he could ever be."

His whole body goes tense, and he grabs a piece off the board and hurls it viciously at the wall.

I jump off the bed and back away from him, heart raging.

He looks at me, utterly distraught. I don't tell him the reason for my sudden, involuntary fear, but he sees it written all over my face: That was something his father would do.

Ballast swallows, miserable. He rubs the tattoos on his arms and takes quick, ragged breaths.

That's when we hear a step outside his door. We both freeze and his eyes snap to mine, wild with panic.

In a heartbeat I'm up in the vent, pulling the grate over the opening, crawling swiftly and silently back to safety. I don't dare stay, don't dare risk the king finding me there. He would kill me. He would kill Ballast. And it would all be for nothing.

It's more than a week before I'm brave enough to return to Ballast's room, to loosen the grate and hop down. I am anxious to resolve the tension between us, to resume our easy friendship. His dressing table is shoved up against his door, but there is no food waiting, no deck of cards or Lords and Ladies board.

Ballast faces me, as cold and unfeeling as his father's mountain. "I want you to leave, Brynja. Don't come here anymore."

"I'll be more careful," I say. "I won't come as often."

His jaw is hard. His blue eyes glitter. "That isn't what I want. This was all a stupid mistake. Don't ever come here again."

Hurt sparks sharp in my chest. "I shouldn't have pressed you," I say quietly. "I shouldn't have asked you why you don't stand up to him. I understand why, better than anyone."

"You understand nothing," he spits at me. "I said *leave*!"

I stare at him, fighting the sudden press of tears. "But we're friends," I say stupidly.

"You're not my friend. You have been taking advantage of me, and if you ever come here again, I will drag you right to my father. Do you understand?"

Terror beats through me with wings, large and dark. "Ballast," I whisper.

He leans toward me, closer than he has ever been before, close enough that I can see his eyelashes are a mix of white and dark, just like his hair. "I never want to see you again," he says. "Now get the hell *out*."

I climb up into his vent and crawl away from his room, clumsy and shaky, the world blurred before me.

I do as Ballast asks.

I never go back.

CHAPTER FIVE

YEAR 4200, Month of the Red God
Daeros—the plains

We abandon our camp and ride hard east after Indridi, into the burgeoning dawn. The wind sears cold past my ears, choking all my breath away. My heart beats, beats, an erratic rhythm. Saga rides beside me, frantic in her anguish. Vil rides ahead, grim as the goddess of death, flanked by Pala and Leifur.

"How do you know?" Saga had asked Pala, desperate in her denial in the flaring lantern light. "How do you know Indridi is an Iljaria spy?"

"Because she rode east, Your Highness, as fast as her horse would take her, and when she glanced back and saw me, she threw flames from her hands. Why would she do that, if she were not an Iljaria spy? *How* would she do it?"

She wouldn't. Because Skaandans don't wield fire magic. That was enough of an answer, for Saga.

So we pound on after her, our horses' hooves tearing into the earth. We see Indridi in the distance as the sun lips above the rim of the world—she's sparking red. But for all her magic, her horse has none, and she's driven it too hard. The animal stumbles. Indridi slides from its back and turns to face us. Fire burns in both her palms; it does not hurt her.

I blink and see Dagmar, the Iljaria boy from Kallias's Collection who was there when I first arrived. Even at nine years old, Dagmar was a master of his fire magic, and Kallias feared him. I was eleven when Kallias slit his throat and dumped his body in the Sea of Bones.

Flames curl up into Indridi's hair as the rest of us slide from our mounts and pace toward her. Vil draws his sword, and Saga just stares at her friend, openly weeping. I am sick through to my core.

The fire burns away the black of Indridi's hair, until her curls are white and gleaming, her brows and lashes, too. She lifts her chin, her eyes locked hard on Vil's.

"I should have known," he says, voice harsh and unyielding as stone. "I should have known no natural person could start such a fire in the rain."

I fight the urge to be sick in the grass. Heat radiates from Indridi, even from ten feet away.

"I don't understand," Saga chokes out. "Ridi, I don't understand. You're Skaandan! You've served me and my family for a decade. You're my best friend. You can't—you can't—"

Indridi shifts her gaze to Saga, and her fire lessens a little. "I never meant to hurt you, Saga."

"You dyed your hair," Saga realizes, staring. "You kept your magic hidden. Why?"

Indridi's fire lessens yet a little more, and I finally see the fear in her eyes. "I was ordered to," she whispers.

"By *who*?" Vil asks viciously.

Indridi flinches. Flames flare hot once more, crawling up and down her arms, circling her brow like a crown. "The Prism Master." She sets her chin, but it wobbles. She looks at Vil like her heart is fracturing into infinite pieces.

On either side of Vil, Pala and Leifur draw their swords.

"You were going to report to him," says Vil. "Somehow meeting the Iljaria on the road yesterday was your signal to go."

"Yes."

"Your *mission* is ended now?"

Indridi is shaking. Saga half collapses against me, and I struggle to hold her upright. She gasps for air. I try to breathe with her, breathe *for* her.

"I have a duty to my people," says Indridi, voice shrill and high. "The mountain does not belong to Skaanda. It belongs to the Iljaria."

"And what would your Prism Master think to do about it, seeing as he doesn't believe in war?"

"Don't *mock* me, Vil!" Indridi cries. "You have your beliefs. I have mine."

"*You* do not have the *right*," he grinds out, "to use my name."

Tears drip down Indridi's cheeks. They turn to steam.

Leifur flicks his eyes to Vil, who gives a sharp nod. Leifur strides forward and grasps Indridi's shoulder, flinching for only a moment before her flames die out altogether.

She sags in the grass. She looks small, vulnerable, her white hair stained orange in the light of the rising sun. Smoke coils up from her fingertips.

Vil approaches her, every line of him hard as steel. "Indridi Hellir, you are charged with high treason against the crown of Skaanda. I sentence you to death."

"No!" I shriek, lunging forward only to be caught by Pala and held forcibly back.

"There is nothing you could do or say to change this," the soldier tells me. Her voice is quiet and filled with regret.

Saga weeps on the ground.

Indridi raises her tearstained face, a hardness coming into her that rattles me to my core. "You do not have the power to deal out death to the daughter of a First One, Vilhjalmur Stjörnu," she says. "I answer only to my people, and it is to them I surrender myself now."

She wrenches out of Leifur's grasp, and flames begin to dance along her arms. The fire runs up her neck and down to her feet, singes the grass where she stands. It pulses hotter and hotter, so that Leifur tugs Vil back, lest he be burned.

Pala releases me, and I stand and watch in sick, helpless horror as Indridi is wreathed all in flame, tongues of fire licking greedily at her hair, making her skin bubble and crack. She gives one long, high scream, and there comes a flash of red so bright that for a moment I am blinded.

There is the stench of burning flesh, the reek of smoke, and the rattle of bones, and when my vision clears, Indridi is gone, reduced to ashes by the power of her own magic.

I collapse to the ground, where Saga kneels shrieking, and I think I must be screaming, too. Tears blur my vision and everything reeks of death and this must be a nightmare except I don't wake and every time I look to the place Indridi was standing there is only ash and shards of bone, gleaming white.

Somehow, eventually, we ride back to our camp, pack everything up, and start again on the northern road. We let Indridi's horse go free.

We ride through the day and some hours into the night before stopping again. Leifur builds the fire and hands out rations from the packs, but it seems no one has the stomach to eat anything. I certainly don't.

Saga sits close beside me in front of the fire, her eyes wet with fresh tears. "I don't understand," she says, helpless and hollow. "How could she be Iljaria? All this time? Spying on us and scheming, pretending to be my friend and pretending to admire Vil—"

"I don't think she was pretending those things, Saga," I say dully. "I think she genuinely cared for you."

"That makes it even worse." Her voice breaks.

"I know." Everything hurts, and I want to crawl into my bedroll and surrender myself to the bliss of unconsciousness, but I am afraid

Indridi's ending will follow me into my dreams. I am afraid I will never be able to think of anything else.

Saga hugs me close for a few long moments, then gets up and goes to bed. I stay sitting by the fire, watching the smoke coil up, trying to comprehend the fact that Indridi is *gone*.

Vil comes to crouch beside me, and I fight off the tears stinging my eyes.

"You were going to kill her," I accuse him. "Right there on the plains."

His face is racked with agony. "She knew *everything*, Brynja. The inner workings of the palace. Our plot to take Daeros and the Skaandan army's paths through the tunnels. *Everything*. She was a horrible risk to us, and with her fire magic, how could we even restrain her? What other choice did I have?"

My insides are writhing and my heart is fractured. "But would you really have done it?"

"I would do anything I have to, to ensure the safety of my people and the success of our mission." Firelight traces the line of his jaw. He looks utterly sick, and adds quietly: "Indridi certainly didn't have much faith in the concept of my mercy. She thought that . . . that dying that way, at her own hand, was better." He shudders and shudders, and I try to ignore the sour twist of my stomach.

Vil tips his head onto my shoulder, and we sit like that for a while, both of us trying to remember how to breathe.

When at last I crawl into my bedroll, I lie for a while in the dark before sleep pulls me under, traced with the scent of smoke and the sound of Indridi's scream.

THREE YEARS AGO

YEAR 4197, Month of the Bronze God
Daeros—Tenebris

There's a new girl in the king's Collection.

I peer down from my cage, watching as the king's steward drags her into the great hall. She's a lot older than the king's usual acquisitions, near my own age of seventeen. She has dark skin and a cloud of tightly coiled black hair. Her clothes are bloodied and torn, and she's wearing only one shoe. She shakes but does not cry. There's a proud tilt to her chin that says she's not broken yet. I wonder what she's lost. I wonder who's missing her. Or perhaps no one is. Perhaps she's like me: wholly forgotten, abandoned to the mountain's whims.

I shove down the old bitterness and turn my back on her, my cage swaying with the movement. I remind myself not to care, because that makes it all so much harder. I made that mistake, early on, with Ballast. I know better now. It's easier to feel nothing but loneliness and fear. That's what's kept me alive all this time.

It's early autumn, so evening light floods still through the glass wall when we're called upon to perform. The king arrives with his current favorite wife, Pelagia, a handful of Daerosian nobles, and two of his daughters, ten-year-old Rhode and five-year-old Xenia. He sets Xenia on his knee as Rhode and the others settle beside him, and then calls for his Collection to begin their performances.

A tiny Skaandan boy the same age as Xenia is first: He is deadly accurate with his throwing knives and can hit extremely small targets from twenty feet away. The Iljaria boy with the Red God's power is long gone. He's been replaced with another Iljaria named Finnur, who's about twelve, his white hair curly, his skin a deep brown. Finnur has the power of the Prism Goddess and can make staggering illusions out of nothing. Tonight he makes butterflies that flutter about the hall and then burst into colorful sparks and fall shimmering like rain. Xenia is delighted, laughing and clapping and hopping off her father's knee to run and chase them. Rhode sits still, wary, tense.

The Skaandan girl is brought out next. She's been cleaned up and dressed in a purple robe cinched with a simple cord belt. Her feet are bare, her hair unadorned.

The king waves at her impatiently to begin. She shuts her eyes, clenches her hands into fists, and opens her mouth. She sings a simple Skaandan melody, but her voice is powerful and raw with feeling. It fills up the whole room. My throat goes dry and tears prick at my eyes as she switches to a ballad about a king who falls in love with a lowly goat girl. The goat girl teaches the king humility, and he comes to live with her in her mountain, forsaking his kingdom forever.

The Skaandan girl's eyes flash as she sings, and I can feel the anger radiating off the king, blistering as fire. He's scowling as he waves her away, and I know she'll be going to bed with bruised shoulders tonight. If she doesn't learn how to keep her head down, she's not going to last here a week.

The king doesn't call for me to perform tonight, which makes worry gnaw at my bones. If he's grown bored with me, *I* won't last another week. I'll have to add something to my routine to catch his interest again. Something dangerous.

It's Ballast the king calls last, and my heart still jerks at the sight of him, despite the fact we haven't spoken in six years. He's grown quite tall since then and remains as lean as any of us. He dines at the king's table but eats very little.

I know because I've watched him.

It's true I have never returned to his room, but I have observed him nearly everywhere else—the library, his father's council chambers, his mother Gulla's room. The only place inside the mountain palace he doesn't go is the great hall, unless his father summons him like he has tonight. And when he is here, he never, not even once, looks up. It's like our evenings together didn't happen, like I dreamed them up in the early days of my captivity to have something to hold on to. Secret evenings with a prince who brought me sweets and books are something, after all, that a child would imagine. But however abruptly it ended, I know it was real.

I can hardly bear to look at him now, all stiff and blank away down below me. The king's steward, Nicanor, hauls in a raging lion, and the king orders Ballast to control it. The beast calms, almost at once, allowing the king to pet it as if it were a kitten, though the murder in its black eyes is plain to see. Then the king commands Ballast to put his head in the lion's open jaws. He does, the slight shake of Ballast's hand the only sign that this makes him nervous.

Little five-year-old Xenia, terrified to see her half brother about to be—in her mind—eaten, starts screaming, and the king wheels on her, enraged. He sends Rhode, Xenia, and their mother from the room with a curse.

This effectively ends Ballast's performance. He looks to be about to go after Xenia, but the king orders him to stay. The nobles and Nicanor, with the lion muzzled and on a lead, file out in short order. I turn my back to the scene below because I know what's coming and I don't want to watch. But I can't close my ears against the sound of the king striking Ballast across the face three, four, five times, like it was *his* fault his tiny sister was scared of the damn lion. Finally, the king sends Ballast away, too. Relief shivers through me. Ballast's suffering is over, at least for tonight.

The king stalks up to the glass wall and stares moodily out into the Sea of Bones, the rising moon sending eerie blue shadows skewing across the ice. There's something feral in him tonight. Something dangerous. Usually tormenting his pets appeases him; usually he stalks away and leaves us to lick our wounds alone. But tonight he curses into the dark, beating his fists against the glass, again and again. "Where *is* it?" he roars. "Where *is* it?" He hisses at the pain in his hands, but it doesn't stop him from pounding the glass. The great hall rings with the noise of it, and I am horribly, horribly afraid that his tantrum will result in one or more of us dragged before him, knives across throats, corpses dumped into the Sea of Bones.

But his rage, at last, subsides. He drops his hands, slick now with blood. He stands a moment more, staring out into the glacier valley. His chest heaves. He utters a final, bitter curse and sweeps from the hall, footsteps echoing in his wake.

In the quiet that follows, the Skaandan singer weeps bitterly in her glass cage. I hunch into myself. I try not to listen.

But it's all I can hear.

CHAPTER SIX

YEAR 4200, Month of the Violet God
Daeros—the tundra

The days grow shorter and shorter. There is no more singing on the road. Vil and I don't dance anymore. We don't have the heart for it. Saga barely speaks, more deeply hurt by Indridi's betrayal than anyone. Leifur is snappy and irritable, Vil withdrawn. In contrast to the rest of us, Pala seems almost cheery.

Saga sticks close to me, always, and as the days slip away and we draw ever nearer to our destination, she starts talking about Indridi. I don't want to talk. But I can listen.

"She was always evasive about her family," Saga says one afternoon, the day already darkening and cold with stinging sleet. "I was only ten when she came to the palace to be my handmaiden; she was thirteen. She was horribly serious at first—I thought she didn't like me. But one day she helped me dump sand in Vil's bed because he was being annoying, and we were fast friends after that." The memory sparks a smile that quickly turns sad. Saga pulls her hood tighter down over her forehead.

I glance ahead to where Vil rides; his shoulders are tight, the grief radiating off him.

"How did Indridi come to be your handmaiden?" I ask, because I feel like Saga is waiting for me to say something.

"Noblemen from all over the country send their sons and daughters to Staltoria City to train as attendants. We can't take all of them, of course. There's a rigorous interview process."

I gnaw on the inside of my cheek. The hood of my cloak is stiff with ice.

"She must have been a good liar," Saga says, "to make it through the training and the interviews. To be appointed my handmaiden. A damn good liar."

"Or someone powerful lied for her," I say.

Saga sniffs and scrubs at her eyes. "Do you think a person should be more loyal to their country or their faith, Brynja?"

I shake my head. "I don't know."

"Your country sustains your body," she says. "Your faith sustains your soul."

I blink thoughtfully into the sleet, the dark. "I guess it all depends on what matters more to you: your body or your soul."

"Indridi's country and her faith were the same thing," says Saga.

"The Iljaria have no faith," I counter.

"Yes, they do. Their faith is in themselves. In their magic and their long lives and their ancestry. But I still can't believe—" She takes a breath, clearly fighting fresh tears.

"What can't you believe, Saga?" I say quietly.

"That the Iljaria would send a child. She was with us for *ten years*, Brynja."

I don't know how to answer. I try not to see Indridi, screaming, fire licking up her hair and smoke curling off her fingers. But I can't see anything else.

"I suppose when you live for hundreds of years, like the Iljaria do, a decade doesn't really matter." Saga gnaws on her lip as she glances over to meet my eyes. "But I bet it mattered to Indridi."

"Yes," I say. "Yes, I bet it did."

Pala tells us a story as we huddle together miserably in the larger tent, barely shielded from the dripping, freezing dark. I doubt I'm the only one thinking of Indridi's fire, warm and red and driving back the rain. Pala doesn't seem like the type of person to care for stories, but perhaps she has grown tired of the sorrow, the silence, that mark our evening campsites.

"Now the Gray Goddess and the Green Goddess are sisters, but they have never understood one another. The Gray Goddess brings decay wherever she treads; beneath the Green Goddess's heels, flowers spring up. They are death and life, each a half of the other, but when they were young, they did not accept that.

"'There is beauty only in life!' the Green Goddess would declare, and she would grow her flowers and trees in her sister's domain, choking out dust and bones.

"'Life is temporary,' the Gray Goddess would reply. 'There is beauty only in the permanence of death.' And she would rip out her sister's greenery and turn spring to the depths of winter.

"Now the Green Goddess loved the Violet God, though he did not know it, and the Gray Goddess loved the Ghost God, who stood vigil with her sometimes at graves. The Gray Goddess urged the Green Goddess to tell the Violet God of her feelings, to make him come and stay with her, whatever the cost.

"But when at last the Green Goddess confessed to the Violet God the wish of her heart, he told her with sorrow that his own heart belonged to another, a human. To spare the Green Goddess further pain, the Violet God bid her a kind farewell, and went to his dwelling place on a high mountain, where he could be alone.

"The Green Goddess wept then, an early spring rain, but she did not regret her words to the Violet God, and she found contentment in the work of her hands, the bringing of life, and growth.

"But the Gray Goddess, seeing all this, was terrified to tell the Ghost God of her feelings, lest he leave her in a similar manner. And so she slew him as he stood with her at a graveside, that she might keep him with her forever.

"But when the Ghost God lay still and cold, the Gray Goddess wept beside him, distraught at what she had done. Her grief shook the foundations of the world. The Green Goddess heard her cries and had compassion for her sister. She knelt beside the Ghost God and sent life into him again. The Gray Goddess rejoiced to be reunited with her love, and from that point on, Gray and Green did not interfere with each other's powers or wishes ever again."

We're quiet for a bit after the story is over.

"And what did the Ghost God think of all of that?" Saga says moodily. She sits close enough to me that I can feel her shaking. "Did he actually love the Gray Goddess? Did he forgive her for killing him? I would think he'd turn his affection to the Green Goddess instead."

"It's just a story, Your Highness," says Pala.

She goes to relieve Leifur of his watch, and I listen to the icy rain, hearing what she didn't say, what the story said for her.

Death isn't always the answer.

It isn't an answer at all.

I wonder if she means Vil's command to execute Indridi, or Indridi's taking of her own life. Or maybe she means our entire plot to take over Daeros and eliminate Kallias.

Whatever she means, I sleep badly, and dream of fire, and wake to the sound of Saga weeping.

☀

It gets colder and colder the closer we get to Tenebris. We dig furs out of our packs, don knit hats and wool leggings. Our breath hangs like smoke in the air, and not even our nightly camp stew and steaming tea can warm us all the way through. Dread weighs on me with each ever-shortening day that passes. Soon I will have to face him again. Soon

I will have to face everything. The tight-knit party that left Staltoria City all those weeks ago is unraveling, thread by thread.

We pass Daerosian farms and villages, scattered almost stubbornly about on the inhospitable tundra. There's a city, too—Skógur—with high stone walls and a forest of trees protected inside them. It's unnatural for trees to grow out here; we lugged wood with us on packhorses from Staltoria City and burned lichen when that ran out. I try to push away the thought of Indridi, who wouldn't have needed any wood at all to make a fire for us.

We camp outside Skógur City, the peace banner waving from the end of Leifur's spear, which is driven into the ground in clear sight of anyone passing by. Even armed with the truce flag, though, Pala judged it best not to set foot in the city.

"It was an Iljaria stronghold, once," says Pala when we're eating our dinner, the coals of our campfire glowing red.

"They abandoned it when they left the mountain," Saga guesses.

Pala nods. "The trees still grow because of them, drawn up from the earth by Iljaria powerful with the Green Goddess's magic. Some say the Green Goddess herself dwells in that forest still. But of course the Daerosians don't believe in the gods. To them, nothing is sacred. So the forest shrinks year by year, not enough trees planted to replace the ones they cut down."

Vil utters an oath to his dinner, and a tangle of grief and longing curls down my spine. "We'll change all that, when Skaanda rules here. When we drive those blasphemous pigs from our shores."

"Green Goddess make it so," says Pala. She rises from her place to relieve Leifur of his watch duty, and he comes to join us by the fire. He eats quickly, mechanically, staring into the flames.

I look toward Skógur City, the walls a silhouette against the rising moon. I'm sorry Pala deemed it unsafe. I would have liked to see the ancient forest for myself.

"'Do not kill,' the Green Goddess instructs us," says Leifur unexpectedly. He doesn't turn his eyes from the fire. It's clear he's thinking of Indridi's death, though he didn't carry out Vil's order of execution in the end. Indridi denied him that choice. That burden. "How does that fit in with the Skaandan philosophy of war?"

"Leave it alone, Leifur," Vil reprimands.

Leifur hunches in on himself, but Saga turns toward him, ready and willing and, perhaps, *relieved* to talk about it. "The Brown Goddess says, 'The earth cries for justice.' What is justice, if not war?"

"And the Gray Goddess instructs us to 'respect the dead,'" I put in. "But does that mean she wishes us to kill?"

"Brynja," says Vil, my name on his lips as soft as a prayer. I can't look at him. I don't.

Saga turns her gaze to me. "'All becomes ashes,' says the Red God, and the Bronze: 'You must pay for your own sins.'"

I have read as many of the old texts as Saga, and I'm not about to let her out-quote me. "And the Blue Goddess tells us to 'be kind to every creature,' while the White Goddess wishes us to 'fill the world with music and therefore beauty.' Neither of those statements can even coexist with war."

"'Light was born to kill the dark,'" quotes Vil, bitterly.

"And yet 'without the darkness,'" Leifur counters, "'there can never be rest.'"

"Leave it alone," Vil commands.

Leifur squares his jaw and ducks his head. "I would have killed her," he says bitterly. Helplessly.

Vil's face goes tight. "She was a traitor, and you were following my order, and—you didn't, in the end. She didn't let you."

"Your Highness—"

"Enough, Leifur," says Vil quietly. "It's over. And if there is any mercy at all in the way that . . . it ended—" His eyes are wet. "At least none of us bears the guilt of her soul. If she even had one." He jerks to his feet and strides into his tent, letting the flap fall shut behind him.

I ache to go after him, to fold myself into his chest, to share the grief that devours us both. But I don't quite know how, and so I remain sitting there with Saga and Leifur, staring miserably into the fire.

"There was nothing else you could have done," Saga tells Leifur gently. "You were obeying Vil, as is your duty. But like he said—in the end, you weren't the one to take her life."

"She didn't deserve to die like that." Leifur's voice cracks. "Why would she—why would she *choose* that? I'm not sure—I'm not certain I could have even done it. I'm not certain I *could* have killed her. And if I'd refused—"

"Then Pala would have done it," says Saga. "Or Vil. Or me." She takes a ragged breath. "Her death was a mercy, Leifur. She could not have lived. We all know that. Skaandans are loyal to their people, to their gods. Indridi did not fit into that equation. She was the enemy."

Leifur bows his head and weeps quietly.

I look away. I can't bear it.

Saga fixes me with her shrewd eyes. "What do you *really* think, Brynja? You listen and listen, and you never say anything."

I take a breath, try to quell the rising storm inside me. "I think she didn't deserve to die. Not like that. Not at all, by her hand or ours."

"And yet she did," says Saga. "Would you have shown her mercy, Brynja? Would you have allowed her, a traitor, to live, let her go running off to the Prism Master to ruin us?"

There is an evil knot in my belly, so tight and sour I am utterly sick. There is no answer I can give her that would satisfy either of us. So I don't reply, standing and turning away from the fire.

I pace toward Skógur City, alone. It begins to snow, and white flakes catch on the shoulders of my coat.

I step up to the city wall and place one hand against the stone. My breath catches in wonder: It's smooth, warm, teeming with Iljaria magic. I close my eyes and let it wash through me, clean and fresh as water from a mountain spring.

A touch on my arm makes me jump and wheel, heart raging. Vil stands there with a lantern dangling from one hand. His head is uncovered, and snow clings to his close-cropped hair as if he's been dusted with icing sugar. His eyes are red. "I didn't know where you'd gone," he says, voice breaking. "You shouldn't have left camp—it isn't safe out here all alone."

The magic pulses at my back, radiating like heat from the city wall. Snow swirls between us, eddying, white.

"Everything feels broken since Indridi," he says. "*We* feel broken. I want to fix it, Brynja. Help me fix it." The grief in his face wrecks me.

I touch his cheek with my hand, brush flakes of snow from his skin. He shudders and puts the lantern down, wraps his arms around my shoulders, pulls me tight against him. His heart beats fast under my ear. He smells like fire and snow and the faint hint of his citrus shaving lotion. For a while we cling to each other, snow collecting in our hair, the night around us frigid but the space between us fiercely warm.

"I can't bear it," he says. "I can't bear that she chose to kill herself rather than appeal to my mercy. I can't bear that I would not have given it to her, even if she had asked for it." A sob wrenches out of him. "I can't bear it, Brynja."

Grief clogs my throat. "I can't, either," I whisper against his chest.

He takes a long breath. "I need you."

I gnaw on the inside of my cheek. Snow falls thicker, colder. Behind me the walls of the ancient Iljaria city pulse with power.

Vil pulls away enough to look down at me, a desperate, liquid wanting in his eyes. But my heart is dull and slow and Indridi is dead and Kallias is waiting in his mountain palace to devour me whole.

He takes a long, ragged breath. "When we get to Tenebris, nothing can compromise our mission. Not Indridi's betrayal. Not our feelings. Mine for you or . . . yours for me."

Shame weighs heavy. I look away.

"We can't have any hidden agendas or grudges," he says. "We have to focus on what matters: seizing the mountain, eliminating Kallias, bringing peace." His jaw works. "We have to trust each other completely. Do you trust me, Brynja? Will you trust me?"

"I trust you, Vil." My whole body is trembling. It would be so easy to pull his mouth to mine, to melt into him like so much snow. But there is too much ahead, and too much behind, and too much uncertainty rattling around in the hollow of my heart.

Once more he touches my face, his fingertips searing my skin. "And I trust you, Brynja Sindri." He smiles sideways at me and picks up the lantern. "Back to camp, then."

We go together, trudging side by side in the fast-accumulating snow, away from the Iljaria city. He takes my hand, his warm fingers engulfing mine, and just for this moment I allow myself to rest in his safety.

THREE YEARS AGO

YEAR 4197, Month of the Violet God
Daeros—Tenebris

I'm asleep when the doors to the great hall burst open and boots grate harshly on the marble floor. I jerk myself upright, bleary-eyed, pulse racing. I glance at the time-glass: It's only the eighth hour—the king never makes us perform in the middle of the day. I peer downward, heart pounding in my throat.

Two guards set an ivory throne down in the center of the room. The king sinks into it. Two more guards drag a Skaandan prisoner between them. He shakes and sweats; he reeks of blood and bile. He's young, perhaps a year older than the new Skaandan singer, and has dark curly hair and liberally freckled skin, like me. A thin gold chain glints around his neck, and a gold bar in his right ear marks him as a guard of the royal house.

My gut clenches. This is not what happens when the king acquires someone new for his Collection. This is something different.

Below me, in her cage bordered with orange trees, the Skaandan singer shrieks and pounds against the glass. She's shouting at the king, shouting to the prisoner, who jerks his head in her direction, a sudden horror in him. In the space of a heartbeat, he wrenches himself from the guards' grasp and lunges toward the glass cage, reaching for the singer's hands between the bars.

They cling to each other, tears pouring down the singer's face while the young man tilts his head against the bars. His words are soft, but they echo in the vast room, all the way up to my cage: "Promise me you'll get free of him. Please. Promise me."

"I love you, Hilf."

"Promise me!"

"I promise." The words choke out of her.

Hilf gives her a single, fleeting smile, lifting one hand to smooth his thumb across her cheek and wipe her tears away. "I love you. Don't worry about me. Remember your promise."

"Hilf—"

The guards snatch his shoulders and haul him away from the cage.

"HILF!"

One of the guards slams his fist into the side of Hilf's head and he goes limp, gasping for breath. They drag him back before the king, throw him at the king's feet.

The singer screams his name, over and over, and tears pour down Hilf's face.

The king sneers at him. "Did you think I'd keep feeding you in my dungeons forever? Did you think someone was coming to rescue you? You have no talent with which to charm me, like your little singer friend."

In my cage I am shaking hard enough to rattle apart. I wish I had magic. I wish I could stop this. But I don't. I can't.

The double doors open again. Nicanor drags Ballast in with him, and my heart plummets like a lead weight. Zopyros, Ballast's half brother—the king's oldest son—follows with a muzzled lion on a lead, the one that two months ago so frightened Xenia.

Dread grips me. I blink and see the mangled bodies of the rats from my childhood, hear the echo of Ballast's ragged, gasping sobs.

Today there's blood on Ballast's face, more blood seeping through the back of his shirt. Rage bursts bright behind my eyes because *how dare his father hurt him like that*. He can hardly stand. I want to burst through the bars of my cage and put a knife in the king's heart. I want to grab Ballast's arm and haul him away from here, away from pain and terror and cruelty. I want to ask him why he told me to stop coming all those years ago, if he truly meant it, or if he was simply afraid of his father.

I look at the king and the lion, at Ballast and the Skaandan prisoner, and the horror cuts deep. I don't move. I don't make a sound. Because I can't stop what's about to happen, and if I protest in any way it could be me down there instead.

I am a vile, gutless coward. I keep silent.

Below me, Hilf begs for his life and the singer screams and Ballast slumps there in Nicanor's grasp, an awful blankness crawling into his face.

Zopyros sneers at Ballast, though his hand shakes as he loosens the muzzle from the lion's mouth. The lion doesn't move, held in check by Ballast's will. Zopyros drops the muzzle and lead, and takes a step back.

"Please," says Hilf. "Please. Spare me."

The king's gaze flicks carelessly over him and fixes on Ballast. "Kill him," he orders.

Bile churns in my gut, rises burning in my throat. *Stand up to him,* I plead with Ballast in my mind. *You don't have to do this. Please, Ballast. Please.* But of course he can't hear me.

Slowly, Ballast straightens, shaking Nicanor off him. He's breathing in quick, shallow gasps, and the effort of standing on his own makes him tremble.

"Do it, boy." The king's voice is cold and hard. "Or I will kill her. And then I will kill you. I have many sons. I don't need you."

Ballast stands there, shaking. Zopyros's right hand twitches at the hilt of his sword.

Hilf has stopped begging, just looks toward the singer in her cage, who weeps uncontrollably. He mouths something to her. I don't know what he says, but I feel the love in him, and I see the moment he accepts his fate.

My heart beats, beats. Everything inside me is screaming. *Please, Ballast. Don't.*

"She will suffer, boy," snaps the king. "She will be in agony. And she will know you are the reason for it."

BALLAST, DON'T!

Ballast bows his head. For a moment all is still.

Then the lion leaps on Hilf, huge jaws closing around his throat. Hilf's scream pierces me, sharp as a spear, but it's cut suddenly short. His neck snaps. His body goes limp. Blood sprays over the floor.

I realize I'm screaming, too, my face wet with tears.

The lion does nothing more. He sits back, docile as a kitten.

The Skaandan singer shrieks in her cage.

Zopyros tries to look as if he's not going to be sick.

The pool of blood seeps wider.

I *am* sick, heaving over my chamber pot.

The king stands from the throne, stepping over Hilf's body like it doesn't concern him in the least. He grabs Ballast by the collar. "Think carefully before you defy me again. You are not important to me. Never forget that."

"Of course I'm important," says Ballast, voice tight and hard. "I'm the very pinnacle of your Collection, your favorite dancing bear."

The king hits Ballast so hard he slides across the floor, skidding and falling in Hilf's blood.

I am sick again, though there is nothing left in my belly but acid. My throat and lips burn with it.

Ballast picks himself up, shaking. He takes a breath that sounds like a sob, and then he walks heavily from the room, red footprints trailing behind him.

I am undone. There is no escape from this horror. No respite. No relief.

The guards remove Hilf's body. A dozen attendants come to clean the floor, and when they're finished, there isn't a speck of blood anywhere, like it never happened. But when I look down, all I see is red.

It's hardly the sixteenth hour when I let myself out of my cage, shimmy down the chain, and climb up into the vents. I'm being reckless—the king isn't asleep yet, no one is, and I could get caught, but I don't care. My body knows the way to his room, though I haven't followed that path in six years. My heart rages and my gut twists. I have to see him, damn everything else.

But when I slip into his ceiling, the room below is wholly dark. I wait for a while, my pulse frantic. Nothing stirs beneath me; there isn't even enough light for me to be able to pick apart the shadows.

The recklessness tightens its grip. I work the vent cover free and hop down, fumbling for the Iljaria light globe that he apparently still keeps on his dressing table. I tap the globe, eyes tearing at the sudden yellow light that floods the room.

Ballast isn't here. The chamber is empty, his bed made, sheets smooth and straight, pillow undented. Except for the bloody shirt slung over the dressing table, I would think that Ballast hasn't been here in a long while.

I scan the room, trying not to look at the damn shirt. There is a small shelf of books on the back wall that he acquired at some point since I was here last. I run my fingers over the spines, perusing the titles. They are books of Daerosian history, politics, strategy, and warfare, not subjects the Ballast from my childhood would have had any interest in. I want to burn the lot of them.

The volume of Iljaria myths isn't here, but jammed in the back corner behind a book titled *War for the Thinking Modern* is our deck of cards. I know it's the same because when I take the cards from their box and look through them, I find the Blue Goddess card with the corner torn, just as I remember. I feel it like a kick to the gut.

He'll come back, I reason. He'll come back, and then I can finally ask him why he sent me away all those years ago. My eyes go hot and damp, and I mutter to myself every foul word I know until the urge to cry subsides.

He'll be back.

I wait for him on the bed with my knees tucked up to my chin. I lay out the cards in a game of Chance, which can be played solo. I try not to think about Hilf, the lion, the pool of blood. I try just to focus on the colors of the cards, drawing them and laying them down, trusting that luck will see me through. It doesn't, though. I lose the game, and the three I play after.

Ballast doesn't come. No one comes.

At last, as my eyelids grow very heavy, I put the cards in my pocket, climb up into the vent, and crawl back to my cage.

It isn't until the morning that I learn Ballast isn't in Tenebris anymore. He has vanished from the mountain entirely, and the king is livid that his son has run away. Or so he says. But he doesn't send anyone after Ballast, and I wonder if part of him is relieved. Because surely he's realized that the scene with Hilf could have played out differently.

Surely he's realized that Ballast could have set the lion on *him*.

It's almost Gods' Fall, the king crows to his wives, his nobles, his general—anyone who will listen. The world outside the mountain is harsh, conditions unlivable. He doesn't believe Ballast can survive long on his own, if at all. The tundra will claim him, he says, or the Sea of Bones, or the darkness.

But I don't believe that. Ballast is stronger than the tundra, the Sea, the dark. Ballast is stronger than almost anything.

He hasn't so much as looked at me in six years, and yet I am bereft in the wake of his sudden departure. I feel desolate, abandoned.

He left without me. Escaped this living hell.

And I'm still here. Captive. Waiting.

Though I'm no longer really sure what I'm waiting for.

Every night, the Skaandan singer weeps in her cage like her heart has broken, like the world has ended. For her, it has.

I still dream of falling, of my body breaking against the ice in the glacier valley. But now I dream of the lion, too. Of blood leaking over the floor and filling up the Sea of Bones, covering all the world. And I dream of Ballast, weeping bitterly in the dark because the Ghost God card was played against him, and he lost everything.

PART TWO

Winter Dark

CHAPTER SEVEN

YEAR 4200, Month of the Violet God
Daeros—Tenebris

The mountain looms ahead of us in the light of the falling sun.

All the air squeezes from my lungs, and I feel suddenly, wrenchingly ill. I fight the frantic urge to wheel my mount around, to ride far and fast away.

Vil looks sidelong at me. "Breathe, Brynja," he says softly, knowing exactly what I need to hear. "Just breathe. I'm here with you. We're all here with you. You can do this."

My heart jerks and I take a breath, long and slow. The bloodied truce banner snaps above my head, and my hand feels numb and tight around the metal shaft of Leifur's spear. Vil thought it would be easier for me if I had something to hold. Something to focus on. I try to let it ground me, try to focus on the freezing wind, the crunch of hooves over crusted snow, the long slanting shadows.

"You can do this," says Vil again.

I almost believe him.

Before we broke camp this morning, Saga did my cosmetics, her work mirroring Indridi's almost exactly. She held up a mirror so I could see my face erased of freckles, the kohl around my eyes drawn sharp enough to kill. Then she crowned me with a jewel-studded gold headdress. It made me look like a queen, she said, a goddess.

But I feel like that same scared ten-year-old child I used to be, dragged into the maw of Tenebris by a cruel and sadistic king. I shake and tell myself it's because of the cold.

A company of Daerosians ride out to meet us, their spears flashing orange in the mingled light of the setting sun and the blazing torches they carry with them. Behind me, Saga utters a quiet curse beneath her shielding veil, and I wonder if she's realizing anew, as I am, that she isn't prepared for this. For being here.

Beside me, Vil sits tall in his saddle. An icy wind rattles the buckles on his breastplate. His right hand rests tense on his sword.

I count the beats of my heart as the Daerosians reach us, a dozen soldiers dressed in scale-armor breastplates and fur cloaks. They're led by a commander as young as Vil, maybe younger, and I recognize him with a jolt as Kallias's oldest son, Zopyros. He's thin and there's a hint of color to his cheeks, thanks to his Skaandan mother. He wears heavy furs that make him seem smaller than he is, and he has steely gray eyes. There is very little of Ballast in him, and yet for a moment Ballast is all I can think of—the shape of his mouth against mine, the warmth of his fingers cupping my face in the dark. A shiver coils through me, and I blink through soft and sudden falling snow.

"We've had word of your coming," says Zopyros shortly, jerking his chin at the truce banner.

Breathe, Brynja. Breathe.

"I am Vilhjalmur Stjörnu, crown prince of Skaanda," says Vil, voice pitched deeper than usual. "With me rides my cousin, Princess Astridur Sindri, along with her handmaid and our guards. We come to treat with Kallias of Daeros."

I can *feel* Vil's anger. It sears off him like Indridi's fire. It's still strange to hear myself referred to as Astridur, something I will have to get used to, now that we're here.

Zopyros folds his arms across his chest, wholly unimpressed. "I require a pledge that you mean His Majesty no harm. Those smears of red on your rag mean nothing to me. What will you pledge?"

Vil clenches his jaw, but we both expected and prepared for this. "I pledge my life," he says, and strips off his coat without another word, the tooled leather vest he wears leaving his muscled arms bare; snow touches his skin and melts instantly. He draws a knife, sets it against his left shoulder, presses hard.

Blood pools and I flinch. I lower the truce banner and untie it from Leifur's spear with numb fingers. I give it to Vil, who presses it against his wound. The fabric soaks up the blood, the lily turning from gold to red. Vil holds the banner out to Zopyros. "The token of my life. Do you accept?"

Snowflakes swirl thicker between our two parties, and Zopyros's lips seem to be turning blue. "His Majesty will hear you," he says. He drapes the truce banner across his mount's withers. "You will follow me." He turns his horse and kicks it toward the snow-shrouded mountain, with his fellow soldiers following and our company just behind.

Vil doesn't bother to put his coat back on. Blood trickles down his arm. I want to wipe it away, want to bind up his wound. But there is no time for that now.

Behind the snow and the clouds, the brief day has ended. Everything narrows to the orange blur of the torches, bobbing ahead of us. My insides knot tight.

What if Saga is wrong, and Kallias recognizes me as the little acrobat who never dared to stand up to him? What if this gamble of mine gets me and Saga and the rest of us killed, neatly trapping the Skaandan army in the tunnels like rats?

"The gods are with us, Brynja," murmurs Saga from behind me. "Skaanda over self. Gods over glory."

"Gods over glory," I echo.

And then the mountain rushes up to devour us.

The gates of Tenebris's grand front entrance are made of huge stone slabs, guarded by gargoyle figures carved of dark stone: They're creatures from a nightmare, with wide black wings and hooked beaks and too many faces. They have eyes that gleam red and seem to watch you when you look at them—more remnants of Iljaria magic. But this is a dark magic, the kind that stings like needles under skin. The gargoyles are said to have been crafted by the Black God and blessed by the Gray Goddess, commanded to kill anyone who did not have leave to enter the mountain. I am not sure if it's true, or if it's just a story, but I don't doubt the gargoyles have the power to bring death, if they so choose, or if they were commanded.

Kallias brought me this way ten years ago, and I shudder as I pass between the statues, as I feel them peering into my insides and realize my childhood memory of them is somehow less horrific than their awful reality. I breathe a little easier when we've left them behind and the awful stinging sensation fades.

We come into a wide stone courtyard, where Zopyros and the other soldiers dismount, and the rest of us follow suit. Pale-faced boys and girls in blue robes and fur caps appear to whisk the horses out through a side gate.

Zopyros orders us to relinquish our weapons, and we hand them over, Vil even offering up three of his six hidden knives. I am nervous without my own daggers, though there is a tiny, needle-sharp blade concealed in my headdress for emergencies. Zopyros nods his begrudging approval, and leads us across the courtyard to the tall arched doors set into the palace proper. They're made of a lacquered dark wood and painted with swirls of silver that seem to move and twist in the torchlight. One of the doors creaks open, pulled by some unseen servant, and my heart leaps nearly out of my chest.

Zopyros steps inside, followed by Vil. I should be next, but my feet refuse to move. My throat closes up, my vision blurs, my knees shake. Then, a hand in mine, squeezing tight for half a heartbeat before letting go again. Saga. Here with me. Feeling it, too.

She's the only reason I find the courage to take that last step, into the mountain.

Then I'm finally here.

Right back where I started.

Nicanor meets us just inside the entrance hall, a high, narrow room that traces the curve of the mountain, the ceiling bare stone. I am startled to find that the king's steward seems smaller than I remember him. He's the one who locked us into our cages, who brought us slop barely fit for pigs, who beat us when Kallias was in a bad mood, or a capricious one. And yet Nicanor is just a pale, sour man of about fifty, with limp brown hair and dull eyes. Unimportant. Unremarkable.

He dismisses Zopyros, who strides off into the palace proper, and then informs us that though the king is busy at present, entertaining the newly arrived envoy from Aerona, he has issued us a dinner invitation. Vil and I exchange glances—we'd discussed the possibility of an Aeronan envoy at Tenebris, so it's not wholly unexpected, but it does make things a little more complicated. We'll have to tread carefully. We're not equipped to take on the empire, not yet at any rate.

Nicanor snaps his fingers and an elegantly dressed servant appears from the corridor, her yellow hair bound in two long plaits that reach nearly to the floor. There's embroidery around the base of her fur hat. "Show them to their chambers," Nicanor orders, and then leaves without another word.

The attendant beckons to the hallway, and we follow her, our footsteps softened by intricately woven rugs spread over the cold floor. Bright lights hum from sconces in the walls, no pulse of magic in them, and yet no candle flame or wick and kerosene, either. I study them curiously, spots dancing behind my eyes. I want to point them out to Vil—he would find them utterly fascinating—but then we turn into another corridor, this one lit by ordinary torches, and the moment is lost.

More hallways, more turns. It's hard to keep track of quite where we are, as I'm used to looking at all this from above, but I'm pretty sure we're entering the guest wing. We come into a corridor lined with plush blue carpets that glint with gold threads. The walls here are straight and square, carved with precision.

Then we're at an elegant carved door, images of flowers and birds painted blue and red, eyes glittering with bits of obsidian. No magic here, just exquisite artistry. A pair of those strange lights glow on either side of the door, which the attendant opens. She waves me through, with Saga and Pala on my heels, and I'm relieved when the door closes behind us. Saga pulls me into a tight hug, and we hold on to each other until our breathing grows easier and our heartbeats slow.

The room is warm, furs spread over the floor and silks hung along the walls to keep the mountain chill at bay. There's a wooden bed piled with pillows to my right, and on the back wall a square window with a sill wide enough for sitting on. It looks out on Garran City. A low archway to the left leads into a washroom with a sunken marble bath. There's also a dressing table with an ornate mirror, a huge wardrobe, and a door leading to what I assume are anterooms.

Saga paces restlessly around the chamber, running her hand along the silk wall hangings, half-heartedly pulling clothes out of our packs, which lay all in a heap in front of the wardrobe. Pala stands guard at the door, her mouth pressed into a firm line.

Saga is to pose as my handmaiden while we're here—it will be just me and Vil who go to dinner, and I don't know if I can bear to leave her in our room. I don't know how I'll face Kallias alone.

"I thought I was going to pass out when I saw Nicanor," says Saga. She chews on her lip. "I shouldn't have come here." She collapses onto the floor, and then she's shaking and gasping for air and I drop down beside her, hold her tight as the panic courses through her body.

"It's all right," I whisper, grief and fear clogging my throat. "We'll get through this. Together. It's all right, Saga."

Tears stream down her face. "I thought I was stronger than this. Stronger than him and what he did to me. What he did to *us*. But I'm not. I'm not."

"I'm not, either," I say softly. "No one could be."

We sit like that for a while, until we've both grown relatively calm again. It's Saga who pulls me to my feet, who shoves me into the bath with stern instructions to scrub all the dirt from the road away.

She drags me back out before I'm ready, then dresses me in a yellow silk gown lined in fur and embroidered with glittering gossamer thread. She once again conceals my freckles with her carefully applied cosmetics, then paints my eyelids red, brushes my lashes and brows with gold powder, and pastes tiny flecks of jewels onto my cheeks and neck. She weaves strands of gold into my dark curls, and crowns me once more with the headdress. Then she tells me to wait, just a moment, and I sink onto the bed as she rummages through the packs.

She returns with a flat wooden box, which she presses into my hands. I open it to find a dagger with an intricately carved hilt, the one she was working on at the beginning of our journey: It has a sun design, the rays wrapping around the hilt, and at some point she inlaid the carving with gold.

"Saga," I breathe. "It's beautiful."

She smiles. "I wanted you to carry light with you, always. Even in this dark place."

I pull her into a crushing hug. "Thank you," I whisper.

She laughs and tugs away from me. "Don't wrinkle your dress!"

Before I go to join Vil for dinner, I kneel to pray with Saga at the little altar she's set up in the corner of the room by the window. She asks the White Goddess for wisdom and protection for Vil and me. I pray to the Violet God to make time pass swiftly.

And then I smooth my thumb over the hilt of my sun dagger and slip out into the hall.

Vil and I are ushered into the dining hall, which I have only glimpsed previously from the heating vents high above the double doors. It isn't unlike the great hall, with its vast ceiling that follows the curve of the mountain and a smaller, purple version of the time-glass on the far left wall. On the back wall, twelve arched windows with diamond panes look out over Garran City. A long table rests on the raised dais in the center of the huge room, chandeliers dripping rubies and sapphires overhead.

Kallias isn't here yet. That's the only thing that keeps me moving to the table, where I'm seated across from Vil a few places down from the ivory throne at the head. Vil looks resplendent, in an elaborate gold collar and a scarlet robe lined with white fur. I can hardly stop staring at him. His earrings flash in the dazzling light from the chandeliers, and there is gold powder brushed along his lashes and brows, to match mine. I try to imagine Leifur applying the powder, then Vil. I fail at both images and conclude that Vil must have been assigned a palace attendant. He catches me looking at him, and I flush. His eyes glitter, and I realize that he is just as struck by my transformation as I am by his. I can't bear the heat of his glance; I am the one who looks away.

A dark-haired young woman with bronze-brown skin sweeps into the room and is shown to the seat on Vil's right. Elaborate braids threaded with gold ribbons circle her head like a crown, with the rest of her hair spilling loose to her waist. She wears a fitted green gown, edged with white fur and sewn with what must be thousands of tiny, glittering jewels. Vil's eyes grow wide at the sight of her: Aelia Cloelia Naeus, crown princess of the Aeronan Empire.

I saw Aelia, once, when we were both children. She came with her parents as part of an imperial envoy, and the king of course had to show off his Collection. Aelia cried through every performance, and later she came to the great hall alone. She peered up at me in my dangling cage. "When I grow up," she said, "I'm going to come back here and free you all, and make that awful king leave this place forever. I swear it in the name of my god." I didn't say a word back to her, but I've never forgotten.

I wonder if she really meant her oath, or if they were just the impassioned words of a child. Because of course she didn't free us. I freed myself.

Now, Aelia inclines her head politely to Vil and me as she takes her seat.

Zopyros comes in next, his scale-armor breastplate looking freshly polished. With him are three of his half siblings: twins Theron and Alcaeus, with milky-white skin and copper-tinged hair, and Lysandra, frigidly beautiful with her dark hair and eyes as blue as her father's—and Ballast's. Theron and Alcaeus are my age, Lysandra a few years younger. The three of them are full siblings, the children of Kallias's wife Elpis. All of them tormented us when we were trapped in Kallias's Collection. All of them tormented Ballast, too.

My throat is thick with an emotion I can't name, and it's hard to give Lysandra an acknowledging smile when she sits beside me, with Theron on her left and Alcaeus opposite. A few Daerosian nobles, whom I know by sight but not name, sit together at the foot of the table. The only vacant seats, now, are the three at the head, including the ivory throne. Dread knots my stomach. Vil catches my eye and gives me an encouraging nod, which bolsters me enough that I stay in my place instead of running screaming from the room. But I don't know how I'm going to force myself to eat anything. This was a *mistake*.

Elpis—Theron, Alcaeus, and Lysandra's mother—comes in alone. She can't be a day past forty, if even that, but she looks far older, shrunken in her fine gown, her eyes hollow and haunted, too much rouge on her pale cheeks. She takes the seat to the right of the head of the table, the place of honor. I know—from spying on other dinners like this one—that the wives clamor for this distinction, that it's only afforded to whichever wife is currently in Kallias's favor. I never saw Gulla here, and rarely Unnur, Kallias's Skaandan wife, but the honor seemed to pass fairly freely between Elpis and Pelagia, Kallias's Daerosian wives. Kallias very pointedly never made *any* of his wives queen, and it strikes me, just now, that these women are just another one of his Collections.

Even though I know he isn't in Tenebris, I find myself looking for Ballast, and being disappointed when each person who comes into the dining hall isn't him. I'm almost caught off guard when Kallias walks in, deep in discussion with his general, Eirenaios, who is decorated with so many medals he jingles as he walks.

All the waiting diners jerk to their feet out of respect for the king, and I numbly echo their movements half a moment after everyone else is already standing. Kallias strides to the seat at the head of the table, not even acknowledging his wife Elpis's deep curtsy and beseeching eyes. And then he's sitting down with a sweep of his blue robes and he's *so close too close* and it takes a heartbeat for me to realize everyone else has taken their seats again and now I'm the only one standing. I sit so fast I jostle the table, and Kallias's eyes flick to mine. I'm frozen in his gaze, an insect pinned to a board.

He knows, screams my terrified heart. *He knows.*

But the next moment he turns his eyes to his general, picking up the conversation they were having as they came in, at the same time raising his right hand and snapping his fingers in the air. I am forgotten.

Attendants lay the first course in front of us, a steaming soup in blue porcelain bowls. I force my hand not to shake as I pick up my spoon, as I take a bite. I nearly choke: The meat is gamy, the broth sweet with a kick of heat that seems to claw at the back of my throat.

"Astridur?" comes Vil's mild voice from across the table.

It takes me a second to remember that's my name now. I look at him and he raises his brows. "All right?" he asks.

I force a smile. "Spicy," I say brightly, nodding at the soup.

"You would do poorly in Aerona," says Princess Aelia from her place on Vil's right. "We eat porridge spicier than this for breakfast."

I think she's mocking me until I catch her genuine smile, the laughter dancing in her eyes. "I'm Aelia," she says.

"Astridur," I manage. "This is Vil—Prince Vilhjalmur Stjörnu, I should say."

Aelia's smile deepens. "You're the Skaandan ambassadors, then. I'm pleased to find you here! Some friendly faces." She lowers her voice and leans in toward Vil and me. "Very welcome in this mountain full of snakes."

I almost laugh. Vil grins. "The pleasure is ours, Your Imperial Highness."

"Just Aelia, please," she returns. "I introduced myself that way on purpose."

This pulls a laugh from Vil.

"It isn't polite to whisper at a public dinner," says Lysandra, from my left. She frowns and stirs listlessly at her soup.

"Our apologies," says Vil. "I don't believe we've been introduced?"

"I'm Princess Lysandra," she tells him primly. "The king's daughter. Soon to be the king's heir."

"Oh?" I say, intrigued. Suddenly her presence at the table, along with Zopyros, Theron, and Alcaeus, makes a lot of sense. Kallias never chose a queen, and so the question of succession isn't a straightforward one. All of them are clamoring for his attention, his favor. Vil isn't the only one with his eyes on the Daerosian throne.

"Of course it will be me," Lysandra snaps. "The boys are a great lot of fools."

"And yet you were not present at the council meeting today, while your brothers were," points out Aelia.

Lysandra scowls at her and waves an attendant over. "This soup is far too sweet. Take it away and bring me something else."

The attendant removes her bowl without a word.

"If you cannot show some manners, Lysandra, I will not have you sully my dining hall again," comes Kallias's cold voice from the head of the table.

Lysandra's eyes grow wide, and she stammers an apology to her father, staring at the vacant spot where her bowl was and visibly struggling not to cry.

Zopyros sneers at her while Theron and Alcaeus openly laugh. Kallias does not reprimand them.

"You are the Skaandan ambassadors, I suppose," he says in a bored-sounding voice, mercifully addressing Vil.

"Yes, Your Majesty." Vil dips his head. "Crown Prince Vilhjalmur Stjörnu and Princess Astridur Sindri. We are honored to be at your table."

Kallias snaps his fingers above his head again, without his eyes ever leaving Vil's.

Attendants take our soup bowls and replace them with scorching-hot plates of meat doused in a creamy white sauce.

"I would have thought you would harbor some ill will toward me," Kallias tells Vil. He cuts off a piece of meat and chews it slowly. "For the death of your sister."

Vil bristles but otherwise keeps himself in check. It helps that Saga is alive and well, a few rooms away. It was her double, Njala, who was killed in the skirmish with Daeros three years ago, but that news was never made public. When Saga was captured on the battlefield, she didn't reveal her true identity to Kallias—she sang for him instead. That's what saved her life; that's how she ended up in Kallias's Collection, shut in the glass cage bordered with orange trees. For Saga's continued safety, and to protect our current mission, her survival has remained a secret known to only a few.

"Peace between our nations is more important than anything, Your Majesty. It is what my sister would have wanted."

Kallias shrugs, unimpressed.

I cut off a bite of meat, shove it in my mouth. I contemplate my dinner knife, the hidden blade in my headdress. The dinner knife would be faster, perhaps, but not as sharp. Either could kill Kallias in seconds.

While the Dark Remains

Vil must read my mind, because he catches my eye, glances at the knife, and then shakes his head ever so slightly.

"And your companion?" says Kallias, nodding to me. He seems to be bored with his meat already, having abandoned his plate after only two bites. He snaps his fingers for the attendants to bring the next course, and they sweep away the meat that no one has had the chance to finish, replacing it with an artfully arranged selection of root vegetables and candied nuts.

"Allow me to formally present my cousin, Princess Astridur Sindri," Vil says.

I attempt a little half bow from my seat, barely able to think around the pounding in my temple and the nausea twisting my gut. *He knows he knows he knows.*

"Are you not hungry, Princess Astridur?" asks Kallias, raising both dark brows.

I open my mouth to reply but nothing comes out. I glance at Vil with full panic.

"It's been a tiring journey, Your Majesty," says Vil smoothly. "The princess is exhausted."

I grimace, meaning to smile and not managing it.

Kallias's blue eyes are sharp as steel in the glittering light from the chandeliers. I hate that Ballast looks like him and I hate that I can't stop thinking about Ballast. Is he still hiding, down there in the dark?

"We will have to find something that will tempt you, Princess," Kallias is saying. And despite the vegetables and nuts having only just arrived, he snaps his fingers yet again. Those plates are whisked away, replaced with slabs of steaming fish and sour pickled apples.

I try to eat, I do, but I can hardly choke down a bite. Kallias's eyes rarely leave mine as he sends course after course away, weirdly obsessed with finding something I will actually eat.

His children and wife vie for his attention, but he ignores all of them.

Finally, twelve courses in and two hours gone according to the violet time-glass, Kallias stands from the table, signaling an end to the awful dinner.

"I will call for you tomorrow," he says to Vil. "We will discuss your treaty, with Princess Aelia to witness negotiations, if that is agreeable."

"I would like nothing more," Vil answers.

And then Kallias strides from the room, his general, his wife, and his children trailing him like the ragged tails of a kite.

"Well," says Aelia. "*That's* over."

"Damn right," says Vil.

She laughs.

I make it all the way back to my chamber before being sick on the floor.

TWO YEARS AGO

YEAR 4198, Month of the Black God
Daeros—Tenebris

I crouch above the false ceiling of the king's council room, muscles tense. I rarely sneak around during the day—it's far too risky—but I'm always a little braver during Gods' Fall. Plus, an envoy of Aeronans arrived this morning, and I want to know what they're here for.

I peer down through a knot in the wood. The king sits at the head of the table with his general, Eirenaios, on his right hand, five Aeronan dignitaries seated all in a row, sipping wine from crystal goblets. Princess Aelia isn't here, to my disappointment. I've looked for her every time an envoy arrives from Aerona, twice a year or so, but she's never returned.

Ballast isn't here, either. I'm not sure what reason he would have had to flee to Aerona or, if he had, why on the Green Goddess's earth he would come back, but I still find myself searching for him. I shove away the familiar pulse of loss that his absence has carved out of me.

An Aeronan man who introduces himself as Talan stands to address the king. He's tall and holds himself well, his eyes dark, his sharp jaw smoothly shaven while his hair curls a bit at the nape of his neck. He can't be more than twenty, and the medallion he wears on a chain at his breast marks him as someone of high social status.

"We've been more than patient with you, Kallias," Talan says, his tone brisk and cool. "All the food Daeros can eat to fill your soldiers' bellies and allow your ridiculous war to continue, in exchange for the designs for your lamps and the materials to make them—but my emperor grows weary. The lamps are not what you originally promised him, you ask for more and more food, and the war drags on. Make peace with Skaanda, Kallias. Establish trade with *them*, and stop draining the empire—or is that your plan?"

The king bristles, knuckles straining white around his wineglass. "Wars take time, Your Grace. I understand that the lamps have been *more* than useful in Aerona—and you misrepresent that they are all we have given you."

"Drills," says Talan shortly, "a box that gives heat without fire, timeglasses that do not need to be wound—they are trinkets. Party tricks. A decade ago, you promised us something else, and I will be plain with you, Kallias: If the Iljaria weapon is not in Aeronan hands by the end of next Winter Dark, the food shipments will stop, and my emperor will send his army to seize Tenebris and look for it himself."

I go numb, heart slamming in my throat. *The Iljaria weapon.* I haven't heard even a whisper of it all the time I've been here. It's an old story, little more than a half-forgotten myth, claiming that before the Iljaria fled from the mountain, they buried something in the heart of it: an ancient weapon with the power to split the world in two. I never thought the king was the sort to put much stock in stories.

The king clenches his jaw and waves one hand at the Daerosian man who hovers near the sideboard: Basileious, the king's engineer. He's short and pudgy, neither young nor old, his skin more pink than pale. Limp hair curls above his too-broad forehead, and a pair of spectacles seem to be squeezing the very breath out of his nose.

"Give your report," the king snaps at him.

Basileious clears his throat. "As I was explaining to His Majesty earlier, we've hit a vein."

"A vein?" Talan's brows go up, his eyes fixing intently on the engineer.

Basileious nods. "A vein of iron, mixed with silver. We believe it will lead us, at last, to the mountain's heart."

"Why this vein in particular?" Talan presses. "You have found them before, and they led nowhere."

The king smirks and waves at Basileious to go on.

"We have, Your Grace," the engineer says to Talan. "But this vein *glows*."

Above the ceiling, I stifle a gasp. *Magic*. They've found a vein of Iljaria magic. Where else could it lead but to the mythical weapon?

"How deep does this vein run?" asks Talan. "How long until you reach the mountain's heart?"

"I am not certain, Your Grace. Our drills and axes shatter every few feet—"

"Give us two years," says Kallias. "We can reach the mountain's heart in two years, can't we, Basileious?"

"Probably," says Basileious, and then, at Kallias's sharp look, corrects himself hastily. "We can."

Talan frowns. "That is not the timeline my emperor requests."

"That is the timeline I can offer you." The king's eyes lock on the Aeronan's. "And when it is found, the weapon will first be used to obliterate Skaanda."

"Careful, Kallias. You overstep yourself. I will make your case to the emperor for the two years, but when the weapon is breached, it will belong to the emperor. He is the one who will decide how to wield it."

"Your emperor does not rule me," says the king coldly.

"My emperor *owns* you. Do not think to turn him into your enemy—you could not bear the cost of it."

The king laughs. "I can do what I've always done, Talan. Whatever the hell I want."

He stalks from the room, and fear jolts through me—I've lingered far too long. I scurry back through the vents and slip into my cage a heartbeat before Kallias bursts into the great hall and takes his fury out on one of the poor bastards from his Collection. I don't know who it is, and I don't want to. I turn my back and shut my eyes, but I can't close my ears, and I can't stop my mind from wheeling over all I heard in the council chamber.

After dinner we're made to perform for the Aeronan dignitaries. Talan sits in his chair with his arms folded tight across his chest, his lips pressed into a thin line. The other Aeronans seem equally unimpressed and uncomfortable with the king's Collection, though none of them move to stop it. So the king parades us out, one after another. I perch in my parrot's cage, waiting for my turn to be called.

It's been a little over a year since Ballast disappeared from Tenebris. The king seems to have forgotten him. Everyone seems to have forgotten him, except, of course, Gulla, who is constantly watching the door of any room she's in, spelling out his name with her fingers like a prayer. Rhode and Xenia miss Ballast, too, I think, though Rhode is old enough to know not to say anything about her half brother and quick enough to hush Xenia before she says anything, either.

I dread the day when Rhode and Xenia begin to emulate their older siblings, who sneak into the great hall and torment their father's captives, poking hot irons between the bars or slinging in sacks of excrement. Theron and Alcaeus like to practice knife throwing in here, which means not even my elevated cage exempts me from their cruelty. Once, they brought a crossbow in, sent quarrels hurtling up toward me. I dodged most of them, though one grazed my shin before Nicanor discovered what they were about and hauled them from the room.

He didn't send the physician in to tend to me—it was Gulla who came, later that night, after I had already performed for the king with a gash in my leg. She spread salve on the wound, bound it up. And she brought me a book to read, which she had done sporadically in the years after Ballast ordered me away from his room. Before Ballast fled from Tenebris, I liked to imagine that she did all those things on his behalf, that he asked her to do them because he still considered me his friend. That was nonsense, of course. A hope to cling to in the long Winter Dark. It was Gulla, and Gulla alone, who offered me these kindnesses.

But that doesn't keep me from wondering where he is now, if he's well, if he ever thinks about all the things he left behind. If he's even alive.

My mind jolts back to the present when the Skaandan singer is brought from her glass cage. The king takes one look at her, frowns, and waves her away before she even opens her mouth. She must be eighteen now, or near it. That's the age when the king loses interest in us, when we are no longer children, no longer deemed remarkable. I'm five months past my own eighteenth birthday, and though I'm still scrawny and small—thank the gods—I know it's only a matter of time before the king checks his records, sees my true age, and surrenders me to the Sea of Bones.

He calls me to perform next and I do, leaping from ropes to chains, doing a complicated tumbling passage on the wire that stretches the length of the hall: cartwheels and flips, handstands and somersaults, my stomach lurching as the room tilts upside down and then rights itself again. Then an intricate routine on the aerial silks, followed by a series of swinging bars. Sweat pours down my shaved head and runs into my eyes.

Last is a series of dizzying leaps onto impossibly small platforms. I throw myself across the gaps, vision narrowing to those tiny squares of wood. One, two, three, four, five. Another leap, and my sweaty palms seize the last chain. I slide down it and let go, jerking my body sideways to land on a nearly invisible wire. I teeter for a moment and then tuck my head down and run along the wire as fast as I can.

A heartbeat before the wire ends, I hurl myself forward, fingers stretching, stretching, to one last lonely silk.

For an instant there is nothing beneath me but air and a plummeting drop to my death.

But then the silk tangles in my hand. I grasp it and let go, allowing myself to fall. I count heartbeats. There's no time for breath.

The floor rushes up to shatter me. I grab the silk at the last moment, catching myself before I collide with the ground. The jolt of it jerks my shoulders so hard it feels like my arms are being ripped out of their sockets.

I hit the floor, ducking my head and somersaulting to land in a perfect bow at the king's feet.

I'm breathing hard, my whole body shaking and pouring sweat. I don't dare lift my eyes before the king acknowledges me, so I stare at his feet, slippered in silk and gleaming with diamonds.

I wish I could haul him up onto my wire, push him off, watch him fall. I wish I could give him the end that he deserves.

Fingers grasp my chin, tilt my face up.

"I grow weary with your routine, acrobat," he says, his voice as brittle as the ice outside his mountain. "Same thing, every time. I'm always hoping you'll fall, liven things up a bit."

I swallow around his fingers, staring up into his colorless face, his piercing eyes. It's not my right to say anything, and so I don't.

The king studies me and drops my chin. "I've just acquired a new acrobat, as it happens. I saw her perform in Garran City yesterday."

Fear pierces me. It feels like falling.

His eyes narrow. "How old are you, anyway?"

The fear boils over. My throat is dry. Words won't come.

"Well?" demands the king, shaking my shoulders.

"I am—I am sixteen, Your Majesty," I lie, hating the shake in my voice.

Humor lights his face. "I see little use for two acrobats, especially when one bores me so greatly. And it seems to me you have been sixteen for a while." He releases me and waves his hands at Nicanor. "Put her back in her cage. For now."

Nicanor grabs my arm and jerks me away from the king, shoving me into my cage and locking it before hoisting me back up to my parrot's perch.

I huddle on my sleeping ledge, counting the beats of my heart until, below me, the room empties, and there is no sound in the great hall but the children's quiet weeping.

I've seen the king murder children from his Collection more times than I want to think about. That will be me soon.

I'm out of time.

But I'm ready. I've been ready for a while. It's a relief. A release.

I get up from my sleeping ledge and tuck my knife into my waistband.

I glance around the cage dispassionately, then let myself out the door and shimmy down the chain.

I find myself slipping past the Skaandan singer's glass cage, bordered by orange trees. The scent of citrus is sharp in the air.

A hand grabs me by the wrist and yanks me against the glass. I jerk my head up and look into the singer's dark eyes.

"Please," she begs, her grip hard as iron. "Please, you have to help me. Kallias means to kill me in the morning."

I stare at her through the glass bars of her cage. Tears streak her brown cheeks, and the skirt of her robe is torn and bloodied. What did they do to her, after her nonperformance? Pity twists in my gut and I hesitate.

"I can't," I say. "I'm sorry." But I don't move. Because I can see her twisted and broken on the floor, her blood pooling around her, her corpse tossed like so much refuse into the Sea.

"He said he'll make me sing an aria," she whispers, "that he'll—that he'll cut my throat while I'm doing it."

Black *God*, I'm going to be sick. Behind me, the level in the timeglass rises.

"Please," she says. "My family thinks I'm dead. I have to get home. I *have* to." Something in her hardens, and all her being fixes on me. "Don't leave me here to die. Please. I appeal—I appeal to the gods."

I go still and cold. She's invoked the Skaandan code of honor: An appeal to the gods is a life bargain, a binding oath. My mind wheels as I frantically recalculate my escape plan. I could still ignore her. I could turn without an answer, slip back up into the vent, leave this damn mountain behind forever, and go home, at long, long last.

But how can I do that? How can I leave her to join Hilf's moldering bones at the bottom of the glacier sea? Her memory would haunt me forever.

And yet helping her would change *everything*.

Her jaw clenches. She shoves back her sleeve and shows me the underside of her wrist, where she rubs away a layer of dirt to reveal a white eight-pointed star. "I am Saga Stjörnu, crown princess of Skaanda, and I *command* you to free me from this cage and take me home to Staltoria City."

My mouth drops open. For a heartbeat more I just stare at her.

And then I pick the lock on her cage and do as she asked.

I take her with me.

CHAPTER EIGHT

YEAR 4200, Month of the Violet God
Daeros—Tenebris

"He knows who I am," I say for the hundredth time.

Vil's guest suite has a receiving room, and he, Saga, and I have been sitting here for the last half hour, filling Saga in on the events of dinner and discussing strategy in tense voices.

"He doesn't know," says Vil, also for the hundredth time, "but *gods* he makes my skin crawl."

I pick at the tray of food Vil sent for me to replace the rich dinner I lost in my room. Everything turns my stomach.

"Aerona's presence complicates things," Vil goes on, "as does the uncertain nature of Kallias's heir."

"Aerona has essentially been Daeros's ally in the war with Skaanda," Saga agrees. "They haven't sent soldiers, but they've kept Daeros's fed, which is nearly the same thing."

Vil nods and turns to me. "We need to know the exact nature of the relationship between Aerona and Daeros—what does the empire want? What exactly are they getting in exchange for their shiploads of food? The next time Kallias has a private meeting with the Aeronan envoy—"

"I'll be watching," I say.

He smiles. "Good. I also want you to find out everything you can about who Kallias means to name as his heir, as well as keeping tabs on the Daerosian nobles. If there is even a *hint* of disloyalty toward the king in any of them, I want to know about it. Are the nobles all here?"

"There's a handful still to arrive," I tell him. "I'll let you know when they do. Most of them stay in Tenebris for the whole of Gods' Fall, so that should make things easier."

Vil gives another nod. "I'll meet with them all, see which ones might make good allies, like we planned. The terms of our peace treaty should win a few over, and hopefully, when we depose Kallias, they'll agree to a smooth transition of power."

"No Daerosian wants a Skaandan king," says Saga quietly.

Vil quirks a smile at her. "Are you chiding me for my idealism, little sister?"

"Do you really think we'll be able to seize Daeros uncontested? The nobles want power, like anyone else, as do Kallias's children. They're all going to be a problem, and you're going to have to get your hands dirty before this is all over."

"Skaanda over self. Gods over glory. Have a little faith, Saga. It's all going to turn out just as it's meant to."

Saga sighs. "I don't suppose you're going to give *me* a job?"

"Get the attendants to gossip—and don't let Kallias see you. Stay in your and Brynja's room as much as possible."

"Don't know how I'm supposed to listen to gossip if I can't go anywhere," Saga grumbles.

"Cheer up, Saga," I say lightly. "At least you don't have to look Kallias in the eye while actively restraining yourself from stabbing him in the throat."

"No stabbing, Brynja," says Vil. "We have to get ourselves invited to stay here for the whole of Gods' Fall, remember?"

I make a face at him and try not to think about Kallias's glittering gaze, sizing me up, seeing right through me.

Vil squeezes my shoulder, his fingers warm through my sleeve. "It's going to be all right," he says. "Trust me, Brynja. I'm going to keep you safe."

I take a breath and tell the turmoil inside me to be still. "I know," I say. And I even think I believe it.

Back in my and Saga's room, I don't miss any time shimmying up the wall and prying off the heating vent. I squeeze in. My body has changed a lot since the last time I did this, but thank all the gods, I still fit.

"Don't be long," Saga says. "Be careful."

"I will," I promise.

I crawl forward, and my old hidden paths welcome me back with open arms.

※

I wake with a start to Saga shaking my shoulder, the chamber alive with lantern light. My cheeks are wet with tears, and a headache presses sharp between my eyes.

"What time is it?" I croak out.

"Nearly the fifth hour," she says apologetically. "I let you sleep as long as I could, but Kallias—" She takes a breath. "The peace treaty talks are in half an hour."

My stomach wrenches. I spent far too long creeping about last night and didn't even learn anything useful, unless you count that Ballast's room is empty—and why wouldn't it be? Had I expected him to be back in Tenebris, waiting to join my plot to take down his father?—and that Gulla doesn't live in the wives' wing anymore. I refuse to wonder if Kallias killed her.

The nobles had either gone to bed early or were out seeking various diversions in Garran City. Lysandra did a great deal of shouting at her attendant, probably to make herself feel better following Kallias's reprimand at dinner. Zopyros, Kallias's eldest son, rooms in the barracks, so I didn't see him, while twins Theron and Alcaeus played cards in their shared room and drank three bottles of wine between them. Rhode and little Xenia, Kallias's youngest daughters, slept cuddled together in their old bed in the nursery, even though they each have their own rooms now. Princess Aelia spent the evening reading. Kallias was with one of his wives—I got the hell out of his ceiling before I saw which one.

"Come on, Bryn," says Saga. "Let's get you dressed."

It still feels wholly wrong to have Saga wait on me, but I'm too tired to protest. She works a cream through my curls to stop them being limp and oily, then does my cosmetics and buttons me into a red gown lined with fur. I choke down a mug of coffee and a little toast, and then Pala is knocking on the door to let us know that Vil is waiting.

I join him in the hall, curling my toes in rabbit-fur-lined shoes, far too aware of the beats of my heart.

He takes my arm and I'm grateful for it; he lends me the courage I do not have on my own.

"Trust me," he says quietly.

"I do," I tell him.

He squeezes my arm.

We follow another elegantly dressed attendant down the twisting corridors to another room I have only ever seen from above. The council chamber is more cave-like than a lot of the palace, with curved walls and only a small hole of a window, set messily with glass and giving the merest glimpse of the Sea of Bones—or it would if there were any light to see by. The sun will be making only a brief appearance tonight before Gods' Fall swallows it whole for the next three months. Already I can feel the oppressive darkness gnawing at my heart.

Most of the room is taken up by an oval table and the high-backed, carved wooden chairs surrounding it. A sideboard at the back of the room is overburdened with pastries and fruit, pink wine, and steaming coffee. Heat pours in from the vents near the ceiling, coiling around my shoulders like a purring cat. The chamber is lit with more of those lamps that hum as they glow, burning somehow with neither flame nor magic.

Kallias stands at the window, sipping from an etched gold goblet. Lysandra is beside him, looking smug and furious all at once, with her brothers Theron and Alcaeus already seated and each tucking in to an absolute mound of pastries.

Eirenaios, Kallias's general, comes in after us, followed by Princess Aelia and Talan, the Aeronan ambassador from two years ago who threatened Kallias with imperial occupation if he didn't find and deliver the Iljaria weapon to Aerona. Nicanor, Kallias's steward; Basileious, his engineer; and three Daerosian nobles—two men and a woman—round out the group.

A handful of attendants hover around the sideboard, ready to fill cups and plates. Aeronan, Daerosian, and Skaandan guards crowd at the door, all of them scowling at each other. I'm glad Pala and Leifur are both here—we'll have a fighting chance if Kallias changes his mind about wanting to negotiate.

Once again I find myself almost unconsciously looking for Ballast, even though my rational mind knows he isn't here. I have felt his absence like a phantom ache since we parted all those months ago, but it is keener, here, in this place where he used to be. With an effort, I push the thought of him away.

Kallias turns, yawning, from the window, and waves for everyone to take their seats. Aelia sits on Kallias's right, with Talan beside her. Vil sits on Kallias's left, with me next to him. I don't pay attention to the rest of the seating arrangements, though I catch Lysandra's scowl from the corner of my eye. I am fixed on Kallias's presence, so close so close *too close*. I dig my nails into my palms to keep myself from shaking. I bite my lip so hard I taste blood.

"Good morning, Astridur," says Aelia to me, smiling.

I realize I'm staring at Kallias, and I jerk my gaze to hers. "Good morning," I manage.

"Shall we begin?" Aelia asks Kallias.

He yawns again while he nods at her and waves his empty wine goblet toward the attendants, one of whom rushes up immediately to fill it.

"His Majesty asked if I would moderate these discussions," Aelia tells Vil and me, "as an impartial party."

Vil nods, though his jaw tightens. Aerona isn't impartial—Aerona is with Daeros.

So many people are packed into this small room that the heat coiling in through the vents grows oppressive. I begin to regret the warmth of my fur-lined gown.

Vil launches into his speech: "As heir of Skaanda and representative of their majesties Valdis and Aasgier Stjörnu, I hereby propose a treaty with Daeros resulting in a permanent cessation of hostilities, and a mutually beneficial establishment of trade between our two countries."

"You propose certain terms, I imagine," says Kallias. He takes a long draught of wine, then a large bite of a ginger cake dusted with sugar. He licks his fingers one by one, and I'm going to be sick again.

I wave at an attendant, ask for coffee, and am handed a steaming mug. I drink too fast and scald my throat.

Vil nods at Leifur, who leaves his post at the door, and starts handing out bound sheaves of paper to everyone at the table.

"This is our proposed treaty and the terms we request," says Vil. "Everything is laid out in detail there, but to speak generally, Skaanda requests a permanent cessation of hostilities and the establishment of free trade between our nations, including food in exchange for metal and gems, and shared, uncontested access to the Altari Forest. We also offer to Daeros Skaanda's army, in the event that Iljaria break their vow of peace, or"—Vil's eyes flick sideways to Aelia—"there is other threat of invasion."

For a brief moment I wonder why Vil and Saga aren't here in earnest, seeking true and lasting peace. But then my glance snags on Kallias, and I remember why. Kallias could sign his name to a thousand treaties, but Violet God's heart, he would never abide by them if they didn't serve his purpose.

He doesn't want to treat with Skaanda. He wants to rule it.

"And these are *our* terms," Kallias replies. "*Generally speaking*, Skaanda has much to answer for." He snaps his fingers at his steward, Nicanor, who also hands sheaves of paper to everyone in attendance. When I get mine, I rub my finger along the smooth cream parchment, wondering how late Kallias's scribes were up writing these—he had a day to come up with terms; we've been working on ours for months.

"I propose we take the day to consider both documents," says Aelia. "We can reconvene tomorrow morning with any objections. All in favor?"

Everyone voices their assent, already thumbing through the pages. Attendants pass out drinks and pastries. I stare at the Daerosian list of terms, the letters swimming before my eyes.

"Tonight," says Kallias, not even bothering to look at his set of papers, "you are all requested to attend my Winter Dark celebration. After dinner, I will have my Collection perform in your honor." He raises his wine goblet in my and Vil's direction, and I choke on my coffee.

"Does the Princess Astridur ever speak?" asks Kallias mildly, his blue eyes fixing once more on mine.

I'm too busy coughing for a moment to properly answer him, and he smirks at me, eating another ginger cake without his gaze ever leaving my face.

"Of course I speak," I snap, not at all meaning to.

Kallias smiles. "I'm glad to hear it." He goes on staring at me as he licks powdered sugar from his fingers again.

I can't quite seem to tear my eyes away. There is a faint scar on his upper lip I don't remember from before; I am pleased that something, at least, had the power to mar him.

Kallias's eyes glitter, like he can read my thoughts, and he turns to Vil. "If I had known the Skaandans would send me such a beautiful ambassador, I would have requested a treaty long ago."

"You didn't request this one," Vil says hotly, hand going protectively to my arm. "And my cousin Astridur was sent for her shrewdness."

I barely register Vil's defense of me. I want to cast my*self* into the Sea of Bones—Kallias of Daeros just called me beautiful.

"It seems we have quite a lot of reading to do," says Vil, visibly reining in his temper.

I stare again at the list of Daerosian terms, which starts with the laughable demand to expand Daeros's borders so far into Skaanda there would be hardly any Skaandan land left.

This is all a game to Kallias. Of course it is. Everything is a game to him.

"I am not certain we will be able to come to an agreement in a single day," I say, remembering our objective. "Or even several."

I glance up to see Kallias watching me again. He of course has caught my not-so-subtle hint. "You should stay, then," he says, "until an agreement *can* be reached. Stay for all of Winter Dark—miserable travel conditions until the new year."

"That is very kind of you, Your Majesty," says Vil.

"The Aeronan envoy will stay as well," says Aelia.

I glance at her—I hadn't realized she was following our conversation.

"We would like to be here for the duration of negotiations," Aelia goes on. "The empire has a vested interest in your peninsula, and a workable treaty between Daeros and Skaanda will go far in persuading my father that imperial action is not needed."

My heart drums dully in my chest—this has always been larger than Skaanda and Daeros, and Aelia just threatened both of us. Talan's words to Kallias two years ago echo in my mind: *"If the Iljaria weapon is not in Aeronan hands by the end of next Winter Dark, the food shipments will stop, and my emperor will send his army to seize Tenebris and look for it himself."*

I don't know why Aerona wants the Iljaria weapon, but everything I've learned about Kallias tells me he has no intention of giving it to them, even if he *does* find it. Such a weapon would give Kallias the power to be free of the trade agreement with Aerona, to end the conflict with Skaanda, even to bend the Iljaria to his will, if he were to be that bold.

Uneasily, I think of the Iljaria party we met on the road, of their leader's promise to send an envoy to help negotiate the treaty. I wonder if those Iljaria will be the ones who come, or if it will be another group entirely.

"Daeros is very pleased to have you stay, my dear," says Kallias smoothly. He takes Aelia's hand and raises it to his lips.

I feel her rage, radiating off her like a signal fire, but she only draws her hand back again and smiles brightly. "Thank you, Your Majesty. Now if you'll excuse us, Talan and I will retire to our rooms to review these documents before the ceremony tonight."

The Aeronans leave, and Kallias looks after them with thunder on his brow. He fears Aelia and her threat of imperial occupation. He hates her, because she is one of the very few people in all his world he can't control.

Kallias jerks up from his seat and stalks out. My stomach drops, and I know where he's going: to visit his Collection. To remind himself of his own power, and to wield it on those who have none of their own.

TWO YEARS AGO

YEAR 4198, Month of the Black God
Daeros—Tenebris

I don't believe in miracles, but I'm not sure how else Saga and I make it out of Tenebris undetected.

We can't take my usual route through the vents. Saga tells me through gritted teeth that her foot is broken—but even if it weren't, I don't think she could have managed the climb. But there are no guards outside the doors to the great hall, and we meet no one as we creep slowly through the dark corridors.

We stop at a forgotten laundry, where I've been stockpiling supplies for years in preparation for my escape. I planned it all carefully, slowly gathering things a little at a time so nothing would be missed. I shrug into one of the two thick winter coats I stole and hand Saga the other, which she buttons with shaking fingers. She's in no state to carry anything, so I take both bulging packs, wearing one on my chest and one on my back.

I try not to think about why I have two sets of everything and fail miserably: I was going to convince Ballast to escape with me; I had plotted out every last detail. But then he went and left without me and I stayed, waiting for my moment. I didn't imagine it like this.

Now, in the forgotten laundry, I break off the end of a broom and give Saga the handle to use as a crutch. I don't like how much she's sweating, or how much her wound is leaking through the rag tied tight around her ankle, but there's no time to examine it right now.

"Let's go," I tell her.

She nods, her eyes glassy.

One more dark corridor, with a wooden door at the end of it, and we come out at the base of Tenebris, a few yards away from a sheer drop into the Sea of Bones. Over our heads, stars peer through swiftly gathering clouds, and far, far north toward Aerona, I catch a glimmer of green, dancing and shifting in its strange quiet song.

"We're on the wrong side," Saga realizes as she hobbles forward, leaning heavily on the broomstick. "Skaanda's that way." She waves her free hand, pointing west past the mountain.

My eyes flick west, then east. Were it not for the Sea of Bones and the scant starlight, I don't think either of us would have known where we'd emerged. "We must have taken a wrong turn in the dark," I say.

Saga curses, shuddering in the frigid wind. Over our heads, the clouds knit tight together, wholly obscuring the stars. Darkness blankets us like a shroud, and it begins to snow, thick and wet. "What do we do? We can't go back into Tenebris, and we sure as hell aren't going to try our luck with the Iljaria."

"No." I set my jaw, digging in the pack for an Iljaria light globe that I stole once from the king's council chamber, just to see if I could. It pulses a pale, warm yellow, its magic warm and purring in my hand, and it casts a small glow, just enough to see a few steps into the darkness. "We'll have to go around."

Saga shields her eyes as she peers west again, toward the front gates and the watching guards. I know exactly what she's thinking—we'll never make it.

But we have to try, trusting that the dark and the snow will hide us.

There's no other choice. We duck our heads into the wind and start west. I hold the light close to my chest, enough for us to see a few inches in front of us, but hopefully not for the guards to spot us from the gates.

Saga hisses in pain with every agonizingly slow step, the broomstick digging a furrow in the snow beside her. The gates are both too far and too near, and already I feel the dark magic of the Black God's gargoyles writhing through me. Nausea churns in my gut, and it feels as if all the air squeezes out of my lungs. I shift the second pack to my chest to join the first. "Get on my back," I tell Saga. "I'll carry you."

She doesn't protest, just climbs on as I kneel down, arms wrapped tight around my shoulders. She's staggeringly heavier than I anticipated, and I nearly face-plant in the snow. But I find my balance and creep forward.

The snow falls thicker, faster; the cold has teeth. The gates loom close, and the gargoyles' eyes flare red. I gasp at the pain of it, fire in my veins. And then a shout from the human guards—we've been seen!

I can't run with Saga on my back. I let her slide off and we both crawl, bellies in the snow, fear and dark magic raging through me. There comes the whine of an arrow over our heads, and the feathered shaft quivers in the ground a hairbreadth from my hand. Saga curses as she crawls, as more arrows wing over us, gleaming and deadly in the halo of our light. I shove the light into my pack and we crawl on blindly, fingers digging into the freezing ground. Pain slices through me as an arrow grazes my shoulder, and I bite down hard on my lip to keep from crying out.

We crawl, crawl. Pain and magic gnaw at me. I try not to imagine the guards lurking behind us in the dark, swords drawn and ready.

But the arrows cease, and the gargoyles' magic fades, and the pain in my shoulder diminishes to a dull ache.

"Are you all right, Saga?" I whisper.

She doesn't answer, just squeezes my ankle.

We crawl on and on, numb in the dark and the snow, until at last I dare to pull out the light again. I look back—we're not as far from the gates as I would like, but there doesn't seem to be any pursuit. There might be, though, when the storm stops. We have to keep moving.

While the Dark Remains

I pull Saga to her feet, trying not to see how gray she looks, sweat pouring from her brow, lips pinched together.

"We'll shelter against the mountain," I tell her. "We just have to go a little further first."

She nods; we both know it won't be enough. We need to get out of the cold, and Saga needs medicine—Saga needs a physician.

But we can't stop here. Not yet, not yet.

I have her lean on me and we stagger forward, the mountain on our right, the wind spitting snow in our faces.

Saga's breathing is quick and shallow, and her foot leaks dark liquid onto the frozen ground. I make her get up on my back again, but that just slows our progress. The light wavers in her hand. I'm terrified she'll pass out.

"Brynja," she says, her voice a mere thread of sound in the storm. "We should pray."

"The gods can't help us out here," I say tightly.

Saga laughs a little. "Have you lost *all* your faith? The gods saw us safely this far. They won't abandon us now." And she prays in a singsong voice, her words somehow bright against the darkness. I cling to her prayers without meaning to and find comfort in them.

The bulk of Tenebris melds into the massive mountain range that marches steadily west, nearly all the way to Skaanda. The stories say that inside the mountains twist labyrinthine tunnels, carved by the Iljaria centuries ago. But the Iljaria abandoned the tunnels long before they fled to the east, and the entrances are lost, or hidden.

Still, I keep the mountain on my right, dragging my hand across the stone, searching fruitlessly for a way in. The stone is rough and cuts my fingers, blood trickling down. I'm so cold I don't feel the pain.

Saga has stopped her praying, and I shake her a little. "Tell me about him," I say.

"Who?" she whispers.

"Hilf."

She makes a choked sound and nearly drops the light.

I stumble on, searching desperately for any crack in the stone large enough for us to shelter in for a while, out of the bulk of the storm.

"He was my bodyguard," she says at last, trembling against me. "It was my double, Njala, who they killed in the skirmish last year. Everyone thought she was me."

Hence the reports of Saga's death.

"Hilf was taken prisoner, along with a handful of us. It was my singing voice that saved me. I—I thought it would be better to live, to have a chance to get home again. But I didn't know that—that—"

"That the king would lock you in a cage like an animal."

She gnaws on her lip, visibly getting hold of herself. "Why don't you use his name, Brynja? He's not—he's not some faceless king. He's a murderer, our sadistic, cruel captor. He's Kallias, and you should name him. Not show him deference. Not give him that power over you."

"Names have power," I say quietly, sick to my core.

"Yes. And you should take his away."

I ponder this as I struggle onward, still scrabbling to find some scar in the mountain. My head is starting to wheel, and the cold numbs every part of me. "Hilf was more than your bodyguard," I say.

Saga chokes back a sob. "We were in love. We were going to find a way to be together. I would have given everything for him, but instead I was forced to watch as—"

"I know." I blink and see blood on the marble, hear her feral cries.

She doesn't say anything more.

I trudge on in silence, exhaustion stealing through me, spots sparking before my eyes.

And then against all hope, my right hand falls away into emptiness. "Saga. The light!"

She hands it to me, and I raise it high. There's a rift in the stone, crowded with snow and dead scrub. I ease Saga from my back and dig as fast as I can, dirt grinding into the cuts on my hands. I dig until the crack is wide enough for both of us to squeeze through. I go first, with Saga, gasping in pain, following after.

We come into a small cavern, shadows stretching long in the light of the Iljaria globe. Saga slumps on the floor while I build a fire with the brush I dug from the crevice. Flames roar to life, heat coiling through the cave. Saga crawls near, and I wrap her in blankets, make her drink a little water, eat a little of the food from our packs.

She's sweating *so much*, and I eye her foot uneasily, fresh blood seeping onto the stone.

I grit my teeth and finally examine her wound, cutting off the messy makeshift bandage. Bone shows white through her skin, and the oozing blood and yellow pus scream of infection.

Black lines crawl behind my eyes, and I fight the urge to be sick. But I force myself to dig medical supplies from the packs, wash the wound as best as I can, and smother it with a bottle of foul-smelling ointment I filched from the infirmary. Then I splint her foot with a piece of branch and bandage it with strips of clean cloth. I can't do anything about the infection, about the fever that's beginning to rage behind Saga's eyes.

"What are we going to do?" Saga says, tears dripping down her cheeks.

I shake my head. "Wait out the storm." I don't say what I really mean: *Wait and see if your wound heals, or if the infection kills you.*

My eyes rove about the little cave, and I'm startled to glimpse markings on the back wall: snatches of Iljaria writing, the colors still vibrant, though half the words have rubbed away with time. I jerk up, heart pounding, and go to examine the writing.

"Brynja?" says Saga from her place by the fire.

I brush my fingers over the words, feeling the echo of their power. That's when I see the outline of a door cut into the stone. For a moment I just stare, reassessing my doubts about divine intervention. There's a carving in the center of the doorway, a medallion of twisted flowers and vines, painted a vivid green.

"Brynja?" Saga repeats.

But I only have eyes for the medallion. I put my palm against it. I press.

The door slides into the wall.

CHAPTER NINE

YEAR 4200, Month of the Black God
Daeros—Tenebris

I suffer through dinner, forcing myself to choke down as much of the rich food as I can. Kallias has rearranged the seating so that Aelia is on his right and Vil on his left, with me beside Vil. Zopyros, Alcaeus, and Theron are seated farther down, along with Pelagia, Kallias's other Daerosian wife. She's heavily pregnant and looks miserable, barely picking at her food.

Lysandra isn't here; she must have done something to offend her father, or is trying to punish him by not attending, unaware or refusing to believe that he simply does not care about her at all.

The rest of the Daerosian nobles have arrived, and all are in attendance: the governors of the four largest cities, the overseers of the mines and the greenhouses, and the head arborist, who reportedly regulates the logging of the ancient forest inside Skógur City. They are all men except for Lady Eudocia, governor of the Bone City, and the arborist, Lady Thais.

As we dine, Kallias looks at me far too much, and I have the uncomfortable realization that he can't be any older than forty, if even that, far younger than I perceived as a child. Kallias would have been scarcely older than I am now when Ballast was born.

Ballast isn't here, I tell myself, and once more shove the thought of him away.

Dinner doesn't take as long as last night, thank gods. The sun is just rising as we finish, and we all leave the table and follow the beckoning attendants down the corridor toward the great hall. My skirts whisper across the cold floor in a riot of blue and silver silk; a red velvet half cape lined with thick fur weighs warm on my shoulders. I'm wearing the headdress again, comforted by the presence of the hidden blade even though I can't use it tonight.

I step through the double doors of the great hall with Vil beside me. The room seems smaller than it used to, and tears prick unbidden at my eyes. I have to fight to keep from looking up at my iron cage suspended from the ceiling.

Vil looks. "Black God's *bastard*," he curses.

I gnaw on my cheek, hard enough to taste blood. Vil's shocked anger on my behalf eases something inside me, like his witnessing the shadow of my trauma legitimizes it in my own estimation.

I try not to look for the other cages, scattered around the edges of the room, but I can't help it. I see Saga's orange trees, and the spot on the floor where Hilf once lay in a widening pool of blood. I blink furiously. *Don't* cry, *Brynja!* I shout at myself.

Vil grips my arm, lending me strength, pulling me out of my nightmares and into the present.

Chairs have been set up in a semicircle facing the glass wall. Light refracts blindingly through the glass, the sun having already reached its zenith. It gilds the whole room in liquid gold. I'm thrown back to last year, and so many years before, watching this same scene play out from above, stretching to prepare for my performance.

If Vil were not beside me, I would bolt from the room. We don't go and sit down, not yet, just stand off to the side watching everyone else come in.

Pelagia enters, hands clutching her belly, and takes a seat. Two of Kallias's other wives, Elpis and Unnur, sit beside her. There is still no sign of Gulla, and I try to push my worry for her away, but it remains, gnawing at me.

Kallias's children parade in: Zopyros, Theron, Alcaeus, and Lysandra, then thirteen-year-old Rhode and eight-year-old Xenia, Pelagia's daughters. Rhode holds tight to Xenia's hand. The elder four sit in the front row, with the younger two by their mother.

Kallias's general, steward, and engineer enter and take their seats, along with the Daerosian nobles.

Princess Aelia sweeps in with Talan, and Vil turns to greet her. They exchange pleasantries, but I can't concentrate on their words, thinking of Aelia as a child, angry and fierce, swearing to free us all when she was grown. Why is she here, now, of all times? Did she really mean what she said back then?

An attendant offers me a glass of wine and I grab one, taking a too-hasty sip. It's so strong I nearly choke.

"Princess Astridur," says a smooth voice at my elbow.

I jump and the glass falls from my hand, shattering on the stone floor as the red liquid leaks out. I stare at it, trapped in the horror of Hilf's death and Ballast's bloody footprints.

Kallias watches me, bemused, his white fur cloak heavy with diamonds. "I did not mean to startle you."

I look at him, and I don't understand how he is so . . . so very human. So very mortal. A monster cannot become a man, but a man can become a monster, and perhaps that's what makes humanity so frightening: You cannot tell, just by looking, who is monstrous, and who is not.

"Do come and sit with me, Princess," Kallias insists, taking my hand in his and drawing me forward.

I throw a panicked look at Vil, who is still conversing with Aelia and somehow hasn't noticed the king's arrival.

Kallias's hand is warm, and it unsettles me. He leads me through the half circle of chairs to the front row, and gestures for me to take the seat next to his. I do because I don't know how to *not*, and my panic subsides a little when Vil sinks into the chair on my right. He did notice, after all.

Kallias sits and rests his hand on my knee. I want to throw it off. I want to claw his eyes out. I want to hurl him through the glass wall and down into the Sea of Bones. But I just sit here, tense and nauseated, and do nothing.

"I am very glad you were chosen as an ambassador," says Kallias, content as a lion after a successful hunt. "I look forward to knowing you better over the next three months."

"I imagine," I choke out, "we will be much occupied revising the treaty."

He settles deeper into his seat. His hand does not leave my knee. "I am sure we shall. But that will not take up the *whole* of every day." His free hand touches my cheek, and I recoil. He laughs, tugging on one of my short curls. "I will do my best to make you feel at ease here, my dear princess."

I'm caught in a nightmare, and I don't know how to wake up.

"Look," says Vil on the other side of me.

Outside the glass the sun sinks into the glacier valley. Gods' Fall is almost here.

Kallias momentarily lets go of my knee to clap his hands for the ceremony to begin. A dozen children approach the waiting crowd: the majority of the king's Collection. I recognize most of them, including Finnur, the Iljaria boy with Prism magic, but a few are new since I escaped. The youngest is five or so, a tiny, pale-skinned Daerosian girl with enormous eyes. Finnur is probably the oldest at about fifteen. All the children are barefoot, clothed in thin robes of a shapeless gray.

I can't bear to look at them. I turn my eyes to the Sea of Bones.

Kallias snaps his fingers, and the children burst into song, their voices echoing all the way up to the domed ceiling. They sing an old, old hymn in haunting counterpoint that makes my blood freeze: a hymn of rebellion against the tyranny of kings, a hymn of supplication to the gods.

While the Dark Remains

I am stunned into looking over at the children again. They sing with their eyes shut, all holding hands. There is power in their voices, in the ancient song that is clearly not the one they were commanded to perform. Magic shimmers around Finnur's body, colorful sparks glowing in his white hair like embers.

The onlookers shift in their seats, some uncomfortable with the display, others uncertain as to whether this is actually the intended entertainment. Nicanor blanches paler than ice, and Kallias's little daughter Xenia cries quietly into her sister Rhode's shoulder.

Kallias, momentarily stunned, jerks up from his chair. "Cease!" he barks.

But the children only sing louder, and the sun chooses that moment to drop below the horizon.

"I SAID CEASE!" Kallias cries.

The hymn wavers, stops, and the children peer at Kallias. I feel their fear—but also their triumph. He will punish them for their defiance. He might even kill a few.

I'm consumed by a deep, overwhelming shame. I never stood up to Kallias like that. I could have driven a knife into his heart while he slept. I could have spat in his face when he told me to amaze him. I could have freed the whole Collection, if I'd been brave enough. But I wasn't. And I can't help but think sometimes that these children are still here, still suffering, because of me. Saga tells me that isn't true, that I was myself a powerless child, trapped in circumstance as well as a literal cage. But in moments like these, I don't believe her.

Nicanor and a half dozen attendants appear out of nowhere and seize the children, jerking them back into the shadows. They won't be punished yet. Not until after the hall is cleared. My hand reaches up to my headdress, fingers tracing the tiny latch that will release the hidden blade.

"It's going to be okay," Vil says, low in my ear. "Trust me."

I bite my cheek, hard, and bring my hand down to my lap again. *No stabbing.*

Kallias flops back into his chair, whole body tight with barely concealed rage. But his tone is level when he leans toward me and says, "The rest of the performances will be more to your liking, Your Highness. The children truly are remarkable, you know, and so grateful to me for taking them in, caring for them out of my own pocket and the goodness of my heart. They were orphans before they came here. They would be living penniless on the streets if not for me."

I try to smile at his lies as my stomach twists, and I sit here, sit here, damned to a hell of my own making. Not even Vil's warm and steady presence has the power to comfort me.

Light flares in the hall as attendants turn up the lamps. I blink at the afterimage of the sun, lost in the glacier sea. I mourn its passing. Already the darkness twists through me, hungry and mocking.

Attendants quietly pass out more glasses of wine, and Kallias stands, lifting his glass high as he leads us all in the traditional Daerosian benediction. I have heard these words many times, but never said them before: "Sleep well with the night, come again with the morning, leave us not forever in the Winter Dark."

We speak as one, our voices murmuring around the hall. Kallias takes a long draught of wine, then hurls the glass as hard as he can against the floor. It shatters instantly, and if anyone was unaware of Kallias's anger before, they know it now.

"Bring out my Collection!" he shouts.

He grabs my hand as he sits down again, threads his fingers through mine. I try to pull away, but he just holds tighter. Panic is a wild thing inside me. My vision washes white, and I can't think around the vicious pulse of my heart, the pressure of his grip, like he means to crush my bones.

I am vaguely conscious of Vil on the other side of me, thigh pressed against mine, fingers light on my arm. He won't let Kallias hurt me, won't let him trap me like a beetle in a jar. Vil asked me to trust him and swore to keep me safe. I believe him.

I focus on breathing, even, slow. The panic dulls a little. I flick my glance to Vil and wonder if he knows how many times tonight he has already saved me.

Two girls are escorted to the space before the glass wall, both pale-skinned Daerosians. The first is tiny, no more than five; the other is thirteen or so. An attendant sets up an easel and presents the older girl with paint and brushes. The small girl faces the audience, opens her mouth, and begins to sing. She has a brilliant, powerful voice for such a tiny body. Behind her, the other girl paints in swift, sure brushstrokes. A scene unfolds on the canvas, an almost exact depiction of the great hall, of the sun sinking into the Sea of Bones, of everyone watching, glasses raised to toast Gods' Fall.

"Exquisite, aren't they?" says Kallias, smug again. "I found the little one just a few months back, singing for her mother's funeral down in Garran City. Snatched her up at once. The other was the daughter of one of my own attendants. Imagine, such talent in a servant!"

I fight not to reach for the blade in my headdress. Bronze God, I can't bear this. But at least my fury is less debilitating than my fear.

The song ends, and the older girl finishes the painting. She kneels to present it to Kallias, who waves her away and gives the painting to me instead.

The performances go on, knife throwers and musicians, a tiny Skaandan girl with an impossible memory. Kallias commands her to recite obscure lines from ancient epics, and she does so, flawlessly, in her little thread of a voice.

Then Finnur is brought out. At fifteen, he's all elbows and knees, with hands that are too big for him; he looks for all the world like a gangly hound pup in the middle of a growth spurt. His Prism magic, which two years ago was already impossibly strong, seems to have outgrown him. It staggers me.

At a mere word from Finnur, a dragon rises out of the Sea of Bones, lunging at the crowd before exploding into colorful sparks. He makes a tree grow from the marble floor, a hesitant silver sapling that shoots ten feet into the air, then unfolds dappled leaves that smell of cinnamon. Unlike his previous illusions, the tree doesn't vanish—Finnur has made something out of nothing. The tree stays, glimmering, even when Finnur is taken back to his cage.

Kallias stands to address the onlookers, his eyes flashing in the lantern light. "You have seen and heard things tonight to impress and amaze, but there is one act left to thrill you with daring and danger. I give you . . . the acrobat of Tenebris!" And he points upward.

My neck strains to the ceiling and I take in a scene horrendously familiar to me: a girl stepping from her cage onto the wire, a scrawny girl with pale skin. Her dark hair is cropped short against her head and she shakes, but her eyes don't leave the wire.

She does a tumbling passage onto the wire, and I go numb. I can't watch. Instead, I fix my eyes on the impossible tree, letting the audience's gasps and smattering of applause tell me when my ghost has successfully made another leap.

"Do you have no stomach for acrobatics?" says Kallias coolly. His fingers are still tangled in mine, hard and cold as bones.

"I am afraid of heights," I tell him past the acrid taste in my mouth.

"My acrobat is not," he returns. "Look." He grabs my chin and tilts my head upward again. I'm forced to watch with his fingers digging into my face as the acrobat makes one final, death-defying leap over an impossible distance, catching herself at the last possible second on a pair of aerial silks.

The audience applauds wildly, and Kallias stands again, clapping with them.

I flee the hall before I'm even aware of my intent, with Vil hard on my heels.

The doors shut behind us, and I run, run, not stopping until I hurtle into my chamber, leap up the wall, and haul the vent off. I cram myself through and crawl to silence, to safety, somewhere in the depths of the mountain. Kallias cannot reach me here. Nothing and no one can.

I curl up into a tight ball, and I sob until I choke.

※

"Brynja."

I jump at Saga's quiet voice as I slip into the bed we share; I'd thought she was asleep.

"You're not alone here. You know that, right?"

I shut my eyes, which are swollen from crying. I don't answer, and she grabs my hand, squeezes it.

"Vil told me about Kallias. About having to watch the performances tonight."

I gnaw on my lip until it's bloody.

"We're here to end all that. To end *him*."

I don't trust myself to speak. I am all raw nerve, tense and jangling.

"Have you gone to see them yet?" Saga says quietly.

I blink into the dark.

"The children."

"No. How could I?" My voice is ragged, rough.

"Because it's part of the plan. And because—it would do you good, Brynja. If you confront your ghosts, maybe they won't haunt you anymore."

I see the new acrobat leaping across dizzying space, snatching the aerial silk, spiraling down. I wish I could claw it out of my mind, but I can't, I can't. Fear and horror fight to consume me. "What about your ghosts, Saga?"

It's her turn to be quiet, and I hate myself for making her think of Hilf, of his dying scream, of his broken body and his blood on the floor.

"Why do you think I'm here?" she says.

I thought I'd had my fill of crying, but fresh tears leak out onto my pillow.

TWO YEARS AGO

YEAR 4198, Month of the Black God
The Iljaria Tunnels

I tell Saga the story, because she hasn't heard it before, one of the stories I read in Ballast's book: Long ago, the Iljaria lived under these mountains, carving beauty into the earth, raising cities of stone, filling the darkness with light in a place that will never see the sun. But they abandoned the tunnels, sealed up the entrances. Forgot them. And then they went east.

If the stories are to be believed, Saga and I could very well be the first people to set foot here in hundreds of years, stumbling by accident through one of those very entrances.

Now we stare in awe at the vast, echoing cavern beyond our cave. The air is whispering and frigid, our presence as insignificant as pebbles in the ocean. Stalactites gleam and drip above us, phosphorescent and strange, stretching up and up, out of the halo of our light. I wonder if the Iljaria were the ones to carve such lyrical shapes in these underearth shadows, or if these caverns were formed in the beginning, crafted by the First Ones themselves.

And yet for all that, the darkness makes my skin crawl. I get the sense we're being watched, unseen eyes stripping us down to bone.

"The gods have been kind," says Saga, soft, reverent. She leans against me, keeping all the weight off her broken foot.

While the Dark Remains

I flinch. "The gods are never kind. Not to me."

Saga says no word of admonishment, but I see it in her swift glance. "We have a chance now," she says. "If the tunnels run all the way through the mountains—"

"We have no way of knowing if they do."

"Do you have a compass, Brynja?"

"Of course I have a compass." It was one of the first things I stole when I started planning my escape.

Saga grins and puts one hand on my shoulder. "Then we go as far west as we can. We'll be out of the snow, sheltered from the elements— the tunnels are a gift, Bryn. A divine gift. We can't squander it."

I grimace, not remotely sure that we're safer in these caves than out of them. "And if we run out of food? And if we reach a dead end? And if we can't get back out of the mountain again?" *And if we discover why the Iljaria fled?* I didn't tell Saga quite the whole story.

"Have a little faith. Did you even think we'd get this far?"

"Dragging a one-footed princess past Kallias's guards through a *blizzard* in the *dark*? Absolutely not."

She throws back her head and laughs at that, and I don't like how her laughter echoes, eerie and overloud, bouncing off the stones, where anything might hear her.

※

We sleep a little, by the fire, then nibble rations from the packs and fill our waterskins with melted snow before heading west through the cavern. Saga moves very slowly, her makeshift crutch tapping and her foot dragging on the stone. Every step clearly still pains her, but at least nothing foul is leaking through her bandage anymore.

I itch to move faster, uneasy in the echoing cavern and the winding tunnel beyond. The mountain suffocates me, and I can't shake that sense of watching eyes, somewhere in the dark, the itch of magic under my skin, foul and forgotten.

We walk for hours, that first cavern and tunnel blurring into countless others. Multiple passages lead out from every cavern, and we choose the westernmost ones, though they don't always run true. Many of the tunnels are painted with breathtaking murals depicting the gods and scenes from the old stories, or covered in line after line of colorful Iljaria script. The walls seem to live and breathe.

The shadows do, too.

We come out of a tunnel into another cavern that's half as big as the first one, crowded with stalactites and stalagmites that look like rows of giant teeth. That sense of being watched grows stronger, and there's a rustling noise somewhere over our heads.

Saga notices it at last. "Brynja," she says carefully. "*Why* does no one live here anymore? Why did the Iljaria abandon the tunnels?"

I don't want to tell her, fragile and unsteady beside me. But she can guess the answer anyway, so I do, low and tense. "The stories say the shadows grew wings and claws and teeth. The Iljaria fled because of the monsters."

She whimpers and I gulp stale air. I give Saga the light to hold; she cradles it in her palm while I draw my knife, hardly adequate protection against whatever lurks in the dark.

"My life for a sword and a foot strong enough to stand on," says Saga.

But all we can do is inch forward, bit by bit, and pretend we're not frightened out of our minds. Saga prays to the Prism Goddess and the Red God and the Yellow God, her words tripping over themselves, endlessly repeating.

Halfway across the cavern, I trip over something, and Saga lowers the light to reveal scattered bones, yellowed with age, and among them a sword.

I stare at it, heart pounding in my ears, while Saga whispers a prayer of thanks and lets her broomstick clatter to the floor.

Wordlessly, I pick up the sword and give it to her. We stand back-to-back, the Iljaria light in Saga's left hand not nearly enough to banish the dark.

"The gods are with us," says Saga, low and tense. "The gods will protect us."

I don't see how.

And then a shadow peels itself off the cavernous ceiling with a scrape of leathery wings and dives straight for us, knocking the light from Saga's grasp. It clatters among the scattered bones and she shrieks, slashing at the thing with her sword while I do the same with my knife.

Neither of us wounds it, and it hisses and flies out of our reach, then wheels and dives again. It's about the size of a cat, and I glimpse dark wings, teeth as long as my fingers, and thick, needlelike hairs that cover its twisting serpentine body. Its head is narrow and lupine, its tail ends in a knot of white bone, and it has wicked, gleaming claws on each of its four scaly feet. Its eyes are bloodred. But worst is the sensation of its oily magic, writhing under my skin.

"YELLOW GOD, SAVE US!" Saga cries as she swings the sword again, throwing herself off balance and landing hard on her broken foot. She screams, scrabbling to get away from the bones, her hand closing once more around the light.

Saga holds it up, and the creature emits a high, eerie screech that seems to shake the whole mountain and reverberates down to my soul.

The monster wheels above us, still shrieking, and I get the feeling that it's calling to its kin, that soon the whole cavern will be swarming with these creatures, or something even worse.

Saga pushes herself to her feet, the sword in one hand, the light in the other. She holds it high.

I eye the winged monster, heft my knife, and hurl it upward. *Fly true, fly true,* I beg, but whether to the blade or the gods, I don't know.

The knife hits its mark, and the creature falls, screaming, to the stone floor. Foul black liquid leaks out of it and it grows still, but the red eyes don't close; they seem to watch me as I snatch my blade back, wiping it clean on the leg of my trousers.

Saga's eyes catch on mine. Sweat pours down her brow, and her body is taut with pain. Her wound is oozing again, and my gut clenches. She tightens her grip on the damn sword.

I stand back-to-back with her once more, heart ramming in my throat.

We hear them before we see them: a rush of leathery wings, a clatter of claws on stone. Saga shakes. "Gray Goddess, guard our souls," she whispers.

I try not to think about the bones on the floor. I try not to think that we will join them soon.

Then there's no time for thinking.

The monsters come all at once.

There are too many of them; they block out the light. All is whirring wings and clacking teeth, scraping claws and thrashing tails, bone-shattering cries and awful magic that slides into my veins and eats me from the inside.

All is dark, dark, dark.

I hack and slash with my knife, managing to kill or wound most of the creatures that come at me. Saga more than holds her own, even with her broken foot. She slays monsters one by one; they pile up at her feet. But it isn't enough. There are simply too many of them.

Claws rake through my shoulders and my belly; the pain is cold and wrong—these shadows drip with poison.

I curse as I fight and Saga prays, her voice at odds with the shrieking, hissing creatures. There are other monsters besides the winged ones: wolfish beings with snakelike scales and tails that sting, feathered creatures that stand upright like men and wield claws of iron.

Saga's prayers turn to weeping as she falls to her knees and drops her sword back among the scattered bones. I stand over her, trying to protect her, but it's no use.

The winged monsters fall on me, claws tearing at my back and my scalp. Pain and death rush up to devour me whole. I never wanted to die like this. Not in the dark. Never in the dark.

And then—

A sudden blur of orange light, somewhere outside the shadows.

An earsplitting roar and a whirl of white.

Monsters torn off me, slashed and broken and flung to the ground. A flash of teeth and the black eyes of a massive arctic bear. It towers over me, nearly twice my height, grabbing at the creatures, killing them with a single swipe of its enormous paw.

The monsters flee from the arctic bear, screaming in fear and pain, and the bear roars after them, its teeth dripping black with their blood.

I cling to Saga among the bodies, the bones, and we shake, shake.

A voice, sharp and smooth as sunlight: "Peace, Asvaldr. They have gone."

The bear backs away from us, dropping down to all fours, and that's when I see the man holding the torch at the back of the cavern.

That's when I see Ballast.

CHAPTER TEN

YEAR 4200, Month of the Black God
Daeros—Tenebris

Kallias is slouched like a sulky child on the couch in his private receiving room. The couch faces an elaborate metal screen on the left wall, heat coiling out of it. I'm in my usual hiding spot in the ceiling, wisps of heat escaping from the vents to whisper tantalizingly around my freezing face.

Both Nicanor and Basileious, the king's engineer, are standing by him. Nicanor looks exhausted, the heavy dark circles under his dull eyes making his face appear even paler than usual. His knuckles are bruised, and there are flecks of blood on the cuffs and hem of his elaborate fur robe. Rage twists through me. I know where he's been—tormenting the whole of Kallias's Collection for singing their rebellious hymn.

But I'm not sure Kallias even knows Nicanor is here: His whole attention is focused on Basileious.

"You've been promising me for *years* that we're almost in," he snarls.

Sweat beads on Basileious's broad forehead, his spectacles slipping down his nose. "We—we are, Your Majesty," he stammers, shoving his spectacles nervously back up again. "But the rock is . . . *resistant* to our drills, our axes. We're trying. We're working as diligently as we can."

"THEN TRY HARDER!" Kallias shrieks, jerking up from the couch and grabbing Basileious by the collar. I flinch as Kallias flings him to the floor in front of the heating grate, and the engineer just stays there, frightened as a rabbit.

My heart drums overquick. I haven't heard anything about Kallias digging for the Iljaria weapon since that conversation two years ago, when the Aeronan ambassador Talan gave his emperor's ultimatum: Find it and surrender it to Aerona, or be invaded. I think of Vil's caginess when Leifur brought up the story of the weapon on the road, the night Indridi—

I push that memory away and refocus on the scene below me.

Kallias paces the floor beneath my hiding spot. He has never, I suppose, learned to look up. Perhaps Vil and Saga are right. Perhaps he *doesn't* know it's me. My foot cramps and I grimace.

"If I may, Your Majesty," says Basileious from the floor.

"Get up, fool," the king snaps at him.

Basileious obeys. Nicanor just stands tensely by the couch, forgotten.

"We have made a hole," Basileious explains. He straightens his robe and shoves his spectacles up onto his nose again.

Kallias frowns. "A hole?"

"Yes, Your Majesty. One of our drills penetrated the last bit of rock that keeps us from the mountain's heart. It's a small hole—the width of a child's finger."

Kallias wheels on him. "Then make it *bigger*."

Basileious gulps, sweating so much the edges of his hair are damp. "That is what we are doing, Your Majesty. We got through once. We can get through again."

My heart beats, beats, as I recall the discussion from two years ago with greater clarity: *A vein of iron, mixed with silver. This vein* glows.

Impossibly powerful Iljaria magic, somewhere deep within the rock—I shudder to think what Kallias might do with such a weapon.

"How much *longer*?" Kallias demands. "That Aeronan bitch is breathing down my neck. It's only a matter of time before the emperor stops blustering and sends his army in place of his daughter. I need that *weapon*, Basileious. Without it, I'll never be able to stop Aerona from invading, won't be able to call Skaanda and Iljaria *both* to heel."

A chill shudders through me.

"I know, Your Majesty." Basileious fidgets with the cuff of his sleeve. "I promise you the weapon will be yours soon. Before the end of Winter Dark."

"You swear this to me?"

Basileious dips his head. "On my life."

Kallias sneers at him. "Don't disappoint me, or that's exactly what it will cost. You're dismissed."

The engineer bows and leaves the room in a hurry. Only then does Kallias turn to Nicanor.

"What happened during the ceremony? Who taught them that hymn?"

Nicanor holds himself perfectly still, the fear clear in his eyes. "I am not certain, Your Majesty, but it will not happen again. They've been properly punished, unless you wish me to dispose of them altogether."

My heart seizes and Kallias swears. "Not while we have visitors."

"Very well, Your Majesty."

"In the meantime, find out everything you can about the Skaandan ambassadors. I don't trust them."

"Yes, Your Majesty."

"And Nicanor?"

The steward meets his gaze, a muscle jumping in his jaw.

"You have served me a long time," says Kallias. "But if anything like that happens with my Collection ever again, I will put *you* in a cage. I'll make you play the part of an acrobat, and I will laugh when you fall and dash your brains out on the floor."

Nicanor dips his head, so white he looks to be made of snow. "I understand, Your Majesty."

Kallias sighs, like these conversations have worn him out. He plops down on the couch again, staring moodily at the heating grate.

"Anything else I can do for you, Your Majesty?"

"Bring me Elpis. I could do with a bit of company."

Nicanor bows and goes to do his bidding.

I scurry away as quickly as I can, sick to my very core.

※

"I know you're there," says Aelia without looking up from her writing. She dips her pen in the bottle of ink on the desk. "You might as well come down."

For a moment I just crouch in what I thought was my hiding spot above her room, blinking through the cracks in the ceiling. Then I crawl across the wood planks, squeeze into the heating vent, slip my hands through the grate, and deftly loosen the screws until one side of the vent swivels free, exposing me.

Aelia watches me mildly as I hop down and settle myself cross-legged on the chaise by her writing desk. This room is a little larger than mine, but furnished the same.

Diamonds dangle from Aelia's ears. She sets her pen on the desk and caps the ink bottle.

"Astridur Sindri," she says. "Somehow I'm not surprised." She smiles and rises from her seat, eyeing me pointedly as she sweeps by. "You move like a dancer, you know. Or an acrobat."

I go cold. Have I really only managed to keep my secret for two days?

She settles again on a plush chair facing me. Her earrings flash in the lamplight. "I do wonder what you're doing here, back in the court of the king who tormented you, acting the spy for a Skaandan prince."

She's trapped me neatly and she knows it, but there is no malice in her gaze. She leans back in the chair and folds her arms across her chest. "Perhaps you don't remember me. But I remember you—how could I forget? I was certain you would fall to your death a dozen times during your routine, all those years ago. But you didn't. And here you still are. Surviving." She lifts her eyebrows, clearly waiting for me to speak.

I'm prepared for a lot of things, but not this. How much does Aelia know? How far is she in her father's confidences? And why is *she* here after all these years? The emperor wants the hidden Iljaria weapon, that much is clear—but does he really trust his daughter enough to send her to fetch it for him?

"I am simply here to negotiate peace for my people," I say carefully, "and to give Prince Vilhjalmur all the tools he needs to accomplish that."

Aelia nods, but there's a glint of something dangerous in her eyes. "I should warn you that we are a bit at cross purposes. Aerona's arrangement with Daeros is drawing to a close. We have nothing more to gain from them, and they take much more than they give."

"What is it, exactly, that Aerona wants from Daeros?" I ask, keeping my voice as neutral as I can.

For a heartbeat, her eyes narrow, but then she smiles again, airy and light. "Daeros offered us the designs and building materials for all of Kallias's inventions."

My heart stutters. I knew this already, in the vaguest of terms, but not the details. "What kinds of inventions?"

"Lamps, mostly, that burn without fire or fuel. They are useful, of course, but hardly worth the endless shipments of food Daeros has demanded. My father originally signed the trade agreement because Kallias promised—" She cuts herself off, frowning at her slip, and changes the subject. I curse, inwardly—she very nearly started talking about the Iljaria weapon.

"To be frank, Astridur—" She gives a little laugh. "Why do I get the feeling that that isn't your real name?"

I grimace, and she studies me intently for a moment before laughing again, like it doesn't matter.

"To be frank," she repeats, "the imperial army will be here by summer. They will seize Daeros and absorb it into the empire. And then they will turn their gaze on Skaanda."

I want to poke at her more, press her to talk about her father's plans for the Iljaria weapon. But I can't do that without admitting that I know about it, too. "Why are you telling me all this?" I ask her.

"Because I *like* you, Astridur, because I believe in the Skaandans' bid for peace, and I wish very much it could come to fruition. Because whatever my father's philosophies, I have not his hunger for more land and people to rule. And because there is a chance—only a chance, mind you—that if the Skaandans send proper tribute to my father, he will stay his army and let them become an independent province instead of an occupied one."

It's my turn to laugh—there isn't a chance in hell that Vil and Saga would agree to *that*.

Aelia waves one hand dismissively, her eyes boring into mine. "But most of all, Astridur, I am telling you this because I have a personal mission I mean to achieve sooner than the summer."

"And what's that?"

Her face grows tight with anger. "Putting an end to Kallias's Collection."

My gut twists. Gods' bones, I'm going to be sick again.

She sees it; she softens. "You're part of the reason I'm here, you know. I refused to leave that acrobat to her fate, locked like a parrot in a cage. I'm glad you got free. I'm sorry it took me so long to come back."

I try to smile, but I can't manage it. "Do you think he knows?" I whisper.

"Kallias? About you?" Aelia shakes her head. "Do you think he'd let you stay here, alive and unchallenged, if he did?"

"Maybe. He likes his games."

Aelia puts her hand on my shoulder. "Then let's beat him at this one. You have my support, Astridur, for the duration of Winter Dark. I am on your side."

I hear the *for now* that she doesn't speak.

"What about the Iljaria?" I ask her. "Does your father mean to conquer them, too?"

"It seems that the Iljaria are best left alone," says Aelia carefully, "unless one has at their disposal a power sure of beating them."

Vil's ordered fruit and cakes to his receiving room, with steaming mugs of tea ready on the end table. He and Saga and Pala are waiting for me when I hop down from the vent, with Leifur keeping watch in the hall.

Pala hands me a rag to wipe the grime off my face and hands. I perch on a footstool and grab a mug of tea but I don't drink it, just watch the steam curl up.

"You heard something," says Saga, reading me easily. "Out with it, Bryn." She's carving a new knife handle, shavings falling off onto the floor.

Vil offers me a plate of food, but I shake my head and he sinks back into his chair.

I give my report while Saga's carving takes shape: It's another sun design, every ray hung with a smaller star. We are all of us longing for the light again, I think, though we are a single day into Gods' Fall. The winter will be long.

I tell them about my conversation with Aelia first, which makes Vil go tense and grim—he hadn't reckoned on having to ward off an imperial invasion quite so soon. Saga just frowns and carves faster.

Then I take a bracing breath and tell them about Kallias's discussion with his engineer.

Vil's whole demeanor changes. He goes tense and jumpy, jiggling his knee and glancing at his sister nervously. I think about his staunch dismissal of the subject when it was brought up on the journey here and realize he hasn't been wholly forthcoming about his plans in Tenebris.

Saga puts down her carving knife, brows bent together. "The Iljaria weapon from the stories—it really exists? Kallias truly believes he can find it?"

Vil grimaces and Saga watches him warily.

"It sounds like he's been digging for years," I say. "And two years ago, they hit a glowing vein."

"A glowing *vein*?" Saga's mouth drops open.

"Why didn't you *tell* me how *close* he was?" Vil demands of me.

I stare at Vil, hurt pulsing sharp in my chest. His sudden intensity makes me wary, or maybe it's my nascent perception that perhaps he's not quite as steady or as safe as I thought.

"That was the night I escaped," I tell him, "the night I dragged your sister and her broken foot out of Kallias's clutches, through a blizzard, and into the tunnels. And *then* I was struggling to keep the both of us alive while battling *cave demons*—so forgive me if mythical weapons and glowing veins went right out of my head."

Vil swears at me. "This changes *everything*, Brynja. How can you not understand that?"

I jerk up from my seat, temper flaring, and swear right back at him. "It would have been nice if you'd bothered to *tell us your entire plan* before dragging us on this godsdamned mission!"

"*What* changes everything?" Saga demands. "What didn't you tell us, Vil? What *is* this weapon?"

I flick my eyes to her. "The stories don't say what it is. But if the Iljaria feared it enough to bury, it must be capable of horrific destruction."

Vil shakes his head, a feverish light in his eyes. "The Iljaria hid the weapon away because they rejected its power, not because they feared it. They couldn't bear the thought of us Skaandans—the people who were once their kinsmen!—becoming as strong as them."

Saga wheels on him. "You seem to have quite determined opinions about something that's supposed to be a *story*."

He flicks her a guilty look. "The weapon must have the power to change the fate of the entire peninsula—why else would the Iljaria bury it?—and I mean to be the one to wield it. Not Kallias. Not Aerona. Me."

Unease ties me in knots. "Vil—" I start.

Saga stabs her carving knife deep into the table, making both Vil and me jump. "What. The. *Hell*, Vil!" she cries. "Were you even going to *tell* me about the weapon before you had it in your hands?"

"I can explain."

She squares her jaw. "Then explain."

My stomach churns. I don't like this side of Vil. It makes me think of how he was out on the plain, ordering Indridi's execution, and it scares me.

"I'm sorry, Saga. I wasn't keeping you in the dark on purpose—or at least not maliciously. I needed to find evidence that the weapon really and truly existed before hanging all our hopes on it. Now we have it."

Saga scowls at her brother. "I am the crown princess of Skaanda, Vilhjalmur Stjörnu. You don't get to decide what I do and don't need to know."

His lips thin.

"I agree with Saga," I say. "This was never a part of our plan. If you would have told us this from the beginning—"

"Then what?" Vil snaps at me. "You wouldn't have come along?"

Hurt burrows deep. I don't understand what happened to the Vil who kissed me in the moonlight, who told me to trust him, who promised to keep me safe. "I would have advised you against it."

Saga isn't finished. "How did you find out about the weapon in the first place? What, exactly, do you think it can do?"

Vil rubs at his forehead, irritation roiling off him. "When the reports came that you were dead, I dedicated myself to destroying Daeros. I researched everything I could get my hands on: maps and generals' reports, ancient records of the time when the Daerosians first came to our peninsula and the Iljaria fled east. In one of those records was an account of the weapon, said to be a power greater than the sun itself, bound in rock and ice, meant to be buried, forgotten.

"I thought that if it existed, if it could be found . . . Skaanda would never want for anything, never *fear* anything, ever again. It's a miracle from the gods, Saga, meant to be wielded by Skaandan hands alone:

the means to at long last right the wrong the Iljaria did us so long ago. A chance at true peace, true freedom. No more darkness, no more fear."

My heart is beating too fast, too hard. I pace along one side of the room, trying to calm myself down.

Saga huffs out a breath, not mollified by her brother's speech. "Do you think yourself a *god*, Vil, that you imagine banishing the dark? Will you even be content ruling only Daeros?"

He towers with sudden rage. "What the *hell* is that supposed to mean?"

Saga stares him down. Both of them seem to have forgotten I'm even here. "You know exactly what it means. You have envied me ever since the priestess marked me as heir, and not you. I thought—I thought we had worked past all that. I guess not."

"Saga—"

"I have trusted you all this time, Vil," she says quietly. "Don't give me a reason to stop."

I'm unwilling to remain in the middle of this festering sibling rivalry. "I'm tired," I announce. "I'm going to bed."

I climb up into the vent before either of them can object, although I'm not sure they even heard me.

A little while later Saga joins me in our room, where I'm already tucked into bed. She crawls in and pulls the blankets up to her shoulders. "You knew about the weapon, too," she accuses.

"I didn't know it was part of Vil's plans."

"You still should have told me."

"I'm sorry, Saga. I should have."

She sighs.

"Are things all right? With you and Vil?" I ask her.

"I don't know. I can't stop being angry at him. I don't want to be afraid that he resents me enough to seize Skaanda for himself . . . but . . ."

"But you are."

She takes a slow breath. "I am."

171

"He's ambitious," I say. "But he loves you. He was ready to tear apart all of Daeros for you."

She huffs out a laugh. "So he was."

I blink up into the dark.

"In any case," she says, "we can't let Kallias wield that weapon. It would be better in Vil's hands."

"Or yours?"

She shifts on the mattress. "Is there anything else you haven't told me, Brynja?" she asks me quietly.

I count the beats of my heart. "No," I say.

"You promise?"

"I swear it on the gods."

"All right." She turns her head toward me. "Have you visited the children yet?"

My gut twists. "No."

"Why not?"

I gnaw on my lip. "I'm a coward."

"They deserve hope, Brynja. You have to go."

She falls asleep before I can reply, but I am awake a long while. When at last I sleep, I dream I'm once more in my cage, dangling from the peak of the great hall. But the cage has no door and the room is filling up with blood and I can't get free. I drown, choking, in crimson.

TWO YEARS AGO

YEAR 4198, Month of the Black God
The Iljaria Tunnels

Bronze God, I'm hallucinating.

Pain radiates down my spine, the shadow creatures' poison crawling through my veins. I squint, but Ballast doesn't vanish. He's wearing tan trousers tied about the ankle and knee with strips of leather, a deep-blue shirt that's ragged around the hem, and a heavy white fur cloak clasped about his shoulders. His light and dark hair gleams in the torchlight, contrasting sharply with his brown skin, his blue eyes. He mesmerizes me. I can't stop staring.

The arctic bear lumbers over to him, bowing its head.

"Thank you, Asvaldr," says Ballast, and bows back.

Asvaldr strides past him, disappearing into the tunnels, while Ballast comes toward us. The torch flares bright.

Saga is tense and frantic beside me, slick with blood, fever and pain and poison raging behind her eyes. I don't think she really sees Ballast. I don't think she knows it's him.

But she screams as he comes near, scrabbles backward among the ancient bones and the bodies of the shadow creatures. She grabs the sword and brandishes it at him, cursing and crying.

He stays just out of reach. "Gray Lady," he swears softly. "You're hurt. Let me help you."

She shrieks at him, her blood leaking onto the stone.

"They'll come back," he says. "The monsters will come back. We can't stay here."

"Saga," I say.

She stops screaming.

Ballast flicks his eyes to me and my heart jolts. "Can you walk?"

I nod uncertainly and push to my feet, trying not to fall over.

He hands me the torch and scoops Saga up into his arms so quickly she doesn't have time to protest. She's not fully aware of herself, her surroundings. The fever is taking her, or the monsters' poison, or both. Her eyes are glassy and dull. In any other circumstance she would never allow Ballast to touch her.

"Come," Ballast tells me.

He walks swiftly, like Saga weighs nothing, and I stumble along after him, fighting delirium. We pass through the cavern and into a stone passage beyond, leaving both Saga's sword and the Iljaria light I stole from Tenebris to molder with the forgotten bones. I still have my pack, at least, though it's ripped and dark with the cave demons' blood.

Shadows stir and simmer above our heads, but they let us pass unhindered. They are wary, I think, of Ballast's light, and the arctic bear lurking yet somewhere in the darkness.

The tunnel doesn't run very straight, and Ballast turns down several branching passageways until at last he steps into a bright cave, a fire burning at the center of it. Smoke curls up through a crack in the stone, escaping out into the wider cavern. There are blankets spread out near the fire.

There are no monsters here.

Saga has gone limp and still in his arms. He lays her down on the blankets and crouches back on his heels. "What happened?" he asks me, without turning. "Where is she hurt?"

She's hurt everywhere, thanks to the shadow monsters, but I know what he's asking. "Her foot is broken," I manage around my dry throat. "The wound is infected."

He peels back the bandage and swears, with heat. "Violet Lord's bleeding *heart*."

Spots dance before my eyes. The air in the cave feels too warm, too close. Pain and poison rage under my skin, and I am torn between anger and relief, hurt and joy to have him here. "Will the monsters come back?" I whisper.

"Asvaldr bought us time. They will lick their wounds awhile yet." He brushes his fingers lightly over Saga's festering foot and begins to speak, strange tripping syllables that spark bright in the air as they leave his mouth. I feel the silver coolness of his magic, so opposite the oily darkness of the shadow monsters. It curls out of him and into Saga, making the redness fade, the pus evaporate, the bone withdraw behind her skin.

Tears pool in my eyes. I have never watched him work anything besides his animal magic. I blink and see the lion tearing out Hilf's throat; I hear Saga's ragged weeping from behind the glass bars of her cage. And yet Ballast has the hands of a healer.

He keeps up his singsong chant, letting go of Saga's ankle and placing his hand on her forehead. He leans over her, his magic sparking so strong I can taste it, the barest whisper of ice and honeysuckle nectar on my tongue.

Beneath his touch, the wounds from the shadow monsters close and heal, the poison pulled out of her veins. Her skin resumes its normal color. She begins to breathe evenly.

Only then does Ballast withdraw his hand and finally look over at me. His eyes are guarded. "Hello, Brynja."

"So you haven't forgotten me." This comes out rather more bitterly than I intended.

He winces. "I'd better see to your wounds, too."

"I'm fine."

"You're not."

The poison is more stubborn than I am; I feel weak, sick. "Fine," I grind out. I tug off my coat, my outer shirt, and kneel on the stone in only my shift.

He comes over to me, carefully examines my back. His nearness makes me shiver. "The wounds aren't deep," he says quietly. "But that doesn't matter, when they're poisoned." He takes a breath. "I will have to touch you, to draw the poison out."

My heart jerks. He has never touched me before. Not even when we were children. We always kept that careful distance between us, him on one end of the bed, me on the other. "All right," I say.

He puts his hands on my shoulders, starting up his singsong magic again. I shut my eyes and revel in the sensation, drinking it in, parched, greedy. The poison pulls out of my veins and my skin knits itself back together, the pain fading to a dull ache. He withdraws his hands, and I want to snatch them back again.

Ballast won't quite look at me. "You should rest now," he says.

I mean to protest. I mean to ask him why he's here and how he found us, if what he said to me all those years ago was true. I mean to shout at him and tell him I missed him and dig our deck of cards out of the pack and demand he explain all those evenings we spent together if he really didn't count me as his friend. But the weariness overpowers me. I curl up on a blanket he lays out for me and I sleep, swift and dreamless.

When I wake, monsters are wheeling outside of the cave and Ballast guards the entrance, a torch in one hand and a sword in the other. The creatures shrink from the light, but they don't fly away.

"There's food by the fire," says Ballast without turning his head. "And water."

I drain almost a full waterskin without meaning to, then devour strips of something charred and soft. The flavor is salty and smoky, and it practically melts in my mouth. Fish, I realize. I haven't had it in so long I forgot what it tasted like, and I've never had it prepared like this.

Saga still sleeps on beside the fire, her face relaxed, peaceful, though I know all hell will break loose when she wakes up and realizes who saved her.

I pad hesitantly up to where Ballast sits, keeping a wary eye on the monsters, watchful and tense.

"Will they attack?" I ask him.

"Not at present. They don't like the light, and they sense Asvaldr lurking near. They know I won't hesitate to call him."

"Can't you order them away?"

"They are creatures of foul magic. Speaking into their minds—their darkness corrupts me. Makes me little more than a beast."

"Then you've tried it."

His mouth goes grim. He still doesn't take his eyes from the beasts to look at me. "I've tried it."

"Will Saga be all right?" I ask him.

"In time. She just needs to rest while her foot finishes healing. My mother could have helped her more."

"You held her back from the Gray Goddess herself," I contradict.

He shrugs, like it's no great matter, and rubs his thumb along his sword hilt.

"Is that what your mother was teaching you during all those afternoons you spent with her? How to wield magic beyond the power given to you by the Blue Goddess?"

Ballast eyes me at this free admission of spying on him. "Animal magic has always come easiest to me," he says, "but yes, my mother taught me a little about how to channel it elsewhere. Her patron is the White Lady, her power in her voice. But growing magic, healing magic—that has always been very natural for her, too, and she believes that any Iljaria, no matter their patron, could learn to wield every kind of magic. Though I don't think all Iljaria are as naturally powerful as my mother."

I think of Gulla, maimed and silent, teaching me her finger speech as we looked together out into the starry darkness of the Sea of Bones. Of her hands, binding the wound on my leg, bringing me soap and books.

"My father doesn't realize it, but he didn't nullify her power."

I had always suspected this. "When he cut out her tongue." It's cruel to say it, but I do anyway.

Ballast flinches.

Out in the passage, the shadow monsters writhe and hiss, flying ever a little nearer to our cave before wheeling away again.

"You *left* your mother," I accuse. "You left her with *him*." My chest tightens and I say a little more quietly, "You left me."

He brandishes the torch at a monster that comes closer than the rest, and it jerks back screaming, horrible eyes glowing red. "Has he hurt her?" Ballast asks, very low. "Has my father hurt her?"

"I don't know." Anger writhes inside me. "You said when you were old enough, you were going to kill him. But you didn't, did you? You ran away."

"So did you!" Ballast retorts. "You could have killed him, too. What exactly was your plan, to get eaten by ancient monsters down here in the dark?"

"I didn't *plan* this! I'd be nearly home by now if it weren't for Saga's foot and the Gray Goddess's damned blizzard."

"Home in Skaanda?"

"Yes, of *course*."

He turns his head at last to look at me, and there's tension in every line of his body, in every cell of mine.

One of the monsters takes advantage of his distraction and dives straight toward us. Ballast leaps to his feet with a yell and hews the thing's head off.

I yelp and jump back to avoid its vile blood.

The rest of the monsters stay away, though they seethe with anger in the tunnel, wings a whir of knotted shadows.

Ballast stands there, panting, sword once again loose in his hand. "I wasn't brave enough," he says quietly. "I wasn't brave enough to kill him."

"But you could have."

His eyes go shiny in the light of the torch.

"You could have turned the lion on him, instead of—instead of—" I can't finish. My mouth floods with the taste of bile.

There is such agony in his face that I want to take my words back, to tell him it's all right, that I understand better than anyone the cruelty and control his father wields. But it *isn't* all right. It doesn't matter that I understand because *it isn't all right.*

"You command one of the strongest magics I have ever seen," I say, "half Iljaria or no. You could have used it to save yourself, your mother. To save us all. But instead you ran. Hid. Left us to our fate."

Like you left all the others, whispers my own conscience. I tell it to shut the hell up.

In the passage, the monsters hiss and shriek, and Ballast shuts his eyes, lips moving soundlessly.

"What are you doing?" I demand.

"Calling Asvaldr," he says.

The monsters attack, a whirl of claws and shadow.

Saga wakes with a cry, jerking upright in a tangle of blankets. She sits frozen as Ballast dispatches the monsters with brutal efficiency. Only one makes it past him and into the cave. I kill that one, with a feral shout and a thrust of my knife into its wretched belly.

Asvaldr takes care of the rest, galloping into the tunnel in a maelstrom of teeth and claws. Then all the monsters are dead, littering the floor of the passageway, their blood reeking, their red eyes sightless. Asvaldr lumbers away, unaffected by the carnage.

Ballast turns to face Saga and me, black blood dripping from the point of his sword.

For a moment Saga is perfectly still, but I tense, every nerve alight.

Then a keening, raging cry rips out of her and she hurls herself at Ballast, knocking him into the mess of slain monsters.

"Saga. Saga, *stop.*" I try to pull her off him, but she shoves me viciously away, tears pouring down her face as she wrenches the sword out of Ballast's hand and puts it to his throat.

He doesn't struggle, doesn't move at all, just looks at her.

"Saga, please," I beg. "He saved us from those monsters—twice. He *healed* you. Please let him go."

But she presses the sword in harder under his jaw, and he winces as it cuts him, red leaking bright down his neck. "Give me one reason why I shouldn't kill you right the hell now," she snarls at him.

His throat bobs as he swallows, his face smeared with the monsters' dark blood. There's a helplessness in his eyes that makes my gut clench. "I can guide you through the labyrinth nearly all the way to Skaanda," he says quietly. "I can guard you from the monsters."

She swears at him and he flinches, bracing himself for her killing blow. But she doesn't drive the sword home. She trembles with emotion, chest heaving. Her face hardens. "You will guide us through the tunnels, and then come to Staltoria City to face judgment for what you did to my kinsman."

There is nothing in Ballast's eyes now but despair. "I will not come with you to Staltoria City."

"Then I'll kill you now."

He just watches her, a muscle jumping in his jaw.

"Saga—"

"Stay *out* of it, Brynja!"

I snap my mouth shut. My eyes flit to the passageway, and I wonder how long we have before more monsters come.

"Swear to me that you'll lead us true," Saga orders.

Ballast looks at her. "I swear on the Blue Lady I will not betray you. I swear on her name I'll guide and guard you true."

Her eyes go wet and she lowers the sword, letting it slide to the stone floor. I wonder if she's thinking about Hilf. I wonder if he swore a similar oath when he became her bodyguard.

Ballast stands, slowly, the cut on his neck still leaking red. "We'd better go," he says. "Before more of the cave demons come to avenge their brethren."

Saga struggles to stand, swearing as she puts weight on her injured foot, and nearly topples over. I catch her before she can fall.

"I haven't yet mastered the art of knitting bone back together," says Ballast apologetically. "I did the best I could, but it'll take a bit more healing."

"I didn't *ask* you to *heal* me!" she screams at him.

I'm left thinking how awful it is that Ballast's magic is strong enough to heal, to preserve life, and yet his father forced him to use it to kill instead.

The distant shriek of monsters echoes down the passageway, and I shoulder my torn pack, hoping it will hold together, while Ballast shoves blankets into a pack he has waiting by the back wall, then shrugs into it. He grabs the sword and the torch, and offers Saga a wooden staff that was leaning against the wall. She snatches it from him.

He looks like he wants to say something to her, but reconsiders.

Then he leads us out into the passage, stepping over the bodies of the monsters he slew, their blood still wet on his hands.

Saga follows, teeth gritted, staff clenched hard in one hand. I come on her heels, a riot of confused emotions.

Ballast is here.

But I have no more answers than I did before.

CHAPTER ELEVEN

YEAR 4200, Month of the Black God
Daeros—Tenebris

Saga isn't there when I wake, bleary-eyed, to the smell of sausages and tea. A lantern glows orange on the table, and Pala watches from her post at the door.

Fear grabs me. "Where's Saga?" I ask.

"Down in the kitchens," Pala replies mildly, though the crease between her brows tells me she's not happy about it.

"Vil told her to stay in the room. She'll be caught."

Pala shrugs. "Her Highness is not exceptionally pleased with her brother right now, and in any case, she claims it would be *more* suspicious if she never mingled with the other attendants."

Saga's still angry that Vil didn't tell her about the weapon, then. Not that I blame her. I'm not especially happy with him right now, either. I sigh and sit down to breakfast, trying to shake the remnants of the awful dream from my mind.

Saga comes back in time to help me dress for the treaty meeting, her eyes bright and fierce, but I wave off her choice of gown. "I'm not going."

"Why not?"

"Perfect time to scout, with everyone of any importance shut in the council room for at least an hour."

Saga makes a face. "Fine. I'll send word that you're not feeling well. I guess I didn't need to be back so soon, then."

For a moment I study her, noticing fresh, dark earth on the hem of her dress. I wonder why she lied to Pala about going to the kitchens. I wonder where she went instead.

Scouting proves fairly fruitless. I briefly search Kallias's receiving rooms, and the guest suites of all the visiting nobility, finding nothing of note beyond a detailed record of Basileious's drilling into the mountain. There's over a decade of accounts that I'd like to read through, but I don't dare take the book with me—it would be too quickly missed.

After a quick perusal, I slip back into the vent.

I don't mean to take the path to the great hall—or maybe I do, my dream haunting me, Saga's words stuck deep in my mind. *They deserve hope, Brynja.* Gods know that's what I needed, for eight long years.

I spend a while staring out of the vent above the time-glass before gathering enough courage to jump down into the echoing room.

Above me, I hear the ghost of myself shifting in her dangling cage, but I'm not ready, yet, to face her.

I go to Saga's cage, first, the one bordered with orange trees. A Daerosian girl of perhaps twelve sleeps on the floor behind the glass bars, but she lifts her head as I approach. She has dark eyes and pale skin, and her blond hair hangs straight to her waist. She scoots to a sitting position as she blinks out at me, tense and trembling.

"I'm not going to hurt you," I tell her, agony tightening my throat. "I wanted to tell you that . . . we're here to save you. My friends and I. Not yet, you must wait still a little longer, but when Gods' Fall is over, when the sun rises again—then it will be time. So have courage. Have hope."

Tears brim in the girl's eyes. I'm not sure she believes me.

"What's your name?" I ask her quietly.

"Gaiana, my lady."

"Have courage, Gaiana. I will come to see you again, to help you bear the long winter night. All right?"

She nods, chewing on her lip. She turns her head away so I can't see her crying.

I go on this way around the room, telling every child I meet that they are not forgotten. That in a few short months, they will be free. I meet dark-haired Pór, a Skaandan cellist who has even more freckles than I do. He's ten and so, so far from home. I speak with Finnur, who is shut fast in an iron cage, his deep-brown skin a sickly gray. It's the iron, dampening his magic, making him ill. I tell him he'll be free soon. Free to flourish and to grow and to *be*, like the tree he made with his Prism magic that yet stands shimmering in the great hall.

I don't rush around the room, though the treaty meeting must be over now, and there's a chance someone might come into the great hall and find me here. I can't bear to leave without speaking to everyone.

My old cage is one of the last that I visit, climbing up the chain and crouching outside the bars, the new acrobat looking out at me, her eyes hard.

"Who are you?" she demands.

Anger seethes out of her. Hatred and bitterness and despair.

The breath freezes in my lungs; words stick in my throat. I force them out anyway. "I'm you. You're me. I was—" I fight to breathe, furiously blinking back tears. "I was Kallias's acrobat, before he took you."

Her jaw hardens. "You're a fool, then. To come back."

"I'm here to save you. To save all of you."

"If that's true, let me out of this cage."

"I can't. Not yet. Not till the end of Gods' Fall. I just wanted you to know that there is an end in sight. I wanted to give you hope."

She curses at me. "I don't want hope or empty promises. Get the hell out of my face."

I don't move, staring her down. "What's your name?"

She folds her arms across her chest. Her chin wobbles. "Rute."

"I'm Brynja," I tell her. "And I swear to you, I'm going to get you out of here. In the meantime—"

She raises her eyebrows.

"Don't fall."

She curses at me again, more vehemently than before. I shimmy back down the chain, my head wheeling.

I visit the last few children and come to another iron cage at the very back of the room. My heart seizes. Gulla's inside.

She lifts her head at my approach, and her appearance rattles me. There are scars on her face that weren't there two years ago; she looks impossibly weary.

Brynja, she says in her finger speech.

"You know me," I reply quietly.

She smiles. *The shape of your body has changed. You are older and healthier. You've covered your freckles; you've grown out your hair.* She traces her fingers along her scalp. *But yes. Of course I know you.*

I press one palm against the bars of her cage. "What has he done to you?"

Made me again what I once was: part of his Collection. But do not worry, Brynja. I am well.

I grimace, touching my cheek where hers is scarred. "He hurt you."

She averts her eyes. *He was angry when my son did not come back. When I made a fruitless attempt to follow him.*

Ballast's image plays out behind my eyelids, his black-and-white hair painted orange in the light of the torch he holds, his shoulders strong against the dark of the caves. "I saw him," I whisper, gripping the bars and leaning closer. "When I escaped, I saw him, and he was—he was well. He spoke of you. He missed you."

Her forehead creases. She shakes her head. *He has become too much like his father, desiring only power.*

My heart jumps into my throat. "What do you mean, Gulla? Have you seen him? Did he come back? Where is he now?" I am wild with sudden hope or sudden horror; I'm not sure which.

But Gulla turns away. She says nothing more, and I am left without any answers to the questions that pound against my skull.

Saga's gone again when I slip back into our room, as is Pala. I'm restless on my own, impatient. I wash in the sunken bath, but I can't scrub away the torment of the children, my desperation to free them *now*, not in three months. But with Tenebris still under Kallias's control, where would they go? Vil and I would be suspected and treaty negotiations cut off. The Skaandan army would be stuck marching their slow way through the tunnels, leaving Daeros free to sweep into Skaanda and take it unhindered. No. I have to wait.

Saga returns as I'm stepping out of the bath, and she avoids my eyes when I ask her where she's been, though she's glad when I tell her I finally went to visit the great hall.

I'm expected at dinner tonight. Saga hurries me into a violet gown trimmed with fur, then threads strands of tiny working clocks into my curls. The whole ensemble is meant to evoke the Violet God—the god of time.

Vil comes to collect me at the thirteenth hour, and he looks in unhappily at Saga, who refuses to speak to him, still upset about him keeping the existence of the Iljaria weapon from her, and shoves me unceremoniously out into the hall.

I pace with Vil down the corridor, my arm tucked into his. Whatever weirdness has arisen between us on the subject of the Iljaria weapon, we are allies in this place. We have to be. I try not to let Saga's unhappiness gnaw at me, and I vow to speak with her in earnest after dinner.

Right now I need to speak with Vil. "It doesn't change anything, does it?" I ask him in an undertone. "What we . . . discussed last night?" I'm being purposely vague in case the attendants are listening.

His dark eyes lock on mine. "No. Of course not."

There is gold powder brushed across his temples, like he's a gilded thing one ought not to touch. He smells of citrus and cedar.

While the Dark Remains

He takes a breath. "I shouldn't have kept it from either of you. And I shouldn't have gotten so angry. I'm sorry."

His pulse flutters in his wrist beneath my fingertips.

"Can you still trust me?" he says quietly.

"Yes," I tell him. But this time, I'm not quite sure it's true.

We walk a few paces more in silence. "How were negotiations this morning?" I ask then.

"An absolute joke. Kallias made his general push for us to relinquish practically all of Skaanda while he laughed at me behind his wineglass. Thank gods the Daerosian governors were there—they spoke earnestly, at least, and seemed grateful for the food coming from Skaanda."

I nod. As a gesture of Skaanda's good faith in pursuing true peace with Daeros, Vil preemptively ordered a shipment of food from Staltoria City that was only a few days behind us on the road, and should arrive very soon.

"I've set up meetings with each of the governors in the coming week—if I can win even a few of them over, it will help a lot toward our goal."

A peaceful transition of power, I think. Is it truly possible? Saga doesn't think so. Unease blooms in my gut.

We reach the dining hall far too soon for my liking, and to my extreme discomfort, the attendants seat me to the left of Kallias's ivory chair, with Vil to my own left. The seat to Kallias's right—the place of honor—is vacant. Lysandra isn't here tonight, but Zopyros, Theron, and Alcaeus are. All three of them practically radiate anger, which I can't see any concrete reason for.

Until Kallias sweeps in with a boy at his side.

A boy I once kissed in the dark.

My heart trips at the sight of him, striding tall across the room. *Ballast*, dressed in silk and fur, jewels in his ears and rings on every finger. *Ballast*, whom I never thought I'd see again, *Ballast*—

Belatedly, I notice the white silk patch tied around the left side of his head with an indigo ribbon. Angry red lines show from beneath the patch, half-healed wounds cruelly given.

Ballast, with only one eye.

I know I'm staring. I can't wrench my gaze away. I feel flushed and frantic, my desire to flee the room at war with the draw of Ballast, who takes the seat of honor. The one across from me. His gaze locks on mine and he looks ill, sweat on his brow and a feverish gleam in his single eye.

I can't think, can't breathe. All is a roaring kind of numbness punctuated by the lodestone pull of him, four feet from where I'm sitting.

"Princess Astridur," says Kallias, turning to me. He takes my hand and raises it, briefly, to ice-cold lips. "I was sorry to miss you at the proceedings this morning. I do hope you're feeling better."

I force myself not to recoil and stammer out something in return, but I have no idea what I actually say. Kallias follows my gaze to Ballast.

"Allow me to introduce my son, His Highness Ballast Heron Vallin," Kallias says. "I do apologize for his regrettable appearance. He's part Iljaria."

Vil tenses beside me and puts his hand almost possessively on my leg under the table. He's heard all about Ballast from Saga, and she didn't exactly paint him in a flattering light, despite what he did for us in the tunnels.

"I am honored to meet you, my lady," says Ballast, still staring at me every bit as much as I'm staring at him. He holds himself stiffly, like he's in pain and trying not to show it.

Gods gods *gods*.

"This is Princess Astridur Sindri," says Vil coolly, collecting himself. His hand is warm and heavy on my leg.

Ballast's lips thin as his gaze slides to Vil. "And you are?"

Vil stares him down. "Vilhjalmur Stjörnu, crown prince of Skaanda."

Ballast's brows go up again. "Indeed?"

"They are here to negotiate peace," offers Aelia.

"I see."

"But not well," says Vil pointedly. "I would imagine."

Zopyros, Theron, and Alcaeus—who have been following this exchange with rapt attention—snicker behind their hands.

Ballast's jaw works, but he doesn't rise to Vil's bait. The attendants lay the first course in front of us, and I eat without registering what's on my plate. The world is spinning and I'm too aware of Kallias at my elbow, Vil brooding on my left.

Ballast, just across from me.

Ballast, with only one eye.

How can he be sitting here at his father's table after everything Kallias did to him, to Gulla? How can he even be back here at all? Gulla's words burn in my memory: *He has become too much like his father, desiring only power.*

I don't understand and it's driving me mad, like my mind is incapable of understanding the shape of him across from me, so very close, but farther away than he has ever been before. I fight to keep hold of the conversation around me, fight for the awareness of anything at all apart from him.

"I am surprised," says Aelia to Ballast as she sips at her wine, "not to have seen you before. Have you been away?"

Ballast fiddles with his fork and table knife, awkwardly stabbing at a thick slice of ham and cutting off a bite. His hands shake.

"My son has been in the infirmary," Kallias answers for him. "Recovering."

I stare at those red lines under Ballast's eye patch, horror squirming in my belly. They can't be more than a week healed, if that. He was here. The whole time Vil and Saga and I have been in Tenebris, Ballast has been here, too. I didn't know. And it guts me.

"I told him he'd had enough time to languish, and he'd best get himself to dinner to meet my guests." Kallias smiles sweetly over at me.

I gag and turn it into a cough, pretending to choke on my meat.

Vil squeezes my knee under the table. He means to comfort me, perhaps, but right at this moment I don't want him to touch me.

"May I inquire what happened to your eye?" says Vil, icy as the Sea of Bones.

His hand stays on my knee, and I realize with a sort of distant incredulity that Vil is *jealous* of Ballast. It's almost hilarious. I haven't seen Ballast in nearly two years, and thus far tonight I haven't spoken a single word to him.

"My son has made some . . . regrettable choices in the past year or so," says Kallias, as if Ballast can't speak for himself. "But he's here, now—home, where he belongs. And he has earned his way back into my good graces."

A muscle jumps in Ballast's jaw, and I see the fear in him again. Visceral. Raw.

"Some of us have no need to earn our way back into your graces, Father," says Zopyros overloudly from his place next to Aelia. "*I* never left your side."

I have the sudden, horrific suspicion that Ballast is here, like his half siblings, angling to be named Kallias's heir. Is *that* what Gulla meant? And if he is . . . is the secret of my identity safe with him?

"I am man enough," says Ballast quietly, "to own when I am wrong. And to bear the consequence for my misdeeds." He attempts to stab another bite of meat with his fork, missing it at first and hastily correcting himself. I realize that having only one eye has thrown off his depth perception, and it sickens me to my core. *What did he do to you, Bal?* I want to ask him. *Oh gods, what did he do to you?*

Kallias leans over and brushes his thumb over the silk eye patch. Ballast goes gray and still, not even blinking. Kallias smiles that satisfied-cat smile before drawing his hand away.

After that, Ballast doesn't eat anything, just stares at his plate, fingers clenched tight around the handle of his table knife, that feverish glint in his eye grown worse.

I can't pin down my thoughts, can't convince my heart to stop its mad racing. It can't be, it *can't* be that Kallias put out Ballast's eye as some twisted test of loyalty.

But Bronze God. I know that it *is*.

All the rest of that interminable dinner, I will Ballast to look at me. But he doesn't. He's the first to leave the table, and I'm trapped with Kallias awhile longer, able to make my escape only after I swear to him I'll attend the treaty talks in the morning.

By the time I slip out into the corridor, Ballast is long gone.

"He's a problem," says Vil for the hundredth time, pacing the width of his receiving room. Vil and Saga have reached a tentative peace in light of Ballast's sudden reappearance, and she's crouched stonily on the footstool, knees pulled up to her chin.

"He knows who you are, Brynja," Vil goes on. "He knows Saga's not dead. I'm sure he can guess the rest."

"Aelia knows who I am, too," I point out.

"She has no reason to reveal you to Kallias," Vil replies. "Ballast *does*."

Every cell in my body is screaming at me to go and find Ballast, to speak with him, to understand what he's doing here, to beg him to tell me he's not back playing his father's games. To ask him why—

I shove the thought away with an inward curse. "Ballast wouldn't be back here, wouldn't have put himself back under his father's control, unless—"

"Unless *what*, Bryn?" Saga snaps. She pulls at a loose thread on the footstool, pulls and pulls until there's a ragged spot on the cushion. Her face has a haggard look, and I think of the dirt on her hem, the things she's not telling me.

I don't remind her that she owes her life to Ballast. That we both do. She's thinking of Hilf, seeing that last awful moment of his life played out over and over.

"He's Kallias's son," she says after a breath. "And that's the *only* thing that he is. I agree with Vil. He's a problem."

Vil flicks her a grateful smile. "Keep a close eye on him, Brynja. Track his movements, his meetings, especially with his father. We need to know how close he is in Kallias's confidences, and if Kallias is likely to choose him as his heir—we need to know if Ballast means to reveal us."

I clench my jaw. I have no intention of spying on Ballast. How could I? After everything we went through together—I jerk up from my seat, but Vil grabs my wrist and holds me back.

I pull my hand from his. "Ballast would never betray me. He hates Kallias too much for that." That's what I thought before tonight, anyway, but I'm not about to admit my uncertainty to Vil and Saga.

A muscle twitches in Vil's face, and I wish Saga hadn't told him everything about what happened in the tunnels. With Ballast. With me.

"While we're here in Tenebris," says Vil, low and tight, "you have agreed to be under my command. Find out everything you can about Ballast. That's an order."

I stare at Vil, hurt pulsing through me. Ever since we left Staltoria City, I've seen a different side of him, one I don't at all like. He claims he wants to protect me, and yet he pushed me to come on this mission to Daeros. He ordered Indridi's execution and was ready to see it through. He's been petty toward Ballast and concealed his knowledge about the weapon in the mountain. The man I thought Vil was is unraveling before my eyes, and I'm beginning to wonder if that man even exists, or if I just wanted him to.

"As you command, then," I say brusquely.

"Brynja—"

But I stalk back to my and Saga's room without another word, fighting to conceal my hurt. Saga follows on my heels, her anger pulsing off her like Indridi's fire.

She doesn't speak to me until the lights are out and we're in bed, blankets pulled up to our chins, heat curling into the room. "You *know* you can't trust Ballast."

I screw my eyes shut tight; I feel every pulse of my heart, and I remember the taste of his magic.

"What happened in the caves, what you thought he was to you there—it was nothing. It meant *nothing*. He's a *murderer*, Brynja, and the son of one. Please tell me you know that."

I dig my nails into my palms, press hard enough to make tears prick. "Have you ever killed anyone, Saga?" It's not what I want to ask her, but I sense she's in no mood to be telling me her secrets.

She's quiet for a long while. I wonder if she's angry at me for not answering her question, or for asking her that one.

"Yes," she says at last. "I fought in the skirmish. I fought *well*. But the Daerosians overwhelmed us. And then Njala was killed in my place, and Hilf was captured, and I—I—"

She doesn't have to finish. "I know," I say.

I let her decide what I mean by that.

Saga sleeps, and I slip out of bed. I don't scramble up into the vent, despite the nearly overwhelming urge to go and find Ballast. I don't trust myself, and as much as I hate to admit it, I'm not sure I trust Ballast, either. Instead, I wrap an extra blanket around my shoulders and curl up on the windowsill, staring out into darkness lit by cold, wheeling stars until another sunless morning comes.

TWO YEARS AGO

YEAR 4198, Month of the Black God
The Iljaria Tunnels

Ballast leads the way, torch in his left hand and sword in his right. Saga hobbles along after him, by degrees silent and cursing, and I bring up the rear, casting frequent, fearful glances behind us. The passageway reeks of the shadow monsters, tangled with a faint musk of bear.

No one speaks as we go; the silence is unbearable. I am on constant alert for the sound of wings and claws and tense at every slight noise, imagined or otherwise. Every time I glance at Ballast, the torchlight tracing him in shifting shadows, my heart seizes. I never thought I would see him again. Yet he's here, a savior unlooked for, lighting our way through the dark.

He's grown taller and broader since he left Tenebris. I wonder what he's found to eat down here that sticks to his bones more than the rich food at his father's table. Or maybe it's simply that he eats now, when he didn't before.

We come to a tunnel that's wider than most, painted with murals in the Iljaria's trademark vivid colors. I study the murals as we pass.

There's the Violet God, tall and thin, his skin dark, his white hair cropped short around his ears. He wears purple robes and holds an orb of light in his hands. I tell myself his story: Once, the Violet God could manipulate time, change it according to his whims. But the other gods grew angry at the disorder of things. They killed the woman he loved to punish him, and hid her soul where the Violet God could not find her. So he withdrew from the world, secluding himself on a high mountain, lonely and sorrowing until eternity's end. And so time marches on as it was meant to.

I've always been drawn to the Violet God. His story is sad and hopeless and unfair. I can relate.

The Gray and Green Goddesses are here, too, shown standing together as sisters, one life and one death. The Black God is wreathed in shadow and the Red God in fire. The White Goddess stands in a garden, her mouth open in song while the Blue Goddess kneels near her, one arm around a lion. The Yellow God holds the sun high in his hands, illuminating the world. The Brown Goddess has her arms plunged deep into the earth. The Bronze God, god of minds, sits mutilated and alone, and above them all the Prism Goddess floats in the air, her hands outstretched, wielding the powers of all the other gods. I have to hunt to find the Ghost God, lurking in the Black God's darkness, apart from the others, but always watching.

I wonder how long ago the Iljaria painted these murals, how long their beauty has been forgotten. And then I see that the paintings are marred with streaks of dark blood, and I look down and there are bones on the floor.

"Brynja!" Ballast cries, and I jerk aside in time to avoid the hurtling dark shadow of a cave demon.

He takes its head off with his sword, and I throw my knife into the heart of another, while Saga shrieks and brains a third with her walking stick.

We all stand panting, after that, bracing ourselves for another attack, but though the shadows hiss and writhe, it seems they have granted us a respite. I retrieve my knife, wipe the blood off on my filthy trousers once again. I'm sweaty and shaking. I don't know how many more of these creatures I can face.

I'm relieved when Ballast brings us into another small cave off the main passage. He builds a fire with a mysteriously convenient bundle of wood and shrugs out of his pack. Saga looks ready to pass out from exhaustion, and her skin is worryingly gray again.

We eat more smoked fish, and Ballast settles in the opening of the cave, face to the passageway, sword on his knees.

I sit close to Saga, wanting to comfort her but not knowing how.

"The gods are testing me," she says quietly, for my ears alone. "They ask me to trust my enemy, down here in the dark."

"Is that why you didn't kill him?" I ask her, equally as low. My stomach churns. I would have stopped her, if it came to it.

"He deserves to die."

The lion leaping at Hilf's throat, his strangled cry, the blood on the marble.

And yet.

"He saved us," I say.

"That doesn't make him guiltless."

"None of us are guiltless."

Her face creases. She makes no reply. She sleeps after that, breaths even and slow, and then it's just Ballast and me. Dread and guilt and relief and longing knot up my insides.

I pace over to him, settling with my back against the stone near the cave entrance. Ballast gives me a single swift glance before looking out into the passageway again, fingers tracing the hilt of his sword.

"Who guards you when you sleep? Or don't you need to?" It's not at all the question I want to ask and comes out sharper than I intended.

Ballast shrugs. "Asvaldr, when I ask him to. But sometimes his family needs him."

"And then?"

"Then I sleep lightly, with a sword in my hand."

I ponder this, picking at a stray thread on my shirt. "How are you here, Ballast?"

His jaw tenses. "I stumbled into the tunnels by accident, through a forgotten door in the palace cellar. I was . . . lost, when I left Tenebris. I was . . . feral. Raging. Despairing. And then I tried to control the cave demons, and my magic turned on me.

"Asvaldr is the one who found me, saved me, brought me back into my right mind. He asked me to help his cub, who'd gotten himself trapped in a rockslide and sliced his gut open. So I did. I lived with them for a while, Asvaldr and his family. He showed me underground streams where I could fish, showed me the passages in and out of the mountain, taught me how to fight the monsters."

"You've been down here this whole time? It's been nearly a year, since—"

"I know how long it's been," he snaps.

I bite my lip to keep from snarling at him. "What about the wood and the blankets and the rest of your supplies? Where did it all come from?"

"The wood was down here already. I spent weeks collecting it, leaving it at various points in the labyrinth so I'd always have it on hand. Some of the caves are filled with things the Iljaria left behind. I've found kettles and dishes, books that go to dust when you touch them, dried-up paint and ancient jars of food long since turned to mush. The Iljaria built a whole civilization here, before the monsters came."

"I know that," I tell him pointedly. "I read it in your book when we were children. Before you decided we were no longer friends."

He recoils like I slapped him, and I grind my jaw.

"Surely the Iljaria were powerful enough to destroy the cave demons," I say, when he offers nothing further.

"Perhaps. But the Iljaria do not like to kill, and they were the Black Lord's children, after all."

I glance out into the passageway, where winged shadows scrape against the rock. I try not to shudder.

"Are you going to hide down here forever?" I ask him quietly.

His shoulders go taut. "Where else am I supposed to go? To the Iljaria? They turn up their noses at half bloods like me. Skaanda, then? They would cut me into a thousand pieces and scatter me about the plains. What about my father? Do you think I should go back to him? Do you know what he *did* to me, Brynja?"

I jerk upright, filled with a wild, vicious anger. "I don't know, *Your Highness.*"

He flinches.

"Has he starved you?" I demand. "Whipped you? Kept you dangling in a cage over his head and made you risk your life every damn time he snaps his fingers? Don't think that just because he ordered you to make your pets do tricks for him, you're the same as me. As Saga. As all the rest of us. You had a *choice*, every time, and you always chose to mind him. Even when it meant murdering an innocent man. He was Saga's bodyguard. They loved each other. And now he's *dead* because of *you*."

He hunches in on himself in the entrance to the cave. I'm shaking with rage, spots dancing in front of my eyes. But the next moment I'm sliding down to the stone floor again, crying so violently I can't breathe. I sag against the rock, wrapping my head in my arms, sobs choking me.

A hesitant touch on my shoulder breaks me from my hysteria enough that I stop crying, manage to catch my breath again. I look at him through bleary eyes.

"There is nothing I can do," he says quietly, "to atone for the things I did then, and the things I didn't. To atone for my father's cruelty. But this is me, now, making the other choice. I won't be his any longer. I will not bow to him, I will not obey him. I've been lost here, slaying monsters in the dark instead of facing my own. But I was going back, Brynja. To save my mother. To save . . . everyone else. To stop him. That's why I was near enough to help when you and Saga stumbled in."

He watches me, face tight with grief and regret. He knows exactly what his father did to me—to all of us. Because he was there, enduring it, too. "I'm sorry," he says. "I know it doesn't mean anything. But I'm so sorry." His voice breaks.

"Why did you send me away?" The air catches hard in my chest. "Was it your father?"

"My mother was there that night, outside my door. She—" He swallows. "She was afraid of what he would do if he found us out. To you. To me. And he very nearly did. She had come to warn me that he was on his way. It could just as easily have been him who heard us that night."

The tears are pressing hard again. "You could have told me that."

He shakes his head. "The fear of discovery would have lessened, bit by bit. You would have come to see me again eventually. I couldn't risk it. But I caused you pain, Brynja. And I'm sorry. You can't know how much."

I gnaw on my lip, not quite able to meet his eyes. "It meant everything to me. My visits to your room. Our friendship."

"It meant everything to me, too," he says softly.

The knot in my heart loosens, but there is only anguish in Ballast's face.

"Go and sleep some," I tell him. "I will guard the door."

He considers this, eyes heavy with exhaustion. "All right. Just for a little while. Promise you will wake me if the demons come." His eyes snag on mine, and I forget, for a moment, how to breathe. Then he lays his sword in my lap, and I turn to watch the passageway in his stead.

There are too many noises out there in the dark, too much empty space writhing with monsters. I think of the Iljaria, centuries ago, carving tunnels through the mountains, making them beautiful, never fearing the dark, because they carried light with them, always: the light of magic, power, strength. At least until the shadows came. And I think of Ballast as a boy, doing his very best to protect me from the monster who tormented us both.

CHAPTER TWELVE

YEAR 4200, Month of the Black God
Daeros—Tenebris

The food shipment from Skaanda arrives before breakfast, three mounded wagons brimming with rice and corn and flour, barrels of beans and stalks of sugarcane, jars of honey and chests of tea.

A group of us comes out to watch the wagons trundling through the great front gates, and I goggle at how much there is—Vil is truly serious about selling this treaty to Kallias and his nobles, and I admire him for it. For his part, Kallias eyes the shipment with his arms crossed and a hard line between his brows.

His governors seem to be rather more impressed. Lord Seleukos, who governs Garran City, steps up to Vil and requests a private meeting, as do Lady Eudocia, governor of the Bone City, and Lord Phaedrus, who oversees Kallias's fields and greenhouses and is in charge of food distribution throughout Daeros. Vil agrees cordially to each meeting, and I see the tension in his shoulders slowly ease away. This is what he wanted—everything is going according to plan.

Not to be outdone by this Skaandan show of wealth, Kallias announces that in lieu of negotiations today, Vil and I are to be shown what Daeros has to offer Skaanda, in the event the treaty is eventually signed. We are to tour the mines, the barracks, and the greenhouse, and then attend the Lantern Festival in Garran City.

We return to our rooms for breakfast, and then Saga gets me ready for the day, though she won't quite look me in the eye. Ballast's presence in Tenebris is a thorn between us, and I don't know how to work it free.

I wear a red gown lined with rabbit fur and a long wool coat that buttons up to my chin and brushes against the tops of my boots. The coat has a hood in case it snows, but that doesn't keep Saga from threading silk flowers into my curls. Foolish, I think, flowers in winter. But I'm not about to deny Saga anything.

Vil meets me in the hall, wearing a similarly long coat, with a bearskin hat embedded with jewels. I am distantly aware of how handsome he looks, but the thought won't stick in my brain because I'm too busy wondering if Ballast will join our party today. *Ballast.* My head spins, and I fight to calm my jangling nerves.

He's a problem, says Vil in my mind, tangling with Saga's voice: *What happened in the caves, what you thought he was to you there—it was nothing. It meant* nothing.

Gulla's words are there, too, the memory of her fingers spelling them out in the great hall: *He has become too much like his father, desiring only power.*

But I think of colorful cards laid out on his bed and his childhood gifts of food and quiet company. I think of his back to mine, battling monsters in the dark, of his fingers tangled in my newly grown hair and his magic sparking inside me, hot enough to burn. I think of his conviction and his longing and his grief. And I can't believe that he is like his father. I refuse to believe it.

We meet the others at the stables, which are built adjoining the mountain. Like Vil and I, everyone is dressed warmly against the bitter wind: Kallias, Aelia, Zopyros, Theron, Alcaeus. Lysandra has managed to garner herself an invitation to this outing, too, her pale face nearly blue with cold under her hood. Also in attendance are Lords Seleukos, Phaedrus, and Damianus, who oversees the mines, as well as Lady Eudocia. Leifur is here to accompany me and Vil, and there is also an Aeronan guard and a handful of Daerosian soldiers.

But Ballast *isn't* here and I feel his absence keenly, like a blade to the heart.

"Astridur?" says Vil, far too many ears around for him to use my real name. "You all right?"

With an effort, I yank my gaze away from the door that leads into Tenebris and fix Vil with the brightest smile I can manage. "I'm fine, Vil. Just a little cold."

He grimaces but doesn't press me further.

I sneak another glance at the door. It remains firmly shut.

Attendants make short work of saddling the horses, and I swing up onto mine, trying not to notice Kallias watching me with glittering eyes.

The soldiers at the head of our company hold torches to light our way through the winter darkness, and they've just started moving out when an attendant leads one last horse out of the stable.

My breath catches as the door to the mountain creaks open and Ballast appears, wearing a green and silver coat he hasn't buttoned. His head is bare, his white-and-black hair dappled in the torchlight. The patch over his eye is tied with a green ribbon.

I'm staring again and I duck my head, struggling to think past my racing heart. Beside me, Vil swears under his breath.

"Bastard can't be bothered to come on time," says Zopyros in an overloud voice.

But then Ballast is mounting his horse and we're all riding two abreast on the road toward the mines, the first stop on our tour.

I struggle to stay present, to keep myself from peering over my shoulder at Ballast, somewhere behind.

Vil rides next to me, his bad mood coiling off him like so much smoke. "Why do you care about him so much?" he asks me shortly.

"I don't," I say, but that's a lie and we both know it. I gnaw on my lip and try to give him a real answer. "We were friends, when we were children. And he saved me. He saved both of us, down in the tunnels. We would be dead a hundred times over, if not for him."

Vil mutters another curse, and it rankles me.

"I didn't think I'd ever see him again," I say quietly.

"Is that supposed to make it better?" Vil demands.

I glance over at him in confusion. "Supposed to make *what* better?"

He clenches his jaw. "You didn't think you'd ever see him again. So you settled for me. But now that he's here, you have no more use for me, do you?"

"*Use* for you?" I nearly shout.

Lysandra looks back from her place ahead of us and frowns at my raised voice.

I take long, slow breaths, trying to calm the confused rage pounding behind my temples.

"That isn't it at all, Vil," I say then. I can't quite look at him, so I study his hands, knuckles tight about his reins. "I swear."

He huffs in disbelief. "Then what is it?"

My heart pulses overloud in my ears, and I fight the urge to glance behind me and find Ballast among the erratic torchlight, desperately wanting to assure myself he's really there.

"I was shocked to see him. It doesn't mean anything beyond that."

"Then you don't have feelings for him?"

I'm startled into looking at Vil, the torchlight gleaming on his dark skin.

"Do you have feelings for him?"

Anger stirs behind my breastbone at Vil's arrogant assumption he has the right to ask me such a question. "We have a mission to complete," I tell him tightly. "I don't have time for feelings."

I've hurt him, now, but no part of me wishes to rescind my words, to soothe his ego and assure him that any feelings I do have are for him. Because that isn't true. I thought I had found family in Vil, safety and security. It was a nice dream. But that's all it was. A dream.

We don't speak for the remainder of the half hour it takes to reach the mines, which lie north and a little west of Tenebris. I don't know what I was expecting, but the vastness of them staggers me, acres upon acres of digging sites, with tunnels spaced out at regular intervals. Men and women swarm like ants, coming in and out of the mine shafts, hauling carts heaped with ore. Hundreds of torches illuminate the dark; the smoke stings my eyes and makes me cough into my sleeve.

Lord Damianus, the overseer, leads us down into one of the shafts, where a massive main chamber branches out into a dozen winding tunnels. Metal cart tracks lead into each tunnel, and the mine is lit with more of those lamps that seem to have no fuel source.

A worker comes out of one of the tunnels, pushing a cart along the tracks, and he comes to a startled halt at the sight of us. He looks young, no older than me, but his eyes are haunted.

"Carry on," snaps Lord Damianus, and the young man bows and trundles his cart past us.

The overseer then launches into a detailed explanation of the types of ore mined in these fields and the amounts garnered each year. Despite the careful distance Vil has put between us since we arrived, I can tell he's impressed, and that Daeros is even richer than he thought. I wonder if he's already calculating exactly what to do with it all, once he sits crowned in Tenebris. He is more than capable of making Daeros flourish, but for the first time I wonder if Saga's accusation is true, if what he really wants is the power he was denied upon her return, and the plot to annex Daeros is his way of getting it.

Our group, for the most part, keeps silent. I can't help but look for Ballast; he stands a little apart from the rest of us, tense and wary, like he's ready to bolt for the exit if he needs to. I try to catch his eye, but he doesn't seem to notice.

"You should set Ballast to work here, Father," says Theron when Lord Damianus pauses for breath. "He could compel the rats and worms to dig, and you'd have no need for other men."

Alcaeus and Zopyros laugh at this, while Lysandra stands fidgeting with her sleeve, like she fears the joke might soon be turned on her. I want to tear all their stupid heads off.

Ballast grows very still, but he makes no answer.

Kallias gives him a feline smile. "Would you set bird and beast to work for me, boy?"

"If you asked me, Father."

My stomach twists. I want to scream at him for standing there, for bending his neck to his father's blade when he's so much stronger than that, so much better than that.

Kallias turns to his other sons. "If you are so eager to change the way things are done here, Theron, I can find you a mine cart."

Theron stammers an apology, his face going even paler than usual.

From the mines we ride to the army encampment, skirting around the northern edge of Garran City. Like the mines, the encampment is much larger than I expected, the barracks and mess hall and training grounds bordered by a high stone wall. General Eirenaios leads the tour here, with Zopyros, Kallias's eldest, attempting to help.

We tramp through the encampment and I take everything in, mentally calculating Skaanda's chances against a far greater force than we had planned on, with more yet to come. According to Eirenaios, deployed soldiers are being called back to Tenebris on the strength of the truce with Skaanda. Vil and I exchange glances, this news enough to halt our feud; he gives me a little nod—we'll discuss the army and figure all this out with Saga later.

We have lunch in the mess hall, and I find Ballast sitting directly across from me at the long table we all share. He studiously avoids my gaze, and his face is pinched and drawn, like he's in pain. I try not to stare at his eye patch and feel utterly sick. I don't eat much.

Our last stop before Garran City is the greenhouses, which lie southeast of the palace. There are two dozen of them, massive structures made of metal and glass.

Lord Phaedrus, who oversees the greenhouses, leads us into one of them, and we're immediately folded in warm, bright light. Crops march the length of the building in neat rows, green and flourishing, and the air smells of rich earth and spring dew.

My eyes turn up, to the dazzling lamps that illuminate the greenhouse, no wick or oil in sight. Vil studies them, too, his eyes wide with awe. I feel myself softening toward him again, the anger from earlier fizzled out.

Lord Phaedrus begins to explain the crop-planting schedule and the average yield of the harvest, but Kallias waves one hand and Lord Phaedrus bows and closes his mouth.

"The lamps are of my own design," says Kallias, and I find him suddenly very close to me. "Do you like them, Princess Astridur?"

He looks down at me with a smug sort of triumph, and the oil in his beard glitters in the light.

I curl my hands into fists behind the fur cuffs of my sleeves and try to look as if I am in awe of him. "Are you an inventor, Your Majesty?"

He grins. "I am."

"How do the lamps work?"

"Electricity," he says, and laughs at my blank look. "I will share the secrets with Skaanda's engineers, as I have shared them with Aerona." He nods toward Aelia, who is standing near with her arms crossed.

"You have not shared *everything* with Aerona, or might I remind you that, in my homeland, your inventions and machines can only be assembled by the Daerosians you send along with the materials, because you have not fully handed us your knowledge, despite your pledge."

Kallias shrugs off her words with a laugh, and to my horror he grabs my hand and tugs me down one of the rows of plants. Strawberries grow in a tangle of green, and he crouches to pick a handful, then offers them to me.

My heart rages inside my chest—where in the gods' names is Vil?—but I can do nothing except eat them. They are delicious, the sweetest strawberries I have ever tasted, and yet I want to spit them out like so much poison.

"Father?"

I turn to find Ballast there, the red lines that show from under his patch stark and angry in the bright lights. He doesn't look at me, but

I feel his intent all the same. I fight to stay calm, to keep myself from grabbing his hand and running with him far away from this place.

"What do you want, boy?" Kallias snaps.

There is fear in every line of him, but he simply inclines his head and says, "Lord Seleukos is eager to have our guests enjoy the festival."

Kallias's lips thin and Ballast tenses, like he's bracing for a slap. But Kallias simply brushes the strawberry tops out of my palm and, coiling his hand around my wrist, tugs me back to the rest of our party. Ballast comes after us, but I don't dare glance at him.

Vil is deep in conversation with Lord Phaedrus about the lamps and crop rotation and designs for building even larger and more efficient greenhouses. My stomach knots. Vil *swore* to me he'd protect me from Kallias, and he didn't even notice when the king pulled me away.

Ballast was the one who came to my rescue.

We ride down to Garran City after that, torches bobbing, horses' hooves crunching through snow. The city greets us with lanterns on high gates and lights in every window, with the smell of candied nuts and roasting meat. The lingering taste of strawberries turns sour on my tongue.

We dismount just past the city gates, attendants taking our horses. Vil comes up beside me and slips his arm through mine. "Notice how Kallias *showed* us all of that in answer to our gift of food," he says in a low voice, "and yet he *offered* us nothing."

I nod; Kallias's arrogance has not escaped me.

"But there's so much *potential*." Vil's eyes spark, his enthusiasm palpable. "Think of it—"

"Not here, Vil," I remind him.

He squeezes my arm. "You're right." His glance flits nervously away before fixing on me again. "I'm sorry about before."

I shake my head and try to smile. "It's fine, Vil. Everything is fine."

He opens his mouth to say something more, but just then Kallias calls for the whole group of us to follow him in a fur-swathed parade into the main city square, crowded with merchant stalls.

A white marble fountain occupies the middle of the square, water frozen in shining arcs. Pierced tin lanterns hang on poles around the fountain, illuminating the dark with fractured pricks of multicolored light. They are far more beautiful, I think, than Kallias's harsh electricity.

But the arcs of frozen water make my heart thud against my breastbone: Iljaria magic, the power of the Gray Goddess, who rules death and winter. Garran City used to belong to the Iljaria, just as Tenebris did.

Musicians play near the fountain: an old woman beating a pounding rhythm on a pair of hand drums, a boy wielding an assortment of haunting pitched bells, and a pale-haired girl on a lightning-quick violin. The girl and boy can't be more than ten, young enough that I inwardly beg them not to play so well, for fear Kallias will take them for his Collection. But today, it seems, he has other things on his mind.

He turns to me with his satisfied-cat smile, smoothly sliding his hand under my elbow. I can feel the heat of him even through my wool sleeve. "Let me show you the delights of Garran City," he says low into my ear. "I think you will like it even more than the strawberries."

I set my jaw, tell myself not to shake, not to pull away, not to vomit all over his silver-embroidered furs. But by the mutilated Bronze God, I don't know how much longer I can keep up this charade.

"Forgive me, Your Majesty," says Vil, suddenly beside me again, "but Princess Astridur promised to accompany me this afternoon. Would you allow me to steal her from you?"

Kallias raises his brow at Vil, who is perhaps being too protective of his "cousin." But mercifully Kallias doesn't comment on it, just gives a careless shrug and draws his hand back again. "Take my son with you, then. He hasn't been enough in company of late, and I fear his manners could do with some polishing." He snaps his fingers at Ballast, who obeys his father's summons like a dog. It rankles me.

"Father?" he says, taut as a bowstring.

"Show our Skaandan friends the city. Spare no expense. And be sure to have them in the arena by the thirteenth hour, or I'll take your other eye."

And then Kallias sweeps past us, hailing Aelia, with Zopyros, Theron, Alcaeus, and Lysandra following him like pathetic furry chickens, while the governors go off in a group of their own.

The tension doesn't leave Ballast's frame as his eye sweeps from me to Vil and then back again. I brace myself for Vil to make some cutting remark. He doesn't, just takes my hand, resolutely threading our fingers together.

I pull my hand free, more than irritated that Vil feels some masculine need to stake a claim to me in front of Ballast.

Vil squares his jaw but doesn't reach for me again.

"Let's go," says Ballast brusquely, and stalks off into the square.

We follow, Vil radiating irritation beside me.

We thread our way through a host of merchant stalls selling food and jewelry and trinkets, books, maps, finely spun linen. There's a booth displaying small wooden chests, intricately carved, another offering blown glass, and yet another gears and cogs and bits of metal, for crafting clockwork. It makes me think of my sister, and my heart wrenches.

A change comes over Ballast as we go, and it startles me. He stops to speak with every one of the vendors and seems to know most of them. He asks the middle-aged Daerosian woman selling the carved wooden chests if her daughter has recovered from her bout with Gray Fever. He chats with a grizzled old fisherman about the season's catch and asks his advice on the best-quality fish to purchase and have sent up to Tenebris. He squeezes into a filthy alleyway to retrieve a child's dropped coin, and as he's giving it back to her, a young woman about my age slips up to him and tugs on his sleeve.

"Lord Prince, can you come?" she asks him. She's really pretty, which annoys me.

Ballast glances at me and Vil and then back at the woman. "Of course."

Vil is getting annoyed at all Ballast's detours, but we follow him and the woman to a booth at the edge of the fair, where leather goods are displayed on a green table, from belts to boots to satchels.

A boy sits on the ground by the table, cradling a bundle of fur in his arms that I think is a hound pup, or was. It's mangled and bleeding.

Ballast kneels beside the boy, who wordlessly hands him the pup. The creature, to my shock, still seems to be breathing. Ballast shuts his eyes, and his magic coils out of him, blue and silver, healing as honey. I can still taste the memory of it on my tongue, and I shiver where I stand.

Vil shifts beside me, uneasy in the presence of Ballast's magic but fascinated, I think, in spite of himself.

The hound pup's wounds knit together, and he begins to wiggle and yip in Ballast's arms. The boy gives a joyful shout. The young woman—his sister, I think—smiles. Her eyes well.

"Thank you, Lord Prince," she says as Ballast gives the pup back to the boy.

He stands and she bows to him, very low. He pulls her to her feet again. "I am happy he was not beyond my aid." And then Ballast smiles, too.

We head back into the maze of the fair, then, an ease to the set of Ballast's shoulders I'm not sure I have ever seen before.

I look at shoes and scarves, peruse a whole booth filled with the pierced tin lanterns that hang all around the square, and another selling small glass spheres with supposed drops of Iljaria magic trapped inside.

Ballast has grown tense and antsy again, and I'm not sure why beyond the lateness of the hour. "You have to buy something," he snaps in my general direction after I wander away from the sphere booth. "My father will be angry if you don't."

My eyes snag on the green ribbon holding his eye patch in place. I gnaw the inside of my lip. I want to shout at him. I want to pull him close.

"There was some jewelry a few stalls back that would suit you, I think," says Vil helpfully.

Gods, I don't want either one of them buying me jewelry, and certainly not on Kallias's coin. I try not to glare.

While the Dark Remains

Instead, I pick out a beautifully illuminated map of the peninsula, a blank book for writing, and a set of new pens and nibs. Then I go back for one of those glass spheres. I choose the one that claims to hold the magic of the Red God, in honor of Indridi. Clearly it's just a bit of red dye trapped in the glass, but the merchant swears that if I break it, the magic will be set free. I could start a fire, he says, even in the rain.

Vil's eyes go wet and I feel sick again, Indridi's scream echoing awfully in my ears. I let Ballast pay for the sphere, and then I slip it into the pocket of my coat, hard and cold. I wrap my hand around it, but the glass never seems to warm.

In the next booth down is an Iljaria storyteller, a young woman with light-brown skin, her white hair bound in two braids so long they touch the ground. She wears thin silk robes in blue and green, not needing heavy furs—her magic keeps her warm. Her eyes fix on mine, and she beckons us over, rings on every one of her fingers.

I step up to the booth, with Vil and Ballast flanking me, and she presses a mug of steaming chocolate into my hands. I don't know where she got it from—it wasn't there a moment ago. She produces mugs for Vil and Ballast, too, then draws back the curtain of her booth and waves us inside, the space lit with calm yellow light, though there is no source for it.

We sit on silk pillows, and I am, suddenly, intensely aware of Ballast, the shape and scent of him, his hair brushing against the shoulder of my coat.

"Listen to a tale of my ancestors," says the storyteller, "and I will tell you what it is you need to hear. The Yellow Lord was the youngest of all the First Ones, and so, too, was he the haughtiest. He did not like bounds to be set on his power; he did not like that the Black Lord still ruled for part of every day, no matter that the Yellow Lord had defeated him.

"The Yellow Lord's guardian was the Prism Lady, and she made for him a great dwelling place in the very heart of the sun. But he sneered at her gift, for he wanted to shine his light in the world, not bind his power to that of a mere star.

"But as time wore on, the Prism Lady pressed him to accept the house she had made for him, and warned him that if he did not choose to dwell in the light, he would instead be bound in darkness. The Yellow Lord did not heed her and scorned her authority over him. She had a piece of the power of all the First Ones, to be sure—but what, in the end, is more powerful than light?

"So the Yellow Lord left the palace of the Prism Lady and the dwelling she had made for him, and went to make his own way in the world. He brought his light to the winter, to the graves of the Gray Lady, gilding death in light. The Gray Lady was furious and drove him out.

"For a time, he dwelt with the Green Lady, for springtime and sun go hand in hand. But his light burned too hot for her tender plants, and she, too, sent him away.

"Where can light go? It clashes with time, which contains everything and is yet nothing. It clashes with fire, which is a light and heat of its own. It does not belong in the depths of the earth, where creatures sleep, where seeds put forth roots, where bones decay. And so the Violet Lord, the Red Lord, the Brown Lady—all denied the Yellow Lord. So, too, did the Blue Lady and the White Lady, because with animals and music, they had no time for light. The Yellow Lord did not visit the Ghost Lord, afraid to have his power nullified.

"So the Yellow Lord burned with resentment, with anger. He refused to return to the Prism Lady and the dwelling that awaited him in the sun's fiery heart. He determined to have all the First Ones notice him. To bow to him.

"And so he called down the stars from the sky. He razed the earth. He turned oceans to steam and mountains to ash.

"And the First Ones came on wind and wing. They came in death and fire, with singing and rage. And they bound the Yellow Lord in darkness, as the Prism Lady had warned him, so he could not destroy the whole of the world with his arrogant light."

"Is that your tale, storyteller?" says Ballast, his voice tight.

The Iljaria woman kneels before him, putting them on eye level. She reaches out one gentle finger and brushes it against his patch.

His jaw tightens, his single eye welling with tears. It guts me. I wonder if he sees himself as the Yellow Lord, inevitably bound anew in his father's court. I want to reassure him that if any of us is the Yellow Lord, it isn't him.

"That is my tale," says the storyteller softly, crouching back on her heels.

"What is the point of it?" Vil grinds out.

She flicks her glance to him. "The point is whatever you need it to be. To not abuse power, perhaps. To not refuse a gift freely given. That there are better ways to gain acceptance."

"That binding power is the only way to manage it?" says Ballast. "My father certainly believes that."

"He is still bound," I say quietly. "The Yellow Lord is still bound."

The storyteller's eyes fix on mine. She stares deep, parsing truth from lies. "Yes," she says. "He is still bound. But for how much longer, I wonder?"

I jerk from my seat, heart unaccountably pounding, and stalk from the booth without even waiting to see if Ballast pays her for the story.

We're quiet as we tour the rest of the square, as we sit at tables near the fountain, listening to the trio of musicians and eating strips of meat from wooden skewers.

"I suppose I should thank you," says Vil to Ballast, voice low and tight.

Ballast doesn't even look at him, his body angled away from us, face pointed toward the frozen fountain. "For what?"

"Saving my sister," says Vil quietly.

Ballast doesn't reply.

I blink and I'm with Ballast and Saga again, battling cave demons in the dark, taking turns watching the entrance so we could sleep, playing cards in the firelight, the flash of Ballast's teeth when he smiled at me.

Now he won't even glance in my direction.

We rejoin the rest of our party in a massive wooden hall in the midst of the city. There is a wide curtained stage at the back of the hall, with carved chairs filling the rest of the space. Kallias claims the seat next to mine and lays his hand once more on my knee while he orders Ballast to buy refreshments from the porter at the door. Ballast obeys with a solemn word and a stiff bow, and yellow-robed attendants come to serve us spiced wine and lacy ginger cookies.

The lights dim and the curtains are drawn back, revealing an elaborately painted backdrop of high mountains and flashing stars.

Ballast sits on the other side of me, and I'm vaguely aware of Vil behind me, saying something in a quiet voice to Aelia. I will Ballast to look at me, but he doesn't, shoulders stiff, gaze trained straight ahead of him. He's close enough for me to touch, and yet he's far out of my reach.

Performers enter the stage, and musicians strike up an eerie tune from their hidden alcove. I am startled to find the tale from the storyteller in the square playing out now before our eyes: the Yellow God, forsaking his home with the Prism Goddess, and growing angry as he fails to find a place with any of the other gods.

There must be an Iljaria somewhere, creating the illusions that enhance the pantomime. Perhaps even that same storyteller. Magic twists and sparks and burns, making it really seem as if the Yellow God pulls stars down from the sky.

For the entire performance, Kallias keeps his hand on my knee, possessive, smug. I grow sicker and sicker with every moment that passes. I am so afraid that I haven't fooled him. That I haven't fooled anyone. That I am no better than the Yellow God, plucking stars from heaven. That I will pay dearly for my arrogance.

TWO YEARS AGO

YEAR 4198, Month of the Gray Goddess
The Iljaria Tunnels

Saga's foot won't seem to fully heal. She insists on traveling more and more each day—or what passes for a day down here—and it's getting worse instead of better. But she won't hear of resting. She won't hear of Ballast using his magic on her again, either.

We've been traveling the tunnels for days now—I'm not sure how many. I've grown used to Saga and Ballast's presence. I know their shapes, their silences, their footsteps. The world has narrowed to just the three of us, the only souls left in all this unending darkness, save the monsters that continue to haunt our paths—and I'm not sure they count.

Ballast and I haven't spoken much since that first day. It feels impossible when Saga is here, her hatred radiating off her in nearly visible waves. But he looks at me, often, and there is a warmth growing between us that pricks at my heart. We are friends again, I think. Or something like it.

There comes a day when Saga collapses, cursing, to the stone floor of the tunnel we're passing through. Ballast lowers his torch to examine her foot and finds it's infected again. Saga sweats and swears. Ballast glances at me, uneasy.

One of the cave demons dives down from the shadows, and Ballast tosses me his sword—I slay the thing, and it drops reeking and foul right beside Saga. Ballast kicks it away as hard as he can.

"You have to let me try and heal you again, Your Highness," he says to Saga, all politeness and regret.

She shakes her head, though her jaw is tight and her eyes shift uneasily.

"Then we'll find a place to rest for the day."

"No."

Ballast sighs. "Then I will carry you while Brynja guards us."

"NO, GRAY GODDESS DAMN YOU!" Saga screeches at him.

All three of us freeze, staring at each other, and there's a rustle of many wings over our heads.

"Fine," Saga grinds out. "Heal me."

Ballast watches her. "I will have to touch you, Your Highness."

She huffs out an angry breath, but I don't miss the tears gleaming in her eyes. "I said *heal me.*"

He nods and puts one hand on her ankle, then shuts his eyes and starts his singsong magic. I feel it, warm and thick as honey, coiling through the air.

Saga weeps silently as he heals her, her head turned away, her tears dripping down to dampen the stone.

Then Ballast lets go, crouches back on his heels.

She scrambles upright and puts weight on the injured foot. It holds her, and there is no trace of pain in her eyes.

"Better?" says Ballast quietly.

She nods. She doesn't thank him.

A flurry of cave demons dive at us, shrieking, and we meet them head-on, Ballast with his sword and me with my knife and Saga with her stick. We dispatch them in short order and leave them to rot in a stinking pile.

We go quickly after that, Saga abandoning her walking stick for another sword she finds in the tunnels. She weighs it approvingly in her palm. "Skaanda would have helped drive the monsters from this place," she says. "The Iljaria were too busy killing us to even ask."

"Do you think it's true, Your Highness?" says Ballast from the front. "The accounts of genocide?"

"History doesn't lie," Saga snaps. "Unless to make the truth more palatable, and there's nothing pleasant about children being slaughtered because they were born powerless."

Ballast has no answer for that.

We walk some hours more before we pass under a massive stone archway that shivers with magic, infused there long ago by some ancient hand. There are words cut into the stone, painted brightly, and they speak of music and protection and peace.

"The demons do not come here," says Ballast. "These halls were hallowed by the Brown Lady herself. The oldest stories say the Iljaria were not the labyrinth's first occupants, or even its makers, but that the First Ones formed it in the beginning."

I read that in Ballast's book as well. His eyes flick to mine, like he's remembering, too.

Prayers of awe and thanksgiving trip from Saga's lips, and her words follow us to our next resting spot, a little room cut into the stone, with a blackened fire ring, waiting wood, and a kettle.

We feast on more fish and heat the kettle for tea, which Ballast has squirreled away in his pack. The atmosphere between the three of us borders on courteous, though Saga still does her level best to not speak to Ballast, or even look at him.

She's weary from the long walk on her newly healed foot, and falls asleep by the fire shortly after we eat.

But I'm restless. Awake. And it seems Ballast is, too.

"Do you want to explore a little?" he asks me.

I glance at Saga, sleeping soundly.

"We'll be back long before she wakes," he promises. "We won't go far."

My stomach wobbles. I want very much to go exploring with him. I nod. "All right."

So he picks up the torch, and I follow him farther into the tunnel, which is wide enough for the two of us to walk side by side. I have to nearly trot to keep up with him, and realize how slowly he's been going, for Saga's sake, even with her healed foot. The torch casts slanting shadows on the stone, and the chill of the tunnel curls around me.

"The torch is magic, isn't it," I realize. "It never goes out."

He gives a huff of a laugh. "Indeed. This way." He grabs my arm and tugs me into a tunnel on the left.

My pulse jumps, fear slicing unexpectedly through me. I jerk away from him, and he releases me immediately.

His eyes find mine in the torchlight, anguish written all over his face. "I'm sorry. I won't touch you again."

For a moment we just stand there, staring at each other. He never touched me when we were children, always keeping that careful space between us. I understand why, now. He is perpetually, excruciatingly aware that he is the son of my tormentor; he doesn't want me to be afraid of him, doesn't want me to equate him with his father. Yet Kallias hurt him, too.

I take a breath. "You only startled me," I say lightly.

He nods but doesn't say anything more, just turns and strides on into the narrowing tunnel, his shoulders tight.

I gnaw on my lip and follow him. Our footsteps echo, strangely loud, and there comes the distant sound of running water. I blink and see Hilf, his throat ripped out by the lion, blood on the floor. I see Ballast, stripped to the waist in the great hall, whipped by Nicanor in the sight of us all, to prove that Kallias would not spare even his own son, so imagine what he might do to us? I see Ballast and me sitting on opposite sides of his bed, the deck of cards spread out between us, cake crumbs on his sheets. I see Gulla, running into the great hall and begging Kallias to leave Ballast alone, to not hurt him again. I see Ballast looking up at me through the hole in his ceiling, hear his oath, born of anger and pain: *When I am older and stronger, I'm going to kill him.*

The sound of running water grows louder. Ballast glances back, his dark-and-light hair glimmering in the torchlight. "Nearly there."

He leads me down a few more passages before we step into a cavern that stretches far beyond my sight line. Water rushes black over smooth rocks; stalactites drip gleaming droplets into the underground river.

"Beautiful," I whisper, my voice lost in the echoing roar.

He shouts to be heard over the water: "It runs quieter down a ways!"

So we pace along the river, the spray leaping up to touch my face.

"Here," says Ballast, leading me down a winding path through the rocks, to where a pool has collected from the river's runoff. It's clear as air: In the light of the torch, I can see all the way to the bottom, crystals flashing blue and green among the silt. Best of all, when I dip my hand into the water, it's *warm.*

"There are hot springs near here," Ballast explains. He smiles at me and produces a bar of soap from some hidden pocket. "I thought you might like a bath. And don't worry. The cave demons never come here—this whole stretch of the labyrinth is protected by the Brown Lady."

I gape at him. I haven't had a bath—a real bath—in half a lifetime. Every few months in Kallias's mountain, Nicanor would drag us from our cages to be cleaned, which meant we stood in a small stone chamber, stripped naked with others of our sex, and were doused with freezing water and scrubbed with brushes so coarse they made us bleed.

But this—

This is a gift.

Violet God's eyeballs, I might cry.

"You go first," says Ballast, suddenly awkward. "I'll wander downstream a bit. Shout if you need me."

"Thanks," I say brusquely, to cover my own awkwardness.

He gives me the soap, then wedges the torch between two obliging rocks and walks away.

I pull off my clothes and the filthy scarf that's still wrapped around my head, then duck into the water. It feels like magic, warm, powerful, safe.

I wash, scrubbing what feels like a mountain's worth of dirt from my skin, not to mention the blood of the cave monsters caked on my hands. It's been nearly two months since I last shaved my head, and my hair's grown, fuzzy against my fingers, not quite long enough for my curls to have made a reappearance. I consider shaving it again, but I'm done with the Brynja who stayed locked in a cage for eight years, the Brynja so afraid that her hair would catch in chains and silks and cause her to fall. No. I'll let it grow. I'll just keep it wrapped up until it's a little longer.

That decided, I wash the scarf, too, spreading it out to dry on the stone as I float on my back in the water. For the first time in a long, long time, I feel peace.

"Brynja?" calls Ballast, a little while later.

"Not yet!" I call back, and scramble to get out of the pool. I dress hurriedly, winding the scarf around my head and knotting it at the nape of my neck. "All right!"

Ballast appears, and I wander downstream while he takes his turn, watching luminescent fish dart through dark water.

When he's finished, we head back to our camp.

"Thank you," I tell him. "I haven't had a bath since before—" I falter, and he glances back at me.

"Since before my father," he says. "I know."

I take a breath. "Really. Thank you."

He offers me a soft smile. "It is the very least that I could do."

He's wrong, though. Saga is awake when we get back.

She's sitting against the wall of the cave, her knees pulled up to her chin.

While the Dark Remains

"Where have you been?" Her voice shakes, and I realize with a jolt how afraid she was, waking up to find herself alone.

"I'm sorry, Saga," I tell her. "There's an underground river, a pool. I had a bath. I remember the way—I'll show you."

Her lips go tight but she nods, so I take her to the pool while Ballast stays behind. I wait with Saga as she slips into the warm water, turning my back to give her privacy. I try not to listen to her sobs.

When she climbs back out of the pool, dripping and shivering, she's calm again, but her sadness hangs on her like a shroud. She dresses quickly, and we start the walk back.

"He isn't kind," she says quietly. "He healed me. He saved us. But he isn't kind."

I blink and see Ballast carrying Saga through the tunnels, infinite in his gentleness. I see his smile in the torchlight as he hands me the soap, see the books and the games he shared with me when we were children. I hear his voice, broken as he is broken: *I know it doesn't mean anything. But I'm so sorry.*

"He killed Hilf." Her words waver. "He killed Hilf."

I gnaw on my cheek to keep the tears from coming. "I know, Saga."

"I will never forgive him," she whispers. "He deserves to die for what he's done."

My stomach twists. "It was Kallias," I remind her. "Kallias made him."

"But he didn't have to do it! He didn't have to do it and he *did* and Hilf is *gone* and—"

She breaks down crying again, and I kneel with her on the stone, numb, hollow.

It takes a few minutes for me to look up and realize that Ballast stands there in the tunnel, torch wavering in his hand. He won't meet my eyes.

We are all three of us forever changed by Kallias; I think that part of us will always feel like we're children wandering alone in the dark, even now we're free of him.

221

Saga glares at Ballast and pushes to her feet, hanging on to my arm to steady herself. "Could an army come through here?" she asks him, her voice rough and low.

"The Skaandan army, you mean," says Ballast. "To catch my father unaware in his mountain."

Saga clenches her jaw. "Yes."

"It would take a long time for many soldiers to travel these routes—the passages narrow so often. And there are the cave demons to contend with."

"But it is possible," says Saga. She snatches at his sleeve and drags him back to our camp, where she pulls a piece of charcoal out of the fire. She nudges it toward him with her foot. "Draw the route," she orders.

His face tenses, but he doesn't pick up the charcoal.

"Draw the route," she repeats. "The route my army will take through the labyrinth."

"I won't let Skaanda take my country."

"But you'll let your *father* rule it?" Saga demands.

He flinches. "I have no love for my father."

She laughs, bitter. "You are your father's prize hound. What will he do to you, I wonder, when you at last come slinking back to him?"

Ballast recoils as if she's slapped him. For a long moment they just stare at each other, Saga's chin trembling, tears of rage dripping down her face.

Then Ballast bows his head and picks up the charcoal and draws a map on the stone.

CHAPTER THIRTEEN

YEAR 4200, Month of the Black God
Daeros—Tenebris

It's late when we finally leave Garran City, nearly the nineteenth hour. We take a different route back to the gates to avoid the chaos of the merchants packing up their carts in the main square, and we pass a large stone building that Aelia, who walks near me, explains is the orphan house. My heart seizes. More than one of the children Kallias took for his Collection came from here.

The door to the orphan house creaks open, and a young woman slips out, the lantern she holds illuminating her smooth dark skin and cloud of black hair swept up onto the top of her head. For a moment I freeze, staring, and her eyes catch on mine. I barely stop myself from calling out her name before she ducks her head and hurries past.

I reach our room before Saga does, and I'm waiting for her with my arms crossed when she does eventually appear, the hem of her dirty cloak dragging across the floor.

She sets down her lantern and makes to move past me, but I snatch her arm and haul her over to the couch.

"Sit," I order, and she does, hunching guiltily.

"What in the *hell* were you doing in the orphan house in Garran City?" I demand.

Saga gnaws on her lip, anger sparking in her eyes. There's a dagger at her hip that I don't recognize, though I can tell the hilt is one she carved herself: It's a tree design, with the branches entwining.

"Do you really expect me to sit still all day, waiting for you?" Her voice is hollow, her shoulders tight. "This place is agony for me, Brynja. I know you understand that." She draws the dagger from its sheath, weighing it in her palms. "I refuse to waste my time here."

I stare at the dagger, at the old, dark stain on the blade.

"I carved this for him," says Saga softly. "For Hilf. He wore it into battle, and it was on him when they dragged us to Tenebris. I've been searching for something of his since we came here, slipping into storeroom after storeroom, digging through piles of junk and cast-off trinkets. But this—" Tears choke her, and she curses.

"A palace guard was wearing it, and I bribed him to give it to me. He was keeping it, he said, because he hoped one day to kill a Skaandan bastard with their own blade." She curses again and hurls the dagger across the room, where it rebounds off the stone wall and nearly hits me in the head.

I pick it up. I hand it back to her.

And then she's weeping uncontrollably, and I go to her, wrap my arms around her, hold her tight.

When she's calm again, I ask her about the orphan house, and she tells me she's been going there nearly every day, to occupy her hands and her heart. There is a great need for people to help there, and the children hunger for more than food.

"I would forget all this treaty and spying nonsense and come with you," I tell her quietly. "If I could."

She gives me a bitter smile. "I know."

※

We kneel on the edge of the Sea of Bones, Saga and I, snow cold and damp on our knees. Stars wheel overhead, and sorrow grips tight, tight.

Hilf has no proper grave to mourn at, so we have come here, to the glacier sea, where bodies are surrendered to the ice. His is down there, somewhere, bones upon bones but not, as so many others are, forgotten.

Saga sings for him, war songs and ballads, a tender love song and a mournful dirge. I pray with her, to the Gray Goddess to keep his soul well, to the Prism Goddess to reward him with riches beyond measure among the heroes of paradise. To the Bronze God, that when Saga goes herself into paradise, Hilf will remember her. I weep with Saga beside the glacier sea as the cold bites deep and snow begins to softly fall.

There comes a quiet step behind us, and I turn to see Ballast there, a lamp in his hand, his face drawn and stricken; he must know why Saga is here, weeping and singing and praying on the edge of the Sea of Bones.

She doesn't hear him, and for a moment his eye seeks mine. I shake my head at him. I spell to him the sign for *go* with my fingers. His jaw hardens at this reminder of his mother, locked in a cage in his father's hall. He turns. He goes.

We are very late to bed tonight, and Saga drifts off almost at once, but I am far too restless for sleep. There is an agony of confusion inside me, an uncertainty that gnaws down to bone.

I slip up into the vents in an attempt to quiet it, because like Saga, I am not content to be still.

※

Ballast's room is a lavish suite that adjoins Kallias's chambers, meant to house a queen. Kallias never crowned one, so he keeps Ballast here, a dancing bear in a pretty cage.

He isn't here now, though the evidence of him is: There's a box of silk ribbons on the dressing table in all different colors, and a smaller box beside it filled with what I recognize with a jolt as eye patches. There's a half-empty bookcase on one wall, the books scattered all about the room as if thrown in a rage. Medicinal vials crowd his nightstand, at least a dozen of them in various sizes.

I fight back a wave of nausea and go search for Ballast elsewhere.

I find him at last in the infirmary, lying on a narrow bed while the palace physician leans over him. I crouch in the ceiling, staring down through the cracks in the wood and trying very hard not to cry. Ballast's eye patch and silk ribbon wait for him on a nearby table.

"It is healing well," comes the physician's voice as he straightens up again, giving me a brief glimpse of Ballast's ruined face, his empty eye socket. I press my hand against my mouth. *Oh, Bal, what has he done to you?*

Ballast sits up, grabbing the patch and tying it on quickly, as if he can't bear to be without it.

"How is the pain?" asks the physician, turning to grab a vial of medicine from a shelf on the wall.

Ballast eases himself off the bed. He stands like a nervous child with his hands behind his back. "It is . . . mostly better."

"And the nightmares?"

Ballast clenches his hands into fists, tension radiating all down his spine. He doesn't answer.

The physician sighs, turning from the shelf and offering Ballast the medicine. "Take it, Your Highness. It will help."

Ballast nods, and his eye flicks suddenly to the ceiling. I freeze, holding my breath. Surely he can't see me?

But then he thanks the physician and leaves the infirmary.

He returns to his room, and I follow silently through the vents. I watch as he considers the vial from the physician and then puts it on his nightstand with the others, untasted. He unties his eye patch, takes off his boots, crawls into bed. He curls up on his side, blankets pulled up to his chin.

His weeping is quiet, but it makes his body shake.

I am wrecked by his anguish, sick to my core. With everything in me I want to go down to him, to crush him close against me, hold him until he stops crying, lend him what comfort I can. But, Bronze God, I don't know why he's here, I don't know how deeply enmeshed he is in Kallias's schemes. And I don't trust myself to keep my head around him. If Ballast asked me to, I think I would abandon all my plans, spill every secret, break every promise I've ever made.

I can't bear to watch him like this anymore. I whisper a prayer for him. And then I force myself to crawl away.

※

The digging never stops, not even during the night. The workers take it in shifts, the shafts illuminated by Kallias's electric lamps. There are no false ceilings down here, no safe hiding places, so it's taken me a while to creep into the maze, ducking around corners and melting into the shadows as best as I can.

The vein Basileious told Kallias about is impossible to miss, a jagged line of pulsing blue in the rock. It fascinates me.

I watch a pair of workers, a man and a woman, attempt to dig into the vein. The woman swings a pickaxe at the rock, and when her blade snaps in a burst of red sparks, the man takes his turn with a whirring, grating drill that sits on what looks like an altered mine cart. But he drills for only a few minutes before the bit breaks and he has to change it for a new one. The woman swings a fresh pickaxe until it breaks, and they go on and on like that, sweat on their brows, stone dust sticking to their skin. But for all that, they're making steady progress, and the vein seems to be growing thin.

Dread twists deep. It's too soon, far too soon. We've counted on the Skaandan army having the whole of Gods' Fall—all three winter months of Black, Gray, and Ghost—to make their way through the labyrinth of the Iljaria tunnels and take Daeros unawares. But if the weapon is found before then, if Kallias seizes it—as I have no doubt he means to—he will be far more powerful than any army, and all this will be for nothing.

I'm about to turn and slip back through the tunnel to report this to Vil and Saga when boots ring out on the stone. I flatten myself against the rock wall, praying that the god of darkness will conceal me.

Kallias sweeps right by my hiding place, flanked by Basileious and Ballast.

I press my nails against the stone, my heart slamming against my rib cage. Ballast looks impossibly weary, his face drawn, the ribbon on his eye patch tied in obvious haste. He stands tense beside his father as Basileious inspects the vein.

The engineer leans close to the pulsing stone but does not touch it with his bare hand. He turns back to Kallias, relief on his pale face. "We are close, Your Majesty. The progress is better than I hoped."

Kallias gives a clipped nod. "How long?"

"A few weeks," says Basileious. "No more."

"Good," the king says. He glances at Ballast, who tenses.

The two workers have paused with their axes and drill; they step to one side of the chamber, heads bowed.

Kallias dismisses them and shoves an axe into Ballast's hand. "Dig, boy," he says. "The blades last longer when an Iljaria holds them. Devils know why."

And then Kallias turns with a flip of his cloak and strides back down the tunnel, Basileious on his heels.

My chest tightens as Ballast hefts the axe in his hands, as he turns to the vein and swings. He misses, the axe glancing off the bare rock and nearly gouging his shoulder. He tightens his grip, swings again. And then he's hacking at the vein with reckless abandon, cursing as he works.

I want to go up to him. I want to ask him why Kallias is punishing him, and why in the gods' names he is doing everything his father tells him to. But it scares me too much, because what if I cannot bear his answer?

So I wind my way back up to the palace proper and go report to Vil.

He's up, though it's the twenty-fourth hour. Weariness drags on my bones—I need to sleep, but there isn't time, not now.

Vil pours me coffee, and I perch on the arm of the couch, sipping slowly. Saga is still in bed, and I don't have the heart to wake her, not after last night's vigil at the Sea of Bones. So it's just Vil and I, with Leifur at the door.

Vil swears quietly when I've finished my report. "You'll have to find a way to delay the digging. Can you do it, Brynja?"

"I can try."

"Any word on who Kallias means to name his heir?"

"Not that I've heard."

He frowns, dragging his finger around the rim of his own coffee mug. "And Ballast?"

My gut clenches. I didn't tell Vil about my visit to the infirmary, or of Ballast's presence in the digging shaft. "What about him?"

"What have you found out? How close is he in his father's confidences? Is he in the running for heir?"

"I don't know."

Vil scowls. "Damn it, Brynja! What have you been doing all night?"

I curse at him and set my mug down so hard coffee splashes over the rim.

His eyes lock hard on mine, and I think again of what Saga told him about what happened in the Iljaria tunnels. But at last he just sighs and reaches for a rag to wipe up the spilled coffee. "Go to bed, Brynja. You look dead on your feet."

I obey without another word, though I sleep for only a few hours before Saga wakes me with apologies and a pot of tea, to get me ready for the treaty meeting.

TWO YEARS AGO

YEAR 4198, Month of the Ghost God
The Iljaria Tunnels

We leave the Brown Goddess's hallowed halls, and the cave demons return with a vengeance. Ballast finds me a sword, which is more effective than my knife, and the three of us spend the better part of each day battling our way through one stone passageway after another. We've passed far out of Asvaldr's realm, so it's only Ballast and Saga and me against the shadows.

We sleep in shifts, one of us always awake to guard the others. We walk, fight, eat, sleep. Wake and do it again. Our path winds often near the underground river, and Ballast catches blind fish in nets while Saga and I keep the monsters off him. He smokes the fish in the coals of our fires.

"Do you charm them into your net?" Saga mocks him one day as he settles by the fire with his latest catch. "Do you call them to their deaths and laugh?"

I'm watching the cave entrance, so I don't look back as he draws his knife, begins to scale and gut the fish.

"No," he says. "I put out the nets. I thank the fish that swim into them. And I tell them that I'm sorry."

Saga doesn't say anything else. When she comes to relieve my watch, I take her place by the fire and notice she's eaten very little.

We come one day to an abandoned Iljaria city, a massive cavern carved with statues and stone pillars, murals covering the walls, with an ancient well in the center of a flagstone square. The whole place is illuminated with magic, glowing and golden as the summer sun. It hurts my eyes until they begin to adjust, and Saga and Ballast stand blinking and tearing on either side of me.

"I have never been here before," says Ballast. "It feels—"

"Ancient," I say. "And yet somehow new."

He nods. "Like the First Ones themselves might step around any corner."

"There are no shadows," I realize. "None at all."

"Because the light touches everything," says Saga, "every crack, every mote." And she begins to softly pray.

Slowly, we pace through the cavern. I wonder if it's the light that's keeping the cave demons from swarming this place or if it is something else.

All around the cavern there are dwellings carved into the stone. They're decorated with brilliant carpets and intricately carved furniture, with shelves of brightly illuminated manuscripts. There is a half-finished painting on an easel, with jars of opened paint beside it, and a brush that looks to have been only just laid down. Nothing has been touched by dust or spiders, decay or time.

On one end of the cavern, we come upon a sunken bath around a column of stone pillars, watched over by more statues, with a fountain in the center depicting what can only be the Prism Goddess, water spilling out of her open palms. I kneel and dip my hand into the water; it's clear and warm. I blink at the bath, the brimming magic tingling all up the length of my arm.

It's been weeks since the pool by the hot springs, and all three of us stare at the magical water with open longing.

"You go first, Saga," I tell her. "Shout when you're finished."

She nods her assent, and Ballast and I pace back into the central square. We sit on the edge of the fountain, the water here also clear and flowing.

I study Ballast as I have never seen him before: in dazzling light. He's shed his coat, and his sleeves are rolled up to the elbow; his brown arms are a map of scars where his swirls of Iljaria tattoos used to be. Kallias cut them out with a knife when Ballast was thirteen or so, to make him more Daerosian, but a few overlooked specks of blue remain.

There are scars on Ballast's jawline, too, and a nick in his right ear along the upper rim. I remember when Kallias did that—he was in a rage because the dogs had gotten loose in the palace, torn his private chambers all to pieces. He thought Ballast had done it, but it wasn't his fault. It was mine. *I* had let the dogs out of their cages and sent them hurtling toward the king's rooms in an act of righteous defiance. And I hid in my cage while Kallias carved a piece out of Ballast because of it.

Ballast turns toward me, catching me in my scrutiny, and I am struck anew by his eyelashes, which, like his hair, are a mix of black and white. He reaches out one tentative hand, his fingers brushing the edge of my headscarf. I tremble, and he mistakes the meaning of it. He lets his hand fall and sags where he sits.

I don't know how to tell him that I want him to touch me, that I long for it, a sharp ache beneath my ribs.

"You're right," says Ballast, to the ancient flagstones. "I always had a choice, and I shouldn't have *let* him . . . hurt you. Hurt all of you. I should have stopped him. I could have. But I was too afraid of how he might hurt me. Of how he might hurt my mother, even more than he already had."

"I was unfair before," I tell him, the music of the fountain echoing in the wide arch of the cavern. "He did hurt you. Over and over. And your ear. The dogs . . ." I speak around the lump in my throat, racked with guilt. "That was me."

He glances over again, a strange expression on his face. "Don't be sorry about my ear. If not for the dogs, he would have found another reason. He cut off one of my toes because I couldn't make a snake play a violin." Ballast gives a bitter, awful laugh.

I feel utterly sick.

But then he shrugs, like it's no big matter. "Whatever else I was to him, I am my father's son. I don't think he would have killed me, if it came down to it. Not like you. Not like all of you. You were expendable. Toys to amuse him and throw away when he got bored."

He's right, and I have no reply to that.

"I could have helped you. I could have stopped him, put an end to his damned Collection and saved dozens of lives. But I didn't because I'm a coward." He slams his fist into the edge of the fountain, cursing as his knuckles split and blood beads bright. He lifts his face to mine, tears gleaming on his cheeks, and runs his uninjured hand through his snow-and-earth hair before turning away again.

My throat hurts, my heart pulsing too fast, too hard. I want to wipe his tears away; I want to comfort him, to pull him into me and banish his tormented thoughts into the darkness where they belong. But I don't know how, or I am not brave enough. And if Ballast is a coward, I am one, too. I could have saved him. I could have saved everyone. But I didn't.

"You are one of the most powerful Iljaria I've ever seen," I tell him quietly. "You can do whatever you want: Free your mother. Remove your father from his throne." I study Ballast, his form lanky and taut in unnatural light. I am struck suddenly by his beauty, enough to steal my breath. "It *isn't* your fault, what happened to me and Saga and all the rest of us. That was your father's doing. It wasn't yours."

"I killed a man." His voice is raw and ragged. "Just because my father told me to."

My heart tears. "You did it quickly," I counter, "as mercifully as you could. Your father meant to be cruel, and you denied him that."

"But he's still dead."

I try not to hear Hilf's cry in my mind, try not to see his blood pooling over the marble.

"Ballast." His name sticks in my throat, and he looks at me again, his eyes wet and bright. "Hilf would be dead, with or without you."

He takes a shuddering breath, and I reach out to touch his arm, his scars rough under my skin. He turns his wrist and grips my fingers like he's dangling from the edge of a cliff and I'm the only one who can pull him to safety. I grip him back, so tightly I can feel his heart beating with mine, ragged and wild. His heat sears me, like I've caught hold of an open flame.

I want to pull him closer, but I'm terrified I will be burned.

"I don't want you to be afraid of me," he says frankly, gaze locked hard on mine. "I don't want you to look at me and see my father."

"I'm not," I say. "I don't."

His eyes go wet and he lifts his free hand, tracing it ever so lightly over my cheek. I shiver and lean into him. His hand is rough and warm.

"Brynja," he says quietly, "I—"

"Get away from her!"

I jump nearly through the roof at Saga's voice, jerking apart from Ballast. Saga stands there, dripping from her bath, eyes blazing with hurt and fury.

My heart is beating too fast, too hard. I can't seem to catch my breath.

"Don't touch her," Saga says to Ballast, low and cold. "Don't you dare touch her."

Ballast stares at the floor. I'm still having a hard time remembering how to breathe. "Saga, he—"

"Shut up," she snaps. "Shut *up*. Let's go."

We do. Neither Ballast nor I take our turn in the magical bath. We shoulder our packs, and he picks up the torch. We take the westward passage out of the Iljaria city, into the waiting embrace of three dozen cave demons. Saga doesn't look at me as she fights, the monsters' dark blood immediately undoing the effects of her bath. I'm not sure she'll ever speak to me again.

I do my best to work through my feelings with my sword.

CHAPTER FOURTEEN

YEAR 4200, Month of the Black God
Daeros—Kallias's Mountain

Sabotaging digging progress turns out to be harder than I expected.

The broken tools—pickaxes and drill bits—are collected at the end of every day and brought to the smithy, where they're melted down and reforged. I manage to steal a whole bin of them, but more metal is just brought in from the mines, and not much time is lost.

The workers are housed all together in a dormitory near the servants' wing of the palace; I lace their food with lobelia, and the whole lot of them get violently ill. But then soldiers are called up from the barracks to take their places until they recover, and I have made a lot of people really sick for no reason.

I explain all this to Finnur, the Iljaria boy Kallias keeps in his Collection, on one of my visits to the great hall. I come to see the children every few days, bringing them little treats or gifts, like Gulla used to do for all of us. But I haven't been brave enough to speak with Rute, my acrobatic replacement, after our first encounter.

"You'll have to strengthen the magic that's protecting whatever the Iljaria buried," Finnur says when I've finished telling him. "It's the only way to truly delay the digging, and no one will suspect it—they'll just think the vein is more resilient than they first thought."

I watch the gangly boy behind iron bars, folding flowers and animals out of the scraps of paper I brought him. His fingers move quickly in the semidarkness of the hall, his white hair seeming almost to glow.

"How am I supposed to do that?" I ask him. "I don't have any magic."

He flicks his eyes briefly to me before refocusing on his paper folding. "I'll do it."

Unhappiness makes my gut tighten. "Finnur, I can't take you down there. I can't even take you out of the hall, not till the army comes."

He gives a little nod, but I see the disappointment in the slump of his knobby shoulders.

"It's not that I don't want to—"

"I know," he says. He finishes the animal he's folding, a cat, and lines it up with the others. He grabs another piece of paper. "If you let me out of my cage, I can try and make something here that you can take down into the diggings."

"You'd really do that?"

His eyes meet mine, and there is a fierceness in him, a power that the iron can't quench. "Yes."

I bite my lip. "I'll have to lock you back in when—"

"I know. I swear I won't try to escape. I'll wait with the others."

I blink back the sudden press of tears. I let him out.

It's incredible to watch him work his Prism magic, there on the floor just outside his cage. He closes his eyes and lifts his hands, his fingers moving as if he's again folding paper and not air. Four small stones glimmer into being, spinning weightless in front of him. When he opens his eyes again, they fall; he catches them just before they hit the marble.

Finnur gives me a crooked smile as he offers them to me. I weigh the stones in my palm, heavy and cool.

"Concentrated healing magic," Finnur explains. "At least, that's what they're meant to be. You'll have to push them into the vein, and they should expand and clot, like a wound scabbing over."

"Thank you, Finnur," I say quietly.

He nods but doesn't reply, his eyes darting around the room. I tense, knowing I don't have the power—or the heart—to stop him if he chooses to run. But he doesn't. He just gives me a sad smile and steps back into the cage.

"I'm sorry," I choke out as I shut and lock the door.

"Come again soon, Brynja," he says. "I want to know if they work."

I promise that I will, and he ducks his head and goes back to folding.

I shimmy up the wall to the heating vent and make the mistake of looking over at my old cage. Rute watches me, wrath in her eyes. "You're no better than *him*," she spits out, "using a child to do a trick for you and then locking him away again."

Her voice echoes overloud in the arched room. I have no answer for her. I crawl away, cursing at myself to stop crying, but by the time I'm down in the depths of the mountain again, my cheeks are stiff with salt.

※

I have spied down here often enough now to know there is the briefest period of time between shifts when the digging site is unattended—when one pair of workers leaves with a cart of broken tools, and another pair comes with a cart of fresh ones. A few minutes, no more.

It's the only chance I have to use Finnur's magic.

I time it badly today, arriving in the tunnel mere moments after a shift begins, and am forced to wait in a narrow crevasse in the rock for hours. When the workers finally leave with their cart, my muscles are screaming from immobility, but I squeeze out of my hiding spot and pace toward the vein.

My heart pounds as I bring Finnur's stones up to the pulsing magic, fear of discovery making spots dance before my eyes. I press the first stone into the vein and jerk back as my finger touches the glowing blue, choking back a scream. The magic has burned me, a glaring red welt on my skin, and pain skitters, sharp and raging.

I'm more careful with the other stones, holding them in a strip of cloth and keeping my fingers well clear of the vein. The fourth one has just been absorbed when I hear the workers coming, boots and cart wheels loud on the stone.

There isn't time to flee down the tunnel before I'm seen, so I squeeze back into my hiding place for another long wait.

I get to see the fruits of Finnur's labor, at least: The pickaxes and drill bits break faster; the hole in the vein has closed up. The workers curse as a fourth axe breaks in as many minutes, and shout down the shaft for assistance. Another worker comes running up, and she's sent to find Basileious to inform him that there's been an unexpected delay.

※

Ballast is in the council chamber when Vil and I arrive, his ribbon and eye patch both a deep forest green. He sits on Kallias's right, face drawn and tired. There are blisters on his palms because Kallias made him dig in the heart of the mountain again last night, after receiving Basileious's report of the delay. But not even Ballast could make much of a dent in Finnur's magic. It wrecks me that his blisters and exhaustion are my fault, that I'm here to undo the hurt Kallias has caused, and all I've done so far is add to it.

For his part, Kallias is yawning and drinking *quite* a lot of wine for it being only the fourth hour of the day, his chair tilted back and his feet up on the table.

Lord Seleukos and Lady Eudocia are present, but none of the other governors are. Zopyros, Theron, and Alcaeus are grouped together, with no sign of Lysandra. Aelia and her steward, Talan, sit across from Vil and me, and Aelia greets us with a smile.

Ballast glances over at me and I tense, fixed by his one blue eye. My pulse hammers in my throat, and for half a moment, it feels like we are the only two people in the room.

And then Vil takes my hand in his, and I'm startled back into reality. Ballast looks away.

"Should we begin, Your Majesty?" says Aelia coolly when, after some minutes, Kallias has shown no sign of calling the session to order.

"Ballast," says Kallias with another yawn. He takes a long swig of wine and turns aside to General Eirenaios and starts telling him about "the girls from last night" in such explicit detail it makes my cheeks heat.

Vil stiffens beside me, and Aelia grows absolutely frigid.

"My father has asked me to lead the meeting this morning," says Ballast, turning to address the room.

Zopyros, Theron, and Alcaeus look at Ballast with murder in their eyes, but none of them dare object.

"He wishes us to discuss changes to the borders between Skaanda and Daeros." Ballast unfolds a map on the table, heroically and doggedly ignoring his father's ongoing topic of conversation. "We must come to an agreement about the river towns here and here"—he points to each—"as well as the guard posts on the plains, here and here."

"Skaanda isn't relinquishing *any* of those," snaps Vil. "There's not a chance in hell."

"Every one of them was taken *from* Daeros," Ballast retorts. "Negotiation is give and take. On both sides."

"Don't school me in etymology, you one-eyed bastard!"

I grab his arm. "*Vil.*"

He shuts his mouth.

Ballast's eye flicks over to me, and I feel sharp and hot with horror. I let go of Vil; his sleeve is rumpled where I gripped him.

For a moment I'm caught in the maelstrom of tension that hangs between the two of them, sucking all the air out of the room and tying my stomach in knots. I want to cry and scream and knock their fool heads together.

"I will remind you," says Ballast coolly, looking at Vil again, "that you are here on my father's goodwill. It is in your own best interest to be civil."

"Now you're *threatening* me?" Vil demands, jerking up from his chair.

"I think," says Aelia, with a dazzling smile, "that we had best move on to other terms and leave the border discussion for another day. Don't you agree, Your Highnesses?"

It's something I ought to have said, if I'd had my wits about me. I curse myself.

Ballast nods. Vil slumps back in his seat. I take a long, slow breath.

Kallias's voice rises in the silence. "While the dark-haired one had the most *delightful*—"

"Let's return," says Aelia hastily, "to the basis of what we all wish the treaty to be: lasting peace between nations. Skaanda showed great faith toward that end with the food shipments, and Daeros in return displayed all it has to offer."

"Though offered none of it," Vil says under his breath.

The conversation limps on, Lord Seleukos and Lady Eudocia discussing trade options with Vil, who seems to finally remember he's trying to ingratiate himself to these people, and keeps a better check on his temper. Vil and Lady Eudocia are conferring about a possible tour of the Bone City when Kallias jerks his feet off the table and settles his chair on the floor with a sudden *thump*.

We all look over at him, and I'm startled to find that he no longer seems drunk. "I have decided to name an heir," he announces.

Zopyros, Theron, and Alcaeus all sit up very straight.

"Who, Father?" says Zopyros, puffing out his chest.

Ballast eyes him uneasily, a muscle jumping in his jaw.

"The naming ceremony will be tomorrow evening," says Kallias. He smiles his feline smile, and it slithers under my skin and sticks there.

Zopyros sags a bit in his chair but doesn't repeat his question.

The announcement effectively ends negotiations, and I stand with relief, ready to crawl into bed and sleep the day away. Vil is deep in conversation with Aelia—he won't need me for a while.

I jump when Kallias grabs my hand. He looks up at me with eyes that are both lazy and cunning. "I have not gotten to know you as well as I would like, Princess Astridur. We will have dinner together, you and I. A private dinner. Not tomorrow evening, of course. The evening after."

I gape at him. "I couldn't accept, Your Majesty," I stammer.

He just grins, showing his teeth. "I look forward to it."

I extricate my hand and flee into the corridor, pausing for a moment to tilt my head back against the wall in an effort to slow my raging pulse.

"Br—Astridur?"

I turn to see Ballast standing there, hands nervous about the trim of his shirt. Veins of red run through the white of his eye, and the shadow beneath it is darker than it looked in the council chamber. He smells strongly of medicine and herbs, and I think of him weeping silently onto his pillow, of the vials on his nightstand, of the physician asking him if the pain is better, if the nightmares have gone. This isn't what he smelled like before, in the caves, in the dark.

Words stick in my throat and I am ill, ill, because he's here now and I want desperately to fold myself into him but I can't, because I don't know what he is, and I don't know what I am, and everything is wrong.

But the intensity in his one-eyed gaze makes my heart stutter.

"You shouldn't be here," he says quietly. "It isn't safe. There are—there are things going on that I can't explain, but you need to leave. Before everything gets worse. Before—"

"Before you're named your father's heir?" I snap. "Are we enemies, Ballast? Is that what we are now?"

"No. No, of course not."

"Then what are you warning me about? Yourself? Why in the Gray Goddess's hell are you back here, bowing and scraping to your father's will? You could have destroyed him. And yet you're—you're sacrificing everything for a wild grab at power?"

"It isn't like that!"

"Then what is it *like*?" I'm shouting and I shouldn't be. We are hardly in a private part of the palace, and I need to hold my tongue.

His chest heaves, his face stricken with grief or anger or some other emotion caught between. "I'm trying to save them," he says softly. "I'm trying to save all of them." His eye seeks mine, begging me to understand.

But I don't understand. I think of Gulla, locked in her cage, bruised and alone and forgotten. "Have you even gone to see your mother since you've been here?" It's a cruel question.

His jaw goes hard. "I can't antagonize my father."

I scoff. "What's your game, Ballast? Get yourself named heir, take over from your father, and then what? Start a Collection of your own?"

Something breaks in his face, and I utterly revile myself for saying that to him.

He turns distant, cold.

I take a step toward him. "Ballast. I'm sorry. I know that isn't you."

"Do you?" he says. He shows his teeth in an echo of Kallias's feline smile, and it chills me to my bones.

"You're better off with your Skaandan prince," he says, eye glittering, "although I'm not sure anyone believes he's your cousin."

My anger flares and I shove past him, but he grabs my wrist. Holds me back.

I look at him, pulse wild. Fear rages through me, fear of him, of his father. Of this mountain and all the secrets buried in the heart of it.

"Don't interfere," says Ballast, tone clipped. "If you know what's best for you, you and your Skaandan prince will leave Tenebris and never come back."

"He's not my Skaandan prince," I practically snarl at him.

For a moment more we stare at each other, his fingers hot through my sleeve.

Then he releases me, and I sweep on down the corridor.

I don't look back.

TWENTY-ONE MONTHS AGO

YEAR 4199, Month of the Yellow God
The Iljaria Tunnels

Saga won't speak to me. She barely even looks at me. She will never forgive Ballast for killing Hilf. And she will never forgive me for permitting Ballast's touch.

The only time she interacts with Ballast is every night after we make camp, when he scratches out the map with charcoal on the stone, and she copies it down, making certain she has it memorized. Other than that every day is an agony of silence, of hewing our way through the cave demons, of careful distance between all three of us. Sometimes I catch Ballast watching me, but when I meet his eyes, he glances away. I want to tell him I am not Saga, that the memory of his hand on my cheek sends fire through my veins. I want to tell him that I care for him, that he means something to me I don't even properly understand.

What pass for days down here spin on, and I sense very keenly that there are not many left, that no matter how often I have felt we will be trapped here in the mountain with the shadow monsters forever, it isn't true. We'll reach the end of the tunnels soon. It will be time to leave Ballast behind. The very thought is a keen-edged agony. I will miss him when we have gone. Already it gnaws at me. I don't know if I will be able to bear letting him go.

"We're close, aren't we," says Saga one day as we break camp, scattering the ashes of the fire, smudging out the twin charcoal drawings on the stone floor. "Close to the exit."

Ballast looks at me for one long and steady moment before turning his back to us and raising his torch into the darkness, sword loose and ready in his other hand. "Yes," comes his quiet agreement. "We're close."

My stomach wrenches.

"How close?" says Saga.

"We will camp only once more."

She huffs out a breath. "Good."

We walk awhile in silence before Ballast says: "I'm not coming with you to Staltoria City."

Saga's jaw tightens. "I know. I will not force you to come—and with that, I consider my debt to you for guiding us repaid. But if I ever see you again, I'll kill you."

"I know," Ballast echoes.

There are no monsters today, which makes me more restless than usual—it's easier to hack through a horde of cave demons than to be confronted with my own thoughts, forced to reckon with the reality of having to part with Ballast, when I have only just found him again.

I dread making camp, but Ballast stops sooner than I'm ready for, in a little cave off the main tunnel. The underground river flows nearby, its laughter reverberating off the stones.

We eat and sip our tea. Saga draws the charcoal map once more on the ground, and Ballast looks at it and nods.

Then there are only the blankets to spread out by the fire, and one last sleep before leaving the caves behind. I take first watch, peering out into the wider passage, listening to the fire crack and pop. But nothing stirs, and I don't think anything will. I take the torch from where Ballast propped it against a rock and pace down the tunnel.

While the Dark Remains

I follow the sound of the river until I find it, running smooth and dark along its stony bank. I sit, study the gleam of the water in the reflected torchlight. Bright-blue pebbles seem almost to glow beneath the surface, and I scoop out a handful of them, spreading them out on the bank to dry. I study the pebbles as I force myself to contemplate my future.

I have to go back to my family, and I try to understand my resistance to do so. My sister has been gone many years now, and yet when I think of home, I think of her—her quick brain and quicker fingers, her spectacles smudged with grease. The way I'm not sure, even now, if she was properly aware of my existence, so wrapped up in her inventing that she had little thought left to spare for anything or anyone else.

There is my brother, of course, but we were never particularly close. He was sickly, when we were little, always being attended to by physicians, closeted away from his rambunctious sister. That's when he started reading so much, when he decided to become a scholar. He's the one who told me all the stories of the gods.

My parents had little time for me. They could have found me in Kallias's mountain, but they didn't. They don't know if I'm alive or dead. I'm not sure it matters to them, either way.

What is there for me, really, at home? But where else would I even go?

"Brynja?"

Ballast's voice is warm and soft in the darkness, and I don't turn as he sinks down beside me, close enough that his sleeve brushes mine.

My skin pricks with awareness, yet my heartbeats quiet, steady. I am easier with him next to me. I'm glad he came. I wanted him to.

For a while we don't speak, just stare into the water, listen to it flowing over the stones.

"The cave demons won't come again, will they?" I say.

He shakes his head. "We are too near the light. They stay in the deeper parts of the labyrinth, where they can be assured of the darkness.

We're perfectly safe now." He picks up one of the blue pebbles and turns it over and over in his hands. "Will you really go with Saga?"

"Yes," I tell him.

"Why?"

"She asked me to. And I have nowhere else to go."

"You could stay here," he says quietly. "In the tunnels."

I hear what he doesn't say: *You could stay with me.*

I want to stay with him. I want to so badly it hurts. But not here. Not now. This isn't how it's supposed to go. "I can't live in the dark, Bal."

He turns to face me. The torchlight dances in his white-and-dark hair, licks along his skin, and turns him all to molten gold. His eyes gleam with moisture.

"You can't stay here, either," I say. "You belong in the light."

"I'm a monster. I belong in the shadows with the rest of the monsters."

His words wreck me. I want to erase the very essence of them, but I don't know how. "You're not a monster."

"But I am. Saga is right. I deserve to die for the things I've done."

"Saga is not a god, to deal out life and death."

Pain writes its way across his face, like his whole soul is filled with it. "Can I touch you, Brynja?" he whispers.

My heart presses against my breastbone. I give him the barest of nods, which doesn't convey even an iota of how much I want him to.

He cups one hand around my face, smooths my cheek with his thumb. I tremble as he tugs the scarf from my head, lets it fall to the ground. I lean into him like I'm drawn by some unstoppable magnetic force. He brushes his fingers across my newly grown hair, infinitely gentle. My skin sparks at his touch. I want him closer. I need him closer.

"I don't know why you don't hate me," he says. "Why don't you hate me?"

"Because you are a good person, Ballast Vallin, whatever you might think." The words stick in my throat. I believe them of him; I want to believe them of me, too. "And because you are my friend."

His eyes are wet, his hand warm against my cheek. "Brynja," he says. "Can I kiss you?"

I am hot and cold, wild and still, a maelstrom of emotions that narrow down to one I can understand. I want this. I want *him*.

"Yes," I whisper. "Gods, Bal, yes."

He looks at me with such intensity my insides go all to jelly, and then he dips his head and his lips find mine, hesitant, soft. I kiss him back, careful and a little unsure, my heart raging inside me. His mouth is warm and wet. He tastes of salt and tea and something untamed that I yearn to know more of.

The stone is cold at our backs; the river rushes steady beyond it, its music echoing in my very soul.

Our kiss deepens, turning feral. His unshaven cheek scrapes against my smooth one, and his lips become fire, desperate and wild. His hands are in the tangle of my newly grown hair; mine are around his shoulders, pulling him harder against me. I can't bear that there is yet space between us. I need him closer.

Blue sparks suddenly before my eyes as magic rushes into me, exploding in my mind, ripping me to pieces.

I jerk away from Ballast with a half-swallowed scream. Blue dances still in the field of my vision, and the pain sears.

He's breathing hard, his eyes unfocused, his fingers still wound in my hair. "What is it?" he gasps. "What's wrong? I'm sorry if I—I thought you wanted—"

"I do." My eyes are hot with tears. "But I can feel your magic, Bal. It's bursting out of you. It burns."

"Violet Lord," he curses. "I'm sorry." He cups my face with his hands, trembling.

I'm shaking, too, and desperately blinking back my tears. "Don't be sorry." I look at him in utter misery. I want to pull him close again. I want his skin on mine, I want to feel the hard and soft planes of him. But his magic terrifies me.

We hold each other for a while in the dark, my head tucked under his chin, his hands tracing slow circles on my back. His heartbeat calms me, pulsing under my ear, but it breaks me, too. My tears soak through his shirt.

I don't want to leave him here alone when we reach the end of the tunnels. I don't want to leave him at all. I want to kiss him again but not in the dark. In the light of the blazing sun.

I lift my head after a while, and we study each other in the torchlight, the river lapping quietly at its stony bank.

"Stay with me," he says. "Please. I don't—I don't think I can bear to be without you."

My heart wrenches. "I can't stay, Bal."

"Why? Saga doesn't need you."

"I need to go home. I need to find my family again."

He traces the line of my collarbone with one finger, and I shiver. "When you've found them, then. Will you come back for me?"

I can hardly think around the hard pulse of my heart. "I don't want to make any promises I can't keep."

"Then keep it," he says.

The river rushes on, soft and steady.

"I can try and hold it back," says Ballast. "My magic."

My breath hitches. "Yes," I whisper.

And then he is crushing me once more against him, his mouth wild and wanting on mine. I feel him reining in his power, or attempting to. It's there just beneath the surface, ready to ignite. Magic sparks on my tongue, burrows into my mind. All is blue, all is heat. Our kiss is a living thing, bound between us, barely contained. I don't think I want to contain it. His magic grows stronger as he loses hold of it. It burns me, eating me up from the inside. But I don't care. I want him closer, I need him closer. I—

Steps sound on the stone, and I come back to myself in a rush, jerking away from Ballast.

I gulp air in desperate mouthfuls, feeling wildly disoriented. Ballast's eyes are unfocused, and he's breathing hard, too. "Brynja," he says, soft as a prayer.

And then Saga is beside us, the torch she carries fully illuminating the wrath and hurt in every line of her face. "Get up," she snarls. "Both of you, GET THE HELL UP."

We obey, stiff and shaky on our feet.

"What are you doing down here?" she demands. "Why did you leave the camp?"

She sets her jaw when neither one of us answers, and then she looks at Ballast, her jaw tight, her right hand gripping her sword hilt. "How far are we from the exit?"

Ballast flicks his gaze to mine, agony written all over his face. "An hour's walk," he says. "No more."

Saga swears at him. "We're leaving. Now."

We follow Saga back to our cave, where we smother the fire and shoulder our packs for the last time. I feel tight and hot and full to bursting. Ballast catches my hand with his, and I turn to speak with him, but Saga yanks me away. "Touch her again," she says, low and cold, "and I'll take your damned head off."

He ducks his chin to her in deference and makes no further move toward me.

None of us speak as Ballast leads us through the tunnels, as our path winds up and the stone morphs to dirt beneath our feet. A screen of tangled brambles obscures our exit. We pull them free, thorns snagging at our sleeves, our hands. The pain grounds me but doesn't stop the tears from pressing hard against my eyes, threatening to fall. I don't want to leave him. How can I?

We break through the brambles to see light spilling across the tundra, gleaming a fiery red on the icy snow. Now I do weep, openly, at the touch of the sun on my skin. I can't seem to stop, sagging against the mountain, wrenched apart by grief, by joy, by deliverance. Kallias cannot reach me here. I am free of my cage. Free of the mountain. Free of everything, perhaps, but myself.

Ballast touches my hand and I lift my face to him, see that he is crying, too. "It has been a long time," he says, "since I saw the sun. It's beautiful."

I choke off my tears, swipe my sleeve across my nose and eyes. "Don't shrink from it," I tell him. "Don't go back into the dark."

He nods, his eyes fixed on mine. "I will try not to, Brynja of Skaanda."

I flinch. This is goodbye. I will never see him again, never have another chance to tell him that I—

Saga jerks me away from him. Her jaw is clenched; her eyes are wet. She shines in the sunlight. "We are going now," she tells Ballast. "Remember what I told you: If I ever see your face again, I will not hesitate to kill you."

He bows to her, very low, as if she is a queen. "Thank you for your mercy."

She has nothing else to say to him and, grabbing my wrist, pulls me with her onto the tundra. I glance back at Ballast, panicked. I shake Saga off. "Give me a moment, Saga."

She shakes her head, angry but resigned. "Catch up, then," she says shortly. "I'm not waiting." And then she stalks ahead, like she cannot get away from Ballast and the mountains fast enough.

My heart stammers as I turn back to Ballast, as I look at him in the full light of the sun. He is so very beautiful it makes me ache. I shiver at the memory of his heat and his magic, his mouth on mine. I want to kiss him again, want to pull him against me. But I don't dare. If I did that, I would never let him go, and I have to. My family, my future, is waiting.

There is a depth of feeling in his eyes as he studies me, the sunlight turning his face all to gold.

"Come back to me," he says, "when you have done what you need to do. Please come back to me."

While the Dark Remains

I can't promise him that. I want to, but I can't. There is too much I want to say to him, and not enough time or words to say it. So all I tell him is: "Don't dwell in the darkness, Bal. Not anymore. Stay in the light."

He gives me half a smile, but I don't miss the sadness there. "In the light, Brynja."

He touches my brow with warm fingers. My breath catches.

"Lords keep you," he says softly.

I echo his Iljaria phrasing: "Lords keep you."

One last look between us, fraught with feeling, with loss.

And then I follow Saga west across the tundra, my boots squeaking in the hard-packed snow, the sun warm on my face.

I glance back, just once, to the mountain.

But Ballast is already gone.

CHAPTER FIFTEEN

YEAR 4200, Month of the Gray Goddess
Daeros—Tenebris

There is no formal dinner tonight. Attendants bring food on trays to our rooms instead, leaving time to prepare for the naming ceremony, which is to be at the fifteenth hour. I eat a few half-hearted bites of roast pork and braised vegetables, but my stomach is too unsettled for anything else.

I sit at the dressing table while Saga arranges my hair, threading tiny strands of glittering crystals into my curls. She covers my freckles with the usual cosmetics, then draws dark lines of kohl around my eyes and brushes glimmering powder on my eyelids. I transform, under her hands, to the image of royalty I'm impersonating.

Kallias hasn't announced whom he's naming as his heir this evening, but I know in my gut that it's Ballast. Payment, I expect, for the eye. There is no other reason that I can think of for Ballast to have sacrificed a piece of himself.

I study my fingers in my lap and think about Ballast in the hall last night, his hand locked about my wrist, the twin of his father's smile on his face. His words to me, harsh and cold: *If you know what's best for you, you and your Skaandan prince will leave Tenebris and never come back.*

While the Dark Remains

But I see him in the caves, too, down in the dark by the rushing river, his mouth warm on mine, his breath on my neck and his fingers in my hair. His magic, blazing out of him.

Saga lays down her brush, shaking me from my reverie. "Come and get dressed."

The gown is laid out on the bed; it makes me gasp. On first glance it looks white, but there are thousands and thousands of glimmering beads sewn into the skirt and the bodice—beads of every color. Saga means for me to arrive at the ceremony dressed as the Prism Goddess, flaunting a power superior to Kallias's—and his heir's.

"Are you really sure that's a good idea?" I ask.

Saga squares her jaw. "The Daerosians don't even believe in the gods. If Kallias is insulted, he'll look the fool for saying so. Now get dressed, Brynja. You'll be late."

※

Vil walks with me to the great hall, my appearance evidently robbing him of all speech. In addition to the gown, which impractically has no sleeves, I wear white furs draped around my arms and shoulders. I feel foolish, overdressed, conspicuous. But there's no changing now.

Vil wears dark trousers and a long white robe, embroidered in multicolored threads that complement my gown. He is handsome, shining, and yet I am scarcely moved by the sight of him. It isn't wholly false, what he said to me before. *You didn't think you'd ever see him again. So you settled for me. But now that he's here, you have no more use for me, do you?*

Part of me, I think, has always been waiting for Ballast. He's the reason I could never quite allow myself to commit to Vil, even though I wanted to accept the safety, the family, I thought he was offering. But I got Vil wrong, just like he got me wrong, and I don't know what to do about it. Maybe there's not really anything I *can* do.

We come into the great hall, and I have to fight the urge to flee. My head spins, but Vil grips my arm, grounding me. I'm humbled and grateful. I lean into him.

Chairs have been set up in a semicircle facing the ivory throne, where Kallias lounges, sipping wine and laughing with a pair of Daerosian women who are dressed in strips of gauzy fabric and little else. One of them is in his lap, and the other is draped over the arm of his throne, both simpering up at him, trailing their fingers along his neck.

Aelia turns to greet us, wearing a blue velvet gown with animals embroidered in silver all down her skirt. I glance around to see that most everyone here is wearing blue, except for me and Vil. Blue is the color of the goddess of animals. Blue is Ballast's color.

"Sit with me?" says Aelia, and beckons Vil to the chair next to hers. I take the seat on the other side of him.

Lysandra sweeps in, looking absolutely livid, her thick mask of cosmetics doing little to disguise that she's been messily crying for a solid hour at least. She's wearing gray, the color of death, decay, mourning.

Kallias's other children file in after her, Rhode and little Xenia holding hands, Theron and Alcaeus dressed in matching gold and gray, heavy with furs and gold chains about their necks. Zopyros is in his lieutenant's uniform, stony and solemn. They all sit together, though Lysandra shouts at Xenia until she starts crying, and Rhode tugs her sister into another row.

Pelagia, Elpis, and Unnur, Kallias's wives, sit behind their children, but Gulla isn't here. I try not to look for her cage on the outskirts of the room, try not to wonder if Kallias has hurt her more since we last spoke, if Ballast has done anything at all to help her. Pelagia's belly is even more swollen than before, and I hope she's being properly attended by the palace physician. She looks ready to give birth at any moment.

The audience is rounded out by Talan, the Daerosian governors, and Kallias's general, steward, and engineer.

Through the glass wall, northern lights pulse above the Sea of Bones, green and pink and violet. I think about all the times I watched them from my iron cage, beautiful and strange and wholly, wildly *free*.

I take a breath, force myself to forget about Rute, my replacement, dangling above my head even now.

Nicanor, Kallias's steward, steps up to the king and says something low in his ear. Kallias yawns, stands, and shoos away the barely clothed women with a look of marked regret.

Ballast comes in, and I think my heart stops.

He wears a long red robe, embroidered with swirls of silver. His eye patch and ribbon are white, and his one eye has been outlined in gold kohl, his white-and-dark lashes dusted with gold powder to match. Tiny crystals have been pasted along his jawline, and he glitters as he walks. He is so beautiful I can't bear it, my mouth dry, my whole body trembling.

And then he stops at the ivory throne, kneeling before his father and bowing his head low. For a moment all I can see is the lion, ripping Hilf's throat out.

"Rise," says Kallias, formal and foreboding. "Rise and take your name, Ballast Heron Vallin."

Ballast stands, and I'm surprised to realize that he's several inches taller than his father.

"By my name," says Kallias, "and by your blood, I seal you as heir apparent to the throne of Daeros, with all the power, privileges, and responsibilities afforded you by that role. Do you pledge your life and blood to Daeros, to its people and its stones?"

Ballast dips his head. "I pledge my life," he says, his voice quiet yet strong enough to echo around the hall. "I pledge my blood. To Daeros, to its people and its stones."

"Do you bind yourself to this throne, until your life is spent or taken?"

"I bind myself to this throne." Ballast's hands shake. "Until my life is spent or taken."

Kallias nods, satisfied, and draws a dagger from his belt.

Ballast holds out his already scarred right arm without a word.

I clamp down on my lip as Kallias cuts Ballast's arm, once, twice, three times, in a crisscrossing pattern just below the elbow. Ballast stands stone-still and lets him do it, his face blank, his eye fixed on some invisible point in the distance. This is not the first time Kallias has hurt him. I don't even think it's the first time Ballast volunteered for it. When the cuts heal, the scar will look something like a spiderweb—the mark of the Daerosian heir.

But right now there are only the wounds, and the blood leaking out. Nausea churns in my gut, and I hate this. I hate all this. I want to save him. I want to pull him far from this place, where Kallias can never hurt him again.

Kallias dips one finger in the wound and traces a line of blood across Ballast's forehead. Then he opens the square, flat box offered him by Nicanor and takes out a gold circlet. He lifts it for all to see. "By the mark of your blood, the bond of gold, and my own word and faithful witness, I name you, Ballast Heron Vallin, heir to Daeros."

Kallias lays the gold circlet on Ballast's white-and-dark hair.

Then it is done, and Ballast turns to the crowd, gilded and shining.

I blink and see Gulla's words, traced through the air in this very room: *He has become too much like his father, desiring only power.*

I look at Ballast. And I see Kallias. And I wonder if she might be right. It rattles me to my core.

I spend most of the following day hiding in the ceiling above the sprawling, cavernous library. I am angry at Ballast. Wildly, viciously angry. I try to parse out my anger, and I can't quite do it, or don't quite want to. Because underneath the anger is hurt. How could he so align himself with his father and his father's agenda? How could he put himself further under Kallias's power? How can he claim he is saving his mother and all the rest and yet stand back and do nothing?

The voice of guilt screams in my own mind that I am also doing nothing, that Gulla and the children remain caged, and Kallias is yet on his throne, and nothing has changed. I tell myself I am following the plan, that in less than two months Vil and Saga and I will put an end to everything that Kallias stands for.

But it doesn't make me feel any better, and I don't know if I'm more angry at Ballast or myself.

Kallias hasn't forgotten his private dinner invitation, and when I ask Vil to get me out of it, he tells me it isn't worth offending the king by refusing to go.

"We have to keep up our facade, Brynja," he says, pouring himself a cup of wine from the sideboard in his receiving room. "That means we have to do hard things."

I swear at him, up and down the pantheon, as colorfully as I can. "What hard things are *you* doing?" I demand. "You promised me you'd keep me safe!"

Vil turns to look at me, a stoniness in his face that is there now more often than not. "You are safe, Brynja. And the hard thing I'm doing is not taking Ballast's damn head off his damn shoulders."

I grind my jaw and swear at him again, to hide the fact that I'm trying not to cry. I go back to my and Saga's room without another word.

Saga dresses me in a gold gown with a skirt that flares out at the hips, then weaves strands of little suns through my hair, and clasps a heavy gold collar—also in the shape of a sun—around my neck. Gold powder on my eyelids, brows, and cheeks, and gold kohl around my eyes complete the look, a not-very-subtle nod to the Yellow God—the god of light.

Saga nods, satisfied, though she won't quite meet my eyes. I've been avoiding her today, not ready to discuss with her in detail the ramifications of Ballast being named heir, though last night she gave me a taste of her feelings: vindication that she was right about his grasping ambitions, and further fuel on the fire of her hatred. In her eyes, Ballast truly is no different than his father.

I thank her for helping me get ready, then step out into the corridor to meet the waiting attendant, feeling very, very alone. I almost turn back to beg Saga for the headdress with the hidden blade, because as it is, it will only be me, unarmed, before the king. I tell myself that *surely* there will be dinner knives, and the thought braces me enough to keep going.

It takes a full fifteen minutes of various twists and turns through the palace corridors before the attendant deposits me in front of an arched, ivory door carved with suns. He opens it and waves me into a small parlor.

A pair of doors at the back of the room lead out onto a balcony carved from mountain stone. Kallias waits there, turning at my step. He's dressed in a black velvet robe embroidered in gold, with a heavy coat of black furs. He smiles. "How lovely you look this evening, Princess."

I think about dinner knives and force myself to curtsy.

He lifts me to my feet again, his hand cold and hard around mine. "You must be hungry. Come."

He pulls me through the doors and out onto the balcony, where a small round table is set for two. A pillar of fire blazes impossibly in one corner, lending a measure of warmth to the frigid winter air: Iljaria magic, sparking red and gold.

Kallias draws out a chair for me and lays a white fur over my knees. He takes the seat across from me, eyes glittering in the light of the fire pillar, and I remember how very, very afraid I am of him.

An attendant with a pitcher steps out to fill our wineglasses, and it takes me a moment to register the silk patch tied over his right eye. My heart tries to claw its way out of my rib cage. I have to force myself not to stare.

"Don't mind him, my dear," says Kallias in a lazy drawl. "I have to keep an eye on him, or he gets himself into mischief. Just one eye, of course." He laughs at his joke, but Ballast doesn't react, just withdraws to the balcony doors, awaiting our pleasure like any ordinary servant.

"Please," says Kallias. "Eat."

I turn my attention to my plate, which is piled with eleven different kinds of cake, candied nuts, sugared peaches, and more sweet things than I have ever seen presented all at once. I've had my fill after only a few bites, but I keep nibbling. Anything is preferable to looking Kallias in the eye. I sip my wine, too, furious. He has offered me only dessert, and so there are no knives on the table.

Kallias snaps his fingers, and Ballast comes back, stiff and wary in the light of the magical fire.

"I thought I would treat you to a little private performance before we get down to business," says Kallias, smug. "Did you know my son has some delightful Iljaria tricks?"

My gut wrenches, and I regret every bite I took of Kallias's damn desserts. It is a horror to me that Ballast has sacrificed everything to be named his father's heir, and nothing at all has changed. "That isn't necessary," I say in a rush. "I am not certain why you invited me this evening, Your Majesty, but—"

"Oh, you'll be charmed." Kallias gives a careless wave of his hand, then turns his shrewd glance on Ballast. "Boy."

Ballast's eye flicks to me for a heartbeat before returning to Kallias. "What is it you wish me to do, Father?"

My heart is a wild thing, frantic and raging. Oh gods, I wish I were anywhere but here.

"Surprise me," says Kallias.

Ballast shuts his eye and takes a step back from the table, his lips moving soundlessly. I can feel his magic whispering out of him, shivering through the air, glancing past my cheek. I can't help but remember the taste of it. The fire of it. My insides turn to clotted cream.

I blink, and there comes the rush of white wings as a flock of owls descends on the balcony. Their low-throated calls are somehow chilling, their flapping stirring my hair and making the pillar of fire flare hot. One of the owls lands on Ballast's shoulder; another takes a tiny cake from my plate and gulps it down whole. A third owl snatches the gold chain from Kallias's neck, letting it fall onto his lap.

I blink again, and the owls fly away.

Ballast opens his eye.

Kallias laughs, but there is no mirth in it, and dread curls down my spine.

"Forgive him, Astridur. I will make him do something more exciting next time."

"No need," I say, fighting to keep my tone even. "It was most thrilling."

"You are too kind." Kallias sighs, bored, and orders Ballast to bring us coffee.

He does, in etched bone cups. I heap sugar and cream in mine, but I can't quite combat the bitterness, and every sip makes my gut churn worse.

"I am surprised you haven't asked me yet, Your Highness," says Kallias as he drinks deep, as the fire pillar blazes too bright for me to see the stars.

"About what, Your Majesty?"

"My Collection. You don't seem as thrilled with it as I had hoped. I am planning another performance soon."

I am hyperaware of Ballast, stiff and still in the corner of my eye. I have to fight not to be sick, to face Kallias and say, as evenly as I can, "The children are . . . remarkable."

"The acrobat, particularly, wouldn't you say?"

His eyes bore into mine and *oh gods he knows* but I simply force a smile through gritted teeth. "I am not particularly fond of acrobatics, Your Majesty. The heights and leaps make me feel faint."

He grins. "Which one was your favorite, then?"

"I am . . . uncomfortable choosing a favorite among children kept in cages." My pulse thrums in my throat, and I am so afraid he's found me out, that Kallias's sweets and acrid coffee will be the only things in my belly when I die.

But he just raises his brows, laughing at me. "I had not thought you especially tenderhearted, Princess. They are very well looked after, you know. Orphans, all of them. They are fed and educated. The cages are only for show."

His bald-faced lies enrage me, but there is nothing, *nothing*, I can do besides keep pretending, as he is, to be something I am not. "Why children, though? What is your fascination with them?"

"I was a prodigy myself, you know," he returns, tapping on the side of his coffee cup. "Mathematics and science—they made sense to me, from a very early age. My tutors praised me and my parents made me work out complicated equations for my relatives and visiting dignitaries, showing off my brain as if they were responsible for it."

I am shocked at the resentment in him, years past but still eating him up from the inside.

Kallias drains his mug and snaps his fingers at Ballast, who comes to dutifully refill it. "But the older one gets, the less remarkable one's skills," Kallias says, "at least in the eyes of others. My father did not think I deserved power, or was capable of wielding it. I was only good for equations, for party tricks. But he underestimated me. *Everyone* underestimated me." He clenches his jaw, and fear knits hot and tight inside me as he smiles, sharp and deadly.

"I came to the throne at sixteen," he says, "when my parents were found dead in their bedchamber during Winter Dark. Poisoned, both of them, by my uncles, who thought to seize Daeros for themselves. They are just bones now, scattered in the glacier sea. I had them executed for murdering my parents." His eyes glitter, malicious laughter on his brow.

I try not to show my horror—I knew in the vaguest of terms that Kallias had become king at an early age, but none of the sordid details. And I understand exactly what he's saying without saying it: *He* poisoned his parents, then pinned the crime on his uncles, neatly eliminating them while securing the throne for himself.

He must have played his part to perfection, for the Daerosian governors to accept his version of the truth and not stand in the way of him becoming king. That, or they're a greater lot of fools than I ever thought.

"I have ruled well, in the twenty-three years since," Kallias goes on. "And soon I will wield a power stronger than my father could have ever imagined."

Everything inside me pulls me toward Ballast, but I don't even dare look at him. "What power would that be, Your Majesty?" I say carefully.

Kallias sets down his coffee mug and stands. "Ballast!" he barks. "Move my chair next to Princess Astridur's."

Ballast crosses the balcony and puts his hands on his father's chair, but he doesn't move it. "Does Her Highness wish you to be so close to her, sir?"

"Are you in the position to question my commands, boy?"

Ballast moves the chair.

Kallias sits next to me, his thigh touching mine. He takes my hands in both of his, trapping them in a cage of skin and bone. His rings press hard against my knuckles, and I try not to gasp at the pain.

"I am very glad," he says quietly, almost tenderly, "that the Skaandans have such a beautiful ambassador at their disposal. The treaty was a wise idea, and sending you to tempt me into agreeing to it was even wiser." He eases the pressure on my hands a little, smooths his thumbs along the backs of them.

My heart beats, beats, but I don't struggle. I know that's what he wants. I try to breathe. I tell myself that Ballast won't let Kallias hurt me, even though I'm not at all sure that's true. I can sense his loathing of me, from his place at the door.

"Your little country is weak, its military spread too thin. Skaanda could no sooner conquer Daeros and seize Tenebris than win a war against the gods you barbarians cling to. But a treaty. A marriage pact to seal it." His smile is oil and steel. I want to crawl out of my own skin. "That would do very well, I think."

I tug my hands out of his, and his rings scratch me. I twist my fingers in my skirt, my whole body aflame. "No woman would bind herself to a man who already has so many wives."

Kallias shrugs and lays a possessive hand on my neck. "They mean nothing to me. I'm forced to seek the company of other girls because my wives bore me so. And you forget I have no queen."

I jerk from my chair and am halfway out the double doors before Kallias grabs my wrist. Holds me back.

Ballast is a dark shape in the doorway, his rage coiling off him. Every nerve inside me is screaming, but I force myself to be still.

I am caught in a waking nightmare, trapped by my childhood tormentor, who means to put me in a different kind of cage than the one that housed me before. But it would be a cage all the same. I've seen the way he treats his wives, the way he treats his newly named heir no better than a bear trained for party tricks. Everything is a game to him, every person a prize to be hoarded or a token to be sacrificed. It feels inevitable, inescapable. I don't see any way out. Panic rattles through me, and the world goes hazy at the edges.

"You don't need to answer me right away," Kallias is saying calmly. "But an answer I will require, before the end of Winter Dark. The choice is yours—a treaty, sealed by our marriage and a crown for your head. Or death, for you and all your countrymen."

I try to breathe, but my head spins. I collapse and Ballast catches me. For a moment he holds me up, his eye fixed on my face, his fingers warm through my sleeve. The world is right again.

And then Kallias swears and rips Ballast away from me, shoving him hard to the floor. "Keep your hands to yourself, boy!"

Ballast sits there in a heap. He bows his head.

Coward! I want to scream at him. *Coward!* But I'm a coward, too, because I don't go to help him up. My stomach churns and my head wheels and I can't bear it. I can't bear any of this.

Kallias turns back to me with a sickly-sweet smile. "Consider your answer, Astridur." He brushes one hand across my cheek. "Consider carefully."

Then I'm running through the parlor and out into the corridor. I make it only a few steps more before I'm sick all over the stones.

TWENTY-ONE MONTHS AGO

YEAR 4199, Month of the Yellow God
Skaanda

We walk without speaking, heading west, always west, across the snow. It's strange, feeling the sunlight again. I forgot how bright it is, how fiercely hot, even out here on the tundra. I tell myself that's what makes my eyes blur as my feet take me farther and farther from the mountains. I try to push Ballast out of my head, but I can't do it. He's always there, the memory of him pulsing through me like my own heartbeat.

The tension eases out of Saga, bit by bit, as we walk. Her foot is fully healed now and she takes long strides—I nearly have to trot to keep up with her. My legs burn and my breath comes short, but I understand her desire for speed. The day will be brief this close to Gods' Fall; the light won't last very long. We will have to find shelter. Plot our course.

A few hours' walking sees the sun dipping down to the horizon again, and we glimpse a blur of dark in the distance I hope to the gods is a copse of trees. Without discussion, we both break into a jog.

It is indeed a copse of trees, and we reach it as the last of the light fades. I gather wood for a fire while Saga spreads out our blankets and unpacks the last of Ballast's smoked fish. We will have to go hunting tomorrow if we want to fill our bellies again.

I try not to think about Ballast. I can think of nothing else. The taste of his kiss resounds within me, the bright fiery burst of his magic. I want more. I crave it.

"What were you doing?" says Saga, low and tight. "What were you doing with him in the dark?"

The fire leaps high into a night alive with stars. By the twelve gods, I forgot the glory of stars. I take a breath, thinking of the underground river and the bright-blue pebbles, the feel of Ballast's mouth on mine. I don't know why I answer her honestly, but I do. "I kissed him. He kissed me."

She curses, turning her face away so I don't see her tears. "I'm glad you're free of him now," she says in a strangled voice. "Free of his magic, of whatever spell of seduction he used on you."

The fish turns to ash in my belly. "He didn't use his magic on me, Saga."

"Really?" She wheels on me, vicious. "Because that is the only reason I can think of that you would let a murderer, a monster, *Kallias's son*, touch you."

Her jaw works and I feel sick, sick. "I'm sorry, Saga. I didn't mean—"

"Didn't mean *what*? To kiss him? To look at him? To fall in love with him?"

"I'm not in love with him." My heart is beating frantic and wild. I tell it to be still but it doesn't obey me. "I'm not sure I've ever loved anyone besides my sister."

Saga lays her head on my shoulder, and I hold her while she weeps, bitterly, grief in every cell of her.

"I was so afraid," she says, later, when we're both lying on either side of the fire, staring up at multicolored stars. "I was so afraid Kallias would kill me. That I would end lost and forgotten in the glacier sea, reduced to a pile of bones. That I would never see my parents or my brother again. That I would die forgetting I had ever been anything but a girl in a cage."

My chest is tight. "I was afraid of that, too."

We're quiet for a while, listening to the pop of the fire, to the hoot of an owl in the trees. I forgot about things like owls, and I am glad beyond measure to hear its voice.

"I know he saved us," she goes on. "I know he healed me and led us faithfully through the tunnels, and I am—I am grateful. I am. But I wish the gods had sent us a different savior. Because when I looked at him, all I saw was Kallias. All I saw was Hilf dying, over and over and over. I was helpless. Trapped. At his mercy."

"I know," I say.

"I am so glad you are free of him. So glad we never have to see him again."

I don't answer, shutting my eyes and watching him turn a blue pebble over and over in his hands. I see the child version of him, laying out cards on his bed, turning the pages of his beloved Iljaria book. I feel his fingers in my hair, his cheek against mine, his lips hot as fire.

"He was my friend," I tell her softly, longing for her to understand. "Before the tunnels, and—and Hilf—before all that, when we were children, he was my friend. I was a girl alone in a cage, and he was kind to me."

"He grew up to be a monster, just like his father."

My gut wrenches.

"You can't love Kallias's son," says Saga.

"I don't."

She takes a breath. I'm not sure she believes me. I'm not sure I believe me, either.

She says, "Tell me about your sister."

My eyes prick with tears, and I do.

The days run into each other, but not like they did in the caves. Out here the sun rises and sets, the light lasting a little longer every day. The terrain changes constantly, the tundra melting into rolling hills and stretches of seemingly endless plains.

We hunt rabbits and squirrels and, once, a deer. I'm the one who kills and skins and cleans them. Saga can't bear to watch. I don't tell her it makes me sick, that I can hardly force myself to eat the meat, and wouldn't at all if my body didn't demand it.

We are perpetually in motion, which leaves little time for contemplation: eating, walking, hunting, climbing. We cross the Saadone River on an ancient, unmanned ferry—we're north of any of the river towns and their larger ferries, but praise gods this one is serviceable. We are so, so close now, to Staltoria City, and the end of our journey.

One evening, as we feast on roasted wild pheasant and handfuls of purple berries Saga swears up and down aren't poisonous, I stretch out my legs and groan. I ache everywhere, my back and arms and shoulders, but especially my legs. I rub them gingerly while Saga laughs at me from across the fire. Our company has become easier the farther west we've journeyed. I might even say we're friends. As long as we don't talk about Ballast.

I shoot her an irritated look. "Why are you laughing?"

She smiles. "You don't realize what's happening, do you."

I keep rubbing my legs. "What are you talking about?"

"Your pants don't fit, you had what you informed me was your first monthly cycle *ever*—you're welcome, by the way, for explaining that you weren't dying—and it's too warm these days, so you haven't realized, but you can't button your coat anymore."

I blink at her, not comprehending.

"Brynja, you have become a woman," she informs me.

"What?"

Saga holds up her hand and ticks items off her fingers as she talks. "Breasts. Hips. Cycle. And I think you might've grown a couple inches, too, since we left Tenebris. How can you not have noticed?"

I look down at myself and realize Saga is right. The shapeless shirt I pilfered from the laundry so long ago is way too tight around my chest, and my leggings are stretched out so much they're beginning to rip in half a dozen places. And I'm still trying not to think about the fact that I have to suffer a monthly cycle . . . monthly. "But I'm eighteen. I'm too old for this."

Saga shrugs. "You're not trapped in a cage anymore, Brynja, not putting yourself through rigorous training and acrobatic routines. And you're eating properly. Your body finally has room and time and the fuel it needs to develop as it should have years ago."

"Slaying endless cave demons was fairly rigorous," I grumble.

She gives another bark of laughter. "In any case, you've changed so much I'm not sure even Kallias would recognize you." She sobers at the name we seldom speak, and I stare into the fire, trying not to think about the things that will forever haunt us both.

I am glad I'm transforming into a wholly new creature, one who cannot be caged. One who tells herself she is not afraid of the dark, and almost believes it.

We sit in silence for a while after that. The owl calls from his tree, and the wind stirs through the branches. Stars pierce the sky over our heads, blue and gold and green. I haven't worn my headscarf since Ballast tugged it off me, and I like feeling the wind in my short hair, prickling along my scalp, whispering of freedom.

I lie on my back and stare up at the sky. "Are you glad," I ask her, "that our journey is almost over?"

"Everyone thinks I'm dead. I'm not sure of my homecoming."

I think of my own home with a pang, and I shut my eyes, try to picture my sister's face. I can't see her clearly anymore. "They will be overjoyed to have you back with them."

"I hope so. I hope my brother won't resent me for it. He'll be acting heir now, with me gone. I've felt guilty ever since the oracle chose me and not him. He was always meant to be king."

"Tell me about the oracle," I murmur, the owl and the wind lulling me to sleep. "I've never met one."

"You're very strange, Brynja Sindri. Everyone knows the oracle. She lives in a white temple on the top of the hill in the middle of Staltoria City. People go to her for prophecies. For any sort of serious decisions, really. Even my parents. Because it isn't the right of birth that chooses the next ruler of Skaanda. It's the word of the gods. And the oracle is their mouth."

"What's she like?"

"She's . . ." Saga lies back, too, arms behind her head. "Hard to describe. Young but not. Beautiful but . . . not. She has threads of white in her hair and wears a medallion that is—I don't know how to explain it. It's like every color, and no color at all."

I prop myself up on one elbow, staring over at Saga. "She sounds like . . . Saga, she sounds like . . ."

"Like the Prism Goddess," Saga says. "I know."

"A goddess wouldn't live in a temple and answer questions from mortals."

"Perhaps she would. Perhaps she wouldn't."

I digest this information. "You spoke with her?"

"We all did. My parents brought Vil and me up the hill to her temple, past the gates to a garden in an inner courtyard. We sat there, by the pool, and she knelt on a white pillow and turned to look at us. Her eyes, too, were every color, and no color at all. She beckoned Vil and me over to her, and we both went, me shaking all over and him very still. We held out our hands to her, and she dipped both of hers in the water, then grasped Vil and me by our wrists. I felt a searing, awful pain for half a moment, and I cried out. Then the pain was gone, and she released us. She looked me in the eye and said, 'The White Goddess blesses you, you who will rule Skaanda.'"

Saga takes a breath and lifts her right arm into my view so I can once more see the white, eight-pointed star—the mark of the White Goddess.

"I was haughty, for a while," she says, drawing her arm back again. "I thought nothing could touch me, that I could win the war with Daeros, be a hero praised in stories and songs for centuries to come. So I went to battle, with a sword in my hand and triumph on my lips. But I got Njala killed, and Hilf killed, and myself—" She shuts her mouth, turns her head away, and doesn't finish.

I drift to sleep and dream I am back in the mountain again, locked in Kallias's cage. Then I am falling, falling, I smash all to pieces at the bottom of the Sea of Bones. And Kallias laughs.

※

We wake to the ringing of trumpets. Saga sits bolt upright on the opposite side of our dying fire, her eyes bright. "Skaandan war horns," she breathes.

They sound again, sharp and piercing in the cool morning air, accompanied by the dull thud of hooves on soft earth. Saga shouts in happiness, then pulls on her boots and practically tumbles down our hill to the plain.

I rise more slowly, dousing the fire and scattering the ashes. This is my moment, my chance to slip away and no longer be embroiled in the fates of Skaandan royalty.

Perhaps it is because I am weary, or perhaps it is because after all this time I do not wish to be alone, but I don't go. I wait for Saga and her army. And when they come, I swing up onto the horse they give me and I ride with them, dark and swift across the plain, chasing the sun as it climbs the arch of the sky and falls down again toward the horizon.

And in the afternoon of the second day with the army, we arrive, at long last, in Staltoria City.

CHAPTER SIXTEEN

YEAR 4200, Month of the Gray Goddess
Daeros—Tenebris

"I can't do this anymore. We have to move our timeline up."

I sit with Vil, Saga, Pala, and Leifur in my and Saga's room, heat coiling through the vents, a tray of wine and scones untouched on the low table between us.

"Why can't we assassinate the king and hold the mountain until the army comes?" I'm trembling, my head hurting from lack of food, my skin still crawling from Kallias's touch. I try not to think about Ballast, hunched on the floor, about what his father might be doing to him for the sin of touching me.

"We've been over and over this," says Vil in an overly gentle tone, like he's placating a child. "You saw the barracks, Brynja. The five of us can't fight off the entire Daerosian army. We have to stick to our original plan. Wait for *our* army to arrive. Then seize Tenebris from within. We only have to last another six weeks."

"Even if we did try and take Tenebris now, Ballast won't let the mountain go quietly," Saga adds, her jaw tight. "Not now he's been named heir."

"Wouldn't he, though?" I argue. "Wouldn't anything be better than his father on the throne?"

"You think you know him so well," Saga snaps. "But Kallias's blood runs through his veins. He will do everything in his power to hold on to Daeros."

"Ballast has been meeting with the Daerosian governors," Vil adds. "He clearly has his own agenda, and I count him every bit as guilty as his father. He'll be executed along with Kallias, when the time comes."

My stomach drops, and I bite back a curse. "I never agreed to that."

"You agreed to be under my authority," says Vil. "You agreed to trust me."

"*You* promised to keep me safe!" I fairly shriek at him.

"Do you expect Ballast to bow his head and swear fealty to Skaanda?" Saga cuts in.

"Maybe Ballast *should* be allowed to be king," I retort. "Annexing Daeros wouldn't even be necessary if true peace can be struck with Skaanda."

Saga swears. "Why are you *defending* him, Brynja?"

"That was never the plan," says Vil sharply. "And you're forgetting the weapon."

"Right. The weapon." I jerk up from my seat and pace the length of the room, trying to get hold of myself.

Saga's anger roils off her.

"We will hold to our original timeline," says Vil.

"And the marriage pact?" I demand.

Vil goes a little gray. "You have until the end of Winter Dark to give Kallias an answer—that's when the army will come. You don't need to worry about it."

I scrub my eyes. "And must I endure his advances until then?"

"I won't let him touch you."

"He already *has*, Vil!"

"Brynja. Please be calm."

I stare at Vil, and I think that I hate him. He doesn't understand me, and I realize now that he never has. He's just using me for his own purposes, like everyone else. "*You* endure the touch of your tormentor and tell me how easy it is to be *calm*."

I'm up from the table and crawling into the heating vent before anyone can stop me.

"Brynja!" Vil cries. "We're not finished talking! Come down from there. Damn it, Brynja!"

I crawl away as fast as I can, until I can no longer hear him shouting.

※

Ballast is in his new room, the suite meant to belong to the queen Kallias never crowned. I watch him from the ceiling. He sits on his bed, shoulders hunched and shaking. After a while he unties the ribbon that holds his eye patch, lets it fall to the floor. He jerks up, puts his shoulder against a heavy dresser, shoves it against the door that joins his room to his father's.

I take that as my cue to wriggle out of his heating vent and drop down to the floor.

He jumps and curses at my sudden appearance, scrabbling frantically for his eye patch, which he ties back on with nervous haste. For a moment the patch doesn't cover his socket properly, and part of the gaping red wound is visible. Horror knots inside me, not because of his missing eye, but because it so shames him, like he thinks I revile him for it.

He tugs the patch into its proper place then, a shroud over his deep hurt.

I gnaw on my lip. There are cuts on his face that weren't there before my disastrous private dinner with Kallias, and red leaks through the right shoulder of his shirt.

"What are you doing here, Brynja?" He's angry, but he's tired, too; there is pain written in the lines of his face.

My glance flicks to the dresser he pushed against the door. "Does he come in here?" It's an echo of a question I asked Ballast years ago, when we were children. I see recognition flicker in his eye.

"Not often," he says. "We'll hear him in time for you to leave."

I take a step nearer and he stands there, stone-still, watching me. I study him in the yellow glow of the Iljaria lamps, cataloging his differences, straining to reconcile the Ballast from the caves with the Ballast here before me. I want to close the remaining distance between us, want to lift my hand to his face and trace his hurts and sorrows with my fingertips, smooth them all away. But I don't quite dare.

"Why have you allowed your father to snare you so neatly in his web?" I ask him quietly.

He is obdurate as marble, no softness at all in the sharp planes of him. "If you want to catch a spider, sometimes you have to pretend to be a fly. I'd think you, of all people, would understand that."

I flinch. "Your *eye*, Ballast."

Muscles jump in his jaw, and he looks past me. "A necessary sacrifice."

"Like hell it was necessary."

His eye flicks to mine. "Did you think I would languish down in the tunnels forever? You're the one who told me to stay in the light."

"This is not what I meant."

"Then what did you mean?" he says viciously. "What do you want from me, Brynja? Why the hell are you here? You were free of this place, free of him, free of all of it. You should have gone home. What possessed you to come back? WHY DID YOU COME BACK?"

His jaw trembles, and tears spark in his eye. I draw nearer, answering the lodestone pull of him, until there is hardly any space between us at all. Then I do lift my hand and brush one finger gently, gently, over his brow. He shakes and closes his eye.

"You were free," he whispers. "You were free, and now you've put yourself once more at his mercy and I can't think clearly, can't adhere wholly to my purpose because I'm afraid he will hurt you and I can't bear it, Brynja. I can bear everything else but not that."

My heart quavers, and I tilt my forehead against his chest, breathing in the medicinal scent of him, searching for something familiar. His pulse is wild beneath my ear, and his magic crackles around him, power barely contained.

He takes a ragged breath, cups my face with his hands. I look up at him, into his single blue eye. My skin is on fire, and there is no air in my lungs. A muscle jumps in his jaw.

"Brynja," he says.

"Bal," I breathe.

And then his mouth is crushed against mine and his fingers are in my hair and my hands are wrapped around his back, tugging him into me. His magic sears my lips and blazes through my veins but I don't care because I want this, I want *him*, so fiercely I can endure anything. Yet his magic burns and burns, and I am at last forced to pull away from him, gasping.

"I'm sorry," he rasps, realizing. "I'll hold it back. Brynja—"

But I'm thinking a little clearer now, for all it feels as if my heart is going to shatter like glass. I step back, putting a marked distance between us. He respects it, though he trembles where he stands.

"We can't do this," I say past my horribly dry throat.

"Why not?"

I glance at the dresser shoved up against the door, and for a moment we both tense, listening. There is no sound from the other side, but I still don't feel safe. "Because I can't trust you, Ballast. We are at cross purposes, you and I."

He shakes his head. "I don't know why you're here, Brynja. But I am here to right my father's wrongs. To save my country from war and starvation and being called to heel by the Aeronan Empire. You told me I was a good person, down there in the dark. I'm here to prove your faith in me."

"Bal."

He grimaces, pacing to his dressing table and fiddling with a tray of cloak-pins, sharp enough to kill if you drove one in just the right place.

"The only way to do all that is to take my father off his throne and become king in his stead," Ballast goes on. "*That* must be done legitimately, or else the governors would support one of my siblings instead of me, which I can't risk—I don't trust any of them to be better than my father.

"I knew that when I returned to Tenebris, the first thing I would have to do was win back my father's trust. Make him think he still controlled me so that he would name me his heir." His voice goes quiet as he says, "So I gave him my eye."

"Bronze God's *heart*," I swear.

He shrugs off the horror of it, and I want to shake him for treating any part of himself as disposable. He doesn't understand, maybe doesn't even believe, that he has immense value. It breaks my heart. I fight the impulse to forget everything else and pull him close again.

"Now. Are you going to tell me why *you* are here?" He has closed himself off again, gone distant and cold. His earrings glitter in the light of the Iljaria lamps, and he looks every inch his father's heir. I remember that's exactly what he is.

"Skaanda's resources are growing thin," I say. "The treaty is the only way to save her."

Ballast laughs. "What a terrible liar you are. Try again, Brynja."

"We're here to annex Daeros into Skaanda and put Vil on the throne."

He grimaces. "Ah yes. Your Skaandan prince."

"He's not *my* Skaandan prince."

"He thinks he is. What could have given him that idea?"

I glare at Ballast, and he leans against his dressing table, folding his arms across his chest. He glares right back. "Do you really expect me to willingly relinquish my country to my enemy?"

"Then we *are* enemies."

"You're the one here disguised as an ambassador and pretending to work toward peace. I assume Saga's army is coming through the labyrinth as we speak?"

I grit my teeth, and that's his answer.

"Damn it, Brynja."

"What are you going to do?" I demand. "Reveal us? Throw us on your father's mercy?"

"My father has no mercy," Ballast grinds out. "He doesn't know the meaning of the word. And I have no wish to see him dash you to pieces."

"Then ally with me. Ally with *us*. Come and meet with Vil and Saga. We can forge true peace between Daeros and Skaanda, and when our army arrives and we take your father off his throne, I'll convince Vil to back your claim to it."

Ballast scoffs. "He would never agree to that. Your Skaandan prince wants power every bit as much as he wants me dead, or I miss my mark."

I look away, Vil's words burning in my brain: *He'll be executed along with Kallias, when the time comes.*

"What, then?" I say quietly, staring at the floor.

"Ally with *me*."

I glance up again and am caught in the fierceness of his one-eyed gaze.

"I mean to be king of Daeros," he says. "Autonomous. Sovereign. When my father is gone, I will drive Skaanda and Aerona both from my country. Forget about Skaanda. Ally with me."

"You're asking me to betray my country. My friends."

His eye glitters. "I'm asking you to choose me over anything else."

Panic crawls through my veins. "And if I don't? If I can't?"

His face closes. "Then stay out of my way, and don't try and stop me. Or you'll bitterly regret it."

I stare at him, and I shake.

His eye goes wide. He stretches out a hand to me. "Brynja—"

But I'm up and through the heating vent before he has a chance to say anything more. I crawl to safety, away from the royal wing to a hidden hole in a forgotten part of the palace, where no one could ever find me, least of all him.

I fight to get hold of myself, to shake away the lingering sensation of his kiss, to not let his words rattle me. But they do. Because I realize he's changed since the tunnels. I realize he's not who I thought he was.

He sounded exactly like his father just now, and it scares the living hell out of me.

※

There are weeks left yet before the end of Gods' Fall, but I am beyond weary of darkness.

Life in Tenebris takes on a horrible monotony. I long for the same things I always have: light and freedom. It feels like little has changed since the last time I was here—it's only my cage that is bigger. I feel trapped, and I envy Saga, who continues to leave the palace every day to help at the orphan house. Aelia begins to go, too, and the two of them strike up a friendship that makes me even more envious. Vil orders me to stay in Tenebris so I can continue to spy for him, keeping tabs on anyone and everyone who moves within the palace.

I track Kallias's movements, as well as those of his general and his steward. I know if his wives stir from their rooms, and if he ever sends for them. I know what his children do all day: the girls attending to their lessons in their rooms or the library, the boys—with the exception of Ballast—training with the guard. Ballast is in constant meetings with the Daerosian governors, striking bargains with them, making promise after promise in exchange for their support. Every so often he glances up to the ceiling where I crouch, listening, and I know he knows I'm there. I don't dare go and speak with him again. I'm still reeling from our last encounter, and I don't know what the point of it would be. He isn't going to change his goals, and I can't change mine.

I continue to monitor digging progress into the heart of the mountain, and twice more I ask Finnur to craft his stones of healing magic, to make certain that Kallias doesn't reach the weapon before the Skaandan army arrives.

Every few days I sneak down to the cellar, slipping through a secret entrance to the Iljaria tunnels behind a curve of stone that looks like a wall but isn't. Ballast told me and Saga about it, marked it down on his charcoal map—it was how he escaped from Tenebris three years ago. I go there hoping beyond all hope to find the advance scout of the army waiting for me. It's far too soon for that yet, of course, but it doesn't stop me from checking.

In the evenings after dinner—where I do my level best to avoid interacting with either Kallias or Ballast—I make my report to Vil and Saga.

"No change?" says Saga one evening, sitting in her usual place in Vil's receiving room, sipping wine.

I'm too antsy for wine or the cheese and cakes spread out on the low table in front of the couch. I perch on top of Vil's wardrobe, jiggling my knee and wishing I could prevail upon the Violet God to make time move a little faster.

"No change," I confirm. "Finnur's magic should hold until the army arrives."

Vil nods. "Good. And won't you come down from there? You're making me nervous."

I obligingly hop down from the wardrobe, landing lightly on the balls of my feet as Vil turns his questions to Saga, quizzing her on her latest conversation with Aelia at the orphan house, and whether she gleaned anything useful about the Aeronan Empire and *their* plans.

I leave them to it, climbing back up into the vents. I didn't tell them that today was hell, as it always is. I didn't tell them about Kallias's possessive touches and smug smiles at dinner, assuming an answer to his proposal that I have not given him and never will.

I didn't tell them that afterward Ballast attempted to pull me aside, desperate to speak to me, as he has been ever since that night in his room, that I left him without a word.

I didn't tell them that there's to be another performance from Kallias's Collection tomorrow evening, and I'll have to watch, stoic and stupid and dying inside.

I make my way to the great hall, where I leap down into the realm of my nightmares and go to visit the children, emptying my pockets of filched treats, giving all my reassurances to their pale and weary faces.

Last of all, I visit Gulla.

She seems to have shrunk since the last time I was here, hollow and gaunt, though her eyes are bright.

Hello, Brynja, she says in her finger speech.

"Hello, Gulla," I tell her.

I don't have anything to say, really, I just wanted to be with her. Wanted her to know she isn't forgotten.

How is my son? she asks me, her white lashes seeming almost to shine in the pulsing glow of the time-glass on the opposite wall.

I shake my head. "Under Kallias's rule. He claims he wants to save you—to save Daeros, but—"

She sighs and sits with her knees pulled up to her chin. *And you, Brynja?*

"What about me?" I whisper.

She shakes her head, reaches her hand through the bars of her cage, and gently touches my curls. *Are you where you want to be?*

"No."

Why?

I don't know how to answer that. We study each other in the dim light, and I am weary, weary, of all this.

"When the light returns, I'm going to save you," I promise her. "I'm going to kill him, and I'm going to save you."

And after that? What then?

"I don't know," I say quietly.

She gives me a tired smile.

There is nothing left to say, so I just sit with her as the night spins on, as the cold floor numbs every part of me, as Rute watches from her cage, high up at the peak of the ceiling, the ghost of what I was, the ghost of who I am.

CHAPTER SEVENTEEN

YEAR 4200, Month of the Gray Goddess
Daeros—Tenebris

Aelia is having tea with Saga when I return from my morning's scouting, dusty from the vents and hungry for lunch. Both of them look up mildly as I hop down into the room, used to my random appearances. I stretch out my aching back and cramped legs, then join them at the tea table.

"Brynja, you're filthy," says Saga, but makes room for me anyway and hands me a scone. Then she and Aelia go back to conversing about improvements to the orphan house, and how, hopefully, when the treaty is finally signed, some of the war funds can be reallocated there. I listen with only half an ear, trying not to be jealous at their closeness.

Vil bursts into the room not a minute later, his feet bare and hair damp, wearing seemingly little besides a red robe belted tight across his waist—he's clearly come from the middle of his bath.

Aelia's face flushes deeper bronze, but he doesn't have the draw for me he did in Staltoria City. He hasn't in a long while.

"What is it, Vil?" asks Saga.

He takes a breath, and I register the panic in his eyes. "I've been told an ambassadorial party has just arrived from Iljaria."

I stare at him, my heart slamming against my breastbone. "The Iljaria? What are they doing here?"

He shakes his head, grim. "That's not even the worst part. It isn't just any ambassador."

Breathe, I tell myself firmly. *Breathe.*

"It's the Prism Master."

"It still bothers you, doesn't it," says Vil quietly as we pace together down the corridor, a change in the air.

My heart beats, beats. The Iljaria are here. The Prism Master is *here.* Kallias is to formally receive him in the great hall, with all of us present. We barely had time to change, and I'm pretty sure I'm still dusty from the vents.

I have to fight for enough presence of mind to reply to Vil. "What does?"

"Indridi's death. The fact that I was going to take her life, before she took it herself."

Her face blurs in my memory, stained with fire and dust. For a moment it shakes everything else free. I answer him honestly. "It will always bother me, Vil. She was my friend."

He nods unhappily. "I know it's been . . . a lot. What happened on the road. The awfulness of being here again. I haven't been fair to you lately, and I'm sorry. But I haven't forgotten what was forged between us in Skaanda, and I want you to know—I *need* you to know—that *I* need you. I want you by my side, through everything."

I stare at Vil and I feel nothing; I am utterly blank. What I saw in him as protection was his need for control, to have everything in its right and proper place, including me. But that is not what I want, not what I long for, even though I thought it was for a while. Gods above and below, I can't do this. "Not now, Vil. Please."

He takes a breath. "You're right. Forgive me. But we'll talk later?"

I try to smile, but it feels like all of me is fracturing apart.

"This doesn't change anything," Vil goes on, anxious to reassure me. "The Prism Master being here doesn't change our plans."

"How can it not?" I bunch the fabric of my bronze dress in one hand, hating that I'm wearing the colors of the mutilated god. It's better, though, than going to meet the Prism Master wearing the multicolored dress, which was Saga's first idea. She thought it would honor him, but it would be the worst kind of arrogance.

"The Prism Master is here for a reason," I say quietly. "And I think we can both guess what that reason is."

"The weapon," he sighs.

"The weapon."

Vil massages his forehead. "But why now, after all this time? What can he even be planning to do? Unless it's about us. Unless Indridi got word to them somehow before she—" He cuts himself off. "Red God damn me."

Pity and grief twist sharp. "And why wouldn't she have?" I say tightly. "She was the enemy. Isn't that what *you* said?"

"And we're about to meet the man who sent her to spy on us. But why now? It's been hundreds of years since the Iljaria lived in this mountain."

"The Prism Master is hundreds of years old himself, isn't he? The Iljaria can afford to be patient."

"I always forget how long they live. I always forget that they're essentially different creatures than us."

Something vicious and feral rears up inside me. "Was Indridi a different *creature*, Vil?"

He hangs his head and doesn't answer.

I don't want to talk about Indridi anymore, or the Prism Master, either. *Be calm,* I tell myself. *Be still.* I grasp for something else to say. "What do *you* plan to do with the weapon, Vil? When you rule Daeros."

He clenches and unclenches his jaw. "Rule justly. I would never seize Skaanda from Saga—I hope you know that. Daeros would truly be an extension of Skaanda. I would still be under Saga's rule."

"Does that bother you?"

"A little," he admits. "But I would be content, I think, with Daeros."

"The weapon, Vil."

"I would defend the peninsula from the Aeronan Empire."

"Aelia won't like *that*."

"What do I care what Aelia likes?"

"She certainly didn't mind seeing you in your bathrobe."

Vil scowls at me. "I'd keep Skaanda safe, and keep the Iljaria at bay."

"Keep them at bay, or conquer them?"

We walk in silence a few moments, our shoes thudding on cold stone.

"I suppose it depends," he says.

"On what?"

He takes a breath, eyes locking hard on mine. "On what the weapon can do. On how powerful it is."

I have no time to answer; we reach the great hall and step in through the double doors, and it is both a relief and a horror.

Kallias lounges on his ivory throne, which has been centered against the glass wall. All the sky and stars are at his back, as if they, too, are under his control. Ballast stands beside his father, dressed in blue and gray, a gold circlet pressed onto his white-and-black hair. My heart stutters at the sight of him, and I hate that I have not yet taught it to be quiet.

Aelia must have arrived just ahead of us; she's taking her place beside Kallias and Ballast, her white-and-rose skirt pooling on the marble floor like confectioner's cream. Vil and I cross the room in her wake. We bow before the king and Kallias smiles at me, slick and cruel.

"Just in time," he says.

I turn to face the doors as the Iljaria envoys sweep into the hall like great birds of prey. Their leader is jarringly, eerily familiar, and Vil curses under his breath at the sight of him—it's the arrogant young Iljaria man whose company we passed on the road. His hair is still bound in long white braids, crimped at the end with intricately carved metal beads. He wears a shirt of thin silver silk, with loose trousers and jeweled sandals, as though he walks the southern shores of the world, where it's said snow has never once fallen. A jewel bound to his forehead glints every color, and yet none, all at once.

He is the Prism Master, and his magic is even stronger than I remember from our previous encounter. It writhes round him in tangles of violet and orange, silver and green. It twists and twists, never still. He could tell the universe to heel, I think, and it would have to obey him.

Four other Iljaria follow him, different from his companions on the road. They are dressed in green, white, red, and gray, respectively, and like the Prism Master's, their robes are made of thin silk. Jewels are bound to their foreheads, each the color of their robes, their magic, and tattoos swirl up their arms. Their presence and their power suffocate me.

Kallias rises lazily from his throne as the Prism Master and his entourage stop a handful of paces away, but gives no word of greeting.

I bow without meaning to, sinking low, low to the floor, and I realize we all are, even Ballast, even Kallias. Because the Prism Master has compelled us with his magic.

I rise again, trying to think around my anger and the mad pulse of my heart. I am so, so tired, of being controlled.

The Prism Master makes no bow in return, his eyes flicking impassively across all our faces. Surely he remembers Vil and me from the road.

His magic chokes me; I have to fight for breath.

"Welcome to my mountain, High Master," says Kallias. "Welcome to Tenebris." His tone is casual, but I can see the rage in him, and I want to laugh. He is not used to being in someone else's control.

"Tenebris does not belong to you," says the Prism Master. His voice is cool. Dismissive. "It has come to my attention that a truce is being negotiated between Daeros and Skaanda. That concerns Iljaria. I am here to preside over these negotiations."

"We did not ask you to come," says Vil.

The Prism Master's gaze fixes on him. "I never did catch your name, Forsaken one."

Vil grinds his jaw. "I am Vilhjalmur Stjörnu, crown prince of Skaanda. I thought *you* were going to the shrine in the mountains. Since when does anything of actual importance on this peninsula concern the Iljaria, *Prism Master?*"

One side of the Prism Master's mouth turns up. "We do not dirty our hands with your wars, Vilhjalmur Stjörnu, but that does not mean we are not watching." He turns to Kallias. "Is this your welcome of me, little king?"

I think Kallias might implode. He gives the Iljaria man a thin smile. "I met the Prism Master nigh on a decade ago now, here in *my mountain*. You are not him, or you have lost all sense of courtesy since then. Can you change your shape by magic, too, when you grow tired of it?"

A muscle jumps in the Prism Master's face—Kallias has scored a point. "It was my father, Hinrik Eldingar, who you met before."

My mouth goes dry. The Prism Master's oppressive magic is making my head spin.

"And what is your name, sir?" asks Aelia, fearless and angry. "I will give you mine: Aelia Cloelia Naeus, imperial heir of Aerona. I am proceeding over these negotiations on behalf of the empire. Iljaria is not needed here."

He barely looks at her, his gaze fixed on Kallias. "Iljaria goes where Iljaria wishes. You all are so small, your lives so fleeting, like moths, like worms. You forget the whole of this peninsula belongs to the Iljaria. That our ancestors created the world. That your gods still walk among you."

Vil gives a cry of outrage at this flagrant heresy. I grab his arm to keep him from lunging at the Prism Master.

"Are you so far above us, then, that you have no name?"

I glance at Ballast in surprise. He stares down the Prism Master with his one eye, unafraid. I can sense the anger beneath his skin, raging and wild, barely contained.

The Prism Master turns his sharp smile on Ballast. "Do you think to challenge me, half blood?"

"Forgive my son," says Kallias. "I have not yet taught him to respect authority."

My stomach turns over. I'm going to be sick, and *gods* I can't *breathe*.

"We are happy to receive you in Daeros," Kallias goes on. "Allow us to honor you with a feast and ball tonight. Tomorrow, we will revisit the terms of peace between Daeros and Skaanda presided over by Aerona"—he nods at Aelia—"and Iljaria. Witnessed by myself and my heir, Ballast Vallin, as well as Prince Vilhjalmur and Princess Astridur Sindri of Skaanda."

The earth is falling out from beneath my feet. No matter what Vil says, the Iljaria being here utterly ruins his plans. There is still more than a month to go before the end of Gods' Fall and the arrival of the Skaandan army.

"Very well," says the Prism Master. I find his eyes suddenly fixed on me, like he's trying, for a moment, to see straight through my skin. Then his gaze returns to Kallias, and I nearly collapse to the floor with relief. "My name is Brandr Eldingar," he says. "Do not mistake my intentions, Kallias of Daeros. I will attend your dinners and dance your dances, but I am here to reorder the universe according to my will. You will fall in line. Or you will be crushed."

And the Prism Master turns and stalks from the room, the other Iljaria behind him. Their magic lingers on in the air, even when they are gone.

For a moment silence reigns, Vil and I, Aelia, Ballast, and Kallias all brought to the same level.

Then Kallias curses and slams his fist into Ballast's jaw. Ballast falls, his gold circlet knocked loose from his head and clattering on the marble. I grab his hands and pull him to his feet again without thinking. It's a terrible, terrible mistake.

I release him the next second, but Kallias glances between us, a smile on his lips.

Worse, perhaps, is the thundercloud on Vil's brow.

CHAPTER EIGHTEEN

YEAR 4200, Month of the Gray Goddess
Daeros—Tenebris

"Do you think he knows?" says Saga quietly, threading strands of rubies into my hair. My gown is red tonight, the skirt stitched with orange and gold to look like fire.

"Knows what?" My thoughts are scattered, useless.

I catch her gaze in my dressing table mirror. She bites her lip, her eyes red from crying. "About Indridi," she whispers. "She was with us when his company passed us on the road."

My heart wrenches. "I don't know. Maybe."

She finishes with the rubies and sags against the dressing table. I catch her wrist, hold her steady. "It isn't your fault, Saga. *None* of this is your fault."

"I shouldn't have come back here. I shouldn't have gone to battle, thinking I was invincible. If I hadn't, Njala and Hilf and Indridi would still be alive. Vil wouldn't be chasing after some dangerous Iljaria weapon, clamoring to rule *something* since the oracle chose me to rule Skaanda. I shouldn't have—"

"Saga." I turn from my stool, grab her by both shoulders, and look her square in the eyes. "None of this is your fault," I repeat. "*None* of it."

She nods miserably, but I don't think she believes me. She fights tears the whole time she helps me get dressed, but rallies when Vil appears at our door to escort me to dinner.

He's dressed all in white, with black gems in his ears, and he's glittering and beautiful, but I do not want to go with him. He's clearly still furious about earlier, but I don't know if his anger is channeled more at the Prism Master or me.

We talk very little on our way to the dining hall.

"We have to tread carefully," he says. "With the Prism Master here."

He's changed his tune from earlier, but I don't call him on it. I take a breath, fighting to stay calm. "You know we can do nothing against him. He's too powerful."

He nods, jaw tight. "That's why we have to get our hands on that weapon before anyone else does."

"We don't even know what it is. If it was so powerful that the Iljaria buried it—"

"It doesn't matter what it is," says Vil shortly. "Only who wields it."

I gnaw on my lip, unhappy.

"There *is* something between you and the one-eyed prince."

I bristle. "I helped him up, Vil. Is that so severe an offense?"

He doesn't answer.

We reach the dining hall.

※

Kallias has not given the Prism Master the seat of honor. Ballast sits there, the silver powder his attendants have dusted over his cheeks not disguising the rising bruise left by Kallias's fist. He doesn't look up as I'm shown to my place across from him.

The Prism Master—Brandr—sits between Ballast and Aelia, sipping his wine, dark eyes flitting around the room. His gaze catches mine, and he lifts both eyebrows. His magic twists suddenly through me and I gasp at the pain, unable to stop myself. He gives a brief, sharp smile. The magic withdraws. He turns his attention elsewhere.

I'm hardly able to eat any of my dinner, fighting nausea and the sick twist of fear. I'm relieved when the attendants clear the table, when we're ushered back into the great hall for dancing.

Music fills the cavernous space, half a dozen children from Kallias's Collection clustered in the corner, effortlessly playing strings and woodwinds to the insistent rhythm of a pulsing drum. Northern lights dance violet and green beyond the Sea of Bones; I blink at them and yearn for true light, but there is a long while yet before the sun will rise again.

"Dance with me, Princess," says Kallias, suddenly at my shoulder. Before I can protest, he tugs me out into the middle of the floor, where the dancing has already started, couples dipping and twirling to the swelling music.

My body remembers the dances Vil taught me what feels like so long ago, before Indridi died in the dust. But Skaandan dances are not the same as Daerosian ones, and I stumble, tripping over Kallias's feet.

He catches me, both hands on my waist, and I recoil, knocking into another dancer. Kallias just laughs, grabs my wrists, pulls me into the dance again.

"My dear Astridur, you seem far away this evening."

I grimace, scrambling for an appropriate response and coming up empty.

"I wanted to remind you," he says, as he lifts his hand and spins me under his arm, "that you have not yet answered my proposal. The Prism Master's arrival changes things. He will push to have his way, to seal the treaty quickly. My terms are the same: Become my queen, save yourself and your country. Refuse me, and you will all die." He smiles as he says it, like either outcome would give him immense pleasure.

"You think you can best the Prism Master?" I say quietly. "He's the most powerful man in the world."

Kallias shrugs. "Not for much longer. Answer me soon. Before your time is up. And, Astridur." Danger sparks in his eyes. "I do hope that your little display earlier means nothing. It would not take much for Ballast to fall back out of grace. I have other sons, you know. I can choose a new heir."

He leaves me reeling in the midst of the dancers. I hardly have a moment to breathe before magic writhes along my skin and I turn to find the Prism Master standing there. He holds out his hand.

I take it.

We dance. There is a roaring in my ears, blocking out music and light and air, everything but the mad beat of my heart.

The Prism Master whirls us to the outskirts of the dancers, a pace away from the glass wall.

"I am surprised to find a Skaandan princess here," he says. "Especially one I didn't know existed."

I can't quite meet his eyes, can't quite comprehend the shape of him or his wild, teeming power.

I answer his question with one of my own. "I am surprised to find the renowned Prism Master is little more than a boy."

His jaw tightens. "My father is dead. His power passed to me."

I gulp air.

His eyes glint as he turns me under his arm. "How close is Kallias to the heart of the mountain?"

We both cease the pretense of the dance in the same moment, sizing each other up in the eerie glow of the northern lights. I want to lie to him, but I haven't forgotten the probing pain of his magic. "Close," I say. "He will reach it before the end of Gods' Fall."

He smirks at me. "Why are the Skaandans here?"

"To overthrow Kallias and seize Tenebris for themselves." I speak quietly, for fear of being overheard.

"And you have signed your name to this mad plot?"

"I mean to kill him."

He frowns, perhaps disapproving of my murderous Skaandan impulses. "Take care, Princess. The Iljaria—"

"Would you care to dance with me, Your Highness?" comes a quiet voice just behind me.

It's Ballast, his ribbon and eye patch scarlet, bright as blood against his dark-and-light hair. "If you are not otherwise engaged," he says.

The Prism Master is a cool pillar of rage. He regards Ballast as if he were a worm, easily squashed underfoot. He stalks away without another word.

I meet Ballast's eye, trying not to look at the bruise on his face, which has deepened in color since dinner. "You looked agitated," he says. "I thought I'd come and rescue you."

My blood boils. "I don't *need* to be *rescued*, Ballast!"

His brows draw together. "We all need to be rescued sometimes. Even you, I think." He holds out one hand. "But will you? Dance with me?"

Despite Kallias's threat, I take his hand, let him lead me back onto the dance floor. He's clumsy, with just his one eye. Sweat beads on his brow. For a few moments he doesn't speak, concentrating on the dance steps.

He smells of herbs and our dinner wine, and his hands are warm about my waist. Despite everything, I want to melt into him. My heart feels easier with him near.

"I frightened you before," he says then, quietly. "I'm sorry. I don't want you to think that I am like him."

"I know you're not," I whisper.

"I don't know how to keep you safe." His voice breaks. He lifts one hand to tuck a stray curl behind my ear. "I want to keep you safe."

Tears blur my vision, and I tell him my wretched truth: "I don't know who I'm supposed to be loyal to."

He smooths his thumb across my cheek. "Be loyal to me. We'll pool our cards together. We'll win this game of War."

"But the Ghost God card is yet to be played," I remind him. "We could still lose everything."

His eye is bright. "I'm willing to take that risk. Are you?"

A hand on my shoulder pulls me away from Ballast, and I turn to find Vil there, his face creased with anger.

"Leave her alone," Vil says to Ballast, low and cold.

Ballast offers Vil a dangerous smile. "I don't answer to you." He flicks his glance back to me. "Astridur," he says. Then he slips away without another word.

I wheel on Vil. "What do you think you're doing?"

"What do you think *you're* doing?" he retorts. "Why do you let him touch you?"

I shove Vil away from me and leave the great hall, rage writhing in my very bones.

He comes after me, hard on my heels in the corridor until finally I turn to face him.

The tears in his eyes freeze me where I stand.

"I hate all this," he says, his voice breaking. "I wish it was over. I wish we could strike today. I wish—" He takes my hand and smooths his thumb over my skin, and I let him, wrecked by his tears. "I am ready to rule Tenebris, Brynja. And I want you to stay. I want you to rule it with me. I want you to be my queen."

"Vil—"

"You don't have to answer me right now. But please. *Please.* I want it to be you. It has to be you."

I blink at him in the cold stone corridor, uneasy at the eerie echo of Kallias's offer. What am I, to Kallias, to Vil? Do they truly want me? Or do they want only to possess me? Kallias with his twisted games, Vil with his desire for power. And what about Ballast? *It's a risk I'm willing to take.*

"I'm tired, Vil." My voice shakes. "I'll see you tomorrow." I turn to go.

But he catches my wrist. Pulls me back. Raises my hand to his lips. "I'm in love with you, Brynja."

All of me is numb, sick. And I look past Vil to see Ballast in the corridor.

"Brynja?" says Vil.

"You can't call me that outside our rooms," I remind him shortly. "Someone might hear."

Hurt tightens his face.

I leave him standing alone in the hall.

Brandr sits near the head of the table in the council room, magic curling off him like smoke. This morning he wears a robe made of thin white silk, embroidered with a brilliant sapphire thread that glistens in the lamplight, and his sleeves are rolled up past his elbows. Tattoos swirl all along the length of his forearms, in all the colors of the gods. He catches me staring at them and I jerk my gaze quickly away.

I slept badly last night, and my head is already starting to pound. Vil hasn't looked at me once all morning, not even on the long walk from our rooms. I can't blame him. But I also can't give him the answer he wants. I don't know if I'm sick over that, or the fact that Ballast overheard Vil's confession.

Kallias sits in his ivory chair with his head leaned back and his eyes shut. Aelia is next to Brandr, looking particularly fierce dressed in gold. Zopyros, Theron, and Alcaeus are all here, stealing terrified glances at the Prism Master. The Daerosian governors sit across from them, next to General Eirenaios. Kallias's steward and engineer are not here, the former frantically arranging things for the feast and ball this evening, the latter checking on the digging progress.

Ballast is the last to arrive, his face in worse shape than last night, which makes my gut twist. His eye patch and ribbon are gray. He takes the seat on Kallias's left.

Brandr wastes no time taking charge of the proceedings. He stands and snaps his fingers; the room is suddenly, wholly silent, when I hadn't realized it was overloud before.

"Show me the proposed terms," Brandr says.

Kallias doesn't open his eyes, so it's Ballast who hands over the Daerosian documents, while Vil offers the Skaandan ones.

Brandr glances briefly over the pages, then drops them on the table. "You quibble over such insignificant things. The border towns will go to Daeros."

"They will *not!*" says Vil.

Brandr ignores him. "The river city to Skaanda."

"Absolutely not," puts in Ballast.

But Brandr isn't finished. "Hostilities will cease, and both armies will be cut in half. Trade will be established, resources exchanged at no cost to either country. Both Skaanda and Daeros will pay tribute to Iljaria."

"On what grounds?" demands Ballast at the same time Vil jerks up from his seat and starts swearing up and down the pantheon with vehemence.

"Our grounds," says Brandr. "This entire peninsula belongs to the Iljaria; it is only on our goodwill that you are allowed to remain upon it."

"What are you going to do if we refuse?" Vil mocks him. "Rally Iljaria to war?"

Brandr looks at him with absolute impassivity. "There are other ways than war to bring down a mountain. You forget how old we are. How patient we are. But even the patience of the Iljaria must come, at last, to an end."

"*You* forget Aerona," says Aelia coolly. "There is another who would lay claim to the peninsula. My father—"

"Your father does not concern me."

Her lips thin. "His armies ought to. They will be here by summer."

"That was *not* in Daeros's accord with Aerona!" cries Ballast. "There is no justification for the imperial army to land here."

Aelia's gaze flicks to Ballast. "My father has long been unhappy with the governing of Daeros, and the wastefulness of the war with Skaanda. Aerona comes to set it right."

"Invade, you mean. Expand the empire. Don't mince words with me, Your Imperial Highness."

"Aerona is inconsequential," says Brandr. "We are getting off course."

"Imperial occupation is not inconsequential!" Vil objects.

"This whole time," whines Kallias, finally opening his eyes, "no one has said *anything* about the marriage clause."

We all turn to look at him, bile acrid in my throat.

"What marriage clause?" says Aelia, wearily.

Kallias smiles, tipping his chair back on two legs and playing with his wineglass, pleased to have everyone's attention. "Princess Astridur is to be my queen, sealing the treaty between our nations and putting a permanent end to the war."

Brandr laughs. Aelia frowns. Ballast's eye bores into my face, and Vil squeezes my wrist so hard it hurts.

"You forget, Your Majesty," I say through gritted teeth, "that I have not accepted your proposal."

Kallias yawns and sets his chair back down on the floor with a *thump*. "And *you* forget, Your Highness, exactly what is at stake."

Brandr waves a dismissive hand. "None of that matters," he says impatiently. He turns to fix Kallias with the full weight of his stare. "There is something, however, that you have conveniently left off the proposed terms."

Kallias's lips thin. "And what is that, High Master?"

"The Iljaria weapon in the heart of the mountain that you are close to reaching."

Everyone in the room goes suddenly, painfully, still. Vil's squeezing my wrist again and Aelia looks grim and Ballast's face is tight and my vision is going white at the edges.

"If your people didn't want it," says Kallias, his voice low and deadly, "you shouldn't have left it here."

Brandr smiles, the pitying, demeaning smile one gives to a foolish child. "When you breach the weapon, all of us will be there—Daeros, Skaanda, Iljaria . . ." He flicks his eyes to Aelia and adds with disgust, "Aerona. We will decide all together what is to be done with it."

"And if I refuse to agree to this?"

Magic licks all up and down Brandr's arms, and I shudder. "Then you will see, little king, Iljaria's other way to bring down a mountain. This council is over."

Without another word, the Prism Master stalks from the room, leaving absolute chaos to erupt in his wake.

CHAPTER NINETEEN

YEAR 4200, Month of the Ghost God
Daeros—Tenebris

It feels like a storm is looming, like the very earth under our feet groans and shifts, readying for irrevocable change.

The Prism Master keeps mostly to himself and his rooms, but every morning he saunters into Kallias's private receiving chamber with his quartet of Iljaria behind him and demands a progress report from Kallias and Basileious, his engineer. I know because I'm always crouched above the ceiling, watching.

"Closer," says Basileious every day. "Soon. But not yet."

And then the Prism Master leaves again.

Skaanda and Daeros sign the peace treaty in the great hall, all the palace watching: Kallias and Ballast first, me and Vil after. Aelia looks on, cold and angry in her fur-lined gown. Brandr signs, too, accepting the pledge of tribute from both nations. Kallias doesn't seem to care about the treaty whatsoever, but Ballast sparks with rage, and Vil seethes with it.

"It isn't real," Saga and I have told him, over and over. "It means nothing."

But *does* it mean nothing now, with Brandr's name affixed to it in a flourish of silver ink?

Kallias makes his Collection perform to celebrate the signing.

I force myself to sit in the semicircle of chairs, nails digging into my legs through the velvet skirt of my green gown. Ballast slouches in his chair, eye studiously trained on his hands, clenched tight together in his lap. Aelia makes no apologies and leaves entirely. Vil jiggles his knee beside me.

The scenes of my worst nightmares play out before my eyes, and when, *when*, will all this be over?

The Prism Master seems largely unimpressed with any of the children, the only exception being Finnur. Tonight Finnur weaves a sky of stars into being, then plucks the stars down and presents them to the audience as glittering jewels, solid and real in the palm of his hand. He hands one to Brandr, who inclines his head to the boy and turns the jewel over and over in his fingers. Finnur gives one to me, too, and it takes everything in me to keep myself from snatching his arm and pulling him out of this horrible room.

Rute, my acrobatic ghost, performs last. I have to shut my eyes and tell myself a story in order to bear it. When I open them again, Kallias is tugging Ballast from his seat and nudging him to the front of the room.

"Do a trick for us, boy!" Kallias crows.

Ballast is hard and blank before him, and says very low: "I am not one of your pets, Father."

Kallias laughs at him. "Of course you are. Amaze us! That's an order."

Ballast's throat works, and suddenly, awfully, I find his one blue eye fixed on mine.

I feel the magic before I hear it or see it. It hums and breathes and lives. And then the room is filled with moths, whispering and white. They swarm around me, shaping themselves into a living gown, drawing me from my seat and spinning me around on the marble floor. For a moment I'm caught up in the wonder of it all, borne along on their fast-flickering wings.

Then a crack of jarring, awful magic blisters the air, and the moths fall dead at my feet.

Horror twists through me and I turn back. Brandr stands, clothed in fury and power, magic sparking off every part of him. He is the one, I realize, who killed the moths.

"I am not interested in parlor tricks," Brandr says, coldly, to Kallias. "Collar your pets, little king. Inform me the moment you breach the weapon. I have no need of your continued presence until then." He strides from the hall, the other Iljaria at his heels.

Kallias wheels on Ballast but doesn't strike him, not in front of the whole court. "Clean up this mess," he snarls.

Then he's gone, too.

Everyone else starts quietly filing out as well, and Vil grabs my wrist to tug me with him. But I shake him off. So he leaves without me.

Ballast kneels in the ruin of the moths, his head bowed. I kneel with him.

"How soon, do you think?" he says quietly. Until the weapon is uncovered, he means. Until all this is over. He knows that I know.

"Soon," I say.

I cradle one of the moths in my hand, marveling at the tiny silver beauty of it. I blink and it turns to dust.

"You should go." He doesn't look at me. "I can't afford for my father to be any angrier with me than he already is."

I let the dust slip between my fingers. I go.

The advance scout is waiting for me in the hidden cellar tunnel. She's young, no older than Leifur, and her black hair is braided tight against her scalp. She introduces herself as Aisa.

"How far is the army behind you?" I ask her, fighting to keep my voice low.

"At least a week," she says apologetically. "They're moving as quickly as they can."

I nod, trying to get hold of myself. "I'll report to Vil and sneak food down to you later."

"No need, I'm well prepared." Aisa thumps her pack. "I'll await His Highness's instructions."

I thank her and slip back upstairs.

"A week," says Vil, pacing the length of my and Saga's room. "A *week*."

"Can we last another week?" says Saga, perched on the couch, all restless, nervous energy. "What if Kallias reaches the weapon before the army arrives?"

"I can ask Finnur to make more magic to seal up the vein," I say.

"It's too risky with the Prism Master here," Vil returns. "You could be caught. We'll just have to strike early, if the weapon is breached too soon. We'll have to hold the mountain until the army comes."

"You said before that that was impossible," I point out.

Vil flicks his eyes to mine, his jaw hard.

I try not to squirm with the guilt of still not having even acknowledged his confession. *I want you to be my queen. I'm in love with you, Brynja.*

"If we don't, we'll lose any control we could have hoped to have—either to Daeros or, gods forbid, Iljaria."

"But we can't *do* anything against the Prism Master," says Saga. "No one can. And if we're all there when Kallias uncovers the weapon, the Prism Master will be the one to seize it."

I shake my head. "Kallias has a plan. I overheard him discussing it with his engineer," I tell them.

Vil still doesn't like it. "It's a risk."

"It's all a risk, Vil," I retort. "But if we're to strike at all, it has to be then. It will be our only chance."

"I want to be there," puts in Saga, pulling her knees up to her chin. "I want to be there when the weapon is found, when the fates of all our nations are decided. It won't matter if Kallias recognizes me after we've captured him. I'll keep my head down until then."

Vil's jaw goes tight, but he doesn't argue with her.

"So," I say. "If the army comes before the weapon is breached, we strike then."

"And if the weapon is breached first," says Saga, "we strike *then*. Can we count on Aelia's support, do you think?"

I nod. "At least until summer, when the emperor sends his army."

"By then we'll have a means to defend ourselves," Vil says.

"Are you so confident you'll be able to wield the Iljaria weapon?" I ask him.

"I know you have no faith in me, Brynja, but I wish you'd believe me the slightest bit capable."

Something ugly twists inside my belly, and I'm ready to be done with the conversation. I don't answer him.

He leaves a moment later, and Saga glowers at me over her tea. "You should be kinder to him, Bryn."

Tears bite at my eyes, and I stalk over to the window, staring out at blurring stars.

She sets her tea down and follows me. "He cares for you a great deal."

My throat works. "He told me he's in love with me. He wants me to stay with him in Tenebris as his queen."

"And what did you tell him?" Her tone is carefully neutral.

"Nothing."

"Brynja."

I turn from the window, a whorl of anger and grief. "I'm tired of being in the dark, Saga. I'm so tired of the dark. This mountain has taken half my life from me. I can't stay here. I can't. And I don't—I don't *feel* those things for Vil. I don't think I ever will." I realize it's true, down to my very bones, and I can't even quite regret it.

Saga's eyes go soft and angry all at once. "But you feel those things for Ballast."

I see him kneeling in a pile of dead moths, and my heart twists. "I am weary of kings and princes, Saga. I am weary of all this."

She presses her lips into a thin, hard line. "Don't leave Vil in his misery. Tell him the truth."

I swallow past the lump in my throat. "Do you hate me?"

"I don't hate you, Bryn. I understand about the mountain. You've been here too long, experienced too many terrible things. I get it. But I *don't* understand about Vil. And I'm trying very hard not to be angry with you about it."

"I'm sorry." My voice breaks. "Saga, I'm so sorry."

She just shakes her head. "Don't tell me. Tell Vil. I'm going to take a bath." She steps past me and slips into the bathing chamber. I scramble up into the ceiling, curl into a tight ball, and let myself cry.

※

Ballast is asleep when I slip down into his room. I light a candle and he wakes instantly, jerking up in bed and scrambling for the eye patch on his bedside table. He ties it on quickly, but not before I glimpse the raw red emptiness of his eye socket.

He sits there on the edge of his bed, breathing quick, and I realize with a twist of horror that he thought I was his father.

I glance to the door that joins their rooms and gnaw on my lip. "I'm sorry," I whisper. "I didn't know when else to speak with you."

He shakes his head. "You startled me, is all." His voice is rough with sleep.

"I wanted to tell you—" I pause, take a breath. Vil and Saga would kill me if they knew I was here, ready to spill their secrets. But Ballast knows most of them already.

He looks at me steadily, waiting for me to go on.

"The Skaandans will strike soon. The army is almost here."

"You mean to seize the mountain, depose my father, put your prince on the throne instead."

"He's not my prince."

Ballast shrugs. "Do you think the Prism Master will allow that?"

"There's the weapon."

"Yes. The weapon." He gets off the bed and paces to the window that looks out over the Sea of Bones. I follow. The stars are quiet tonight, like they're waiting, too.

Ballast turns to me. "What *is* the weapon, Brynja?"

I'm hyperaware of my pulse, thudding through the whole of my being. "I don't know."

His lips thin. "Why are you here? Why are you telling me this?"

"Because—because I'm worried about you."

He laughs and folds his arms across his chest. "You're such a liar."

"I'm not lying. Your father will be executed, Ballast. And Vil says that—"

"That the same fate awaits me? No. I told you before that I will not allow the Skaandans to take Daeros. *I* will depose my father and rule in his stead. And the Skaandans will get the hell out of my country. Will you go with them, Brynja? Or will you lay all your cards on the table now, and join them with mine?"

I square my jaw. "My loyalty is with Vil and Saga. It has to be."

"Why? What right does Skaanda have to Daeros?"

"What loyalty do *you* have to Daeros?" I retort.

"Do you think because I'm a half blood that I don't belong anywhere? That I have no right to carve out a place for myself?"

"Of course not."

"Then what right do you have to ask me what loyalty *I* have to my own damn country?" He's breathing hard, magic sparking off his skin, cerulean and pink.

Anger twists through me. "What are you *doing* then, Ballast? What are you waiting for? For your father to hurt your mother more or to lock more children in cages? For him to get his hands on a godsdamned Iljaria weapon and burn all the world to ashes?"

"Then you *do* know what the weapon is!" he cries.

We stare at each other, my heart wild and my face hot. "It's power," I say. "Unimaginable, uncontainable power. That's all I know, I swear."

He scoffs at me. "*Is* that all you know, Brynja? Is it?"

I fight to breathe, and I wish to the gods I hadn't come here tonight. This was a mistake. "It's all I know," I say quietly.

He clenches his jaw. "You don't need to worry about me. You just need to worry about staying out of my way. And you can tell that to your precious Skaandan prince, too."

"He's not my prince."

Ballast laughs. "I don't care."

I leave him without another word, leaping up into the vents and crawling back to my room, where I slip into bed beside a soundly sleeping Saga. I lie there a long while, staring up into the dark and reviling myself to the depth of my bones.

I'm still awake when Vil bursts in, his clothes obviously pulled on in haste, rumpled and askew. I jerk up and shake Saga awake in the same moment.

"The weapon?" I ask.

Vil nods. "It's time. We've all been summoned. Get dressed as quick as you can."

He turns his back to us as we scramble into our clothes and wrap ourselves with furs against the mountain's chill.

I make sure to wear my headdress.

The one with the hidden knife.

CHAPTER TWENTY

YEAR 4200, Month of the Ghost God
Daeros—Tenebris

We walk side by side, me and Saga and Vil, with Leifur and Pala at our heels. My heart beats triple time to our quick footsteps, and I pull my fur-lined cloak tight around my shoulders.

"Together," says Vil quietly, looking straight ahead. "We're in this together, right?"

"Together," says Saga. "For the glory of Skaanda."

I take a breath of icy air. "Together."

A male attendant and Nicanor, Kallias's steward, are waiting for us as we leave the guest wing. Nicanor inclines his head to me and Vil, not even glancing at Saga, who ducks her head in sudden terror. "You're to surrender all weapons, Your Highnesses," he says. "And then follow me."

Vil grunts but unbuckles his sword belt and pulls three knives from his boots and hands them to the attendant. I know he has at least one more knife strapped against his chest. Saga relinquishes her dagger with shaking hands, and Leifur and Pala relieve themselves of spear, sword, and more knives than seem possible for any two people to carry at once. I hand over my dagger, praying that Nicanor won't suspect my headdress. But he nods in satisfaction.

"This way," he says. "The king is waiting."

He grabs a torch from the wall, leading us down several corridors to a heavily barred door. Eirenaios, Kallias's general, unlocks it for us, but not before demanding Vil's hidden knife and relieving Pala and Leifur of several more. I'm allowed to keep my headdress.

Nicanor and Eirenaios lead us through the door and down a winding stone stairway. We follow in single file, our footsteps echoing on the cold stone, the torch casting eerie shadows on the rough-hewn walls. My heart beats too hard and fear claws up my throat and it's time, it's time. This will all be over soon.

We go down and down, and the cold grows deeper. Saga's teeth begin to chatter. Vil shrugs out of his cloak and gives it to her.

We reach a landing of chiseled stone, illuminated with globes of pulsing Iljaria magic.

Kallias stands here with his engineer, Basileious, as well as Ballast, Aelia, the Prism Master, and a half dozen Daerosian guards in steel helms.

I sense Vil stiffen, because we didn't count on quite this many soldiers. His eyes flick to mine and I nod. We can still go forward with our plan.

"Welcome," says Kallias, flashing his teeth at me and not even glancing at Saga or Vil. "Now. Before we go any further, I must ask the Prism Master to surrender his magic, for a little while, so we are all on even ground when the weapon is uncovered."

Brandr throws his head back and laughs, the stone around us glowing suddenly red. Heat sears through my furs, and I fight to breathe.

Kallias looks at Brandr mildly. "I do not trust you, High Master. There is nothing to keep you from obliterating us all, seizing the weapon, and melting the earth like so much candle wax. I must insist on this, or I will take you no further." He snaps his fingers, and Basileious lifts an iron collar into view.

"Star metal," says Kallias. "It will dampen your power while you are wearing it, but have no lasting effects."

Brandr's gaze darts around the chamber, landing, for a moment, on mine, before returning to the king. "You forget, Your Majesty, that *I* do not trust *you*."

Kallias nods and takes the collar from Basileious. Without any warning, he snaps it around Ballast's neck. Ballast curses and jerks away from his father, but it's too late. The collar is secure.

"Come here, boy," says Kallias, and to my horror Ballast obeys. His eye patch and ribbon are violet, turned to liquid darkness in the pulsing blue light.

The king draws a tiny jar of honey from his robe and, after opening it, smears a little on Ballast's cheek. He takes out another jar, and my gut wrenches at the sight of the buzzing wasp inside. Kallias lets the insect out, and it goes at once to the honey.

"Can you keep it from stinging you?" says Kallias. "I wonder."

Ballast closes his eyes, his lips moving quickly. But no magic sparks off him.

Kallias waves his hand to agitate the wasp, and Ballast winces as it stings him. His father laughs and flicks the insect to the floor, grinding it under his heel.

"And *why*," says Brandr coolly, "would I submit myself to that?"

Kallias faces him. "Because you are the Prism Master. Surely a mere bit of iron can't make you as powerless as our little half blood here."

Ballast's jaw is tight, and a welt is already rising on his cheek where the wasp stung him, and it's all I can do to keep from slamming Kallias to the ground and ripping out his wretched throat.

"Fine," says Brandr. "I will play your game, little king. When I tire of it, I will kill you."

"How very un-Iljaria of you," Kallias drawls.

Basileious takes out a second collar and steps up to Brandr, who ducks his head and allows the engineer to lock it around his neck with violently trembling hands.

I watch the magic flicker out from Brandr's skin. He seems suddenly frail, as if the barest wind could rattle him apart. But when he speaks, his voice is steady. "Lead on then, little king."

Kallias smiles. He takes the torch from Nicanor and ducks into the tunnel opposite the landing.

We all follow. I find myself walking between Ballast and Saga, and I'm thrown back to those long weeks we journeyed together through the Iljaria labyrinth.

Ahead of me, Ballast breathes ragged and quick, obviously in pain, and it wrecks me.

The tunnel narrows until it's barely wider than my ceiling vents, and I have to duck my head. The sudden taste of magic hits me like a gale force wind, so much stronger than on any of my solo visits. I gasp and stumble, and Ballast turns to grab my arm, steadies me. "All right?" he asks, his eye meeting mine. I read regret there. Grief.

"I'm all right," I whisper. It's a lie.

We keep going.

The tunnel presses in around us, glinting blue and green and silver. It tastes cold and strange and powerful on my tongue, and I struggle to keep up with everyone else.

Finally, the tunnel opens again, and we step into a natural cavern in the rock.

There's hardly time to catch my breath before Kallias is beside me, folding his hand around mine. His eyes glitter as he smiles at me. "There is still time, Princess Astridur, to give me the answer I have been waiting for."

"You are wrong, Your Majesty." I can hardly speak around my tight throat. "We are out of time."

He just grins and pulls me with him into the next tunnel.

We walk straight for a while, past other tunnels that branch out from the main passage. There are marks left by drilling and explosives, the rock scarred, cracked, broken. But the tunnel doesn't collapse above our heads.

From there we wind down again, deeper and deeper. Weird veins of light flicker through the rock, red and green and yellow. The taste of magic grows so strong I can hardly bear it.

Then, all at once, Kallias pulls me to a stop.

We've come into the chamber that is so familiar to me—it takes a great effort of willpower not to glance over at my hiding place in the rock crevice. Kallias smiles and lifts our joined hands to touch the vein in the wall.

I screech and leap back—the vein is scorching hot, lines of blue and silver splintering outward from where our hands touched it.

I am hyperaware of the beat of my own heart, the magic pressing in and in, like it wants to eat me alive.

Basileious, the engineer, steps up to Kallias and hands him a pickaxe that shimmers the same blue and silver as the wall. It must be made of pure Iljaria magic, and I wonder why his workers never used it before, or if it is something he forced Finnur to make for him only recently. That seems the most likely, and I'm thankful it didn't occur to Kallias earlier.

Kallias lets go of me to grip the pickaxe with both of his hands. He turns to address everyone in the chamber, the mingled people of four nations. "Today you witness history," he cries, his voice bouncing about the walls of the cavern. "Today I uncover the power at the heart of the mountain and claim it for Daeros. Today you will crown a man among gods."

"That was not our agreement," says Aelia hotly. "We were to all decide together what is to be done with the weapon."

Kallias just laughs and snaps his fingers, and the Daerosian guards draw their swords, pressing them against everyone's throat but mine, Ballast's, and Brandr's. They are bound in iron, and I am, evidently, not considered a threat.

I take a quiet step back, my fingers quickly releasing the knife from my headdress. I hold it tight in my palm and fight to remain as solid and certain as the blade.

Kallias raises the pickaxe. "For Daeros!" he cries. "For its rule immortal and its power unending!"

He swings the axe and strikes the wall, the shock wave resounding through the chamber. The rock cracks but does not break.

"For Daeros!" he shouts.

He swings the axe again and again, and with every blow, the crack widens.

"FOR DAEROS!"

The rock shatters, magic spilling into the air like blood. Pebbles skitter across the floor, and beyond the opening in the wall, I glimpse what appears to be a huge cube of ice, or stone, bound with chains that trail off into darkness. Kallias sets down the axe, radiating triumph.

But this has gone on too long. I glance at Vil, who gives me a sharp nod.

I slip up next to the king. "I am ready to give you my answer," I say, forcing sweetness into my tone.

Kallias grins like a cat and slides his arm around my waist. "At last you see sense." He bends his head to kiss my neck like he owns me.

That's when my blade finds his throat, pressing hard enough to draw blood.

He curses and tries to back away from me, his blue eyes round with shock. But I pin him up against the wall. Magic pulses behind his shoulders, and the whole cavern echoes eerily, a strange golden music whispering through the air. I blink and see yellow, yellow.

No one else seems to hear or see it. I fight to stay present, my knife biting into Kallias's throat, blood sliding red down his neck. It is strange, to be the one wielding power over him. I feel strong. Free. But my hand trembles.

"Let the Skaandans and Princess Aelia go," I order the Daerosian soldiers. "Or your king dies."

The soldiers withdraw their swords and step back.

Saga and Vil come forward, Vil taking a sword from one of the guards, Saga throwing back her hood to reveal herself. Her ears are heavy with rubies, her hair pulled tight against her scalp and bound in gold.

She stares Kallias down. "I am Saga Stjörnu, daughter of Valdis and heir to Skaanda." Her voice rings sharp and clear. "By my own name, by the nature of your crimes, and by the power of Skaanda, I claim this mountain—and your life."

My heart is stuttering in my chest, my palms sweating despite the frigid air. The magic around me teems and burns, burns, down into my soul.

Vil raises his eyebrows at me, ready for me to turn Kallias over to him—we are to hold the king hostage until the Skaandan army arrives, with Brandr conveniently bound in iron.

I grab Kallias by the arm and haul him away from the wall, my knife still digging into his neck.

But I don't take the king to Vil.

I step past Vil, bring Kallias to the Prism Master. In one swift moment, I unlock the collar from Brandr's neck and release Kallias into his arms.

The Prism Master smiles at me.

"What are you doing?"

Saga's question echoes in the air as the Daerosian guards pull back their hoods, their magically assumed forms melting away to reveal their true selves: Iljaria, white hair bright against their dark or light skin.

"Correction," says Brandr, putting his own knife to Kallias's throat. "The *Iljaria* reclaim the mountain that is rightfully theirs. Skaanda will stand down."

"Skaanda will *not!*" Vil cries. He lunges toward Brandr, sword outstretched, but the cool steel of my blade, pricking sharp beneath his jaw, draws him up short.

One of the Iljaria catches Saga as she bellows an outraged curse and charges at us. Another pair of Iljaria subdue Pala and Leifur. Kallias's general, engineer, and steward are seized in short order, leaving only Ballast and Aelia standing free.

"Brynja," says Vil slowly, careful around the point of my knife, "what are you doing?"

My eyes flick once toward Brandr. "My brother already told you. The Iljaria are reclaiming our mountain."

TWO YEARS AGO

YEAR 4199, Month of the Yellow God
Skaanda—Staltoria City—the royal palace

The palace suffocates me. It shouldn't. It is the opposite of Kallias's mountain: airy and light, filled with plants and color and music. It's built of white sandstone and decorated with carved marble columns. There are huge domed ceilings, laughing fountains, interior courtyards bursting with orange trees. It is life, where Kallias's mountain was death.

Saga has given me the room that adjoins hers, and I have everything I could ever wish for, even the use of her handmaiden, Indridi, who helps wrangle my disastrous, half-grown-back hair into a vaguely presentable state.

Saga's family is impossibly kind to me, especially her brother, Vil. I find myself looking for him wherever we go and have not quite grown used to the quickening pulse of my heart when his eyes meet mine. Saga is thrilled to be home, but my restlessness doesn't escape her.

"We have to find your family, Brynja," she says, when we've been in the palace for a week. "Where are they? Do they live in the city? What is the address?"

So I take her there, dread knotting in my belly, Indridi and a pair of guards accompanying us. We walk the cobbled streets of Staltoria City, the sun warm on our faces. Birds sing in our ears and bees whir through the air, but my heart is heavy, cold.

The house is half falling down, the roof sagging, the paint on the wooden pillars and shutters sun-bleached and peeling.

Saga glances at me, anxious, as we step up to the door and knock.

There is no answer, and I don't expect one. We step inside to find only dust and cobwebs and abandoned, broken furniture.

Saga expects me to cry, maybe, but I feel nothing. I feel less than nothing.

"I'm sorry, Bryn," says Saga softly. "Do you have any idea where they might have gone?"

I shake my head. "They must have moved years ago."

She chews on her lip, her eyes filling, though mine stay dry.

"It's all right," I say, putting a hand on her shoulder. "I haven't seen them in years. A little longer will make no difference." I glance at Indridi.

"I'll make inquiries, Your Highness," she tells Saga. "It might take some time, but I'll find them."

Saga takes a wobbly breath. "Thank you, Ridi."

The walk back to the palace is solemn, though the birds sing no less sweetly.

Vil is waiting for us in the main courtyard, honeysuckle hanging over the walls, fountains bubbling merrily, parrots singing in the trees. He's wearing loose trousers and a sleeveless vest that puts his arm muscles on full display and makes me blush. His earrings are diamond and gold and flash in the sunlight.

"No luck?" he says, reading our moods.

Saga shakes her head, dejected.

I stand there awkwardly as Indridi goes on ahead into the palace proper.

"Will you continue staying with us, then?" Vil asks me.

"Of course she will!" Saga cries. She grabs both my hands, excited again. "You'll stay here until Ridi finds your family. You can go on staying here even then, if they turn out not to be worthy of you."

She means it as a joke, but it stings a little. "I can't impose on you any longer, Saga."

"You're not imposing. You saved my life, Bryn. My family and I owe you a debt we can never repay. Hospitality is the very least that we could offer you."

I let the chattering parrots and laughing fountains fill my ears. I revel in the touch of the sunlight, the feeling of freedom. But I still can't quite bring myself to agree.

"Besides," says Vil, "we could use your help. We're going to end the war with Daeros, once and for all."

My pulse spikes. I meet his eyes. "How?"

"My sister tells me we can send our army undetected through the old Iljaria tunnels. I mean to lead a team posing as ambassadors to infiltrate Tenebris and, when the time is right, depose the king."

"What does that have to do with me?"

Vil glances at Saga and then back at me. "My sister *also* tells me you can go anywhere in the mountain palace unseen. We need that, Brynja. We need a spy."

PART THREE

Soul's Rest

CHAPTER TWENTY-ONE

YEAR 4200, Month of the Ghost Lord
Daeros—Tenebris

Vil's eyes lock hard on mine, his pulse beating quick in his neck under my knifepoint. I feel his anger, his confusion. My head is a wheeling mess of emotions I don't have time to identify, but at least one of them is guilt. Dimly, I register that Saga is cursing at me.

"*I* am the heir to Tenebris." Ballast's voice echoes sharply in the stone chamber, but his skin looks gray, wrong, and his neck is starting to blister where the iron touches it.

Brandr eyes him with disgust. "What are you going to do, half blood? You let your father collar you like a dog, and you deserve to be put down like one." He snaps his fingers, and more Iljaria melt out of the shadows—I am impressed that my brother was able to conceal so many down here, but not surprised. Two of them wrestle Ballast's hands roughly behind his back and bind his wrists together. He struggles and swears, but it doesn't do any good. He goes still all at once, tense and exhausted, sweat running into his good eye. I turn my own eyes away, sick and ashamed.

"Will you seize me, too?" says Aelia coldly, standing alone in the middle of the chamber. "Do you declare war on the peninsula and the mainland in the same breath?"

Brandr frowns. "Aerona is of no consequence to me. You may return to your father if you must, but if he attempts invasion, his blood will be on his own head."

"Brynja," says Vil again, low and angry, "explain yourself."

I will my hand holding the knife to his throat not to shake. I don't trust myself to speak, the bravado from a moment ago seeming to have leaked out of me.

Brandr shoves Kallias at the remaining Iljaria soldiers, and they drag him back into the tunnel we came through. He doesn't struggle or curse or show any emotion beyond stark bewilderment. He seems small to me, like a confused child. The blood from my knife trickles still down his neck.

My brother steps over to me and Vil, his presence, his *magic*, large enough to fill the whole mountain. "There is nothing to explain," Brandr says. "She is Brynja Eldingar, youngest daughter of the former Prism Master, and my own twin sister. You owe her your reverence."

"But you're *Skaandan*!" spits Saga, writhing in the grasp of her guard.

My heart is a dull drum, beating out every second of the last ten years, every secret, every lie. Sometimes even *I* forgot what was real, and what must only seem real, if I were to honor my people.

"No," I say softly. "I am Iljaria. I came here to watch Kallias. To monitor his progress digging into the mountain. My people do not believe in war, but we have never forgotten that this land belongs to us. We devised a way to take it back without bloodshed."

Saga lets loose another string of curses. "I thought you were my friend. I thought you were *helping* us, but you were just buying time until your monstrous brother decided to take over."

"You're a godsdamned Iljaria *spy*," says Vil. "Just like Indridi."

I see fire and dust, and my stomach twists.

"Yes, Indridi," says Brandr, brows drawing tight together as he glances at me. "Where is she?"

"Indridi is dead," Vil tells him viciously. "It is all your kind deserves."

Brandr looms suddenly large in his rage. "Take these Forsaken away," he says, low and cold. "I will deal with them later."

Vil swears as an Iljaria wrenches him out of my grasp. His eyes meet mine for a heartbeat before he's pulled into the tunnel. "We trusted you. You betrayed us."

Saga is hauled out next, fighting and cursing the whole time, then Pala and Leifur, Kallias's steward, general, and engineer. Aelia walks unhindered, but she's escorted by another guard.

Ballast is taken last of all. "I knew it," he says quietly as the Iljaria steer him past me. "I knew that's why you could taste my magic."

And then he's gone, too, and it's just me, my brother, and one last Iljaria, a woman who could be forty or could be three hundred. She has pale skin, like Brandr and I, and her white hair is bound in braids on top of her head. I wish she were someone familiar, but she's not. I don't know why that guts me.

Brandr turns to me, his face splitting into a grin. It doesn't suit him somehow, in his grand role as Prism Master. "An admirable performance, little sister."

"You're only three minutes older," I object, and he laughs.

"Still fierce and argumentative, I see." He wraps me in a sudden, tight embrace that crushes all the breath out of me.

"You won't hurt them," I say, hating that my voice wobbles, hating that I am unsure. I haven't seen my twin in a decade, and he is different than I remember him, in every way possible.

His brows bend together. "Hurt them?"

"The Skaandans and . . . Ballast."

Brandr waves a dismissive hand. "Violence is not the Iljaria way. Or have you forgotten?"

A knot pulls tight in my chest, and I think of my knifepoint, pressed into Kallias's neck hard enough to draw blood. That is a violence I do not regret. Does that make me less Iljaria? "I haven't forgotten."

"Good."

I gulp air and remind myself that I've done it. I've finally completed my mission. My brother is here and I can be myself again. I have honored my people, and perhaps, at long, long last, they will honor me, too.

I smile at my twin and link my arm through his, trying not to wince at the sting of his magic. "I am happy to see you, Bran."

His grin is back, and he shakes his head. "A Skaandan princess. On the road, and then here—at first I couldn't believe it was you! Last I knew you were a parrot in a cage."

My brief pulse of happiness evaporates.

"But never mind that now," Brandr goes on. "Are you ready?"

"Ready for what?"

Brandr turns to the hole Kallias knocked in the magic-infused wall, and the mysterious chained block in the room beyond. In all the commotion, I'd forgotten.

"To fulfill our destiny," he says.

We walk through.

ELEVEN YEARS AGO

YEAR 4189, Month of the White Lady
Iljaria—the Prism Master's house

Brandr and I turn nine today. Next year we'll push up our sleeves and receive the first of our tattoos in the color of our patron Lords. Mine will be bronze, to warn everyone to be wary of my mind magic. Brandr's will be red, though he has none of the power of the Lord of Fire that I can tell, and I've heard my parents speak in low voices that they fear his true patron is the Ghost Lord. But they can't claim him for Brandr. It would mean casting him out of Iljaria society, because my people fear the Ghost Lord's nullifying magic more than anything.

But this year there is only a token gift for each of us from our mother—esteemed architect and adviser to the queen—and a lecture from our father, the Prism Master.

We sit together in our father's office, the diamond-paned window open wide, the summer breeze rushing in over the sea. I would pity Brandr, perhaps, if I were a kinder sister. He is sickly again—he's always been sickly, from the moment we were born, plagued with every illness known to the world and rarely leaving his rooms. He sweats and shakes today, but there is anger in his eyes. He can hardly bear to listen to our father go on and on about bringing glory to our people, serving them with our gifts, being true and being strong.

Brandr is not strong. He has never been strong. And whatever magic *does* flow through his veins wreaks havoc on him. He hates everything, and he hates me especially, because I have all the strength denied him. My lecture is worse. It's all about responsibility, and not taking advantage of those weaker than myself, and how mind magic can easily be used for evil purposes—just look at the Bronze Lord. I squirm in my seat, acutely aware of Brandr's ever-increasing anger, because who else would our father be talking about being weaker than me but him?

My eyes wander to the window. I long to be out of doors, reveling in the sweet scent of summer, basking in the warmth of the sun, which always feels like a miracle after the long darkness of Soul's Rest.

"Are you listening, Brynja?" says Father sharply.

I suck in a breath and snap my gaze to his. "Yes, sir."

Father frowns. "I suppose you can both go to your lessons now. I have things to attend to."

Brandr stands shakily and leaves the room with agonizing slowness, but I hang back.

At first, Father doesn't notice. He assumes I've gone, too, and shuffles through the papers on his heavy mahogany desk, all thought of me and Brandr and our birthday gone right out of his head.

I fiddle with the gift from my mother that I shoved into my pocket the instant she gave it to me: a beaded necklace with a hammered bronze pendant. Brandr got a red one. They're pretty, I suppose, but they don't even *do* anything, which feels like a waste of Iljaria craftsmanship. I wonder if Brandr is mad about the necklaces. I wonder if he's mad that we don't even get a party for our birthday.

Because today is not about us. Not really. It's about our sister, Lilja, who is six years older than us. Her patron is the Green Lady, though I've always thought she must have Prism magic, because her powers are greater than just growing things. She's an inventor, infusing mechanical machines with her magic, like a carriage that doesn't need horses, a self-powered drill, a clock that can cook breakfast, and lots and lots of other things.

Her latest project is a set of wings made of canvas and wood, stitched with power to make the wearer soar like a bird. I watched her make them. I watched her use them, flying so high I feared she would reach the sun. I didn't dare ask her to let me try, though I dearly wanted to.

My parents are taking Lilja to Daeros to show off her inventions to the king, and maybe even sell some of them to him. They don't care about the money, of course. They're really going to see if the thing the Iljaria buried in the mountain so long ago remains hidden. They go every few decades, on one pretense or another. But pretense or not, Lilja couldn't be more proud, and I couldn't be more envious. They're leaving this afternoon.

So I stand in my father's office and wait for him to notice me.

"What is it, Brynja?" he asks after a while, without looking up from his desk.

I worry my lip, embarrassed that he knew I was here all along and was evidently just waiting for me to leave.

"I want to go to Daeros with you and Mother and Lilja. I'm old enough to go."

He gives a little laugh. "You are no older than a dewdrop. You will stay here and look after Brandr." He pulls out a blank sheet of paper and his lips move silently, words scrawling themselves onto the page without the use of a pen.

I ball my hands into fists and glare at the paper, pulling the words my father just put there right off again, and flinging them into a jumbled heap on the table.

"Brynja!" says my father sharply.

But I don't care. I'm not staying home to look after Brandr.

I dart into my father's mind, quick and slippery as a minnow.

A heartbeat later, he smooths the words onto the paper again. "It would be good for you to experience the land that once belonged to us," he says. "You may come, Brynja. Pack your things."

I smile bright as the sun and bolt out of the office before he realizes what I did.

YEAR 4189, Month of the White Lady
Daeros—Tenebris

Lilja is more than a little annoyed that I get to come to Daeros. "She meddled in your *mind*, Father!" she says, over and over. "She ought to be punished, not rewarded."

But Father replies that if I had the gall—and the power—to manipulate the Prism Master, I can't be trusted to be left alone. And I can tell he's at least a little bit impressed, even though I *do* earn myself another lecture.

So I travel with Lilja and our parents in one of Lilja's horseless carriages, rushing swift and silent over the long miles to Daeros, and it is only Brandr who is left behind.

My first glimpse of the mountain takes my breath away, the sun shining on rock and ice, the Sea of Bones crafted in shades of shifting blue beside it. The name is too grim, I think, for such ancient beauty.

We are received in the great hall, the entire back wall made of glass, sunlight refracting so blindingly off the ice it makes my eyes tear. The king of Daeros greets us along with four of his sons, and I can't help staring at them. I am not used to unmagical people, with their dark hair proclaiming they have no power at all.

One of the sons, though, has strands of white mixed into his hair, and magic burns bright beneath his skin. I'm fascinated by him—I've never heard of a half Iljaria before. He catches me staring, blue eyes fixed on mine, and I duck behind my mother, embarrassed.

The king gives us a tour of the Collection he keeps in the great hall, which I'm horrified to find is made up of children kept in glass and metal cages. He explains how one is a brilliant singer, how another can swallow fire, and another is an impressive shot with bow and arrow, even blindfolded.

My belly churns; I'm afraid I'm going to be sick, but neither my parents nor Lilja say even a word against it. I'm relieved when the tour is over and we're all shown to the guest wing.

After that, Lilja and I are made to keep mostly to the room we share. Even Lilja is deemed too young to attend any of the king's grand dinners, which annoys her to no end.

"It's because *you're* here," she snaps at me. "I'd be allowed to go if not for *you*."

I hold my tongue so I don't say something rude. I hate that I worship the very ground she walks on, and all I am to her is an annoyance.

She spends most days tinkering with her inventions, occasionally acquiescing to play at Lords and Ladies with me. But even that isn't much fun. She gets mad if I move my carved wooden game pieces with my mind instead of my hands. She thinks my power is wicked.

"The Bronze God ended up mutilated," she tells me what seems like a thousand times, shoving her silver spectacles up onto her nose. "If he would have bound his power up inside of him instead of letting it consume him, maybe he wouldn't even now be in misery and torment."

"But I'm not wicked," I say, very quietly, because sometimes I'm not actually sure.

"You used your power to get what you wanted, at the expense of Father, and me. What else would you call it?"

I chew on my lip and fall silent.

There are times when Lilja is called for, to show her inventions to the king, and I'm left alone in our room, staring moodily out the window and wondering why, exactly, I wanted to come. Brandr will never forgive me.

We're in Daeros for a week before at last I'm summoned from my room along with Lilja. She's to give a demonstration of her wings to the king, and I'm to be allowed to watch. According to Lilja, he's already purchased several of her inventions and is considering the wings as well.

We troop out onto the tundra as the sun is beginning its slow descent west. The days are not yet growing shorter, but I still feel a pulse of sorrow—I have never loved the darkness. Wind swirls across the snow and I command my coat to be warmer, and it obeys.

My parents are here, of course, with the king and a few of his sons, including the magical one with the black-and-white hair. There's a cut on his cheek, barely scabbed over, and I can't help but wonder how a prince could have received such a wound.

Attendants bring Lilja the wings, and she shows them to the king, explaining how she built them, how she infused them with her magic. She straps them onto her back, fastening the leather straps across her chest, and then steps to the edge of the cliff, the Sea of Bones stretching into deep-blue darkness below her. Wind whips her skirt about her knees.

Lilja smiles, proud and brilliant.

She jumps.

For an instant the wings spark silver and I hold my breath, ready for her to soar up into the air.

But the next moment she's falling, spiraling down into the dark.

"LILJA!" I scream, rushing to the edge.

But she falls, falls, falls.

I try. Lord of Time and Lady of Death, I try to save her.

But the wind and the snow and the ice don't listen. The sun doesn't hear me. The wings do not obey.

And so I watch in horror as my sister falls into the Sea of Bones and her body breaks upon the ice.

ELEVEN YEARS AGO

YEAR 4189, Month of the White Lady
Daeros—Tenebris

I am not sure who pulls me away from the cliff, only that someone does.

The whole world is shaking, ice flying off the mountain, wind turning to knives that slice across my skin and make blood dribble warm and wet down my neck.

"Brynja. Brynja, STOP." My father's voice, bellowing in my ear.

And I realize *I* am doing it: shaking the world, ripping the mountain apart, killing us all.

I stop.

The mountain settles.

The earth calms.

I blink and see Lilja's body beside us in the snow. I brought her back up to us in my frantic mind-storm, too late, too little.

Her neck is twisted, her arms and legs bent at odd angles, bone piercing white through her pale skin. Her wings are little more than sticks and rags now, no magic at all pulsing in the ruin of them.

I stare at her. I can't stop staring.

Somewhere, someone is roaring.

It's me.

My father cannot heal her. Not even the Prism Master of the Iljaria has the power to bring someone back from the dead.

Yet my parents shout petitions to the Gray Lady anyway.

She doesn't answer.

Lilja stays dead in the snow.

And King Kallias watches, his blue eyes glittering. Like he isn't at all surprised.

YEAR 4189, Month of the Prism Lady
Iljaria—the Prism Master's house

We stand on the hill outside my parents' house. Lilja is dead, dead. White face and white hair, wrapped in a shroud of gray. The shroud is silk and embroidered with flowers, but it is still a shroud, and she is still dead. She ought to have lived three centuries or more. All she got was fifteen years.

Father sings the funeral chant as her body rises into the air.

My heart burns with sadness, but my eyes are dry.

Brandr sobs in the chair we brought up the hill for him because he can't stand for any length of time. I didn't know. I didn't know he loved her, too. I hate myself for not including him when I wriggled my way into the trip to Daeros. He didn't even have that last week with her, like I did.

"We surrender Lilja Eldingar to the stars," says Father, and he sings the song of unwinding, a magic that is as old as time itself.

Lilja's body bursts into thousands of glittering sparks: her magic, released from her mortal frame.

And now she's truly gone.

But it isn't over.

Because I know to the depths of my soul that somehow the Daerosian king ruined my sister's wings. That he killed her. And that he must pay.

"Violence is not the birthright of the Iljaria," my father tells me, a few days after Lilja's funeral. I'm in his office again, railing to him against the king, but I don't dare use my magic to manipulate him a second time. "Vengeance does not belong to you."

"But she shouldn't have fallen!" I cry.

"No," he agrees. "She shouldn't have." He studies me, clearly weighing whether he ought to tell me something. He runs one large hand through his curly white hair. "There were iron shavings ground into the wood of Lilja's wings. I have no doubt it was Kallias who put them there."

I shake with rage, with the horror of it. "Then why must we do nothing?"

His eyes meet mine. "I didn't say that, little one. I only said that violence is not the answer."

Hope pulses through me. "What, then?"

Father sits back in his chair, steepling his fingers and peering at me over his white beard. I still can't comprehend how very old he is, but I know his eyes have seen many, many things.

"You know that the mountain once belonged to our people, that we buried something deep in the heart of it. A mighty power that could alter the very nature of the world."

I nod, not wanting to even breathe, lest he change his mind about telling me.

"We want it back, but we will not take it by force, and we don't even know if Kallias is aware of the power, if he is searching for it. We have long wished to install a permanent ambassador in Kallias's court to keep an eye on him, but he won't agree to one because he doesn't trust us. We need to send someone he wouldn't suspect."

I blink at him, not understanding. My eyes catch the movement of a bright-yellow bird, winging past the office window, but all I see is Lilja, falling to her death.

"What would you say to being that someone?"

The question jerks me back to the present. "What do you mean?"

"It wouldn't be easy, Brynja. You might be there for a long time, just waiting, just watching. You couldn't have any contact with us. You'd have to keep your identity a secret."

I still don't understand.

Father gets up from his chair and comes around the desk, kneeling on the floor to bring himself to my eye level.

"You saw the children in Kallias's Collection."

"Yes."

"I want you to *be* one of those children. To stay in the mountain. To watch Kallias. When the time is right, we will come and take back the mountain for ourselves. We'll be able to do that without violence because of you, Brynja. You'll tell us if he's about to breach the heart of the mountain."

I am beginning to comprehend what he's telling me, and something twists deep in my heart. "It will punish him," I whisper. "It will punish the king for what he did to Lilja."

He nods. "Yes."

I take a deep breath. "Am I to live in a cage and perform tricks with my magic?"

"No. For this to work, you must not let on that you have any magic, or even that you're Iljaria at all."

I tilt my head. "What do you mean, Father?"

He smiles. "We're going to turn you into a Skaandan, and we're going to make you remarkable for something other than magic." Grief flashes across his face, raw sorrow stitched with rage. "We're going to make you fly."

☼

YEAR 4190, Month of the White Lady
Iljaria—the Prism Master's house

Every morning, as soon as I wake, I drag myself to the training arena, where my father is already waiting. He brings in trainers from all around Iljaria, and even a Skaandan woman sworn to secrecy. They teach me to push myself past my breaking point, again and again and again, until

I become strong, and then adequate and then, by the close of the year, remarkable.

I break every bone in my body at least once. I push through my routines with fractured feet and splintered collarbones. I grow to embrace the pain, to use it as a tool instead of a burden.

I learn how to walk wires thinner than my fingers, and when I master that, I learn routines on them.

With the power from her patron, the Brown Lady, my mother erects an enormous arena for my use, with wires thirty feet in the air, silks, rings, swinging platforms—anything and everything my father thinks might help to catch the king's eye.

Every evening, after a full day of training, I return to my room to find Brandr waiting for me with a stack of books. We have formed a temporary truce, he for a time satisfied to be teaching me things I don't know. In this area, at least, he is stronger than me.

Brandr educates me about being Skaandan. He finds me a new last name, invents a history for me that is close enough to the truth that it won't sound false—my mother an architect, my father a mirror maker. He teaches me the Skaandan way to talk about the First Ones, and even teaches me how to curse.

"Stop calling them the Gray Lady and the Yellow Lord and so on," he says. "Think of them as gods and goddesses, even in your head. Think of yourself as Skaandan, and no one will doubt you."

So I do. I bury Brynja Eldingar deep in my mind and become Brynja Sindri in truth as well as name.

I am determined to avenge Lilja, to bring honor to my people, to defeat the king. And so I don't falter. I don't back down.

Even though every time I shimmy up the wall or do a tumbling passage on the wires, every time I leap across dizzying air to grab the rope or silk or swinging bar waiting for me on the other side—

Every time I fear it might be my last.

Every time, I see Lilja plummeting to her death, her body breaking on the ice.

331

I am utterly terrified I will meet the same fate.

I have no magic to assist me anymore—I can't call on the air or the wind to save me. My father has locked my power deep inside me so I won't betray myself. I am as helpless as if I truly were Skaandan.

Nightmares haunt me. I dream of falling, my body fractured on the rocks.

But I refuse to give up. My parents and Brandr have invested too much in me. And if I don't go through with my father's plan, Lilja's death will never be avenged.

At the close of the year, a little after Brandr and I turn ten, my father declares me ready. "There is only one thing left," he says. He puts his hands on either side of my head, and his magic slides into me, buzzing across my scalp, twisting hot through my skin.

He withdraws his hands, and I peer into a mirror to see he's turned my hair from white to dark, my brows and eyelashes, too. I stare and stare, realizing that I am truly no longer myself. That there is no turning back.

YEAR 4192, Month of the Black Lord
Daeros—Tenebris

Father promises me before I leave that once or twice a year, an ambassador from Iljaria will come and check on me, to get my report on anything regarding the king digging into the mountain.

I count every day of the first year.

The ambassador doesn't come until I've been here two. He watches the entire Collection perform and later that evening returns to the great hall. I slip from my cage to speak with him. He doesn't ask me if I am well, just inquires about Kallias. I tell him I haven't heard anything about him digging into the mountain yet. The ambassador frowns and walks away.

I don't see him again.

Year after year passes. The ambassador doesn't return. I hear no word of Iljaria at all, not even the barest scrap of news from home.

My father's last words to me echo forever in my mind, uttered on our hilltop as the sun sank west and the wind blew leaves in my hair.

"You are of the Iljaria, Brynja," he told me. "You could live three hundred years, perhaps more. Time does not bind us like it binds others. Our kind doesn't even feel the passing of time—it will be nothing to you. Remember that. And be true to our cause. To our people."

My father was wrong. I do feel the passing of time, in my iron cage in the king's mountain. I feel it acutely. Every second, every heartbeat—they pierce me through like swords, and leave me breathless.

CHAPTER TWENTY-TWO

YEAR 4200, Month of the Ghost Lord
Daeros—Tenebris

It's quiet in the heart of the mountain. I feel its breath, sense its pulse. And I stare at the block wrapped with chains and am very, very afraid.

There is no fear in Brandr. He is all strength, power, certainty. The sickly brother I left behind is no more, and I wonder, as I have since we met him on the road to Tenebris, what became of him.

Brandr puts his hands on the chains, and I shudder because they are made of iron, and how is he not burned?

"Is Father really dead?"

His eyes flick to mine, and I read his irritation that I ask him this question here, now. "Yes."

My throat hurts. "When?"

"About two years ago."

This doesn't surprise me. It's when my hair started turning white again. I kept it wrapped up when I could, in the caves, in the dark. I rubbed charcoal into it when Ballast and Saga were sleeping. And when we finally made it to Skaanda, Indridi helped me dye it, showed me how to hide the roots, how to trace my brows and lashes with staining

While the Dark Remains

kohl that Saga wouldn't perceive. My stomach twists, and I see Indridi as she died in the dust, wreathed in fire.

"Hush now, sister. Let me concentrate."

I nod, lacing my fingers together and clenching them in front of me.

Brandr returns his concentration to the iron chain. He closes his eyes and magic coils out of him, his face tight with power, with pain. The iron pulses with his Prism magic, blue and bronze and every color between. My eyes sting and my skin sears and I try not to scream at the pain of it, my breath hissing through tight lips.

One by one, the chain links burst in a spray of yellow sparks and fall away from the block, which I can see now is made of ice. All around me the mountain is screaming, grinding out its terror in rock and dust.

Then all the links are broken. Brandr steps back as a crack appears in the ice block.

It shimmers silver white, then indigo, then a deep, fathomless black. The block bursts apart all at once, fragments exploding outward as an impossible, all-consuming light floods the chamber.

My eyes burn with pain, and I screw them shut. But even still I can see the magic, feel it on my skin, taste it on my tongue. It sears through me, consuming every piece.

I sense Brandr's Prism magic, slipping silver into my mind, a balm against the power that consumes me from the inside, and I am grateful that he does not let me perish in the light.

I open blurry eyes, and the light has shrunk to a sphere of crackling, pulsing power that hovers in the air where the ice block used to be. My brother faces the sphere head-on, sweat running down his face, steam coiling off his skin. He holds his hands out, every sinew straining, and shouts the words of his Prism magic, keeping the sphere of light contained. Fragments of the iron chain rise spinning into the air, binding together to form an iron collar, marked with whorls of obsidian and gray.

With a word, Brandr flings the collar into the light sphere, and suddenly there is a boy sitting on a stone. A young boy with pale hair and warm brown skin. His eyes are the color of mountain ice. His clothes are tattered; his feet are bare. Chains hang from his ankles, and the iron collar is locked tight around his throat, pulsing in every color of my brother's Prism magic.

I think of Ballast, of the burns on his neck from his own collar, and I'm gutted that he's suffering, that I wasn't able to get it off him before he was dragged away. I swear to myself I will, as soon as I can.

The boy looks from me to Brandr and back again. He snaps his fingers, and little sparks of light dance across his hands.

Brandr takes two steps toward the boy and falls on his knees, bowing his head low to the ground. "My Lord." Brandr's voice is thick with emotion.

I don't have the presence of mind to bow as well. All I can do is stare: at my brother on the floor, at the boy on the stone who I know to be the Yellow Lord, the entity the Skaandans worship as the god of light.

I knew that my ancestors bound him in the mountain centuries ago. His power was reckless, boundless, destructive. They couldn't control it. All they could do was contain him. And so they locked him in iron and wove him with spells and buried him in the ice. But he couldn't survive indefinitely in the darkness. So they bound him to the sun. Allowed him to draw from its energy and its light three months out of every year. During Soul's Rest, the sun is *here*, burning in the heart of the mountain, sustaining the Yellow Lord. It is here now.

I knew all that. I've known all that for years. I just—I just hadn't expected him to be a *child*.

Brandr rises to his feet again. "My Lord," he repeats, "I am humbled to stand in your presence. The Iljaria call upon you once more."

The Yellow Lord blinks at Brandr, the sparks of light still dancing between his fingers. "Remove my bonds, and I will serve you." His voice is thin and strange, hollow and shifting, like he is born and made of flame.

"In due time, My Lord. For now, I have awakened you. Is that not enough?"

"I have not been sleeping." The Yellow Lord weaves light like yarn on his fingers. "I have felt every moment of my imprisonment, crushed under the weight of your cursed mountain."

His words are so like my own thoughts they take the breath out of me.

Brandr isn't cowed. "You will soon have much to do. I am the Prism Master of the Iljaria. I have unburied you, awakened you, and now I bind you to me."

He speaks a word in the Old Tongue, and I watch it appear in the air, a rune that shifts from cerulean to green to bronze to yellow, and every other color of the First Ones' magic. The Yellow Lord's collar pulses in answer as Brandr grasps the rune with his hand and, wincing, presses it into his own forehead. I have heard of these kinds of ancient bindings but have never seen one before; I feel the staggering weight of it, strong enough to call a god to heel.

The Yellow Lord gives my brother a thin smile and inclines his head ever so slightly in acknowledgment of being bound. The chains rattle on his ankles, and his light weaving grows and grows, spilling over his knees and down to the stone floor of the cavern. "And you, girl? Who are you?"

The Yellow Lord fixes his disconcerting gaze steadily on me, and his magic crawls through me like worms. "Your guardian," I say, my voice echoing oddly in the chamber. "I have watched over you these ten years."

The Yellow Lord laughs, a hiss through his teeth. "I have never needed a guardian, much less an Iljaria child with no power."

"We will call for you when we have need of you," says Brandr, dismissing our exchange with a wave of his hand. "Farewell for now, My Lord."

He steps from the cavern and I follow, feeling the Yellow Lord's eyes boring into my back.

With a pulse of magic, Brandr weaves a door back across the opening Kallias made with the pickaxe. He seals it with a disk of liquid black—darkness against light. His hands shake.

"Will it hold him?" I ask.

Brandr takes a deep breath, and I don't know if this glimpse of his uncertainty comforts or terrifies me. "He is bound to me, and to our people. It will hold until it is time to unleash his power. I merely had to be sure of him—be sure that he truly still lived. But come, sister. It is time we crawl out of this wretched hole and celebrate our victory."

He strides toward the tunnel without a backward glance. I follow, padding along quietly behind him, scrambling to put all my burning questions into words that don't sound desperate, demanding, accusatory. "What do you mean to do with him?" I ask at last, though that isn't the thing I most want to know.

Brandr glances back, an orb of magic bobbing in front of his head to light our way.

"With the Yellow Lord, I mean. Father—Father never told me." My voice wobbles. The shock of his death hasn't had time to dull, but it isn't sorrow I feel. I'm not sure what it is. My father honed me into a tool, took away my magic, and sent me to Kallias. Then, for all I can tell, he forgot about me entirely.

"When Soul's Rest is over," Brandr tells me, "when the sun rises again, there will be judgment. The Iljaria will release the Yellow Lord, and his power will consume everyone outside of the mountain—all of Daeros, all of Skaanda. They will pay for what they've done to the Iljaria's sacred land, and when the dust of the Yellow Lord's vengeance has settled, the Iljaria will rule the continent once more, as is our right. As is our responsibility."

I think of Skaanda, of the bustling cities and the airy palace, of Saga's parents and all the people, fiercely loyal to their country, to their gods. Of our shared ancestry, of their resilience. I feel Saga's hands, pressing mine around a cold glass to pull me from my nightmare. I see Vil, teaching me to throw knives in the arena, bringing me books and making me laugh. They were a family to me, when I was forgotten by my own family.

"You're going to kill them all?" My voice is small and steeped in horror.

Brandr stops walking and turns to face me, his magic light bobbing between us; it casts harsh shadows on his face. "It is justice, nothing more. They have defiled our people, our land, for too long. Why do you think our father sent you here? What do you think we've been working toward?"

"But . . . *all* of them? Isn't it enough to drive the Daerosians out? Surely we have no real quarrel with Skaanda anymore."

Brandr frowns, his earrings flashing in the light. "This land is *ours*, Brynja. All of it. The First Ones gave it to us—Daeros stole it, defiled it. The Skaandans rebelled against the judgment of our ancestors. It isn't right for them to be here—they've endured far longer than they ought to have. Have you been playing at being Skaandan for so long that you feel sympathy for them?"

I bow my head.

A memory flashes through me: my father kneeling beside me where I'd fallen from the wire in the practice arena. Sand was ground hard into my face, and my arm was bent underneath me at an unnatural angle. I didn't feel the pain yet, just numbness, and shame that I wasn't better, faster, stronger. That I wasn't what I needed to be.

My father didn't heal me immediately, like he usually did. He just frowned and voiced my own thoughts back to me: "You have to be better than this, Brynja. We're sending you to Kallias in less than a month. You have to be *better*."

Tears welled in my eyes, and I couldn't stop them from falling. My father looked at me in disgust. "We must sacrifice everything we are for the greater good," he said sharply. "You must want this, need this, *be* this. Your sacrifice will save our people. Never forget that."

Only then did he heal me, his magic coiling green and white and blue around my arm, knitting the bone back together.

I didn't understand what he meant, then. I didn't realize I was sacrificing myself. I thought I was infiltrating an evil king's court like a hero from a story. I wouldn't be there long. My family would come for me.

Except they never did.

I do understand his meaning now. I *did* sacrifice myself, nearly to the point of death. And that's what Brandr is talking about. Sacrificing Skaanda and Daeros to restore Iljaria to what it once was.

To erase the defilement of our land.

To bring, at last, true peace.

But I don't know how peace can come out of death, and it makes me feel sick, down to the deepest part of me.

I follow my brother up the long, long way through the tunnels without another word.

I catch Brandr's arm as he's about to head down the main corridor. "There's something we have to do. Now. Before anything else."

He frowns but follows me to the great hall, where he speaks a word and silvery light shimmers into existence, illuminating the vast room. I watch him as his eyes flick impassively around the cages. His mouth presses into a firm line. "Are there other Iljaria here?"

It's my turn to frown. Does he not remember the night he watched the Collection perform? "Yes."

"Lead the way."

I take him to the iron cage at the back of the room, and Finnur looks at me with expectant hope as we approach.

Now Brandr *is* angry, red sparking off him because one of our own has been kept behind iron. "*This* is why we will unleash the Yellow Lord," he tells me shortly. Then he snaps his fingers, and Finnur's cage opens.

While the Dark Remains

Finnur spares only a single glance for my brother before fixing his gaze on me. "Is it time?" he says softly. "Is it done?"

My heart seizes, and I don't know whether to grin or to weep. "Yes," I tell him. "You're free."

Finnur slips out of his cage and bows to me very low. Tears prick and I grab his hand, pull him up. His fingers are cold and thin and tight in mine.

Brandr gives Finnur an approving nod. "You will be given a room in the palace, with all your needs attended to, until this is over. Then you may stay here, or return to your family in Iljaria, whichever you prefer."

"Thank you, High Master," Finnur whispers.

An Iljaria appears seemingly out of nowhere and bows to Brandr, then beckons for Finnur to follow him. But Finnur doesn't move, still watching me.

"Go, then," says Brandr, impatient. "We have a celebratory dinner to attend."

My heart jerks. "Finnur isn't the only one here, Brandr."

Brandr squares his jaw. "Skaandans and Daerosians don't deserve anything from us."

"They're *children!*" I shout. "They haven't done anything to anyone. Kallias has kept them like animals and—" My throat closes up. "I promised them. *All* of them."

Finnur blinks up at me, wisps of colorful magic swirling around his head, now that he is no longer shut in his iron cage.

"Fine," Brandr snaps.

I lead him next to Gulla's cage at the back of the room, with Finnur close beside me. Brandr unlocks the cage with his magic, and she kneels in front of me and kisses the hem of my skirt.

My heart twists, and I pull her to her feet again. "You do not bow to me, Gulla. You have been my savior many times. I'm only returning the favor."

She smiles at me and touches two fingers to my brow.

Brandr is looking at her strangely. "Who are you?" he asks.

This is the new Prism Master? she says to me in her finger speech. *He is very young.*

"Gulla, this is my brother, Brandr. Brandr, this is Gulla, Ballast's mother."

Brandr frowns but inclines his head to her in respect.

We go on around the room, Finnur, Brandr, Gulla, and me. Brandr uses his magic to unlock every cage and the children creep out like terrified rabbits, tears slipping silently down their cheeks. Not a one of them speaks a word, and I realize with a twist of my gut that none of them actually expected me to save them. But they trust me now, following along behind me like an increasingly unwieldy procession.

There is only one cage left now: the iron one above our heads that used to be mine and is Rute's now. Gulla and the others stand with me in silence as Brandr calls it down with his magic. This time I pick the lock myself, stepping into the cage and trying not to let my fear of it overwhelm me. Rute stares at me, tense, wary, but her anger seems to have leaked out of her.

"I'm sorry it took so long," I say quietly.

She gnaws on her lip and then she weeps, her thin body shaking. She lets me lead her out of the cage, and both of us breathe easier, I think, with our feet planted squarely on the floor.

Gulla glances about at the children, barefoot and ragged, many with barely scabbed cuts on arms or legs or faces. She touches my arm. *Let me be their guardian,* she signs to me. *Let me look after them. For as long as is needed.*

Tears press hot behind my eyes, and I sign back to her: *Lords bless you, Gulla. Thank you.*

I swear to myself that when all this is over, I will find a true place for her, and for all these children, too.

I try not to think about the Yellow Lord, about Brandr unleashing him on the world. There must be justice, yes. But I will protect each one of these precious souls with everything that is in me.

I look back at the cage, revulsion and hatred and horror searing through me. Rute makes fifteen children saved, fifteen free, out of far too many others who lie forgotten in the Sea of Bones.

"Where have you put Kallias?" I ask my brother.

Brandr has been growing more and more annoyed with this whole process, impatient with me. He lifts his eyebrows at the mention of the king. "In a cell like the rest of the prisoners."

My stomach twists at the thought of Saga and Vil locked away, of Ballast writhing in the dark with the collar burning his neck. Grief and guilt war within me. "I want him locked in here," I say, nodding to the cage.

Brandr raises his eyebrows, a hint of laughter in his eyes. "So you *have* developed a Skaandan heart. Very well, it will be done."

"Immediately," I press.

He snaps his fingers for the Iljaria guards and relays my instructions. They bow and go to do my bidding.

I wait with Gulla and the huddle of freed children, my heart blazing in my chest. I think it will burn through my bones and my skin. I think it will fall to the marble floor and turn to stone. All I can feel is the children, clinging to me like I'm the only thing mooring them to the earth. I wonder if they know they're the only things mooring *me*. I try not to sense Gulla's frigid disapproval—but how can she think my request anything but just?

It's a moment or an eternity.

Then footsteps ring on the floor.

Kallias comes into view, gripped on either side by two tall Iljaria. Somehow the king manages to look as smug as he did down in the mountain, striking the final blow against the rock. His bewilderment is gone. He holds his head high and sneers at me.

All the children stare at him, stare and stare, like they can't believe their roles have been reversed. Gulla looks at the floor, as if she is ashamed.

"In there," I say roughly, pointing to my cage. My skin is buzzing. Bronze sparks blur my vision.

The Iljaria guards shove the king inside. He perches there, an oversized spider too large for its web.

I lock the cage myself, shutting the door, turning the key. Kallias peers at me through the bars. "I knew it was you," he says. "My wayward acrobat, come home to me. Did you think you had changed so much?"

I resist the urge to strike him. To spit, to swear.

But he sees it all in my eyes, and he laughs at me.

I turn my back to him and nod to Brandr.

His magic curls around the chain, and the cage is hoisted back up to the peak of the roof. Kallias dangles above me, as I once hung above him.

But I don't feel satisfied. I am shaken to my very core.

"We're done here," I tell Brandr. I turn to the guards. I can't look at Gulla, can't meet her eyes. "Find these children and the Lady Gulla rooms in the guest wing. Treat them like kings and queens, or I'll have your heads." I am wildly, viciously angry, and I want to cry until all the rage pours out of me, but I won't. Not here, in front of my brother, who has forgotten he was ever weak.

I leave the great hall. I don't look back at Kallias in my cage, but I feel his eyes, burning into my shoulders.

Did you think you had changed so much?

He was playing with me this whole time. It surprises me, unsettles me. My childhood perception of him as the impulsive, reckless king who couldn't keep hold of his temper isn't quite right. If it were, he would have exposed and killed me the instant I set foot back in Tenebris. But no, he was a lion, toying with his prey, plotting the moment of his victory, and my demise, all the more satisfying for having spun out his manipulative game to its conclusion. The Ghost God card, triumphing yet again.

But none of that matters now. I'm free. The Collection is ended. I can be with my people again, and all shall be well.

All shall be well.

If only I could wholly believe that.

TWO YEARS AGO

YEAR 4199, Month of the Yellow Lord
Skaanda—Staltoria City—the royal palace

It's all I can do to keep the shock from my face when Saga introduces me to her attendant, but Indridi's expression at least remains perfectly blank.

I have only a handful of memories of my cousin—we played together as children, but not often, as her parents' house was not near to mine. But she was my favorite nonetheless. Sometimes I think she loved me better than my own sister did. Indridi left for Skaanda shortly after Lilja was murdered, and my father referred to her many times when he was training me for my own mission to Daeros. *She serves us proudly,* he would say. *She serves us faithfully. Be like Indridi.*

That ought to have been my first clue that I would be in Kallias's cursed mountain for more than a few years. But I was naive. Idealistic. Of course I was—I was a child.

"Indridi is wonderful," says Saga, drawing me back to the present, a breeze smelling of orange blossoms wafting through the airy hallway. "We've practically grown up together. She'll help you with anything you need, just ask."

I force a smile that I hope isn't one of absolute bewilderment, but I'm not at all sure I manage it. Indridi gracefully inclines her head to me.

"Right," says Saga. "I'm off to a bath. A *bath*, Brynja. Have you ever heard of anything more wonderful?"

I force a laugh.

"See you at dinner!" she calls, and ducks into the room next to mine.

For a moment I just stare at Indridi. Her brows pinch together ever so slightly, a warning that I'm not to say a thing in the hall, where anyone could hear.

We step into the room and I shut the door and open my mouth, but she still shakes her head.

"Is there anything in particular you need help with, my lady?" she asks.

I notice the door that joins this room to Saga's, and I understand that there *is* no safe place to speak freely, not within the palace in broad daylight, anyway.

"I need help with my hair," I tell her, unknotting my scarf and showing her the charcoal I smeared messily over my white roots, the mud I've let dry on my eyebrows and eyelashes.

Indridi nods. "A bath first, my lady. And then I know just what to do with your hair."

Saga is not wrong about the bath. It is *beyond* wonderful, and I'm reluctant to get out. But when I do, Indridi is waiting for me with warm towels and a soft robe. I know she sees my many scars, but she makes no comment on them. It's a relief.

"You are truly Lords blessed," she says to me quietly, as she settles me on a stool in front of the dressing table. "What would you have done, if I were not here?"

I shake my head. I truly don't know.

Indridi dyes my hair, brows, and lashes with a concoction of her own making that she's used herself for the ten years she's served as a spy in the Skaandan court. I watch my roots and short curls turn wholly dark again, and I'm relieved I won't have to worry about it anymore.

I try not to wonder why, after all this time, my father's magic has worn off. Because it is the *only* thing that has worn off. My own magic is still sealed tight inside me, out of reach. Sometimes I forget I even had magic. I've spent nearly half my life without it now.

"Is there anything else I can do for you?" asks Indridi, meeting my eyes in the mirror.

"Saga means to reunite me with my family," I tell her carefully. "But I don't know where they live in the city."

Indridi nods, understanding my predicament. Because of course my family is in Iljaria, and Saga can't know that.

"I will find them," she says. "It may take a little time."

I smile at her. "Thank you."

She smiles back, and the warmth of kinship pulses between us like magic.

CHAPTER TWENTY-THREE

YEAR 4200, Month of the Ghost Lord
Daeros—Tenebris

Candlesticks gleam bright on Kallias's dining table, every one of them lit with magic. They spark purple and green, silver and blue, a few a writhing, eerie black. I wonder which of the Iljaria lit the candles, or if it was just my brother, with a casual snap of his fingers.

He sits at the head of the table in Kallias's place, dressed in a thin silk robe of green and yellow. I'm on his right, Ballast's usual chair, and I'm the only one in the room wearing furs, because I don't have my magic to warm me.

I try not to think about Ballast, somewhere below me, locked in agony. I try not to think of Saga and Vil, Pala and Leifur, cursing the day I was born. I try not to think about my magic, about why it's still locked deep inside me even though my father is gone. The magic he used to change my hair must have been of a lesser kind than the sort he used to bind my power. I am afraid that without him, I won't be able to get it back. I try not to think about all those things. I fail utterly.

There are about twenty-five Iljaria around the table, each with a gem the color of their main power bound to their foreheads. I wonder absently if they've brought a bronze gem for me to wear on my own forehead, or if I even have the right to wear one, when I have no magic at my command.

I don't recognize anyone at the table, and my heart sinks when I realize I'm searching in vain for my mother, an aunt, a cousin, *someone*. But these people—my own people—are nothing more than strangers to me.

Brandr introduces me to a few of them, including the woman who was with us earlier in the mountain's heart—Gróa, Brandr's scribe—and a man called Drengur, Brandr's steward, who can't be many years older than Brandr and me. Drengur has dark-brown skin, with swirls of white tattooed on his arms.

Kallias didn't know, of course, that Brandr had brought so many of our people with him. The larger part of the Iljaria stayed hidden in an ice cave a ways out from the mountain, and Brandr snuck them into the palace a few at a time, concealing them with his magic.

I'm not entirely sure what's been done about the Daerosian army encampment, but I wouldn't be surprised if Brandr has another host of Iljaria relieving them of their weapons and herding them into prison at this very moment.

The thought of prison sends me right back to Ballast and Saga and Vil. I don't dare ask Brandr to remove Ballast's collar—not after their earlier exchange. My brother fears Ballast's power. I sensed that, from their first meeting. I still mean to go and free him of it, as soon as I can slip away from dinner. I have no illusions that he'll be on my side. He offered his hand of cards, but I didn't offer mine because I'm the one who had the Ghost God card. Now I've played it, and I can't help but think that everyone has lost the game, even me. Especially me.

I haven't decided what to do about Saga and Vil. I never wanted them to hate me. And I never wanted to care what anyone thought about me, but I *do* care. I've always cared, no matter how hard I denied it. The caring twists through me like hot knives, and I hate myself.

Polite conversation ripples around the table, most of it regarding the success of our people's endeavors in retaking Tenebris—without any reference to me—and of plans to reshape and rebuild the land in the aftermath of unleashing the Yellow Lord's power. The Iljaria whose patrons are the Green Lady and the Brown Lady will be very much in demand, but everyone's magic will be put to use.

All this is discussed so mildly it makes my insides squirm. Is this really what the First Ones want? Annihilation of everything that has gone before, a wholly new beginning? Surely the magic wound into the stones of our most ancient cities will protect them, but in the fury of the Yellow Lord's power—everything else will be reduced to ashes.

I can't understand why this seems to mean nothing to my kinsfolk. It's like we are stones, changing little with time, not heeding the fates of the mayflies who live and die all around us. Maybe it's my own fault, for pretending to be a mayfly. But I don't want to be a stone.

I flick my eyes to Brandr. "How did our father die?" I'm not sure it's a safe question, but then I doubt that any of my questions are safe ones.

My brother takes a sip of wine from a silver goblet and glances over at me as he sets it back on the table. He's lined his eyes with bright-blue kohl, which makes him look both dangerous and regal. I can't help but think that blue is Ballast's color.

"He died of old age," Brandr says.

"But he wasn't old," I object. "Not even three hundred."

The Iljaria sitting nearest us cease their conversation and frown at me for arguing with my brother. They don't know what to do with me. What to think about me.

Brandr gives a careless shrug. "The burden of Prism Master weighed heavily on him. I suppose it was too much for him, at the last."

Frustration buzzes through me. Our father was the strongest, most powerful man I have ever met. He ought to have lived another century at least. "Did he—did he . . . did he send any messages with you?"

Brandr frowns. "Messages?"

I force down my anger, my hurt. "I thought he might want to say goodbye." I don't say what I really wanted from my father: for him to tell me he missed me, for him to acknowledge and regret my sacrifice. Something, anything, to show that he cared.

Brandr waves a dismissive hand. "He bid you farewell when you left us, Brynja. We all did. Why would he need to say it again?"

I gnaw on the inside of my cheek. "What about Mother? Did she—"

"There are other things to discuss besides our family, sister. We bore the rest of the company."

Brandr's scribe, Gróa, and steward, Drengur, give me matching thin smiles, emphasizing Brandr's point.

I ignore them. "*I* want to know about our family. I haven't seen them in over a decade. How *is* our mother? How was Father before he died? What's become of Lilja's inventions? Is Sparrow still hunting mice in the garden?" The memory of my cat makes my heart pinch.

"Brynja." Brandr's tone is cold and final. "We will not discuss this now."

I can't help myself, growing more frantic by the moment. "What about you? How did you develop your magic enough to become Prism Master?"

"He worked very hard," says Gróa, who sits opposite me. "The power was in him always. It's what made him weak, until he learned to control it." Her voice is cool and smooth, and she looks to Brandr with undisguised admiration.

"Father trained me," says Brandr. "After he was done with you."

Resentment bubbles up in me at the bitterness in his words. Here is the Brandr I remember—but what does he have to be bitter about anymore? *He* wasn't sent away and forgotten, wasn't sacrificed for the greater good. He's shed his weakness like a butterfly bursting from a cocoon. He has power now. He has everything he ever wanted.

I take a deep breath and ask another question I know isn't safe. "Father locked my magic away inside of me. Can you unlock it?"

Brandr gives me an infuriatingly indulgent smile. "We will discuss it later, Brynja." He turns to speak to Gróa, who gladly soaks in his attention.

"I have sent word to Her Majesty," Gróa tells him, putting one hand on my brother's arm and tracing his tattoos with her fingers. "I expect her reply via blue kestrel within a day, possibly two, with her arriving shortly after. Drengur and I will of course ready the grandest rooms for her we can find."

"The queen is coming *here?*" I blurt.

Brandr frowns but doesn't answer.

Gróa looks at me with utter condescension. "Naturally our queen wishes to be present at the Yellow Lord's unleashing and the long-awaited cleansing of our world."

"Did you think our father orchestrated this entire plot alone?" Brandr asks me pointedly. "Did you think *I* was here against our queen's will? I am not the ruler of the Iljaria."

You're certainly acting like it, I want to tell him, but don't quite dare.

For the remainder of the dinner, Brandr ignores me. Drengur, Brandr's steward, tells me briefly about how his power of music—his patron is the White Lady—is actually more useful than I might think. If one's magic is strong—which his is—the vibrations of musical notes can be used to manipulate and move matter, similar to the power of the Brown Lady, although her power is generally limited to earth and rock. When I don't display the correct amount of awe at this explanation, he tires of me quickly and turns to speak with someone else.

I have outlived my usefulness, I suppose. Fulfilled my duty. And what good am I now, an Iljaria with no magic? Not even worth the effort of conversation.

As soon as dinner is over, I catch Brandr's arm and pull him into an alcove off the main corridor, where wine bottles are locked in a wood-and-glass cabinet. Their scent permeates the air, sweet and strong.

"Can you unlock my magic or not?" I demand, not even attempting to hide my anger.

Brandr jerks his sleeve from my grasp, magic crackling over his skin. He's angry, too, and his anger terrifies me. "Your magic has nothing to do with me. It never has."

I'm thrown back to our childhood, him shut up in his rooms with his books, me making the plates and silverware dance out of their cupboards in the kitchen, seeing how many I could keep track of at once. The answer was all. All of them, until a servant came in and startled me and every last one came crashing to the floor.

I got shouted at and banished outside, where I tried the same thing with seashells and pebbles on the shore. I was there until the sun set and the stars began to appear, and then my mother came out and found me with sand and fish and water swirling about my head, unsure of how to put them all down again without causing a hurricane. I got quite a few lectures after that.

"My hair color is coming back," I say, "so that spell is wearing off. Why isn't my magic returning? If one reverted on his death, why not the other?"

Brandr sighs, like I'm the most troublesome thing in all the world. To him, maybe I am. "It is possible that locking magic can't be reversed at all. Did that never occur to you?"

It occurs to me now, and I want to scream and rail. I need my magic back, a second heart I've been living without for all these years. I'm not sure how long my other heart, my frailer heart, can go on beating without it.

"Won't you even *try*, Brandr?" I ask him quietly. "You're the most powerful Iljaria alive right now. If there's a way, surely you can find it. And—and you of all people know what it is like to be weak."

It's the wrong thing to say, and I take a step back as his magic pulses off him white-hot.

"Your sympathies with the Skaandans and even the Daerosian children run far too deep. How can I trust you?"

"So you'll damn me to live forever like one of them?"

"I'd imagine you'd be used to it by now."

I bite my lip hard to keep from screaming at him.

"Prove yourself to me, Brynja. Prove your loyalty to the Iljaria, and I will do my best to reunite you with your magic."

"What do you think I've been *doing* all this time?" I demand. "I sacrificed a decade of my life for our people. I betrayed my friends and handed you the keys to the Yellow Lord. I've done nothing *but* prove my loyalty."

His mouth thins. "It isn't enough. Simply calling Skaandans and that half-Iljaria bastard your friends attest that you've grown too much like them, that you don't know what true loyalty even means."

"But—"

"Enough, Brynja. I have things to attend to."

He leaves me alone in the alcove, the scent of wine wrapping around me, my own insignificance crushing me into oblivion.

☼

My room feels strange, wrong, without Saga and Pala in it. I don't know why I'm surprised that no one has moved me to a grander room—Brandr has been installed in Kallias's suite, after all. But then again, which room would I even want? Ballast's? My stomach turns sour. No, this is better.

I don't dare go to the dungeons until Brandr is asleep. He doesn't know about my paths through the ceilings—he doesn't know anything about my years here, my escape with Saga, or how long I've been back. He probably doesn't care. But I still need to be cautious. He'll be able to sense me if I'm near him, and if he catches me freeing Ballast, all hope of getting my magic back will be gone.

I pace awhile, trying to collect myself, trying to reorder my understanding of the world and my place in it. I think of the Yellow Lord, bound beneath my feet, awaiting his fate as all of us await ours. I try to reconcile myself to the necessity of my brother's purpose: the restoration of Iljaria, as it was meant to be.

What *did* I think my father's plan was? To keep Kallias from uncovering the Yellow Lord, to take Kallias off his throne, and . . . then what?

Bury the Yellow Lord again? Set him free? Bring him back to our queen and king?

I curse. Was it really always going to end this way?

For all my recent quarrels with Vil, he's my friend, or at least he was. He and Saga have been family to me, showing more care for me in two years than my actual family did in a decade. I cannot resign them to death by the Yellow Lord's power. I cannot see any justice or peace in the eradication of their entire people. Pacifism is the Iljaria's way of life. Or at least I thought it was.

Lord of Time. If I could, I'd go back to the night of my escape. I would harden my heart to Saga's pleas. I would leave her to Kallias's mercy and go home to Iljaria, as I had planned. I had tried to anyway, leading her east out of the mountain, counting on delirium from her wound to keep her from realizing we weren't going west to Skaanda. But she'd noticed. So I lied to her: *We must have taken a wrong turn in the dark.*

And like a fool, I took her west. Like a fool, I didn't leave her to die in the snow, or in the caves. Like a fool, I went with her all the way to Skaanda, when I had chance after chance to slip away. Like the greatest of fools, I entangled myself into her life, and now I can't bear that my brother means for her to die.

I curse and curse, sweeping jars of cosmetics from my dressing table, hurling them at the wall. I look in the mirror and scream at my reflection, because Indridi's hair dye has worked too well, and there is not a hint of white showing among my dark curls. I try to find the Brynja I used to be, studying every freckle, every scar. But that Brynja is gone. I hid her for too long, and she's never coming back, and I don't know who I am anymore.

It's late by the time I deem it safe to go, the twenty-first hour by the mantel time-glass. I jam a chair under my doorknob and shimmy up into the heating vent.

I pick my slow way to the dungeon, hating myself more with every beat of my heart.

I've been in the dungeon only once before, years ago, when I did my extensive exploration of the palace. I left in a hurry, because I found that it wasn't only the children in his Collection that Kallias liked to torment.

The main entrance is a heavy wooden door, which leads to a wide dark corridor, lined with cells carved out of the rock, all barred in iron. Because, once, this was an Iljaria prison—it was built to contain Iljaria.

Brandr hasn't bothered to post a guard, so I pick the lock to the main door unhindered. I'm forced to carry a light, and I tense as I pace down the corridor. I can't see Saga and Vil. Not now. I'm here only to ease Ballast's torment. Then I can work on gaining my brother's trust. Earn my magic back. Become wholly Iljaria again. Fix all this, to the best of my ability.

"Have you come to crow, Brynja?"

I jump at Saga's voice, turning toward her without meaning to.

She stands with her hands wrapped around the iron bars of the cell she's in, her eyes filled with such visceral hatred that I take an involuntary step backward.

I can't let myself say anything to her. I *can't*. I glimpse Vil in the next cell, sitting against the stone wall with his head tilted back and his eyes shut. My limbs turn all to water. I harden my resolve. I have to. I walk past them both, Saga hurling curses in my wake.

Kallias's children are all locked up, too—my brother has been thorough. Zopyros, Theron, and Alcaeus all share a cell, with Lysandra, Xenia, and little Rhode in the one beside them. The boys don't even look at me as I go by, but Lysandra screeches for my attention, demanding I let her out, telling me it's a mistake, it's all a mistake, she cares nothing for her father, she wants to ally with the Iljaria, she wants—

I ignore her, though my heart jerks at the sight of Rhode cradling a sleeping Xenia in her lap. Those two are as innocent as the children in the Collection, and I make a mental note to speak to Brandr about having them released. To my knowledge, Kallias's wives have been allowed to stay in their warren of rooms. Surely Rhode and Xenia can join them.

I find Ballast in the very last cell on the right. My hands shake as I pick the lock and slip inside.

He's lying on the floor, unconscious. There's dried blood under his fingernails and all around the iron collar on his neck, like he was trying to claw it off.

I fight to breathe, to force the nausea down, to keep control. I kneel beside him. I fumble with the collar, cursing and cursing until I find the latch that releases it. I hurl it at the stone wall, and it falls with a clatter.

But Ballast doesn't wake. There are welts on his throat from the collar. His cheek is still horribly swollen where the wasp stung him. The ribbon that kept his eye patch in place has come loose, leaving his empty socket visible. Gently, gently, I pick up the ribbon. I tie it back on.

I bow my head and weep over him, racked by grief and rage, wanting and loss.

He opens his eye. Blinks up at me.

For a moment there is tenderness in his gaze, a fathomless relief. I see memory crash through him. He hardens. Recoils. Scrambles away from me as fast as he can.

His hands go to his throat. "You should have left me to die," he snarls. "You should have *left* me."

"How could I?" My voice cracks, wavers.

He swears at me, and I bite my cheek so hard I taste blood.

"What's your plan then, Brynja? Because you always have a plan, don't you?"

My heart races as I look at him. I take a breath. I open my mouth and close it again. "I wanted to tell you. I almost did in the caves—"

"What would that have accomplished? Did you think I would just merrily join your Iljaria plot?"

Hurt pulses sharp because I don't *know* what I thought, only that I yearned for him to know every part of me.

His eyes flick past me, to the open cell door, but before he can lunge for it, I'm already through, slamming it shut in his face before he can get out.

"I'm sorry," I say.

He laughs at me, sounding so very like his father that I want to cry again.

"I'll save you," I tell him. "If I can."

He grabs the iron collar from the ground and heaves it at me through the bars. It hits my shoulder, hard, and I choke on a scream because Bronze Lord it *burns*. I think about how it must've felt, locked around Ballast's throat for hours and hours, and I have to fight not to be sick.

I leave the dungeon without a backward glance, Saga's shouts and curses still echoing in my ears even when I'm back in my room again.

I spend the rest of the night in the windowsill, staring out at wheeling stars.

Whoever this new Brynja is, I think I hate her.

TEN YEARS AGO

YEAR 4190, Month of the Bronze Lord
Iljaria—the Prism Master's house

The window to my father's office is open again, the summer breeze blowing in, scented with salt water and honeysuckle. I'm sitting in an overlarge chair, my feet not touching the ground, facing my father behind his desk. I broke my shoulder in training a few hours ago, and it's still knitting itself back together, tingling with the effects of my father's power but no longer painful.

He says it won't hurt when he locks away my magic, but I'm afraid he might be lying.

"I won't—I won't use it," I plead, studying my chipped fingernails so I won't have to meet my father's piercing eyes. "I haven't used it, all these months. You can trust me. I won't betray us."

"You will betray us in small ways, Brynja," he tells me. "You aren't even aware of it, perhaps, but you *have* used your magic, every single day since your training began."

I bristle with anger, but my father holds up one hand to forestall me. "Magic curls round you when you sleep, little one. You can't help it, and you certainly can't stop it. Sometimes, when you're hurrying home, or attempting a particularly difficult leap, you tell the earth to move for you, the bar to swing for you, the air to shift for you. Not consciously, perhaps, but you still do it. You breathe magic, Bryn. Nothing you can do will ever stop that."

I sag in the chair, because I know he's right.

"It won't hurt," he says, returning to his original claim. "And it will be over quickly. But we must do it now. Are you ready, Brynja?"

I bite my lip to hold back the tears because I refuse to cry about this. I nod.

He gets up from his chair and comes over to mine. He stands behind me, gathering my mass of white curls and tying them up. The intimacy of this simple gesture startles me—my father has never even hugged me in all my life.

"Close your eyes."

I do. Color swirls before me, sparks of magic. My father puts his hands on each of my temples, warm and astonishingly gentle, for all the power that seethes beneath his skin.

Suddenly there are needles boring into my skull, a thousand pricks of unbearable, glistering pain. Somewhere outside of myself I'm screaming, but inside my head all I know is magic, boiling and raging, swirling round me, drowning me in bronze and amethyst and cerulean.

It hurts, it hurts so *much*, and yet I have no voice, no being. I am trapped in a moment of time, and I think I will die here.

Then I am walking through a corridor made of magic, whorls of prismatic colors sparking in and out of existence. I have hands again, and I reach out to touch one of the whorls. It creeps into me, filling me with warmth and strength, easing some of the pain.

At the end of the corridor, I step into a small chamber that is seemingly made of stone. A window looks out into blackness, and in the center of the room, a figure crouches over a small worktable, where a single candle burns.

I go up to the figure and find that he is a man, or the ruin of one. His ears and nose have been hewn off, his eyes put out. He has no feet and no hands, but he pinches a hammer between the stumps of his arms, and with it he strikes a small chest.

Sparks fly off the hammer, and the candle flame dances in a breeze I do not feel. I wonder why the candle is there at all; the world is only darkness to him, no matter how much light there is.

I realize that the candle is for me.

"What are you making?" I ask.

He must still be able to hear through the wreckage of his ears. He lifts his maimed face to mine.

Look and see, he says into my mind, for his tongue is gone, too. He turns from the worktable to offer the chest to me while I openly stare at him, not quite believing all the stories I've heard, not quite believing that the Bronze Lord is here with me at all.

"What are you doing in my head?"

He gives a soundless laugh. *Binding magic requires much power.* He sets the chest on the table, nudges it open with the stump of his arm.

The chest is wholly empty.

It is for you, says the Bronze Lord in my mind. *For your magic. Will you give it to me?*

"I don't want to."

Then you would not have come here.

It is disconcerting to look at him, but I am not repulsed by him. His skin is a warm brown; his white hair hangs shining and straight past his shoulders. Once, I think, he must have been beautiful. Surely another of the First Ones could heal him. Restore him to what he once was.

"It is my father who wishes to bind my magic so that I can save our people."

And what do you wish?

The candle flame wavers, and there's a flash of light outside the window. "To make him proud," I whisper. "To make him love me." I hadn't known this burned so fiercely in my heart until this moment. Sorrow and wanting grip me.

The Bronze Lord nods, and I find myself wondering what color his eyes were, before they were put out. *Then you know what you must do.*

"I know." I shake and shake, and I think it odd that I have a body inside my own mind that can do any of those things. "Take my magic, then."

He smiles, but there is no joy in it. His lips form a soundless word that sparks bright, and the chest lifts into the air, spinning slowly. A pair of long silver hooks appear in front of him, and I get the idea that he holds them with hands that no longer exist.

I am sorry, says the Bronze Lord.

The hooks stretch toward me, sinking into my temples.

For a moment I don't feel anything.

Then, pain, brittle, burning. Colors burst behind my eyes, and I am dust, I am stars, I am nowhere, I am nothing, nothing.

The hooks pull and pull, tearing my magic out of me and piling it like glittering sand inside the chest. The pain goes on and on; the hooks take and take.

But the chest is never full.

I sink to my knees in that not-place, surrendering myself to the eternal torment of the Bronze Lord.

And then it's over.

I lift my head to find the hooks on the floor, the chest filled, shut, locked. The Bronze Lord pinches it between the stumps of his arms.

This belongs to you, he says, the words resounding inside me solemn and sorrowful. *You must hide it away yourself.*

The room changes around me, taking the Bronze Lord with it, and I am alone in a stone cavern, the chest of magic heavy in my arms. The cavern is obviously ancient, filled with carved pillars and crumbling statues. It stretches on into infinity in every direction.

Dimly, I'm aware of the self that is outside of all this, screaming in my father's office with his hands pressing against my temples. But here, in my mind, there is no pain. The chest grows so heavy I can barely hold it, and it burns my arms like it's made of iron.

I shove it into a crack in the stone, near the statue of a young woman whose hands and feet, nose and ears, have all crumbled away in an eerie echo of the Bronze Lord.

I turn, shuddering, and find myself in my father's office again, light streaming through the window, honeysuckle and saltwater wind tickling my nose.

My father draws his hands away, not meeting my eyes. I wonder if he feels guilty for lying to me. But I have nothing to say to him. Not now.

I slide from the chair, wiping tears from my eyes, realizing dimly that Brandr has been here this whole time, perched on a stool in the corner, watching us.

I run out onto the hills, away from the house, away from the sea. I run and run, until I find a little hollow where wildflowers lie thick as a carpet, and a shiny green snake winds its way through the grass. I sink down among the flowers and hug my knees to my chest, reaching and reaching for just an ounce of my magic.

But it isn't there.

I am hollow.

Powerless.

I am not Iljaria anymore.

I am Brynja Sindri. A Skaandan acrobat.

I weep there bitterly, for hours. Because I didn't know it would be like this. Didn't know, didn't know.

☼

A week later, I leave for Skaanda.

My father doesn't tell me goodbye.

CHAPTER TWENTY-FOUR

YEAR 4200, Month of the Ghost Lord
Daeros—Tenebris

Gulla is sleeping when I slip into her room in the guest wing, though it's nearly the seventh hour. Two of the littlest children from the Collection are with her, curled up tight on either side of her. The rest are draped over chairs and the sofa, or sprawled about on the floor in mounded blankets.

It's Rute who senses me first, unfolding herself from a fur blanket and blinking up at me with huge eyes.

"I didn't believe you when you said you'd free us," she tells me frankly. "But you did. Thank you."

My heart wrenches. "I'm sorry it wasn't sooner."

She gives me a small smile, and some of the tension eases out of me. "Why are you all in here together?" I ask her then. "I left instructions for rooms to be found for each of you—"

"None of us wanted to be alone. We wanted to be with Gulla. She looked after us as best she could, you know, before she was shut in a cage, too. She's all we have."

I take a breath, blinking back tears. "I know."

"What's going to happen to us?" Rute asks quietly.

"Do you have a family to go back to?"

She shakes her head. "My parents passed when I was little. I grew up in a traveling troupe—that's where I learned all of my tricks. But they were short on money, and they heard Kallias was looking for a new acrobat—"

Ice slides through my veins. "I'm sorry, Rute."

"It isn't your fault. It's *his*. I'm glad he's there now. In our old cage."

"Me too." I give her a tight smile. "But don't worry. I'll find a place for you. I'll find a place for *all* of you, just as soon as . . ." I trail off.

Rute looks me square in the eye. "Is the Yellow God *really* chained in the heart of the mountain?"

I blink at her. "How would you possibly know that?"

She just grins and jerks her thumb at the ceiling vent.

I have to laugh. "Did you pick your lock with hairpins?"

"A cloak-pin, actually. But is he?"

I sober. "Yes."

"And does the Prism Master really mean to—" She cuts herself off as she realizes the children are waking up, including Finnur, who sits up on one of the armchairs and stretches out his long legs; he sparks green and yellow.

"Brynja," he says, and smiles.

I turn to find Gulla sitting up in bed. *Hello, Brynja.*

Rute meets my eyes. "Go and speak with her. Finnur and I will take care of this lot while you do."

I nod my thanks, and Gulla and I slip into the empty adjoining room. A lamp glows orange on a low table, and we settle on either side of it.

"Are you well, Gulla?" I ask her quietly.

Well enough, she signs back. There is weariness in her face, but a calmness, too. *What's wrong, Brynja?*

I take a breath. I force myself to look her square in the eye. "I'm not who I told you I was."

She smiles a little. *You're Iljaria. The Prism Master is your brother.*

I blink at her. "Rute told you?"

About the Prism Master and the Yellow Lord, bound beneath us, she signs to me. *I already knew you were Iljaria. I sensed it the first time we met, like calling to like.*

My eyes go hot and scratchy.

Her gaze softens. *You hid yourself very well from those who could not see. But how could I not recognize a fellow Iljaria in exile?*

Tears sear down my cheeks, and I scrub them away with my hands, taking deep, choking breaths in an attempt to get hold of myself. "Did Rute tell you what my brother means to do?"

Gulla nods. *Unleash the Yellow Lord. Remake the world.*

"I didn't know that this was my father's plan from the beginning. I didn't know I was sent here to bring destruction."

Her gaze pierces me. *If you had known, would you still have come?*

I shrink beneath her scrutiny, because I don't know. "Is this really what the First Ones want?" I ask quietly. "Is this really what our people are meant to do?"

Our people speak of peace, but I do not think they truly believe in it.

"Do you? Believe in peace?"

She raises her eyebrows. *Do you?*

I consider her for a long moment. "How did you come to Daeros, Gulla?"

That doesn't matter now.

I clench my jaw. "How did you come here?"

She sighs. *My sister and I wanted to see Tenebris. We left our home by the sea, traveled by ourselves for some weeks. Daerosian soldiers found us within sight of the mountain. My sister used her magic—growing magic, from the Green Lady—to get away. I was brought to Kallias. No one ever came for me. You know the rest.*

I fight back a fresh wave of tears. "I'm so sorry, Gulla."

She gives me a sad smile. *It was not of your design, Brynja Eldingar.*

"What about *your* magic?" I ask her.

It is harder to reach than it was. But it is not wholly gone. And then she does something I have never heard her do—she makes a sound deep in her throat, a guttural note of rich, powerful magic.

The lamp on the table winks out, smoke curling up. Another note from her and it's lit again, flaring brighter than before.

I stare at her, mouth hanging open, and she gives a soundless laugh.

"What am I supposed to do?" I say. "About my brother and the Yellow Lord? About our people?"

Her brow creases as she studies me, and I'm seized with a sudden wild grief that I will never know what her voice sounded like before Kallias cut out her tongue.

I think you need to figure out where your loyalties truly lie, she signs. *I think you need to figure out what is buried within your own heart.*

I take a deep breath.

I am worried for my son, she says then. *How is he?*

I shake my head. "He's locked up with the rest of them."

Will you save him? Whatever it is he's been up to since he came back, I do not truly believe he is like his father. I know he is not. Will you save him? Her eyes go wet and shiny, and my gut clenches.

"I will try," I promise. "But, Gulla. *Please* tell me what to do."

I can't tell you what to do, Brynja. She blinks at me. *I think you already know.*

※

The Yellow Lord is sitting on his block, playing with a little ball of light that I can't look at directly because its intensity makes my eyes tear. The chains on his ankles clink faintly with his movement, and the collar that Brandr bound him with pulses with prismatic runes. He tosses the ball of light back and forth between his hands, unaffected by its brilliance. The patch Brandr magically regrew over the wall is gone, and I get the idea that, if he really wanted to, the Yellow Lord could leave his prison, bound though he is.

While the Dark Remains

I stand just within the low doorway and wait for him to notice me. After a while, he puts the ball of light beside him on the block, folds his hands behind his neck, and yawns. "So the impotent one has decided to visit me." He sounds and looks so young, but the heat of his magic sears my skin even from a few paces away. "What do you want?"

Gulla's words repeat themselves endlessly in my mind: *You need to figure out what is buried within your own heart.* "My father locked my magic away. Can you unlock it?"

The Yellow Lord looks at me with passivity or boredom or both. He flops down on his side, propping his head up with one hand, bare feet dangling. "What kind of magic did you call your own, Brynja Eldingar?"

"Mind magic."

The Yellow Lord makes a face. "Horrid fellow, the Bronze Lord. I don't even like to think about him." He realizes he accidentally made a joke. "Ha!" He snaps his fingers and the light globe whirls in his palm, a blur of yellow-orange-white.

"Then you can't help me."

"If your father locked your magic, your father will have to *un*lock it."

"But he's dead."

The light winks out. "He is, isn't he. That does make things difficult." The Yellow Lord sits up again. "Come here, Eldingar. Let me look into you."

This seems like a very bad idea, but I'm angry and wrung out and reckless, so I pace over to him. Somehow his magic doesn't burn as terribly this close.

I stand eye to eye with him and am overwhelmed with the sudden sensations of *loneliness* and *sorrow* and *anger*. They taste bitter on my tongue, and I peer at the Yellow Lord with greater understanding. He's been chained down here for centuries. My measly eight years in Kallias's cage don't even compare.

"One person's pain does not negate another's," says the Yellow Lord quietly, reading my thoughts. "I have been down here longer, but that doesn't make your experience meaningless. You have been hurt. Deeply. Haven't you?"

Another wave of *loneliness* hits me, and I gasp under the weight of it.

The Yellow Lord puts his hands on either side of my face, like my father did all those years ago; his fingers are gentle and cool, where I'd expected them to be rough, hot. Magic rushes through me, raging as rivers, quiet as spring rain. For an instant the memory of my own magic sparks bright on my tongue, and I want to weep in relief.

But the next moment it's gone again.

The Yellow Lord withdraws his hands. He studies me, solemn and small, and I think again how very strange it is that a First One who has lived untold centuries looks to be little more than a child.

"Your magic is not gone," he says after a moment, tapping his fingers along his jawline, "but it is buried deeper than I would have guessed. Your father used your own magic against itself. Only your magic can unlock your magic." He grins at me.

I choke back a Skaandan curse. "But I can't *use* my magic."

"Therein lies the dilemma. You still sense magic, as easy as breathing. I perceive the effect I have on you. You see it everywhere, don't you? What does it look like?"

I blink at him, shocked. How could a First One not know? "Magic is color," I say softly. "It turns and twists in shapes and patterns; it sparks or glimmers or pulses. Some magic is sharp and some is bright, some dark, some cold. And it tastes like—" I shrug. "I don't know. It tastes like magic."

"Perhaps you have only to reach for it in the right way. Perhaps it is not as impossible as you think."

I huff in frustration. "Could my brother help me?"

"The Prism Master?" The Yellow Lord laughs. "Certainly, if he could be bothered. But you have already asked him, haven't you?"

I slump in on myself. "Why won't he help me?"

The Yellow Lord looks at me with a sort of regretful frankness. He smiles, thin and haunted. "Because he's afraid of you, Eldingar. Your brother is hungry for power—he is afraid that yours will surpass his."

"But he has Prism magic. I only have mind magic."

The Yellow Lord raises one white eyebrow. "I read your brother when he came to me the first time. He was sickly, once. He could hardly walk. What little magic he had was eating him up from the inside. What happened, do you think, that so changed him?"

Dread worms through me. "He said he learned to control his magic. He said our father taught him."

The Yellow Lord studies his hands, light dancing once more between his fingertips. "Or perhaps he learned how to tap into your father's magic. To sap it from him. Have you ever heard of a Prism Master who died before they reached their third century?"

"Brandr would *never*—"

The Yellow Lord catches my arm, his eyes piercing me as his light dances from his skin to mine. The light doesn't burn me. It isn't even hot.

"Do you truly know," he says, "the things your brother would never do? Do you know him at all?"

Images flash through my mind: Lilja bent over her worktable, her fingers covered in grease, her spectacles sliding down her nose. Me, perched on a stool at her elbow and barely acknowledged. But Brandr isn't there. He never is. He's always shut away in his room, reading. Resenting me.

The Yellow Lord sighs and I see his age, suddenly, behind his eyes—he's older than the mountain, older than the ice, older than I can possibly imagine. He lets go of me, and I take a step back from him.

"Now," says the Yellow Lord, "I must rest before my trial of power in the morning."

"What exactly does this trial of power entail?"

His eyes glitter. "You will have to ask him that. He bid me to silence."

"Must you obey him?" I demand.

"I am bound to the one who unchained me."

"And when he . . . unleashes you . . . you will consume everyone and everything outside of the mountain, except Iljaria."

The Yellow Lord nods. "It is my purpose, Eldingar. It is why I was made."

I take a breath, struck by a sudden realization. "It will kill you. To expend that much power."

He gives me a wry smile. "It is my purpose," he repeats. "It is why I was made."

Grief sticks hard in my throat.

"Young one," he says gently. "Go."

I turn. I go.

I tell myself that at least everyone in the mountain will be safe. At least Saga and Vil and Ballast, at least Gulla and Rute and Finnur and all the children from the Collection, won't be consumed.

Saga will survive. Ballast will survive. I'll make sure of it.

They will hate me forever. But they will survive.

When I emerge from the tunnel that leads to the mountain's heart, I find Brandr waiting in the corridor. There's no disguising where I've been, and I tell myself I don't need to feel guilty—I have just as much right as my brother to speak with the First One.

I fold my arms across my chest and face Brandr with my chin up. "What did the Yellow Lord mean by a trial of power? What are you going to make him do?"

Brandr frowns. "Brynja, I thought you'd be in bed by now."

"I'm not a child, Brandr. It's hardly the fifteenth hour. Now what did he mean?"

A muscle twitches in my brother's jaw. "He's to execute the prisoners in the great hall. You'll be there to watch, never fear."

I stare at him in abject horror. "You can't do that."

"Of course I can. I'm Prism Master, and acting ruler of the mountain. I can *do* whatever I want."

Panic wrenches in my gut, and my heart beats too quick, too hard. "That's not our way, Brandr. That's not the Iljaria way. We don't kill people in cold blood! The First Ones taught us to hold life sacred, to uphold peace, to—"

"And you say you're not a child," he cuts me off, mocking me. "Do you really believe all that, Brynja? The Skaandans, the Daerosians—I don't care who they are or what you think they have or haven't done. They're guilty of defiling the Iljaria's sacred land. They're guilty of dealing out blood and death and war. They're guilty of murder. Justice must be had."

"And you think you're the one to deal it out?" I demand. "You're not a First One, Brandr. You're not even the ruler of the Iljaria. You're just—you're just—"

His eyes go hard, magic rolling off him in prismatic waves. "I'm just what, Brynja?"

I step toward him. I reach out my right hand and touch his cheek, his stubble rough under my fingertips. I lift my hand higher, to his temple.

Power sears me and I gasp in pain, a vision wrenching through me with horrible sharpness.

Brandr sits on a stool in the corner of our father's office, watching him lock my magic inside of me. He hates me. He hates me so much, *because I have been deemed useful, and he is weak and small and alone.*

Brandr sits in the dark of his room, a single lamp burning on the table beside him. He reads an ancient book, its pages so brittle and soft they crumble as he turns them, so he reads as quickly and as thoroughly as he can.

The book is about the Ghost Lord. About the power our parents won't admit that he has, the power that is eating him from the inside. The power he fears so deeply will kill him if he does not learn how to channel it. The book tells him that the Ghost Lord's power does not nullify other magic, as all the tales say. It consumes other powers. Absorbs them. And grows. If he can learn how to wield his gift, he need not be sickly and weak any longer. He can be strong.

It is hard to learn, in the dark, in the quiet. But he does. Slowly. And bit by bit he becomes stronger. Until he can glean pieces of magic from our mother, little specks she won't realize are missing. Until he can absorb power from our father, enough that our father begins, at last, to notice him.

Our father is proud that Brandr's power has finally shown itself, relieved that it is not the abominable gift he feared it was. And our father begins to train him in the wielding of Prism magic. Because he does not know that the magic Brandr uses is his own. He does not realize, until it is too late, that as Brandr grows stronger, he grows weaker.

Then it is too late, and there is nothing left of our father but a hollow shell, and Brandr grows tall and strong, bursting with power. It is Brandr who releases our father's body to the stars while our mother stands near, cold and sad and not understanding why, not understanding how. Or perhaps simply not wanting to understand.

I jerk back from my brother, head wheeling, heart pounding. For an instant, my magic was mine again—it drew those images from Brandr's mind. But now, even though I scrabble and reach, it's gone again, its absence a hollow in my very soul.

Brandr doesn't seem to have noticed any of this. He just frowns at me, like I'm a pesky fly. "Don't worry, little sister. Your despicable king will be the first to die. I'll make sure you have a prime seat."

Without another word, he pushes past me and steps onto the stairs winding down to the tunnel.

Then he's gone.

I stare after him, my whole world inverting itself.

One thing is brutally clear: Brandr doesn't believe in pacifism anymore, if he ever did. I am not sure if any of my people do, not truly, not as I was taught when I was small. Maybe the Iljaria never believed in true peace. Maybe I don't, either. Maybe Vil was right, all those weeks ago, and the Iljaria's professed pacifism *is* a sham. What is the good of near-limitless power if it isn't used to protect and defend, to uphold peace and preserve life?

Whether Brandr intended it at first or not, he killed our father.

And now he's going to kill Saga and Vil. Now he's going to kill Ballast.

Now he's going to kill *Kallias*.

This realization twists inside me like a serrated blade, and I feel every jagged cut. Death by the Yellow Lord is too good for Kallias. He murdered Lilja. He tormented me and countless others. He laughed while he did it. Death by the Yellow Lord is too good for him. Kallias stole my childhood, my family, my magic, my name. He murdered my sister and caged me like an animal. He tormented me, day after day, year after year, kept me trapped and terrified in the never-ending dark. But no more.

No more.

My feet turn toward the great hall before I even tell them to, and somehow there's already a knife in my hand.

CHAPTER TWENTY-FIVE

YEAR 4200, Month of the Ghost Lord
Daeros—Tenebris

Kallias is asleep on my ledge, though it's far too small for him. He's curled up like a child, his head tucked into his arms, his legs dangling into the empty space of the iron cage. I try not to see how much he looks like Ballast. I try not to think about Ballast at all.

I slip up the chain without a sound and hang there a moment, watching him sleep. I don't understand how he can be so helpless, so fragile, this man who held my life in his hands for nearly a decade. I sidle around the outside of the cage to the sleeping ledge. My knife finds his throat.

He wakes in an instant, his body perfectly still, his blue eyes blinking up into mine in the semidarkness of the great hall. "I was wondering when you would be back, little acrobat." His words are quiet, careful around the point of the knife. But he has the audacity to smile.

I press the blade in a little deeper. A trickle of red runs down his throat. "My brother means to execute you tomorrow."

"And you have come early to save him the trouble, is that it?" His eyes bore into mine, fearless and unflinching. "I knew you were my wayward acrobat the moment you paraded in here with those Skaandan fools. There's too much pride in you—and too much fear. Why do you think I allowed you to get close to me? Why do you think I offered to make you queen? Certainly not because I *desired* you."

I fight to keep hold of myself. If I kill him now, I won't have answers to my questions, and he won't know exactly why I mean to end him.

He just smirks at me. He wants me to ask.

"Why?" I grind out.

He shows his teeth. "To mock you. To draw you closer and closer until I could strangle you alive, make you pay for escaping from my Collection and *daring* to come back. I'm not a fool. I knew the treaty was a ruse. But I like a good game, Brynja. It helps to pass the time. And what better game than toying with your Skaandan friends and you? All the sweeter when the long night is over, when I could throw your worthless corpses into the Sea of Bones."

"Shut up." My throat is starting to hurt, the old terror coiling through me.

He smiles and smiles. "And my worthless son, Ballast, near bursting with rage to see you with me—I swear the stupid boy is half in love with you."

"I said shut *up*!"

Kallias raises his eyebrows. "I figured you came here to talk, little acrobat. Or else you would have killed me already."

I'm livid that he reads my mind so easily. I don't withdraw the knife, eyes fixed on the line of red that slides down his neck and seeps into his collar.

"This is about your sister, I suppose."

I tighten my grip on the knife as images flash through my mind: Lilja bent over her worktable, Lilja overseeing the packing of her inventions, Lilja beaming in pride as she showed her wings to Kallias. Lilja falling, falling, falling.

"I should have recognized you, when you joined my Collection, as the Iljaria monster who nearly brought down the mountain on top of us. I shouldn't have been fooled by your dark hair, your sudden flair for acrobatics." He sighs a little. "But in my defense, I barely even noticed you the first time you were here. Your sister vastly overshadowed you, you know."

I gnaw on the inside of my cheek, because I *will not* give him the satisfaction of seeing me cry. "You murdered her."

He gives a noncommittal shrug.

I'm trembling; the point of my knife shakes. "Why?"

"Your sister was remarkable. I wanted her to stay here in Daeros. I wanted her to be part of my Collection. But your parents wouldn't hear of it—I even offered them a fortune, told them she would be treated like a queen—"

"A *lie*," I spit.

"—and they had the audacity to say that their little genius was not for sale." Kallias blinks at me, his blue eyes glassy in the dim light. His lips curl into a smile. "Do you know what they offered me instead?"

A sick dread slides into my veins. I grind my jaw shut, refusing to answer.

"They offered me *you*, Brynja, their youngest daughter, who had the power to control minds. I got the feeling they were afraid of you, you know. Of what you could do. They saw an opportunity to get rid of you, and they seized it."

Spots jump in my eyes, and I bite harder and harder into my cheek, until I taste blood.

Kallias's smile sharpens. "I didn't want you—why would I? I wanted Lilja. I wanted her to join her genius to mine, to create marvelous machines with me, to help me burrow into the heart of the mountain faster, easier. But your parents refused, and it made me angry. If I couldn't have her, I didn't see why anyone else should."

My head wheels, my palms sweat. I adjust my grip on the outside of the cage, muscles trembling in the effort to hold me there. Lord of Fire, I'm going to be sick. "You murdered my sister because my parents told you no."

Kallias tilts his head to one side. "I killed her because I didn't want *you*. It was the easiest thing in the world, you know. I'd heard her brag about her wings. I sent a servant to your rooms. Had him grind iron shavings into the wood, the canvas. So her magic would fail. I didn't count on you, of course, the little Iljaria girl grown so powerful in her rage that she nearly tumbled the mountain down around my ears. The Prism Master himself could barely subdue you, let alone contain you. You could have killed me right then on that frozen cliff. But you didn't have it in you, then. You weren't quite enough of a monster."

My throat feels thick and tight. I am hollow, numb. A tear slides down my cheek without my consent. I focus on the king, the trickle of blood on his pale neck. "Is that why you kill people?" I ask him quietly. "Because you are a monster?"

His eyes bore into mine. "I kill because it makes me feel powerful. It makes me feel alive. When you kill me, Brynja, what will you feel?"

I stare at him, stare *into* him, and see for a moment a soul as fragile and tremulous as my own. "I'll feel peace. I'll be able to sleep at night, knowing there is one less monster in the world."

"And what of the monster chained below, poised to devour the world? What of the monster you call your brother, who dresses in the robes of the Prism Master and means to rule the world when it has been devoured?"

"Brandr isn't a monster," I say, but my voice shakes, because I'm not sure I believe that.

Kallias doesn't reply, just looks at me. For an instant I see Ballast in him, a child who longs to be a man, to prove himself, to be taken seriously. Then I blink and see Lilja falling. I see Hilf dead on the floor in a widening pool of blood. I see the children of the Collection, kept in cages, beaten on his whim. I feel their fear and I feel my own, back when he had power over me.

But it's Kallias in the cage now. And I'm the one holding the blade.

My rage surges back, stitched into every part of me. I tighten my fingers around the handle of my knife.

"What will you do when I'm dead?" says Kallias softly.

"Be free," I whisper.

And then I drive the knife deep into his heart.

CHAPTER TWENTY-SIX

YEAR 4200, Month of the Ghost Lord
Daeros—Tenebris

Kallias's blood is sticky on my hand. I try to wipe it off on my skirt, but it just smears and catches in the silk.

I crouch in the vent that connects with the great hall, scrubbing at the blood, scrubbing and scrubbing. But it just continues to smear, and at last I give up, cursing. I pull my knees tight against my chin. I sob, without understanding why.

I killed him. And Kallias was right. For a moment I felt powerful. And then I scrambled down to the floor and was sick in one of the potted orange trees.

It takes a long while before I come back to myself, lift my head, wipe my eyes. I realize that the night grows short. That there is not much time left before the Yellow Lord's trial of power.

What am I going to do?

I can't let my brother kill Saga and Vil. I can't let him kill *Ballast*. I can't, can't, can't. But how am I supposed to stop him? If I had my magic, maybe I could—what, subdue him and the fifty Iljaria who answer to him? Violet *Lord*, who do I think I am?

Gulla's words spell out in my mind: *You need to figure out where your loyalties truly lie. You need to figure out what is buried within your own heart.*

Where *do* my loyalties lie?

With my family, with my people. Of course they do. Of course.

But.

My father, forging me into a tool, locking my magic away, sending me into the den of a lion without a backward glance. I was just a sacrifice. A useful sacrifice, and a willing one.

But a sacrifice all the same.

Did he ever think about me, after he sent me away? Did he hope I was doing well? Or was he just impatient for news of the Yellow Lord? He didn't send the ambassador more than once.

I am Iljaria. I must be faithful to my people.

But.

The Iljaria are pacifists. We don't believe in war, in death. It is not our way.

Except our history is steeped in war and death. The entire nation of Skaanda fled Iljaria to escape it. To cover our shame, we built a barrier of magic and hid in the haven of power and privilege we created while the rest of the world destroyed one another. And now Iljaria has emerged again, to seize more power and remake the world according to our whims.

To Brandr this is justice. Retribution. He has no qualms at all in sacrificing two peoples to accomplish his purpose.

I can't accept that.

Saga, trusting me to carry her through the snow. Trusting me in the caves, even when she woke to find her worst enemy there with us. Saga, bursting with joy when we met up with the Skaandan army. Pulling me out of my nightmares. Trusting me, always trusting me, even as I plotted to betray her.

Vil, befriending me, making me feel safe, reminding me what it should be like to have a family. Dreaming of bigger and better things for the country he so loves. Offering his heart, even though I found myself unable to take it.

And Ballast. There on the cliff when my sister died, there in the great hall when his father locked me in an iron cage. There in his childhood bedroom, bringing me food and books, giving me the precious gift of light and companionship to hold back the horror of the dark. There in the caves by a rushing river, his mouth on mine and his fingers in my hair. There in his father's prison cell, reviling me, burns on his neck where the collar bound him.

I can't let my brother kill him. I can't let him kill any of them.

I refuse.

My throat hurts. Kallias's blood is stiff and dried on my hand now. I try not to think about him, slumped and dead in the cage. I told him I would be free, when he was dead. But I'm not.

If I don't do something, and do something *now*, that will be Saga and Vil, very soon. That will be Ballast.

Gulla's fingers flash in my memory, spelling out a truth I wasn't quite ready for: *You need to figure out what is buried within your own heart.*

I take a breath.

I think you already know.

She's right.

I do.

I should stop to scrub my hands, to change my gown, before I go back to Gulla's room, but I don't. When I drop down from the vent, Gulla, Rute, Finnur, and a few other of the older children are waiting for me. The younger ones are asleep in the big bed, their dreams making them whimper.

Gulla and the others look at me, and I see the truth of what I've done reflected in their eyes. I don't know why, but I feel dirty, ashamed, like Kallias's blood has seeped through my skin and into my heart. I am a monster now—isn't that what Kallias said I would become? My cheek is raw and tender where I gnawed on it. I bite down again, because I don't have time to cry anymore.

You have decided, Gulla signs to me.

I nod.

"What do you need us to do?" asks Finnur. Yellow and violet spark around his head.

"We're ready," says Rute quietly. "All of us."

My throat hurts and I hate this—how can I ask them to risk their lives after everything they've already been through?

Gulla gives me a frank look. *Time is running out.*

I take a deep breath, send each of them a swift, hard glance. "After the sun rises again, when the Iljaria queen arrives, my brother means to unleash the Yellow Lord and wipe out Skaanda and Daeros. We can't let him."

Rute and Finnur nod. Pór, the Skaandan cellist of about ten, looks determined, while twelve-year-old Gaiana, a Daerosian mathematician, gulps nervously.

"Tomorrow—in a few hours, actually, he's going to execute innocent prisoners, including the prince and princess of Skaanda and . . . and Ballast."

Gulla's eyes go wet, and she ducks her head so I won't see.

"What's your plan, Brynja?" asks Rute. She jiggles her foot, muscles antsy.

I tell them.

It doesn't feel like a plan, really. And there's not much of a chance it will work. But it's all we have.

Rute will come with me through the ceiling to the dungeons, where we'll free the prisoners. She'll sneak most of them into the tunnels to hide, and then go to fetch Kallias's wives and Princess Aelia and bring them there, too. Then she'll raid the kitchen and the cellar to keep everyone fed. Gaiana and Gulla will usher the children into the tunnels, while Finnur and Pór go to free the Daerosian army. I don't like this at all, but Finnur claims he has enough magic to get past a few Iljaria guards.

It's up to me to talk to Saga, Vil, and Ballast.

We don't have any time to spare. I give Gulla a quick, fierce hug; then Rute and I scramble up into the vents.

My heart is a riot in my chest as I drop down outside the door to the dungeon. Rute lands beside me and picks the lock with swift efficiency. I'm glad—I'm shaking too hard to be of much use.

Rute starts methodically unlocking all the cell doors and explaining to everyone with quiet urgency what's going on. Lysandra starts shrieking out demands, but her brothers quickly hush her and join Rute in spreading the word.

I go straight to Vil and Saga's cell, every nerve on fire. Kallias's blood cracks stiff on my hand, and just the sight of it makes my head wheel. Why didn't I stop in my rooms to wash, to change? It's too late now.

Saga is slumped in the corner, her face to the wall, but Vil lifts his head, watching me. He looks pinched, hungry, and I have the sudden horrifying realization that my brother probably never sent any food down here.

"Brynja," says Vil. "What do you want?"

Saga jerks around at his words, her eyes flashing. Rage coils off her.

I take a breath. I gnaw on the raw spot in my cheek. I will myself to have courage.

"My brother means to kill you all tomorrow. I'm here to rescue you."

Saga throws her head back and laughs, then picks up a rock and hurls it at me through the bars. I duck but the rock grazes my face, leaving a raw line of pain in its wake.

"LIKE HELL YOU ARE!" she shrieks at me.

I gnaw on my lip. "The Yellow Lord is chained in the heart of the mountain. *He's* the weapon my people buried so long ago. My brother will make the Yellow Lord kill you, and then, when the sun rises and the Iljaria queen arrives, he's going to unleash the Yellow Lord wholly, and wipe out all of Daeros and Skaanda. Millions of people are going to die unless you help me stop him."

"And how exactly could *I* help the *Iljaria*?" snaps Saga.

I touch one of the iron bars, let its coldness burn me. "I wanted to tell you, Saga," I say quietly. "I almost did, lots of times. But Indridi—"

Saga stiffens, and Vil drops his eyes to the floor.

"She urged me to keep my secret, as she kept hers. She said—she said—" Grief and helplessness roar within me. "She said it didn't matter that we were friends. That if I told you I was Iljaria, I would be arrested. Executed." I chew on my lip. "She was my cousin, you know."

Saga's eyes go wet. Vil curses and slams the heel of his hand into the rock.

My heart beats, beats. "I thought I was serving my people, being faithful to the task my father set me all those years ago. But I couldn't leave you to die, Saga. I couldn't do it when we escaped. I can't do it now. My brother's actions are *wrong*. This land used to belong to the Iljaria. But that doesn't give him the right to take it back again like this. My people are supposed to believe in peace, in the sanctity of life. This is revenge. This is death." I clench my bloodied hand. I try not to think of Kallias, stiff and cold in my dangling cage. I believed that too, once.

"You betrayed us," says Vil, his voice rough and cold. "Why would we trust you now?"

I give a tired lift of my shoulders. "Because I can't do this alone. And because you are my friends. My . . . family. And because—because I'm sorry." My voice breaks.

It's Saga who gets up, who paces over to the cell door. There is still anger in her eyes, but the hatred has, perhaps, lessened a little.

"I was wrong," I say. "I was so wrong, Saga. I won't ask you to forgive me. But will you help me?"

Behind me, Rute and the rest of the prisoners are waiting. I glance back at her and give her a swift nod. She leads them away, ushering

While the Dark Remains

them through an entrance to the tunnels I found on my last visit here, just past Ballast's cell. Pala and Leifur are the only ones who linger.

Vil climbs slowly to his feet and comes to stand by Saga. "What's your plan, Brynja?"

I pick the lock to their cell and pull the door open. They both come out, eyeing me warily.

"The Skaandan army has to be close," I say. "I haven't told my brother about them, so he doesn't know they're coming. Go down into the tunnels, speak with the scout, meet up with your soldiers. The Daerosian army should be free shortly. The combined forces of both armies should be enough to subdue fifty Iljaria. Rute can bring messages back and forth to coordinate the attack."

Vil looks at me doubtfully. "Can't your brother just kill us all with a snap of his fingers?"

I grimace. "That's why I have to get my magic back. I'm going to talk to Ballast. I think he might be able to help me, and I think the Daerosian army will follow him. So all we need to do is—"

"Ballast is gone," Saga interrupts.

I blink at her. "What?"

"After your last little visit, an obliging rat came and brought him the key to his cell. He's gone."

Panic races through me. "Where did he go? Why didn't he let you all out?"

"Why would he?" she snaps. "He has no love for Skaandans."

"He said something about gathering his own army," says Vil.

"The Daerosians?" I ask.

Vil shakes his head. "I don't think he meant a human army."

CHAPTER TWENTY-SEVEN

YEAR 4200, Month of the Ghost Lord
Daeros—the tundra

Saga doesn't trust me. I'm not sure she ever will again, and I can't blame her. Vil barely looks at me, and I wonder if his love for me died the moment he learned my true heritage. I can't really blame him, either.

But it still hurts.

I see Saga, Vil, Pala, and Leifur safely into the tunnels, where the Skaandan scout, Aisa, is still waiting. Saga gives a cry of relief, and Vil's shoulders visibly relax. Leifur and Pala greet her warmly. I feel like the worst kind of outsider. Unacknowledged. Unneeded.

"The army is close," Aisa tells us, "not more than three days away."

Vil quickly catches her up on the change in plan, and Aisa flicks her eyes at me, brows raised.

There's no point in me lingering. "I'll be back as soon as I can," I say quietly.

Saga grits her jaw but doesn't say anything.

For half a moment Vil meets my gaze. "You had better be, Brynja. Betray us again and I'll kill you myself."

While the Dark Remains

My stomach churns with the memory of his pronouncing Indridi's fate. "I know," I say.

Then I'm gone, back up the cellar stairs, around a corner, into the safety of a heating vent.

I stop briefly in my room, long enough to finally wash the blood from my hands and change into sturdy trousers, a heavy shift, tall boots. I shrug into a fur-lined coat and bundle supplies into a pack, and then I'm ready.

It's the twenty-second hour by the mantel time-glass. I don't know how far Ballast is ahead of me, but if I want to find him, I'm going to have to hurry.

I scramble back into the vent and take the shortest route possible to exit the mountain. Ballast knew the Skaandan army was coming through the tunnels—he wouldn't have gone that way and risked running into them.

I slip out a side door meant for dumping wastewater and am hit by a sudden onslaught of frigid, stinging wind. I bow my head and trudge into the dark and the snow, pulling up the hood of my coat and cinching it tight.

When I'm a little ways from the mountain, I shut my eyes and *feel* for the echo of Ballast's magic, to give me some sense of which direction he's gone. I reach, reach, beyond grateful that my sensitivity to magic wasn't locked away with the rest of my power. This, above anything, gives me hope that I'll be able to find it again.

If Ballast can help me, that is.

I reach, reach.

Then—

There.

I catch my breath and open my eyes. For a heartbeat I see a faint spark of blue, bobbing far east beyond the mountain. I blink and it's gone.

I pull an Iljaria light globe from my pack and lift it high, illuminating my way.

"Wait for me, Ballast," I whisper, bending my head into the wind and trudging west, wet flakes of snow clinging to my eyelashes. "Wait for me. I'm coming."

I remember the heat of him, the taste of his magic, and I know very well that needing my own magic back is not the only reason I'm going after him.

※

I walk on, shoving through deeply mounded snow, pulling my hood tight against the wind. The Iljaria light doesn't waver, my only companion in the cold dark.

My thoughts drift again and again to the Bronze God, pulling my magic out of me with long silver hooks. I try to reach him in my own mind, but I cannot find him, or he does not wish to be found, and I am left with my panic, driving me onward.

I am terrified that the Iljaria queen will arrive with an army of her own before the Skaandan and Daerosian armies can join forces. I am terrified that Brandr won't even wait for the queen and will unleash the Yellow Lord at his own whim. I'm afraid that Saga and Vil will die thinking I betrayed them again.

And I'm afraid Ballast won't ever forgive me, and I won't be able to find him, and that both of us will die all alone in the light of the Yellow Lord's power.

Violet Lord, I pray. *Let me reach Ballast in time.*

I trudge onward, uncertain if I've been walking for one hour or ten. But I know time is running out.

Soon Brandr will unleash the Yellow Lord, and all will be lost.

It stops snowing after a while, and I glimpse the sparks of Ballast's magic again. I bow my head into the wind and push on.

The eastern sky begins to glow bit by bit, and it grows so unbearably strong I have to squint against the light. Before my eyes the landscape is illuminated, a wide snowy ridge, with a globe of fire rising beyond.

This isn't Ballast's magic.

It's the sun.

"Yellow Lord," I whisper.

I tilt back my hood and lean into the sunlight, its fingers touching my skin with delicious, impossible warmth. I love the light, beyond welcome after so long a darkness.

I squint against the sunrise, because someone is coming over the ridge.

A lone figure, dark against the snow, the sun, but no—not alone. A mass of shapes follows behind, blurring together, a hundred strong, a thousand, too many to count.

The figure leading them blazes with magic, a pillar of blue fire. Ballast.

I stare as he comes, heart thrumming against my breastbone, all the breath gone out of me.

The sun rises, and Ballast draws nearer, the shapes at his back resolving into an army of beasts: arctic bears and lanky white lions, huge gray wolves and magnificently antlered stags. They are glorious, *he* is glorious, all of them gleaming in the new sun.

Ballast strides tall and fey, a thick white cloak hung around his shoulders, a jewel blazing bright from his forehead. He wears no patch over his ruined eye, the socket red and scarred against his brown skin.

I stand there waiting, undone by the sight of him. I watch him see me, watch the anger come into his face, the tightness into his frame.

He could kill me with a thought, and suddenly I'm terrified that he will.

He stops a half dozen paces away, cloak whipping about his ankles. I drop to my knees in the snow, bowing my head before the rightful king of Daeros.

"I need your help," I say to the ground.

He doesn't answer and I dare to glance up, into his one piercing blue eye. It's so like his father's it makes my gut twist.

Behind him the animals pause in their march, the stags blowing and stamping at the ground, their breath curls of fog in the frigid air. The lions crouch on muscular hindquarters, ready to spring, their sleek white bodies turned to gold in the sunlight. The wolves whine and the bears growl and the whole teeming mass of them smells of musk and damp fur. They pulse with heat.

I force myself to hold Ballast's gaze. I force myself to tell him what I must tell him. "I did what I swore I'd do, all those years ago. I killed your father."

A hard line comes into his face, but he still doesn't speak.

I look up at him, heart raging, the snow seeping in through my trousers and freezing my skin. "My brother means to unleash the Yellow Lord and destroy all of Daeros and Skaanda. I need you to help me stop him. Your magic is the only thing strong enough to stand against him. Yours and—" I take a breath. "Yours and mine."

Still he doesn't say anything, just stares down at me, jaw tight, cloak snapping in the wind.

"I need you to help me unlock my magic." My voice shakes. "I need you to make me whole again so we can defeat my brother and bind the Yellow Lord anew. I need you to help me save our people. All of them."

"You're a liar, a traitor, a spy." His voice is harsh and cold and sends a tremor through me. "Why should I believe anything you say?"

I pull something from my pocket and lift my hand into Ballast's view, unfolding my fingers so he can see the pebbles resting there, blue and shining, washed smooth by the waters of an underground stream. "I almost told you then," I say softly. "That last day, with the river beside us and the stone at our backs." *Your mouth on mine,* I tell him with my eyes, *your magic burning inside of me.*

His jaw tenses. "Why didn't you?"

"Because I was afraid."

"What were you afraid of?"

While the Dark Remains

I stare at the pebbles, trying not to think of Ballast's eye, of everything else we've lost since then. "I was afraid I would forsake everything to stay with you, down there in the dark."

"Why didn't you?"

His question lingers in the air, and I lift my gaze to his. I don't know how to tell him that, in my mind, there was too much left undone, that the pull of my people was still too strong, even stronger than him. I don't feel that now.

"We are the same, you and I," I say instead. "Yearning for light and yet trapped in the darkness. We're bound by the same bloodline. The same fate. Down there in the tunnels—me and you—it was real to me, Bal. And I think—I think it was real to you, too." I take a breath, my outstretched hand trembling with the effort of staying still. "I can't follow the Iljaria, not with Brandr leading them. I *won't*. Please help me. Please."

He considers me, my knees growing numb in the snow. Something in him softens, and he reaches out a hand, closes my fingers over the pebbles again, and pulls me to my feet. For a moment he doesn't draw away, his fingers rough and warm over mine. Power crackles off him, and my heart rages. I am sorry when he lets go of my hand, puts space between us again. I drop the pebbles back into my pocket.

I glance to the animals behind him, a restless, seething swarm, armed with tooth and horn and claw.

Ballast sighs a little. "I suppose you have a plan?"

I tell him.

CHAPTER TWENTY-EIGHT

YEAR 4201, Month of the Yellow Lord
Daeros—the tundra

There isn't any time to spare. I am not sure when the Iljaria queen will arrive—or if she already has—but Soul's Rest is over, and I don't wholly trust my brother to wait for her before unleashing the Yellow Lord. The sooner Ballast and I get back to Tenebris, the better.

Asvaldr lumbers out from amid the host of animals, and bows his head before Ballast, who rubs his neck affectionately and then scrambles up onto the massive bear's back. Ballast reaches out his hand to pull me up after him, and for a moment I balk, staring.

"He won't hurt you," says Ballast. "And it will be faster than walking."

I take a breath. I let him pull me up and have barely settled in behind him before Asvaldr lopes forward, enormous paws plowing through the snow. My stomach lurches with every movement and I hold tight to Ballast, my heart thudding against his back, closer to him than I've ever been, save by the river in the tunnels.

After a while I grow used to the motion and breathe a little easier, hyperaware of Ballast's warmth and power, pressed up against him.

The rest of the animals follow at a slower pace, growing ever fainter behind us.

This first light of the new year lasts only an hour before the sun begins to sink west again, blue shadows slanting long over the snow. Asvaldr lopes along, seemingly tireless, chasing the light.

I can't quite parse out Ballast's mood: He's been pensive, quiet, since I told him my plan. But the tension seems to ease out of him bit by bit as Asvaldr lumbers across the snow.

"How did you find them all?" I say at last, into Ballast's shoulder. "The animals?"

It takes him a moment to answer, and I wonder if it's difficult for him to talk when he's holding so many creatures to his will, that maybe that's the reason he's barely spoken. "I called Asvaldr, and he called the others. When I asked them, they bound themselves to me, every one. They will fight for me."

I feel a rush of pride for him. But even if we manage to stop Brandr, the tension between Skaanda and Daeros and Aerona won't just evaporate. I'll have my work cut out for me, convincing Ballast and Saga and Vil and Aelia to forge a real, lasting peace.

"Why didn't you free the others when you left?" I say. "Saga and Vil. Your own siblings."

He grimaces. "I couldn't have brought them with me—they would have only gotten in the way. I was going to free them when I got back. When Tenebris was mine."

I digest this without further comment.

Ballast glances back at me, as if trying to read my thoughts.

I stare at the marks on his neck, left from the iron collar, and I hate myself for not freeing him of it sooner.

"I wondered if it was you," says Ballast quietly, into the setting sun. "No one could ever forget the girl who nearly brought the mountain crashing down around her with the strength of her anger and her grief."

I bite my cheek to hold back the tears. Ballast was there that day, when Lilja fell to her death.

"I wondered," he says, "when my father brought you to Daeros, when he locked you in an iron cage and hung you from the ceiling. I wondered if it was you. Your hair wasn't white. You had no magic. And yet. The pattern of your freckles was familiar. So were your eyes, fierce and dark. And the haughty tilt of your chin."

"I wasn't haughty."

A laugh huffs out of him. "Yes, you were. But I didn't understand how it *could* be you. It didn't make any sense. But that day I caught you spying on me—"

I flush and am glad he can't see me.

"You told me your name," he says. "And it was the same as hers. The girl who almost brought the mountain down. I was beyond glad when you kept coming to see me, those next few months. The time we spent together—it made me feel human, Brynja. I was devastated when my mother told me I had to end it. She was right, but . . . I wish it could have gone differently."

The old pain pricks at my heart.

"But I didn't forget about you. I watched you for years, and you never gave a hint that you were anything but what you pretended to be. So I thought I must have imagined it." He glances back at me, eye catching mine in the last glimmers of light. "How could you have done it," he says with quiet agony. "How could you have put yourself at my father's mercy, let him debase you, abuse you, torment you, for year after year after *year*? How could you bear it, Brynja?"

My throat goes tight as his eye gleams with moisture. And I know the question is not wholly directed at me.

The sun drops below the western horizon; for a little while more, Asvaldr gambols in its afterglow, paw prints silver in the snow. Ballast sends an Iljaria light globe bobbing ahead of us to illuminate our path as the white bear runs on.

"Tell me about your magic," says Ballast then. "Tell me how it was locked away."

I do, leaving out nothing: my father, the Bronze God, the chest, the silver hooks, the crack in the stone. I tell him how I can still sense magic, see it, feel it.

"You can't find the chest?" he says. "Can't go back to that place inside your head?"

"I've tried, but I can't seem to get there on my own. The Yellow Lord told me—"

Ballast straightens in surprise. "You spoke with the Yellow Lord?"

"Yes. He told me that my father pitted my magic against itself. So that only my magic can unlock it."

Ballast twists around on Asvaldr's back, squinting at me. He puts his fingers on my temples, as my father once did. His skin is rough and warm, and I shut my eyes, heart pounding. His magic slides through me, whisper soft.

But nothing happens.

He withdraws his hands, and I have to restrain myself from yanking them back again.

"I can't sense anything, Brynja. There is nothing for me to hold on to, nothing for me to pull out. I think the Yellow Lord is right. I think you have to unlock it yourself. No one else can do it for you."

"But I've tried! I can't do it."

"Maybe you haven't tried hard enough."

Anger sparks inside me, wild and hard. "What is that supposed to mean?"

"Maybe you need to want it more. Maybe you need to *need* it more."

I grind my jaw and bite back a curse. "But I *do* need it. It's the only thing I need!"

Ballast turns forward again. "When we get closer, we'll try something else."

I press him for more information, but he won't elaborate. I finally get tired of asking and snap my mouth shut.

"Did you really let your father take your eye to earn back his trust?" I ask him a while later, Asvaldr still bearing us onward. Ballast hasn't said anything about Kallias yet, whether he's angry at me for killing him, whether he's glad he's dead. I try not to think about him slumped in my cage, his blood slick on my hands.

Ballast's whole body goes tense, and I regret the question. But he answers me anyway.

"He dared me to do it. He said that if I gave him my eye, he would believe I was earnest in my return. In my repentance." Ballast's voice is thick with grief, or perhaps the memory of pain.

Something goes sick and still in my belly.

"I needed him to believe me," he goes on, quieter now. "I needed to get myself named heir. Afterward I was going to arrange his assassination and seize the throne. I was going to bring justice back into Daeros. I still mean to. But"—he takes a shaky breath—"it was . . . harder . . . than I thought it would be."

I gnaw on my cheek to keep the tears from coming. "I hate that he did that to you."

"I let him." Ballast's voice is thick with emotion.

"He still shouldn't have done it. Everything was a game to him."

"You let him play his games with you, too," says Ballast softly.

I take a breath. "I thought I could win."

He gives a little huff that could be a laugh or could be a sob. "So did I."

I think about my own father. He was also playing a game that I conceded to, a carved piece on a board moved about by his shrewd calculation, no regard for my well-being. Both Ballast and I let our fathers take from us, and I ache for everything that we have lost.

"You would make a good king," I tell him, and find that I mean it.

His jaw goes tight. "I have it in me to be cruel. Like my father."

I see again the deadness creeping into Kallias's eyes, the feeling of his lifeblood leaking warm onto my arm. My gut twists.

"So do we all," I say.

While the Dark Remains

It's still dark when we come to the edge of the Sea of Bones. I hadn't realized we had come north at all, let alone quite so far. Asvaldr jerks to a stop, and Ballast leaps down from his back. After a moment, I do the same.

The land plunges down into the frozen valley, where glaciers claw jagged fingers into the moonlit sky, or lie like the massive broken bones the Sea is named for, scattered across the brittle tundra and the frozen lake. The Sea is miles upon miles wide; I am not sure where we are on the southern edge of it, but we are enough in the middle that it appears to go on forever in three directions. And in any case, we have taken a detour we can't afford.

"Why are we here, Ballast?" I ask uneasily.

But Ballast puts his hand on Asvaldr's giant head and speaks into his ear.

A sudden sound like thunder shakes the earth beneath us.

It's the rest of the animal army, not nearly as far behind as I thought, racing across the snow in a blur of hooves and claws, spotted fur and antlered heads, wide wings and fierce calls. They surge past us, their tangled scents strong in my nose, snow spraying up in our faces.

"We'll catch up," Ballast tells me.

Asvaldr turns around in a circle and flops down in the snow with a grunt. Ballast paces up to the edge of the Sea of Bones. I watch him, but I don't follow.

"It occurs to me," says Ballast without looking over his shoulder, "that if you felt threatened enough, your magic might unbind itself to save you."

I blink at his shoulders, dread squeezing my insides. "What do you mean?"

His cloak whips about his ankles, the mingled light of the stars and the moon tracing him in silver. "Do you trust me, Brynja?"

The quiet longing in his words is enough to draw me to him; I step gingerly up to the edge of the Sea, heart thudding, sweat breaking out under my heavy coat. For a few long moments, I don't look aside at him. I think of Vil, asking me to trust him outside the walls of Skógur, how I told him I did but it was already a lie. I trusted my father, who molded me into his willing sacrifice and sent me away to be devoured. I trusted my brother, my people. But I was nothing to them beyond a game piece, easily discarded when I was no longer of use.

But Ballast isn't asking for something he hasn't already freely given to me.

"I trust you," I whisper. And I think that perhaps I trust myself, too.

Ballast looks at me. The jewel on his forehead shines. "Then jump," he says.

I jerk backward, ice skittering from under my feet and tumbling into the glacier valley. This is very like the place Lilja fell to her death, the place that still haunts my dreams. "I can't do that."

"If you want to unlock your magic, I think you have to."

I shake my head, terror pounding through me. "No."

"Trust me."

"You can't ask me to jump into the Sea of Bones!"

"Your magic was strong."

"I was a child, Ballast! I—I barely remember it."

"*I* remember it. You nearly brought the whole world down around us. Surely you can catch yourself if you fall."

"I *can't.*"

He takes a step toward me and I back away, terror stitched into my soul.

"I'm not going to hurt you," he says quietly. "I would never hurt you."

My throat hurts. "I know that, Bal."

"Then trust me." His voice breaks. "Try."

I look down into the Sea of Bones, wicked and grinning in the moonlight. I look at Ballast, his face racked in anguish.

"I'm afraid of falling," I whisper. Tears blur my vision.

His jaw works. "I know."

My heart beats, beats. I take a breath of ice-sharp air. I turn once more to the Sea.

And then I leap off the cliff.

All the breath is sucked out of my lungs as the frozen wind laughs and tumbles me downward.

Down, down, down.

I'm falling.

Falling.

Terror clouds my vision as images flash through my head: my sister's wings, Kallias's laugh, my roar that shook the very mountain.

But I'm falling, falling, the ice thundering up to meet me with its open, bony arms.

I'm screaming, somewhere outside of myself. Tears freeze on my cheeks. He told me to trust him and I did.

Still I fall, fall.

I scrabble desperately for my magic. But the only thing in my mind is fear.

My eyes close. A deadness steals through me, and I know there are only seconds left before I smash against the ice.

I am nothing, no one.

I fall

fall

fall.

I blink and see the chamber where the Bronze God once sat, mutilated and alone. His table is empty now, the candle guttered out. The hooks lie glinting wickedly in his vacant seat.

But the chest containing my magic is nowhere to be found.

Outside of my mind the wind rushes around me, the ice claws at my hair, the Sea of Bones reaches up to shatter me.

I will be nothing more than a memory, a whispered nothingness in the dead of winter dreams.

Inside my mind, I snatch the silver hooks and run from the chamber into the ancient cavern, where I'm greeted by crumbling statues and stone pillars half worn away. Everywhere, there are cracks in the stone, and I scrabble frantically inside each one, searching, searching, for the place I hid away my magic.

The silver hooks burn in my other hand, bitter fire gnawing down to bone.

My heart beats, beats.

Outside me, I am falling.

I dig into the cracks, anguished with each one that turns out empty.

But then I see a spark in the stone, glittering bronze, and I shove my hand into the rock and draw out the chest.

I sink to my knees as I open it, my magic mounded in a glittering pile. I tremble, because I've found it now, and I don't know how to take it back again.

Young one. What do you seek?

I turn to find the Bronze Lord, there beside me, his mutilated face shimmering in the dim light. He kneels on the stone, the stumps of his arms resting on his thighs.

"My power," I say. "But my father has reduced it to dust."

You did that yourself. His voice echoes strong inside me, resonant as a bell.

I gaze at the ruins of my magic in utter despair. "How can dust become a stone again?" I whisper.

How indeed, says the Bronze Lord. *But must it become a stone?*

I remember the hooks in my hands. I take them, dip them into the gleaming remains of my power. I twist. The dust winds onto the hooks, becoming gossamer threads as thin as spider silk. When the hook is full, I turn it on myself, plunging it deep into my temple. Agony bursts in my very soul. But I don't stop. I can't stop.

Outside, I am falling.

Over and over I wind my magic onto the hooks and drive them into my head. The pain burns and burns, eating me from the inside.

But with each new strand, I sense power returning to me, a trickle at first, then strong as a flood rushing over the plain.

Then there are only a few more specks of dust in the chest. I wind them into silk, lift it to my head. I pause, blinking over at the Bronze Lord. "What have you become, My Lord?" I ask him.

He smiles, raising his truncated wrists. *A story. And one day, I will learn how to rewrite myself. But hurry, young one. You are almost at the bottom.*

I drive the hook into my temple. I *burn* with magic. I know I am whole.

But then I blink and I'm hurtling into the Sea of Bones, and not even my magic can save me.

It's cruel, I think, in the last few heartbeats before I smash against the ice, cruel to have found myself again just to die like I always feared I would. Falling. Into oblivion.

There is a rush of air, a whir of wings, and I collide with something soft and strong. I am buoyed up, up, back toward the top of the cliff.

I curl my fingers around broad feathers and find I am carried by a trio of massive white owls, all of them sharing my weight, beating their wings as one. My heart wrenches. Ballast.

The owls deposit me in a heap at the top of the cliff, and I watch, shaken, as Ballast bows to the magnificent birds. They bow back and take wing, flying west, Asvaldr keeping pace below them.

He turns to me, stricken. "Are you all right?" he says quietly.

I stare at him, my power searing in every part of me. I have been rewritten, from the inside out, but he can't see it. He doesn't know. Then I'm sobbing in the snow and I can't *breathe* and I think that my grief will rip me apart and I don't know don't know don't know why I'm crying but I can't *stop*.

He wraps his arms around me, pulls me tight against his chest, tucks his chin against my shoulder. He holds me, holds me, and it takes a while to realize he's crying with me, his tears damp in my hair.

"I'm sorry," he says. "I'm so sorry, Brynja. It was the only thing I could think of that might restore your magic. I would never have let you die."

I'm not sure how long we're like that, locked together on the edge of the Sea of Bones, but at last my tears stop, at last I come into myself again and lift my head.

I look at Ballast in the light of the stars, and he looks back. He smooths his thumbs across my cheeks, wiping away the remnants of my tears. I'm stricken again by his scarred eye socket. I lift one hand, touch his scars with gentle fingers. My gut wrenches, and it's all I can do to keep from crying again. It hurts, that someone I care about so deeply has endured so much pain.

"Do you hate me?" I ask quietly.

His forehead creases. "Why would I hate you, Brynja Eldingar?"

"I deceived you. Betrayed you." My throat tightens. "I killed your father."

My skin buzzes where Ballast touches me, his hands warm on my skin. There is pain in his glance, in the set of his jaw.

"Are you sorry that he's dead?" I whisper. I feel the blood on my hand, see the life gutter out of Kallias's eyes. It makes me sick.

"I am not sorry he's gone," says Ballast. "But I would have spared you if I could have. You shouldn't have been the one to kill him."

I can't tell my grief from my anger. "Didn't I have the right? Didn't I? He murdered my sister and he *tormented* me for years and he—"

"Brynja." His voice is soft. His touch is softer.

I go still.

"I wanted you to be free of him. Wholly free. I didn't want him to haunt you in death, as he did in life. I would have spared you that. I would have taken it on myself, so you never had to think of him again." His voice breaks. "I should have. None of this is your fault. *None of it.*"

I blink back fresh tears. His kindness, his care for me, is staggering. I am glad that Ballast doesn't bear the weight of his father's death. He has borne enough. "None of this is your fault, either," I tell him. "You know that, don't you?"

He shakes his head and cups my face in his hands. "Do you know how remarkable you are, Brynja Eldingar?"

Hearing my true name from his lips makes me smile.

He kisses me, softly, his mouth warm and full of promise. Longing and contentment stir together in my belly, and I wrap my arms around him, pull him close. I can taste his magic, sharp and bright on my tongue, but it no longer burns me.

Wind stirs over the cliff, blowing snow into our faces, and without even really meaning to, I tell the snow to make a canopy to shelter us. It obeys. I forgot what true power felt like, seamless as a second skin, but it seems the power has not forgotten me.

Ballast breaks our kiss and glances up at the shimmering snow canopy. His eye finds mine again and a slow smile touches his lips. "You unlocked your magic. It worked."

I grin, almost giddy. "It worked."

He whoops with triumph and pushes to his feet, pulling me up with him. He sweeps me into a hug, spinning me around in the snow and laughing like a madman until all at once we're still again, his hands in my hair and mine around his shoulders, crushing him against me. Now his lips are like fire and his stubble scrapes my cheek and the jewel on his forehead presses hard and cold into mine, but I don't care. I don't care because Ballast is here, with me, and all the cards have been played and there are no more secrets between us.

It is some time before we come back to ourselves, breathless and wild, the wind hardly able to cool our hot faces. Ballast smiles at me and brushes his fingers across my brow. "What now, my lady Eldingar?"

I echo his smile, my heart full to bursting. "Shall we go and kick my brother out of your mountain?"

He grins. "That would do nicely. His expulsion is long overdue."

Up from the Sea, I call a chunk of glacier that's as large as a carriage, glittering in the starlight. Ballast gasps, but it costs me little effort, my power stretching and settling inside me, as eager to be used as a long-penned-up hound is ready to run.

This kind of exertion would have exhausted my child self. But I am not exhausted now. The colors of my own magic spark and shimmer before my eyes, blue and violet and bronze. I tell the glacier piece to be a sleigh, and it becomes one, runners and seats and a shining prow made all of ice. It waits before us, sparkling in the snow.

Ballast looks at me sideways, his brows raised and his mouth hanging open. "Are you sure *you're* not the one with Prism magic?"

"I've always been able to sense a spark of . . . *awareness* in all things, like every bit of matter has a mind, in a way. I don't create new things. I ask them to find a new form, or move in new ways. But I'm stronger now. Even than I used to be."

Ballast shakes his head in bewilderment. "I don't think everyone blessed by the Bronze Lord can do that."

I shrug. I wouldn't know. The Iljaria mistrust mind magic—I am not sure my parents would have allowed me to be trained in it even if they hadn't sent me to Kallias.

We climb into the sleigh. I speak a word to the ice and it hums in answer, the sleigh hurtling forward, bearing us swiftly across the tundra.

Toward the mountain, and whatever fate awaits us there.

CHAPTER TWENTY-NINE

YEAR 4201, Month of the Yellow Lord
Daeros—Tenebris

I halt the sleigh when we're still some ways from Tenebris. We've caught up with the animal army, and Ballast holds them in check with his magic while the two of us climb out of the sleigh. I dissolve it with a thought into a flurry of snow. I can sense the sun below the horizon—it will rise within the hour. We need to keep moving, but I won't have us walking into a trap if we can avoid it.

"Can you send one of the birds ahead to scout?" I ask Ballast as we stand together in the mass of creatures, leopards lying at his feet and Asvaldr guarding his back. Stags stamp and blow, rattling their antlers together, while wolves whine and lions growl, impatient at being held fast on Ballast's invisible leash.

Ballast nods, and an owl wings westward, disappearing into the dark.

I pace while we wait, trying to reach out to Saga, Gulla, Rute, and the others, trying to speak into their minds, but they must still be too far away; I can't sense them. I curse in frustration at my fifth failed attempt, and stop trying. Ballast watches me, tense and quiet.

It seems an eternity before the owl comes back, landing on Ballast's shoulder and ruffling its feathers as it leans its head to his ear.

Ballast's eye meets mine.

"Tell me," I beg.

"There is no sign yet of the Skaandan army. Your brother has come out of the mountain, with the Yellow Lord on a chain, and prisoners beside him."

My gut twists. "What prisoners?"

Ballast shakes his head—the owl doesn't know.

"Is the Iljaria queen with him?"

"No. But there is an army of Iljaria camped just outside of Tenebris."

"An army? How many?"

"Four hundred strong at least."

I gasp. I had no *idea* Brandr had that many Iljaria with him—or perhaps they arrived with the queen.

Ballast looks at me with his one eye, waiting for me to absorb this information and recalculate my plans. "We have to assume the Skaandan and Daerosian armies are still at our disposal," I say, "waiting for the signal to attack."

He raises his brows. "What we have to assume is that we're on our own."

"You and I and a few hundred animals can't fight off that many Iljaria."

"What's the alternative?"

The animals are growing more and more restless, lions tussling in the snow, stags trumpeting and bears growling, with the owls flying in circles above them, a wheel of white wings.

"Brynja, you have that look about you."

I eye him sideways. "What look?"

"The look that means you're plotting something I'm not going to like."

I grimace but don't contradict him.

He puts his hands on my shoulders and gazes down at me with his one blue eye. "Brynja."

"Brandr doesn't know I have my magic back," I say. "If I go alone, I might be able to catch him unawares. Stop all of this before it even comes to a fight."

"No way in hell I'm letting you do that."

"Do you trust me, Ballast?"

He blanches in the face of his own words turned back at him, and curses softly. "Promise me you'll be careful."

"I'm always careful."

This pulls a smile out of him. "No, you're not."

I have to laugh. "I will be this time."

He just shakes his head and kisses me, swift and wild enough to make me dizzy.

"I'll be behind you," he says when he pulls back again.

"I'm counting on it," I reply. "Lords keep you, Bal."

"Lords keep you, Brynja."

It takes everything in me to set my face toward the mountain. To leave him.

To sprint across the snow alone.

Dawn draws perilously near. Already there is a hint of light to the east, and the stars are rapidly fading. The daylight will last a little longer than yesterday—two hours, maybe three. I hope I live long enough to see every hour of it; I hope we all do.

I reach out once more for Saga, Gulla, and Rute, but I still can't sense them. I tell myself fiercely that they're all right. They have to be.

I slow my pace as I near the western edge of the Sea of Bones, where a half dozen Iljaria light globes illuminate the small company of people waiting there.

Closer still, and the knot of people resolve themselves into individual shapes: There's Brandr, dressed in gold, with the Yellow Lord beside him, collared and chained, and his scribe and steward, Gróa and Drengur, at his back.

Theron and Alcaeus, Kallias's twin sons, kneel in the snow, wrists bound, as do Nicanor and Eirenaios, the king's steward and general. Vil and Saga are there, too, huddled together, hands tied, with Gulla beside them.

My heart wrenches. I'm not exactly fussed about Nicanor and Eirenaios, but everyone else was supposed to be tucked safely into the tunnels with the Skaandan army. Can everything have gone so wrong?

My mind tells me what my eyes don't see—or rather, *who*. Leifur and Pala are absent, as are Rute, Finnur, and the rest of the children from the Collection. Kallias's other children are missing, too.

There are only two possible answers for why these seven people alone have been dragged out here: Either everyone else is already dead, or Saga and the others gave themselves up willingly to distract Brandr's attention away from the arrival of the Skaandan army, and Finnur's efforts to free the Daerosian one.

I tell myself firmly it's the latter option, that I'm not marching to my death, that there is still hope. I don't dare try to speak into their minds now—Brandr can't know that I have my magic back. Not yet.

I watch my brother catch sight of me, observe my progress over the snow as the eastern sky turns from rose to silver. The others see me, too. Drengur frowns and Gróa looks wary. Saga jerks her chin up, eyes fierce, while Vil straightens his spine and gives me a nearly imperceptible nod. Nicanor blanches paler than the snow—he doesn't look for mercy from me. Eirenaios, though, glances sideways at Vil and seems to catch on to his sudden hope. Theron and Alcaeus are grim as they look past me, waiting for Ballast, the brother they always so despised, to come and save them.

I stop several yards away from Brandr and the rest, staring him down, willing myself not to shake.

My brother crosses his arms and smiles. "So my errant little sister has come back. We've been waiting for you."

"But not for our queen, I see."

While the Dark Remains

I try not to look at the Yellow Lord, but I can't help it. A chain trails from his collar, which Brandr holds carelessly in one hand. The First One meets my gaze and shows his teeth, snapping his fingers and watching sparks fly up like embers.

"Where have you been?" Brandr demands.

A sudden wind blows my coat about my knees, spits ice into my eyes. I remind myself to be calm, and the wind dies down again.

Brandr doesn't notice. "Well?"

I lick my lips. "I killed the king. I was ashamed, so I ran away. But there was nothing for me, out there."

Brandr laughs. "We dumped his worthless corpse into the Sea of Bones, in case you were wondering. But you needn't have bothered. He would be here, groveling for his life in the snow, if not for you."

My stomach twists. "I am surprised you waited for me."

"You have grown confused," he says, a softness in his voice I'm not at all used to hearing. "But you are still my sister. You still share my blood. You don't deserve to die like all the rest of them." He holds his hand out to me. "Come, Brynja. Take your place beside me as I remake the world."

Despite myself, my heart jerks. He truly believes what he's saying. And I can't deny I'm tempted by his offer: belonging. Acceptance. Maybe even love. I had that, for a while, with Saga and Vil, but never from my parents, my siblings.

Behind him, Drengur's frown deepens and Gróa's face pinches tight with anger. They have no use for me. The sky lightens, and I remember what's at stake. I shake my head. "Where is the queen, Brandr? Was she ever going to come?"

"The queen has given me authority here," says Brandr coldly, "to act and to speak on her behalf."

Gróa darts a look at him, and her thought is so strong I accidentally snag hold of it: *That is not the message that came with the blue kestrel. The queen commanded you to bring the Yellow Lord with you to Iljaria, that she might wield his power from there.*

I jerk my awareness out of Gróa's head before she can notice, and refocus on my brother. "I can't let you destroy the world, Brandr. This isn't peace. This isn't life. Please reconsider."

Darkness folds into his face, and he drops his hand. He turns to the Yellow Lord, looses the collar and chain, lets them fall clanking into the snow. "Kill the prisoners," he snaps.

I tremble. Drengur and Gróa step back, sudden fear in them.

The Yellow Lord blinks mildly. He turns to Saga and the others. He raises both hands.

"Wait," says Brandr, all the harshness gone from his tone. "You don't need to kill them. Brynja is right. There's another way to do this. A more peaceful way. A more Iljaria way." He turns his face to mine, takes one step toward me, two. Then he stops in his tracks, hardened with rage. "Damn you," he spits at me.

I shrug. "It's funny how easy it is, to slip into a mind that has forgotten to build any defenses against you. It was worth a try."

He curses at me vehemently and colorfully, which seems bold of him with the Yellow Lord *right there*. The Yellow Lord, for his part, glances mildly between us, his lips curled up in amusement. Drengur and Gróa stand tense, the jewels on their foreheads trembling.

Brandr realizes all at once that he's let the facade of the impervious Prism Master fall, and grinds his mouth shut. I watch him gain control of himself again. Fear boils through me.

"What's your plan, Brynja? Do you really think you can defeat me with nothing but your reacquired magic?"

A flicker of movement in the corner of my eye makes my knees wobble with relief. "No," I say. "I don't."

The Skaandan army pours from the mountain, three hundred strong, with Leifur and Pala at their head. They sing as they come, brash and chilling Skaandan war songs that shatter the stillness, their feet like drums pounding the earth. They shine in the burgeoning dawn, swords brandished high. A thrill sears through me.

Saga gives a shriek of triumph, and both she and Vil jerk to their feet.

Brandr curses and shouts a word into the sky, sending a flare of light bursting up above his head.

Out of the shadows comes the Iljaria army, white hair unbound, jewels shining from their brows. They are on foot as well, wearing thin, light breastplates of tooled leather dyed the colors of their magic. Some carry weapons but most do not, magic blazing in them so bright it's hard for me to look at them. The owl was wrong. There are at least six hundred, maybe more. Gróa smiles and Drengur begins to sing, a quiet melody threaded with power that makes the snow swirl up around his feet.

And then three hundred Daerosian soldiers come marching up from Garran City, with Aelia and Zopyros, Kallias's oldest son, leading them, gleaming in gold-plated scale armor and steel helms. My trepidation eases, just a little—the combined Skaandan and Daerosian forces equal the number of Iljaria, with Ballast and his animals still to come.

Saga meets my eyes, and with a single focused thought, I loose her bonds. The ropes fall silently to the snow. Between one heartbeat and the next, I do the same for Vil and Gulla and the others.

Run, I say into their minds, and they all jerk their gazes to me, startled. *Now.*

I fling up a wall of snow between them and Gróa and Drengur. Saga, Vil, Gulla, and all the rest bolt across the tundra.

Brandr utters a vicious oath as Drengur's song shakes the ground and thorny vines burst out of the earth at Gróa's command, too late to keep Saga and the others from escaping.

"You really think you can stop this?" Brandr demands of me. "You really think two human armies is enough to *stop this*?" He turns to the Yellow Lord. "Kill them," he snaps. "Kill *all of them*. Wipe out every soul in Daeros and Skaanda, save me and my army alone. Thus I command you, and thus I unbind your power."

"My Lord," I beg the First One. "Please spare us."

The Yellow Lord yawns, twiddling his thumbs and watching sparks of light weave in and around them. "I must do as I am commanded," he says without looking at me. The light curls up his arms, winding through him, making his skin pulse yellow. Pain creases the lines of his immortal face. He spares Brandr a single, fleeting glance, before refocusing on the light dancing between his fingers. "You will have to take shelter in the mountain. I cannot control the light when it reaches its fullest power, and the Black Lord's guardians will protect you."

He must mean the gargoyles at the front gates. I shudder at the mere thought of trusting in their dark defense.

"Fine," Brandr grinds out. He glances east. "Give me and my people until the sun crests the ridge. We'll be safe in the mountain by then."

"As you wish," says the Yellow Lord, fixated on the light in his hands.

"Brandr." My heart drums in my ears, frantic, quick. "Command him to stop. Save us. Save our land."

My brother sneers at me. "I have nothing more to say to you, Brynja. You are no sister of mine. You should have died in your cage. No." His eyes are fierce and hard, the prismatic gem on his forehead glistering with power. "You should have died here, all those years ago, instead of Lilja. She would not have forsaken our cause. Our faith. Our people."

"Brandr—"

He shrieks a curse and flings out his hand, thrusting me backward with the force of his magic. Pain sears through my chest and I land hard in the snow, breathless for the moment it takes him to turn on his heel and stride away from the Sea of Bones, Gróa and Drengur at his back. "To the mountain!" he shouts to his army, which comes like the tide over the tundra. "For Iljaria!"

"FOR ILJARIA!" the army echoes, and the clamor of their unified voices rumbles in the earth.

I drag myself up again, my own power hot in my veins. "My Lord?" I say quietly as the First One grows brighter and brighter before me.

"Little one," he says. "I cannot stop it." His voice crackles with heat, with light. "Whatever it is you mean to do, you had better do it now."

I bow to him, though I'm not sure he can see me through his light. Then I bolt through the snow after Brandr.

Behind me, the sun is rising, and the Yellow Lord burns ever hotter and more luminous than that ancient star.

Ahead of me, Saga and Vil have joined the Skaandans, spare swords thrust into their hands, helms shoved onto their heads. I think I see Rute with them, but there's no sign of Gulla. Theron and Alcaeus, Kallias's twin sons, have run the other way, toward the Daerosian army, with Nicanor and Eirenaios at their heels.

Screams shatter the burgeoning dawn as the first ranks of the Skaandan army collide with the Iljaria. Pockets of fire and light, darkness and whirling ice burst from the Iljaria, their magic bitter and deadly against the flash of mortal blades. Roots push from the ground; stone monsters ascend from the cold earth. The Iljaria who are blessed by the White Lady raise a song of death, shrill on the frigid air. The Skaandans scream at the noise, dropping their weapons and clapping their hands over their ears, only for thorny vines or stony hands or living, writhing darkness to rip them into pieces.

Magic bursts in all its colors before my eyes, blue and green, white and yellow, black and gray. And yet everywhere I look, it's red, red.

I scream as I run, desperate to catch up to my brother and stop him the only way I know how. But his Prism magic speeds his steps, and I can't quite seem to reach him.

To my right, Theron, Alcaeus, and Eirenaios reach the Daerosian army just as it clashes with the Iljaria, half of which has turned to face them, while the remainder continues to mow through the Skaandan army like so much wheat. Nicanor has fallen behind the others and is caught by a stray flame of Iljaria fire. In an instant he burns, screaming, into ash. My stomach heaves and tears bite at my eyes and I don't understand how I can feel sick over the death of Kallias's steward, my tormentor, even for a moment.

I run on, aware of Finnur, somewhere in the dark, fighting the Iljaria with magic of his own. Fire turns to butterflies with red-and-orange wings; the monsters made of earth and stone become smoke and blow away. The death song becomes a flock of chirruping canaries. But he is only one, against hundreds, and the canaries fall and are trodden underfoot, and the song of death is sung anew.

A new music rises to combat it. I glimpse Gulla within the fray, her whole body shimmering with power. She stands with her head tilted back, eyes shut and mouth open, a song of life spilling from her ruined tongue. She is stronger than I could have ever imagined, nullifying the music of the other Iljaria. But even Gulla's magic is not enough to turn the tide. The snow is thick with bodies, and only a very, very few of them are Iljaria.

I reach out with my mind and sense Saga and Vil, Pala and Leifur and Rute, still alive, still fighting. Tears slide down my cheeks. They are not yet among the dead.

I reach for Ballast, too. *Where are you, Bal? Where are you?*

The sky grows a little lighter, and the heat of the Yellow Lord pulses stronger and stronger away behind me.

I try to breathe, and barrel on toward my brother. I tell the earth to speed me along, and suddenly I'm within reach of him. I grab Brandr's shoulder, wheel him around, and press my hands, hard, against his temples.

"Get off of me!" he shrieks. "You can't do anything to me! You only have mind magic, and I am the Prism Master. Get off of me!"

Behind me, the roar of an arctic bear shatters the sky. *Here,* says Ballast's voice in my head. *I'm here.* A knot within me loosens.

"No, Brandr," I tell him. "Come with me."

And I wrench both of us sideways, into his mind.

CHAPTER THIRTY

YEAR 4201, Month of the Yellow Lord
Daeros—Tenebris

I blink and lift my head from a frayed carpet covering cold stone. Brandr is here, too, of course, scrabbling to his feet and cursing at me. I stand more slowly, counting the beats of my heart.

We're in a library, old and abandoned, a broken window somewhere letting a cold wind blow through, scattering leaves and dirt over the shelves. It reeks in here of mold, of decay.

Brandr wheels on me, grabs my wrists. "Let me out, *damn* you, Brynja! Let me out!"

"Do you know where we are?" I ask him carefully.

He pushes me away in disgust, stalks to one of the shelves, runs his hands over moldered spines. "In my mind, I suppose, though I didn't know anyone else could come in."

I shrug. "Neither did I."

He's hard, angry, cold. "Send me back."

"No."

"Brynja. When the sun crests the ridge—"

"You have broken our sacred laws," I say quietly. "You have forsaken our people. Our beliefs. Our ideals."

"I bring justice, Brynja! How many times do I have to tell you? I bring recompense. I *follow* our laws. I fulfill them."

Wind whips strong through the decaying room, blowing my curls in my face. "Do you, Brandr? You did not obey the queen's latest command—how many other of her orders have you disregarded? *Was* this mission sanctioned by her? Truly? Or was there no more power for you to seize in Iljaria, so you came here seeking more?"

He regards me with unfettered loathing. "You don't know what you're talking about. I am here to enact the First Ones' judgment—their law is above even our queen's."

I shake my head. "Murder isn't judgment, Brandr. You're talking about the eradication of two entire peoples."

"They are *worms*," he spits, "insects. Blink, and they will be gone. They are not like us."

"Yes, they are," I say quietly. "They have hearts and minds and bodies. They deserve life and freedom. The only thing they lack is our power, and I can't help but think they might wield it more faithfully than we do. You have freed the Yellow Lord. Be content and go back to Iljaria and repent of the blood you have spilled. You are not a First One. Don't presume to claim their power."

"You are a *fool*. The greatest of all fools. Do you truly believe the nonsense you're spouting? Do you truly believe Iljaria has never gone to war, never left destruction in their wake? Do you think our father would be more merciful?"

"You weren't merciful to him," I say roughly.

He drops his eyes, and for a moment I think he's ashamed. But it's rage he feels, and it sears me.

"Our father gave me *nothing*." Brandr's long white hair whips about his face in the cold wind, and he slams his fist into one of the bookcases. He hisses with pain, because it is not a real bookcase. He's only hurting himself.

"He cared about Lilja," Brandr goes on, a little quieter. "He cared, in his way, about you. But he didn't care about me. He was ashamed of me, of my power. So I reinvented myself to please him. Made myself something he wanted, something I wasn't."

My gut twists. "That's what I did, too."

Brandr doesn't acknowledge me, just traces one finger along a dusty shelf. Sparks of silver float to the floor. "I hope he was sorry, by the end. I hope he was sorry that he didn't nurture me from the beginning, that he didn't search with me until he found an answer to the gift of the Ghost Lord's power. But he didn't. I had to find the answer myself, in a rotting book whose pages crumbled as I turned them."

Pity sparks within me. I know what it is to be used. To be forgotten. But that still does not absolve him. "Then this is truly what is in your mind," I say, glancing around the room. "Knowledge. Power. Misused and left to rot. Have you ever met him, Brandr? Have you ever met the Ghost Lord?"

He sneers at me. "Met him?"

I pace through the decaying room, glancing at the ruined books but not touching them. "He is your patron Lord. He would come if you asked him, you know."

"I don't want the Ghost Lord. I don't need him. I made myself. I *am* myself. And soon all the world will bow to me."

I shoot my brother a swift, hard glance. "Then you *do* mean to make yourself a god."

"Power was always meant to be mine, little sister. It belongs to me. I mean to clothe myself in it."

"And when you rule the world, what will you do? Bind the rest of the First Ones and make them do tricks for you, like Kallias did with all of us in his Collection?"

"I will bring justice. The people will weep at my feet and thank me for saving them."

"When you are done with your justice, there will be no one left to kiss the hem of your garment."

He hisses as he cuts his finger on some rough part of the shelf—a nail, perhaps. Red mottles his skin. "I've had enough of your little game, Brynja. You will die too, you know. When the sun fills the sky, when the Yellow Lord unleashes his power. Release me."

I give him a thin smile. "You are the all-powerful Prism Master. Free yourself, if you can. But first, I think, there is someone you ought to meet."

The Ghost Lord comes from between the shelves. He's hard to look at—no, he's hard to perceive. He's wearing gray, I think. He's about my brother's height. But I cannot say if he's old or young. I can't tell the color of his eyes or even his hair.

Brandr turns to face him, and trembles before his patron Lord.

"You have learned well, young one," says the Ghost Lord. His voice is a whisper on a snowy mountainside, sharp as ice and holding back a power strong enough to break the world.

"Go," says Brandr. "Go, I do not want you here."

The Ghost Lord shrugs. He resolves, a little, into the form of a young man. His skin is gray and white, marbled together. His hair is every color there is, and yet none of them. His eyes—his eyes are wholly white. The Ghost Lord is blind.

"You cannot take and take for eternity," says the Ghost Lord. "You cannot hold it all. It will destroy you. And when it does, there will be someone there to take your place, and all you fought for will come to naught. You will be an outcast to your own people. You will be what you always feared to be: nothing. No one."

Brandr curses and lunges at the Ghost Lord, but he wisps out of the way like smoke, reappearing beside me. A coldness emanates from him, seeping down, down under my skin.

"LET ME OUT OF HERE!" Brandr cries, balling his hands into fists.

"No," I say. "Not unless you swear to me you'll call it all off. The Yellow Lord. Your army. Not unless you promise to go home."

He throws back his head and laughs. "You're out of your *mind*, Brynja, if you think I'd promise you that."

I take a breath, eyes flicking sideways at the Ghost Lord. "I *am* out of my mind, in fact. I'm in yours. Thanks for reminding me." From my coat I draw a chest that shimmers in my hands, all colors, and yet no color at all: a prison for Brandr's magic.

"My Lord?" I say to the First One beside me.

He nods, grim and sightless, and two gleaming silver hooks appear in his hands. He takes a step toward Brandr.

My brother's eyes go wild. "Brynja. Brynja, what are you doing? What is this? Stop. You have to stop. You can't do anything to me. You can't—"

I turn. I wrench myself sideways, out of Brandr's mind and back onto the tundra, where the sun is just lipping above the Sea of Bones.

I kneel with my brother in the snow, pressing my hands against his temples, tears coursing down my cheeks, because I remember exactly how this felt when our father did it to me. When it's done, I withdraw my hands, watch him open his eyes in a world where he once more holds no power.

He shoves me away from him with a hopelessness that guts me. "When I learn how to unbind myself," he says, very low, "I will kill you, Brynja. And for all your cleverness, you still can't stop what I have put in motion. I still command my army. I still command the Yellow Lord." He glances at the sun, eyes tearing at the light. "And there isn't much time left." He sneers at me. Turns his back to me. He runs to rejoin the Iljaria.

I let him go.

Mere moments have passed while we were in my brother's mind, and the battle rages on. The air reeks of blood and bile, and the Iljaria are closer to the mountain and the gargoyles' protection than before. They climb over the bodies of Daerosians and Skaandans as if they were mere mounds of earth, jewels flashing from their brows, magic clearing their path in swaths of red.

The remaining Daerosians and Skaandans fight doggedly, grimly, hacking at writhing vines and earth monsters, hurling spears and loosing arrows into the midst of the Iljaria forces, to little effect. I glimpse Saga, fighting side by side with Vil, her helmet off and her face smeared with blood. Gulla and Finnur are still fighting, too, though Gulla's song has grown fainter and Finnur's magic weaker, having spent so much of it already.

Ballast on Asvaldr comes swift across the tundra with his animal army behind him, a rush of hooves and paws, wings and horns. Owls dive screeching at the Iljaria forces while wolves and leopards and foxes leap for throats and arctic bears slash with knife-edged claws. For a moment the Iljaria falter, and the joined Skaandan and Daerosian armies press them back.

But then the Iljaria blessed by the Blue Lady give a great shout, the jewels flashing cerulean on their foreheads. As one, they shift into beasts with dark leathery wings, and rising out of the army, they dive at the animals head-on. I stare, horrified, because they are very like the cave demons in the tunnels, and I can't help but wonder if the monsters that drove the Iljaria out were in fact the Iljaria themselves.

The Iljaria-beasts ram into the animals in a wheel of wings and claws and teeth, halting their advance and allowing the remainder of the Iljaria forces to redouble their efforts against the human armies. Ballast slays one of the beasts that dives at him on Asvaldr, blood spraying all up his arm. Asvaldr roars and swipes at another of them.

I glance behind me. The sun is half above the ridge now. The Yellow Lord stands on the edge of the Sea of Bones, contemplating its coming.

For a moment I shut my eyes, reach out to every mind I can sense. *Stand down!* I cry. *All of you, stand down! Get into the mountain! The sun is rising!*

But though I feel a pulse of uncertainty and confusion, I am not powerful enough to halt three armies with my will alone. They battle on.

I have to stop this. Or at least I have to try. And I can't do it alone.

Ballast! I shout into his mind. *Ballast!*

He turns toward me, ducking the attack of another Iljaria-beast. Then he's leaping from Asvaldr's back and hurtling toward me over the snow. He reaches me, and his hand finds mine.

Then we're running together toward the Yellow Lord, toward the Sea of Bones.

Toward the rising sun.

CHAPTER THIRTY-ONE

YEAR 4201, Month of the Yellow Lord
Daeros—the Sea of Bones

Already the heat and light of the Yellow Lord are too much to bear. My eyes tear and my skin burns and still he grows brighter, brighter. I can't see Ballast anymore, but his hand is yet caught in mine, our feet pounding in unison over fast-melting snow.

Ballast? I say, frantic, into his mind.

His answer comes hesitant, unsure: *Here, Brynja.*

We draw near to the edge of the glacier sea and slow our steps.

The Yellow Lord is impossible to look at. All is light, light, scorching every part of me. My heart sears and my lungs boil and I think I will drown in light.

"STOP!" I shriek at the Yellow Lord. "YOU HAVE TO STOP."

His voice comes out of the brightness, solemn and weary. "I cannot, little Eldingar. My power has been unbound. It will not stop until it has consumed all darkness, on the earth and under it."

Behind him, the sun rises, but I cannot tell him apart from the brightness of that ancient star.

While the Dark Remains

I think of the Sea of Bones, where it's said the Ghost Lord walks, hand in hand with the Gray Lady, guardians of the dead. Ballast and I cannot bind the Yellow Lord anew. But they could.

The Sea, I whisper into Ballast's mind. I only hope he understands.

Then we're running again, hurtling toward the Yellow Lord. The world is white before my eyes.

We slam into him and I cry out in agony. All is heat, light, pain. But we don't stop.

The sun rises and the Yellow Lord burns and we fall with him, into the Sea of Bones.

I lose Ballast somewhere in the light, his fingers slipping from mine. The Yellow Lord weeps as we fall, the power bursting out of him, still growing and growing. It is agony to be near him, but his torment must be worse, boiling from the inside.

We fall and fall, and I feel strangely outside of myself. The fear is still there, the pain, the loss. But there will be relief soon. Rest.

My people have long believed that if they are devout enough in life, they will be rewarded with the power and immortality of a First One after death. I have both served and betrayed my people; I don't know what awaits me at the bottom of the Sea. I only hope we've bought enough time so that Saga and the others can make it to Tenebris, that they'll be saved from the Yellow Lord's annihilation.

Brynja, comes the frantic thread of Ballast's voice in my mind.

Here, Bal.

I grasp for him, but I can't reach him, and that's what makes the fear rush up, the horror and the sorrow of death grip tight.

BRYNJA!

The ground rushes up to greet us. The light burns, burns, and then—

The music of bubbling water, the quiet warmth of an underground chamber.

I blink and see the Iljaria city that Ballast and Saga and I wandered through two years ago. It's illuminated by soft, unseen lamps, and the whole place smells of yeast and honey. There is the fountain where Ballast and I sat while Saga bathed. There are the statues, the murals, the flagstone floor.

I am here and yet not here, for I seem to have no hands, no voice. I wonder if I am already dead, shattered at the bottom of the Sea of Bones, or if this is a vision, the ravings of my dying mind.

I blink again and see the Yellow Lord, kneeling in the midst of the room, his head bowed. Light ripples all along his skin, and tears drip from his eyes and turn to steam.

The Prism Lady stands before him, her hair a river of white that falls to the floor and pools around her ankles. She looks at once young and ancient, her skin very pale, her eyes no color at all, and yet every color at once. With her are the Blue Lady, the Ghost Lord, and the Bronze Lord, who sits in a carved chair, his ruined arms laid on his knees.

"Youngest of us all," says the Prism Lady, crouching down to the Yellow Lord's sight line, taking his chin gently in hers. His light does not seem to harm her, but her face is heavy with sorrow. "You have been unbound."

"So," says the Yellow Lord, agony twisting his features.

"Once," says the Ghost Lord, taking a step nearer, "we offered you a choice, a dwelling place that you scorned."

The Yellow Lord weeps, weeps, and the steam of his tears hisses on the flagstones.

The Blue Lady comes forward, butterflies and bees tangled in her curls, a lion pressed against her hip, a falcon on her shoulder. "Once, you nearly destroyed the world with your power. We will not allow you to do so again."

The Bronze Lord does not speak, but he bows his head and weeps along with the Yellow Lord.

While the Dark Remains

The Prism Lady takes the Yellow Lord's hand and raises him to his feet. He looks at her but cannot quite meet her eyes.

"We offer to you once more the choice that was previously so abhorrent to you," says the Prism Lady. "You will be bound, you will never again be loosed, but we will bind you in light instead of darkness, if you will choose at last the dwelling we made for you."

The Yellow Lord takes a breath. "And if I do not choose that, my lady?"

"Then you will be bound in ice and rock, encased in iron, swallowed up in the domain of the Black Lord, whom you so despise."

"I choose what I should have chosen before," says the Yellow Lord softly. "I choose to be bound in light."

The Prism Lady nods, and the Ghost Lord locks fetters about the Yellow Lord's wrists.

Then the city is no longer around us and we are soaring through the sky in a winged ship, the Prism Lady at the bow and the Yellow Lord in the center, flanked by the Blue Lady and the Ghost Lord, with the Bronze Lord at the stern. The winged ship flies up, up, toward the sun. And then we're sailing into the light, and it welcomes us.

The sun is living, blazing, liquid fire, but it does not burn. The winged ship bears us into the heart of the old star, where waits a tall, fair house with white gates and a river of light running past it.

The Yellow Lord steps from the ship and bows his head to the Prism Lady.

"I did not know," he says. "I did not know that you built for me such a dwelling."

The Prism Lady smiles sadly. "I have never wanted any of my children to dwell in torment. Here your light will burn for all eternity, and harm no one."

The Yellow Lord steps through the gates of his house. There is a flare of light, the searing feeling of *joy*, and then the ship turns around, and flies out of the sun.

I blink and there is no ship, no First Ones. There is only the sun, rising, and me, falling.

Down and down and down.

The Yellow Lord is gone.

And I will end as I always feared I would, falling, shattered, broken.

Fingers tangle suddenly in mine, hold tight, squeeze.

Here, Brynja, says Ballast.

Here, Bal, I say, and I am fiercely glad to not be alone in my nightmare.

I cling to him as we fall down and down.

Into the welcoming embrace of the Sea of Bones.

CHAPTER THIRTY-TWO

YEAR 4201, Month of the Yellow Lord
Daeros—Tenebris

The owls catch us before we smash onto the ice. I could laugh. I had forgotten the owls.

We are too heavy for them to carry us both at once, back to the top of the cliff. I send Ballast first and wait for a little while by myself in the Sea of Bones.

It is quiet down here, the sun casting the glaciers in eerie shades of blue. I think of my sister, and I wonder what she thought of as she fell. I hope she thought of love and laughter. I hope she remembered light. I hope, when the world is reborn, that I will see her again, as she was meant to be. Happy. Inventing things.

Tears prick at my eyes.

The owls come for me, and I let them bear me up, into the wind, into the sky.

Ballast waits at the top of the cliff. The edges of his white-and-black hair are singed. He smells of smoke.

"Brynja," he breathes. He crushes me tight against him, and I muffle a sob into his chest.

I look up at him, and he smooths my hair away from my brow, and we stare at each other, caught in the dizzying awe of what we witnessed together, having walked for a little while in the realm of the First Ones themselves.

I want to melt into him. But there is work yet to be done.

Ballast takes my hand, and we turn together toward the armies. They've ceased their fighting, staring every one at the sun, and I wonder what it must have looked like to them, at the precise moment when the Yellow Lord was bound there.

The snow is dark with blood and gore, and hundreds of bodies—human and animal—are strewn about the ground. Thorny roots lie broken and twisted, and the earth is shattered in the places where the rock monsters rose. The Iljaria-beasts who still live have shifted back into their original forms, though remnants of their wings and claws seem still to whisper about them.

Less than half of the Skaandan and Daerosian armies remain, and the Iljaria forces have dwindled to a few hundred. The air reeks of death, and the cries of the wounded hang brittle on the wind.

Tears bite at my eyes. None of this had to happen, such reckless waste of life. And yet it did.

They wait for us, watch us come: Saga and Vil, Gulla and Aelia, Gróa and Drengur—Brandr's scribe and steward—holding Brandr between them. There is blood on my brother's temple, blood caught in the shock of his white hair. Ballast's brothers, Zopyros, Theron, and Alcaeus, are there, too.

The armies wait, tense and uncertain, hands still gripping tight to sword hilts and spear shafts. The animals have drawn back but not dispersed, held in check by Ballast's will. Again, his power stuns me—there are hundreds of beasts, and all of them obey him.

We stop a few paces away from the waiting armies. Saga's eyes go to my hand, still caught fast in Ballast's, and her whole being hardens. There is blood on her face, and more leaks through a rag tied tight around her left forearm. My throat hurts. I let go of Ballast's hand.

The sun burns warm at my back. It bathes the battlefield with a stark brightness that sickens me. I don't want to look at the bodies, don't want to see the blood staining my boots.

"Lady Eldingar."

I snap my eyes to Gróa, my brother's steward.

"Command us," she says.

I blink at her. "I command no one."

"The Prism Master is powerless. We have no leader."

Brandr doesn't lift his head. His chest rises and falls. His blood drips into the snow.

"We have ceased our fighting upon the sign of the Yellow Lord's binding," Gróa goes on, "but give the word and we will annihilate these barbarians."

"No," I say, voice tight. "No. There will be no more fighting today."

Gróa inclines her head to me. "As you wish, my lady."

"What of the mountain?" says Vil.

I force myself to look at him. His side is leaking blood, his hand pressed hard into the wound, red running through his fingers.

"Skaanda claims the mountain," he says through gritted teeth.

Zopyros wheels on him, sword high. "Get what's left of your army the hell out of my country!"

"You are not a king," Vil sneers at him. "You do not command me."

"And it is *my* army," says Saga fiercely. "Not his."

Vil glances at her and ducks his chin in deference, though his body tenses, and the anger is still in him.

"Tenebris is claimed for *Skaanda*," Saga says, raising her sword so it catches the light of the sun. Behind her, the Skaandans shout a note of their war song and lift their own blades. She is fey and bright, a goddess on a hill. "Daeros will stand down."

"Daeros will *not!*" snaps Zopyros. He lifts his sword, and the Daerosians crouch into a fighting stance.

The Iljaria just stand there, silent and watching, like they truly have no part in this conflict.

Ballast strides fearlessly between them, his blue eye flashing. "There will be no more fighting today," he says. Then, shouting into the sky: "THERE WILL BE NO MORE FIGHTING TODAY!"

The Daerosians knock their sword hilts against their breastplates in a show of respect and obedience. The Skaandans don't move, blades gleaming in the sunlight. Saga's jaw is tense, and her eyes flick to me.

Please, I whisper into her mind. *Let there be no more death today.*

Ballast's brothers look at each other, a wordless agreement passing between them. They kneel all together, bowing their heads and laying their swords at Ballast's feet.

"All hail the king of Daeros," they chorus.

The Daerosian army echoes: "ALL HAIL!"

For a moment Saga stays frozen, sword fast in her hand, rage and wanting bright in her eyes. Then she takes a breath. "Stand down," she orders.

"Saga?" Vil says, the anger holding him fast.

"Stand down," she repeats.

Vil obeys her and lowers his sword, and the rest of the Skaandan army follows suit.

My heart beats, beats. Ballast stands before his army, gilded in light, and his beauty robs me of breath. I think he will never again walk in darkness.

*

Saga can't look at me, her eyes everywhere else in the private tearoom: the window, the table, the pattern on the marble floor. There is food laid out on the table between us, but neither of us has touched anything. The tea has already gone cold.

She fiddles with her cup, running her finger around the rim.

"Are you sure you won't stay?" I ask at last, desperate to hear her voice. "I'm not sure Vil is the best choice to negotiate peace."

She attempts a smile. "I'm ready to go home, Brynja. If I never see this mountain again, it'll be too soon."

I worry my lip. "Vil is disappointed."

"That he doesn't get to try his hand at being king? Yes. But don't tell me you feel sorry for him."

"I do."

This surprises her enough that she raises her eyes to mine. "I thought you hated him."

"I have never hated him, Saga. I blamed him, for a while, for Indridi's death, but he didn't kill her, and I can understand the fierce loyalty he has to his country. The truth is, he was my friend, and was far kinder to me than my own brother ever was."

Saga shifts in her chair. "Was any of it real, Brynja?"

My throat hurts. "Of course it was real. I could have left you when we escaped from the mountain. I could have left you in the tunnels, or on the tundra. But I didn't."

"Am I supposed to say *thank you* for that?" Saga demands. There are tears in her eyes, and I feel them pressing against mine, too.

"Saga." My voice breaks. "I never wanted to hurt you. I never meant to. But I did, and I'm sorry."

She stares at her lap, twists her fingers in her skirt, twists and twists.

"What will you do?" I ask her quietly. "When you get home?"

"Try and forget all of this," she says without looking up.

"I understand. But if you—" I hesitate, unsure of myself. "If you were to write me—"

"I'm not going to write you, Brynja. Why would I?"

I take a slow breath. "I understand," I repeat.

"What about the Iljaria?" she asks after a moment, her voice unsteady. "What about Aelia and the threat of Aerona?"

"Aelia has seen with her own eyes that the peninsula is prepared to defend itself. We will urge her to persuade her father to reconsider his plans to invade. As for the Iljaria—they'll go home. They'll take my brother with them."

"And you?" says Saga quietly.

For another brief moment, her glance meets mine.

"I will stay awhile longer. Help to negotiate peace. And then..." My heart thrums quick, my mind buzzes with magic. "Then I'll go home, too."

"What does it feel like?" she asks me. "Your magic?"

"Like breathing. Like life."

I am eager to tell her more, to share with my friend all the things I ever kept from her. But she doesn't ask, and I have lost the right to tell her anyway.

"The darkness won't come again, will it," she says. "There will be no more Gods' Fall."

I nod. "We'll always have the sun, now, I think."

"I'm glad of that, at least." She pushes her chair back. Stands. Looks me in the eyes. "Goodbye, Brynja. I can't say I'll miss you. But... thank you. For saving me. For saving all of us."

She leaves the room without another word, her skirt dragging over the marble, her perfume lingering in her wake.

The Iljaria leave in the evening, Brandr sullen and silent. I have not told my people that my brother's true patron is the Ghost Lord. I should, perhaps. But I don't. I do tell them he killed our father. I will let them sort out what that means for his homecoming.

"Will you not come with us, Lady Eldingar?" Gróa asks me frankly.

I stand with the Iljaria outside the mountain, snow skittering past my face in the light of the falling sun. The light was long today, stretching for nearly twelve hours, as it usually does only in the height of summer. I think of the Yellow Lord. I hope he is content with his choice; I hope he knows he chose rightly.

"When I have finished with my business here, I will return to Iljaria," I tell her.

Gróa bows to me and swings up onto her horse. "As you say, my lady."

"Brandr."

He stiffens from his place on his own horse, his hands bound. He doesn't look at me.

"I hope you find what you need," I say. "I'm sorry it ended this way."

Brandr curses at me.

I turn and walk back into the mountain.

It's strange, eating dinner with such an eclectic array of people. Ballast and Gulla are here, of course, and Kallias's other three wives, Pelagia with newborn Charis wrapped in her arms. Charis was born during the battle, Pelagia told us, and came into the world hollering. The rest of Ballast's siblings are here, too, including little Xenia. There's Aelia and Vil. Rute, Finnur, and the rest of the children from the Collection.

In the morning, I, along with Gulla and Kallias's other wives—Pelagia, Elpis, and Unnur—will begin the process of bringing the children home, or finding places for them if they have no home to go to. When I'm not busy with the children, I'll be in the council chambers, attempting to negotiate true peace between Daeros and Skaanda, and doing my level best to keep Vil and Ballast from killing each other.

Ballast meets my eyes across the table, as if sensing my thoughts. He smiles at me, and my insides turn to mush.

"Vil."

He turns to face me, pausing in his progress down the corridor. His jaw is tense, his eyes hard.

I'm a jumble of nerves. "I hope that—I hope that my presence here won't deter you from making peace with Daeros. I—I truly want to help."

His lips thin. "Saga is gone, Brynja. You don't have to pretend to be nice to me anymore. And just to be perfectly clear, I rescind my offer of marriage. There. Now we never have to speak to each other again."

My stomach twists. "I'm sorry I hurt you, Vil," I say quietly. "You were a true friend to me in Skaanda, far truer and far kinder than I deserved, and I repaid you cruelly. It meant everything to me, and I need you to know—" I take a breath and forge ahead. "I need you to know that there were times I wanted to bury Brynja Eldingar for good, to forget I was ever Iljaria and become in truth what you thought I was. What you needed me to be, and what I wanted to be for you. But I could never quite do it, and I'm sorry."

He scoffs. "Traitorous bitch. You should have knifed me in the heart the first time I saw you. That would have been easier."

His admission guts me, and from the tightness in his jaw, I know he didn't mean to say it so plainly.

"I hope someday you'll forgive me," I tell him.

But he just curses at me and stalks off down the corridor.

I don't follow him. There is nothing else left to say.

CHAPTER THIRTY-THREE

YEAR 4201, Month of the Yellow Lord
Daeros—the Sea of Bones

I stand alone on the edge of the Sea of Bones. I watch the sun rise, slowly at first, then swift and sudden, dazzling the depths of my being with its brilliance.

"Hello, My Lord," I say. "Good morning."

I know I imagine the Yellow Lord's laughter in my ears, but it heartens me all the same.

I sense Ballast step up beside me, but for a while I don't turn to look at him. We stare together out over the Sea.

"Are you content, Brynja?"

It's not a question I was expecting, and I don't know how to answer it. "Are you?"

He laughs softly. "I think I am."

"What happens now?" I slide my hand into his, feeling a spike of happiness as he laces our fingers together.

"Whatever you want to happen," he says.

"What if I don't know what I want?" At last I turn to look at him, and I trace my free hand over the scarred remains of his eye.

He shivers at my touch. "Stay with me," he says.

"I will stay to see you crowned and until the treaty is signed. But—but then I think I need to go home, Ballast. I don't know who I am anymore. I don't know *what* I am. But I think at least part of me is waiting in Iljaria."

His eye never leaves mine. He tangles his fingers in my curls. "Your hair has gone white," he says, wonderingly.

I laugh a little. "Something I will have to get used to."

"I like it," he says, and kisses my brow.

"Will you come back to me?" he says then. "After you have found what you're looking for in Iljaria, will you come back to me?" It is an echo of his question to me down in the tunnels, when I told him I didn't want to live in the dark.

But there is no darkness here. "Yes," I whisper. "I'll always come back to you, Bal."

He smiles.

I tug him toward me, and I kiss him the way that, down in the dark, I wanted to kiss him: in the light of the blazing sun. His lips are soft and warm and wild, and they move against mine in a liquid, wanting rhythm. His heat sears me, or maybe mine sears him; I cannot tell, after a while, the difference between us. His hands are in my hair and mine are on his shoulders, crushing him ever harder against me. I taste his power, mingling with my own until all is glittering, bright. Something strong, something new.

When the fire has gone out of us, we sit awhile on the edge of the Sea of Bones, feet dangling over empty air. I tilt my head on Ballast's shoulder. I listen to the quiet beat of his heart. The sun rises higher, burning yellow instead of red.

For now, I am at peace, and Ballast is beside me, and all is well. Later, that will change. I suspect Vil won't be content to sign a peace treaty and will make a bid for the throne. I don't trust the Aeronan emperor and his greedy arrogance. I don't trust my brother. I don't trust my people.

But for now—

While the Dark Remains

I blink over the glacier sea. I close my eyes. I watch the spots of light dance behind my eyelids. I squeeze Ballast's hand.

For now, there is peace.

The darkness is gone.

We dwell in the light.

GLOSSARY

The First Ones

The Black God (god of darkness)
The Blue Goddess (goddess of animals)
The Bronze God (god of minds)
The Brown Goddess (goddess of the earth)
The Ghost God (god of nothing)
The Gray Goddess (goddess of death)
The Green Goddess (goddess of life)
The Prism Goddess (goddess of all things)
The Red God (god of fire)
The Violet God (god of time)
The White Goddess (goddess of music)
The Yellow God (god of light)

Calendar

SPRING (the year begins)
Month of the Yellow God
Month of the Brown Goddess
Month of the Green Goddess

SUMMER
Month of the Blue Goddess
Month of the White Goddess
Month of the Prism Goddess

AUTUMN
Month of the Bronze God
Month of the Red God
Month of the Violet God

WINTER (Gods' Fall / Winter Dark / Soul's Rest)
Month of the Black God
Month of the Gray Goddess
Month of the Ghost God

Places

Aeronan Empire—the occupied territories on the mainland, north of the peninsula

Altari Forest—a great forest in the southeast of the peninsula, a point of contention between Skaanda and Daeros

Bone City—a city on the bank of the Sea of Bones, in Daeros

Daeros—country in the north of the peninsula, bordered by mountains and the great Saadone River

Garran City—the capital city of Daeros, just outside of Tenebris

Iljaria—country in the east of the peninsula, bordered by the sea and a magical barrier the Iljaria erected

Saadone City—a city built on the banks of the great Saadone River, on the Skaandan side

Saadone River—the massive river that borders Skaanda and Daeros

Sea of Bones—a massive glacier valley in Daeros

Skaanda—country in the west of the peninsula, bordered by the Saadone River and the sea

Skógur City—walled city around an ancient forest said to be grown by the Green Goddess

Staltoria City—capital city of Skaanda, location of the royal palace

Tenebris—the mountain palace where Kallias rules Daeros; originally built by the Iljaria

Characters

AERONA

Aelia Cloelia Naeus—imperial Aeronan princess
Talan—Aeronan ambassador

DAEROS

Kallias Vallin—king of Daeros

Kallias's Wives
Elpis Vallin—Daerosian wife of Kallias
Gulla Vallin—Iljaria wife of Kallias
Pelagia Vallin—Daerosian wife of Kallias
Unnur Vallin—Skaandan wife of Kallias

Kallias's Children
Ballast Heron Vallin—son of Kallias and Iljaria wife, Gulla
Charis Vallin—newborn daughter of Kallias and Pelagia
Lysandra Vallin—daughter of Kallias and Daerosian wife Elpis
Rhode Vallin—daughter of Kallias and Daerosian wife Pelagia
Theron and Alcaeus Vallin—twin sons of Kallias and Daerosian wife Elpis
Xenia Vallin—daughter of Kallias and Daerosian wife Pelagia
Zopyros Vallin—son of Kallias and Skaandan wife, Unnur

Other Daerosians
Basileious—Kallias's engineer
Eirenaios—Kallias's general
Lady Eudocia—governor of the Bone City
Lady Thais—head arborist of Skógur City
Lord Damianus—overseer of the mines
Lord Phaedrus—overseer of the greenhouses
Nicanor—Kallias's steward

Children in the Collection
Brynja Sindri—a Skaandan acrobat
Corinna—a Daerosian painter
Dagmar—an Iljaria boy who has fire magic
Edda & Frida—twin Skaandan sword dancers
Eirene—a Daerosian singer
Finnur—an Iljaria boy who has Prism magic
Gaiana—a Daerosian mathematician
Pór—Skaandan cellist
Rute—a Daerosian acrobat, Brynja's replacement
Tier—the Skaandan boy captured at the same time as Brynja; a harpsichordist

ILJARIA

Brandr Eldingar—the Prism Master
Drengur—Brandr's steward
Gróa—Brandr's scribe
Hinrik Eldingar—the former Prism Master

SKAANDA

Aasgier & Valdis Stjörnu—king and queen of Skaanda, Saga and Vil's parents
Hilf—Saga's former bodyguard and boyfriend
Indridi—Saga's handmaiden
Leifur—Skaandan commander
Njala—Saga's double, killed in battle
Pala—Skaandan soldier
Saga Stjörnu—crown princess of Skaanda
Vilhjalmur Stjörnu—prince of Skaanda, Saga's brother

ACKNOWLEDGMENTS

I wasn't really sure this book would ever see the light of day *cue semi-unintentional pun* and I am beyond grateful to be meeting you here in the acknowledgments!

Infinite thanks to my agent, Sarah Gerton, who saw something in *Dark* when I queried her with its early incarnation and who pushed me to make it so much better and richer and deeper in subsequent drafts. Thanks for all the brainstorming calls, your thoughtful notes, your cheerleading, and your tireless efforts in getting *Dark* out on submission.

Many, many thanks to Marilyn Brigham at 47North / Amazon Publishing for acquiring this book and connecting with my vision for it. I'm ridiculously happy that *Dark* has found such a fantastic home!

Thanks so much to Lindsey Faber and Marilyn for their editorial insight and for helping me grow *Dark* into its final form. I'm so thrilled and proud of how it turned out (and hooray for more kissing!).

Huge thanks to everyone who read an early version of *Dark* (and freaked out in all the correct places): RJ Anderson, Maria Farb, Claire Trella Hill, Charlie Holmberg, Rosamund Hodge, Hanna Howard, Isla Meyer, Suzannah Rowntree, Amy Trueblood, and my husband, Aaron (sitting next to you while you read *that part* was amazing, ha!).

Special thanks to The Pod, The Thing with Feathers, and the AZ MG/YA writing groups for all your love, encouragement, and cheerleading along the way (and for putting up with all my complaints and despair).

Always thanks to Hanna Howard, my virtual coworker and fellow consumer of excessive amounts of tea. Thanks to RJ Anderson for all the brainstorming and cheerleading and being my emotional-support Canadian. Thanks to my BFF Jenny Downer for that discussion we had about geopolitics; I always appreciate you letting me use your brain (but not, like, in a mad scientist kind of a way).

Thanks to the band the Oh Hellos for their song "Caesar," the ending of which I have always envisioned playing in the scene where Ballast comes over the ridge with the sun rising and his animal army behind his back—that song was one of the main reasons I didn't want to give up on this book, and it still gives me goose bumps.

While the Dark Remains is essentially a love letter to Megan Whalen Turner's *The Thief*. Anyone who has read it will understand why. So thank you, Megan, for writing a book that has inspired me many times over.

Thanks to my husband, Aaron, for living life with me, even when life is hard, and for reading my weird books and not judging me for them (at least not much). Love you always.

And thanks to Arthur, who was a tiny little bean growing inside me when I was first drafting *Dark*, and who will be eight by the time it publishes. You amaze me, and I can't believe I get to be your mom. Love you bunches.

And thank you thank you thank you to my wonderful readers; I am so honored to be able to share my words with you.

Lastly, to the one who holds all things in his hands and who puts stories in my heart. Soli Deo Gloria. *The light shines in the darkness, and the darkness has not overcome it.*

ABOUT THE AUTHOR

Photo © 2024 Vanessa Rose Holman

Joanna Ruth Meyer is the author of five young adult fantasy novels, including the critically acclaimed *Echo North*. *While the Dark Remains* is her first adult fantasy. She lives in Mesa, Arizona, with her husband, son, two orange cats, and a giant grand piano named Prince Imrahil. Joanna loves forests and rainstorms and stories that make her feel things, and in all likelihood, she's drinking tea right now. To learn more about the author, visit www.joannaruthmeyer.com and follow her on Instagram @gamwyn.